ADELAIDE THORNE

IRON HEART OF TERLSAN

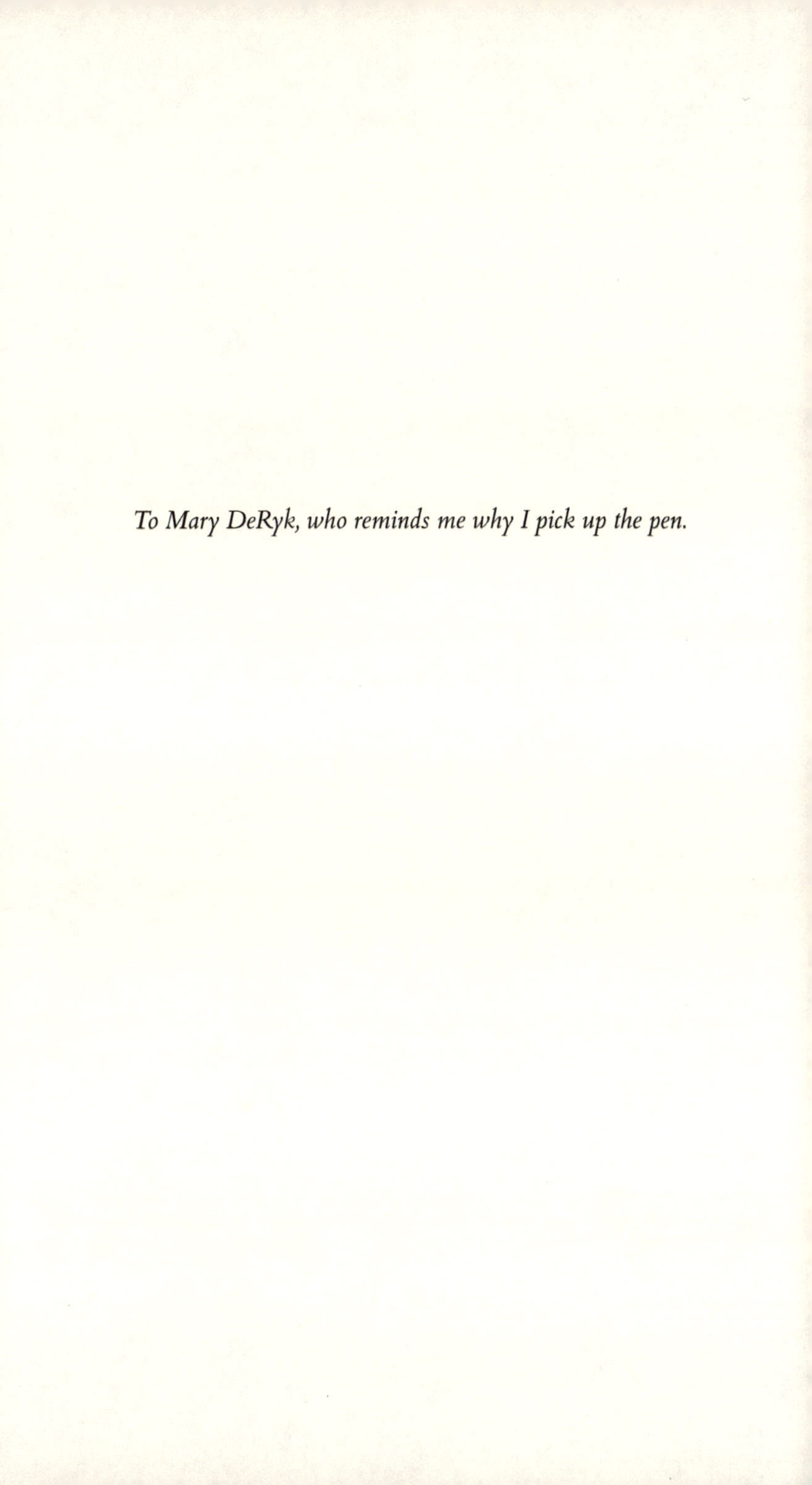

To Mary DeRyk, who reminds me why I pick up the pen.

N
E
S
W
Lowlands
Faargard
Port of Vaspurakan
Bar'Falian Palace
Borku
Gate to Terlian
Ashlamak
Danaki Güyl Mountains
Lake Vaspurakan
The Arati Highlands
Holy Mother's Tears
The Amber Forest
ARAT

PROLOGUE

N ONE HAD KNOWN HOW bleak it was, this realm of death.

Rafe limped along sand black as ash. His injury needed treating. Later. For now, Rafe hunted. The oppressive fog, reeking of rotted egg and decay, weakened his sight. This land was barren, its fate bound to the Lykill, and the Lykill's time had not yet come.

A groan carried on listless wind.

There.

Rafe followed the moaning toward the sea and found his prey on the sunless sand, sheltered by a rock formation. The man lay in his own blood. King, some called him. A title without meaning. Halfdan had claim to nothing.

Rafe stood over him. "Where is it?"

He coughed and did not answer. The crimson-stained sand was growing darker.

"Your wife is with child. Another son."

Halfdan's gaze struggled toward Rafe's. "So you have stolen my letters too."

"He will despise you, accuse you of abandoning his mother." Despair had ever served Rafe as a weapon. It wrung out the heart, robbed men of prudence. He waited for Halfdan to succumb to its blow.

But the man laughed, the sound slick with mucus. "Fall back on your belly, snake."

Rafe dug his heel into Halfdan's wound, finding it without difficulty for he'd put it there. "Where is the Tome?"

Halfdan cackled like a madman. This happened when a man neared death. Rafe had hoped for more time, but he'd wasted countless minutes finding Halfdan and his brother. Niall Mykaois might have escaped, but his life was already forfeit.

Rafe had never stabbed a man before. Today, he'd stabbed two.

Wind carried noise from the cliffs, a harsh sound Rafe did not recognize. He was unfamiliar with this land, its people and their tools, but he sensed approaching danger.

Before they could be spotted, Rafe dragged Halfdan to the cave from which they'd come. He heaved the man through the luminescent gate and came upon nightfall on the other side, gilded by the shine of two moons. The lake flowed softly by. Rafe rolled Halfdan's body into its waters. Halfdan did not protest. He'd died somewhere along the route.

Rafe did not watch the corpse drift away. What use had he for empty vessels?

The dead realm called for his return, but perhaps Halfdan had not hidden the Tome there. Perhaps Halfdan's brother had taken it. Rafe would seek Niall out. If met with no success, Rafe would return to the dead realm and search until his body failed him. And when Rafe was no more, his son would assume his mantle.

Rafe did not fear failure. His line would continue. For there was no end to the Hands of the Lykill.

CHAPTER ONE

"The Order of the Lykill lived a mostly ignored existence until Quirin Lyng entered the scene." – *Why the Order Won't Fade* by Dr. Mariemma Crawley

I F VIOLET HADN'T KNOWN better, she would have guessed their ferry captain was lost. They'd been navigating through the fog for so long, her clothes had grown sticky. She should've joined her siblings in the warmth below deck, but logic seemed stuck in the swirling vat of moisture around her.

Or maybe she just wanted to avoid her brother. She and Oliver hadn't been forced into such close quarters since their cousin's wedding years ago. Then, the usual topic of disagreement had known better than to emerge. Today, nothing prevented Oliver from shoving it out of the shadows.

Said topic nudged from Violet's phone. She read Mariemma's email again.

We're more than a group of old codgers. The Order has youths. They can learn from you. Do consider my offer. It's what your father wanted.

Dr. Mariemma Crawley wasn't wrong. Fa had never asked, but the expectation had followed since Violet was twelve. Who better to take up Fa's mantle than the daughter already accustomed to its weight?

She stowed her phone and finished filing down uneven paint on the ship railing. It burned her fingertips like ice. January's bite stung bitterly this far out on the Atlantic. Sunlight and warmth didn't exist this close to Helheim. Nothing did, not since Ragnarök.

"Don't call it that stupid name."

Oliver's voice was louder these days. Every fiber of him had protested this trip. Violet hadn't wanted to go either. Visiting Helheim was utter madness, not to mention complicated. Had it not been for Fa's renown, the government would have prohibited this trip. Helheim was a place for scientists and archeologists, not families.

But Violet had swallowed her misgivings and made this trip happen. She'd promised Fa he'd see Helheim again. Twenty years ago, his employer had sent him to study the ancient volcanic debris of Mt. Rof. He'd left Helheim as a man changed, driven by the insatiable itch to return. Today, he'd have his homecoming, though not in the way he'd pictured. Fa had never planned to return in a coffin.

"Violet?"

June stood on the deck, shivering as sea breeze rifled through her hair, the same dark shade and paper-straightness as Violet's and Oliver's. Their Scandinavian heritage had given them little choice but to have dark hair and eyes, though Ma had always promised that her great-great aunt was rumored to have blue eyes. Included with that rumor was the suspicion that Hilda wasn't actually anyone's aunt, great or otherwise.

"Where's your coat?" Violet said, already fishing for a handkerchief as she observed her sister's runny nose. She felt her phone, remembered Dr. Mariemma's email, and wished she'd left the device below.

June grinned. "Looking for this?" She waved a handkerchief. "I can blow my own nose, you know. Anyway, I came up to relay Oliver's message. He says we're lost."

Of course he did. "We're not," Violet said.

"Yeah, I figured. I can keep watch, if you tell me what . . ." The rest got flung overboard, stolen by the mist.

"I don't need help. Go back down, June. You'll freeze."

June joined her by the railing instead. Violet frowned. There was a time when June followed Violet's every piece of advice. That acquiescent sister was becoming harder to find. Violet could have blamed it on June being a sixteen-year-old but for the fact that these displays of independence had begun once Fa took a turn for the worse. June had started pitching in, picking up more shifts at work. But Violet was supposed to be the one carrying the Lyngs.

"I've been thinking," June said, fidgeting with her necklace, a new habit since Fa gifted her with it. "Do you think, when we get there, Fathka will . . . you know?"

Violet sighed. June had been tiptoeing around hopes of magical remedies for months. Being Fa's daughter came with unavoidable side effects—namely, too much contact with folklore. "Fa can't come back to life."

"It's not wrong to wish," June said. Vacantly, as if talking to the ocean.

"You're wishing for the impossible."

"Like the Lykill?"

Violet said nothing. She didn't want to disappoint June.

"You're going to look for it, aren't you?"

"I'm going to look for the rock formation. That's all."

"But the Lykill's probably in Helheim. It's not Fathka's fault he never got another chance to go back."

Violet chose her next words carefully. She'd been hoping to tell June this later, when she was less fragile. But if June was going to insist, then it was fair that she hear the truth. "Last week, he told me he was at peace with it. That he knew—had always known, deep down—that he wasn't supposed to find it."

"Not supposed to? That was his whole life!"

"He did all he could. He didn't want to die thinking he'd failed."

"Do *you* think he failed?"

"Of course not."

June folded her arms. "Mariemma will find it, then."

"She's a historian, not an archaeologist. The government won't allow her to come. I still can't believe we got permission. Regardless, we're here to bury Fa. That's all." Violet eyed June the way she used to when June neglected her homework. That June had been fifteen. *This* June didn't droop, but held Violet's gaze until the wind forced her to blink. Then, squeezing her necklace pendant, she left.

Violet touched her own pendant. June's sun pendant was as vibrant as her personality. Violet's, molded from volcanic glass, was her flower namesake, plain and colorless. Fa had pegged her accurately.

The fog began to separate, as if some great mouth was blowing it apart. In a moment, she'd see "Ground Zero"—its technical name, though some called the wasteland "Helheim." Land of the dead. If the island had ever been known by another name, no one alive remembered it. Short of some Viking Age stoneware and weaponry, nothing of Helheim's history had survived Ragnarök. Anthropologists couldn't even determine who'd lived on the island when Mt. Rof had erupted. An entire civilization wiped out in an instant.

She let go of her pendant, wondering what volcano her obsidian violet had originated from—if it had destroyed as many lives as Mt. Rof. *How could one volcano cause so much destruction?*

One thousand years after the eruption, science still failed to provide a satisfactory answer. Admittedly, most weren't as concerned with the cause of Ragnarök so much as trying to survive it. Helheim wasn't the only wasteland now. Ragnarök had spread. It was *still* spreading.

Shortly after Mt. Rof erupted, the marine life around Helheim started dying. The Atlantic kept bringing forth dead fish and blackened seaweed. Next, the east coast of Helheim's neighboring country stopped producing crops, and so the devastation continued. Today, twenty percent of the planet had been leeched of fertile soil, of clean water and air that didn't smell like sulfur. Everyone had seen the satellite images; the Northern Hemisphere looked like it was wearing a black, perfectly round cap. Ragnarök—or "the Outburst," as the scientific community labeled it—crept across the globe in an exact circumference that widened every year, turning all it touched into the Blacklands.

Millions of people had been forced to evacuate their countries—Scandinavia, Ireland, France, Greece, parts of Canada. Over the millennium, Europeans went east. Asia and Africa grew as crowded as the Americas.

Everything changed after the technological boom of the 1800s. Once goods could be easily manufactured and transported, people started moving back into the Blacklands. Most did it out of necessity. Housing was cheap, and anyone in the Blacklands received government stipends in return for helping to alleviate population density. Technology had made the previously abandoned Blacklands livable. Water purification tools were portable; UV lamps made up for the sparse sunlight; crops could survive in green houses.

Fa had always said not even the handsomest salary could tempt him to move back to the Blacklands. He and Ma had grown up there. Violet's ancestors made up the *other* small percentage of migrants who'd willingly returned to the Blacklands. Not to save money, but to preserve their heritage. Violet's parents had been raised in a community determined to rebuild Scandinavia. What natural disaster had erased, they would reclaim. Only, how could one rebuild a culture that had spent centuries mingling with the cultures of dozens of other refugees? Who could say what Scandinavia would have been, had Ragnarök never happened?

In San Diego, Violet had been spared from all effects of Ragnarök except overpopulation. The destruction curved ever-so-slightly up the States, from West Virginia to North Dakota, but the Southwest remained untouched. San Diego was the first place her parents had ever seen a blue sky. Fa and Ma had moved to America as soon as they'd turned eighteen and planned never to look back. Then, Fa got sent to Helheim for work and suddenly, *back* was the only place he looked.

The fog around Helheim grew tired of stitching itself together and gave way with a final sigh. A strip of black took shape. Long moments passed before Violet accepted it as the ocean, lackluster beneath a wintry sky. Beyond that stretched the northwest coast of Helheim. Crags, drawing fog toward themselves, grew out of the ocean like unearthed spires from a world of nightmares.

Helheim was nothing more than a realm of death. No one ventured there except scientists.

And today, the Lyngs.

AS THE ONLY PASSENGERS, Violet's family was easy to spot. Her immediate family could fit onto one bench. Mathka had died when the girls were little, and Fa had followed suit last week, hanging on long enough to let Violet turn eighteen. She was grateful for that. Had Violet been a day younger, she and June would have been shuffled off to distant relatives in Scandinavia, despite their parents' wishes that no child of theirs would be raised in the Blacklands.

Of course, there was Oliver. On paper, a twenty-four-year-old was qualified to parent. But he was tied to the military. And he was Oliver. He'd already made it clear that he couldn't be bothered with family obligations. He'd only come to Helheim because reporters would have wondered why the famous Quirin Lyng's son had ignored his father's burial.

Violet strode to the table. "We're nearly there. I saw the coast."

"Did you see *Harth-skarth* too?" Oliver asked dryly, mispronouncing the name.

"Fathka didn't believe in Harðgjǫrð," June said.

Oliver rubbed the remnants of his military-proper hair. "Some people in the Order do."

Fa had too; he just hadn't thought the sword of stone was magical. "*There's no power in the blade,*" he'd say. "*The power is in the one who carries it.*"

But Oliver didn't care about specifics. One fantasy was as delusional as another.

"And here we are," Oliver continued, "in the middle of nowhere, still trapped by his cult. That's what killed him."

"He died of ALS. Not insanity," Violet said.

"So you admit he was crazy?"

"No, I'm just arguing against your implication."

"Can't you two pretend to love each other for once?" June folded her arms and glared. "*Þú rekr mik shílen,*" she muttered in Scandinavian.

Yes, Violet was well aware that she and Oliver drove June crazy.

"Now," June said, sitting straighter, "what we really need to talk about is Violet's quest."

"For the last time, there's no quest," Oliver said. "Too dangerous."

"Dangerous to explore an uninhabited island?" June's brows rose.

"Lightning storms."

Oliver was right. But how had he known? He'd never cared to crack open a research book or ask Fa a single question about Helheim.

June's bossy mask faltered. "I thought those only happened in the summer."

"That's when they're most frequent," Violet admitted. "They can happen any time."

June went wide-eyed.

"I'll be fine," Violet soothed, but June's voice was already rising.

"You're going to get electrocuted!"

"No, I won't."

"We'll have to bring your body back in little fried pieces!"

"That's disgusting."

Violet's comment was overshadowed by a noise so uncharacteristic that she didn't recognize it—Oliver, leaning back on the bench, was *laughing*.

"You're such an idiot, Junie," he said, tweaking her hair.

"No, I'm not," June said in a half-irate, half-sheepish grumble. She punched Oliver's arm.

Violet couldn't help studying Oliver's laugh. It was unfitting for a military officer in mourning. But, as Violet and June had been counseled countless times, first over Ma, and now Fa, people acted strangely when they grieved.

Is Oliver grieving?

He leaned forward again, elbows on the table. "Are you going to look for the . . . Lykill?" The word slunk out, reluctant.

"No," Violet said, ignoring June's shoulder slump. "I'm just going to find the troll."

"Why?" Oliver said.

"He wanted me to."

"And you're going to obey a dying man who didn't know what he was asking?"

"Yes."

"Why?"

She entwined her fingers on her lap, beneath the table. "I don't want to talk about this with you."

"No, you just don't want to talk. Because then you might be forced to open up like a normal person for a change."

"Stop bickering!" June smacked the table. "*Hrofn-ja*, I'm serious. If you can't agree on anything, keep it to yourselves. We're supposed to be family."

Violet and Oliver shared a final glance before each looked elsewhere.

She'd been twelve when he signed himself over to the military the morning of his eighteenth birthday. When Fa saw the emptied bedroom, he wept. June, reacting to the sight of Fa coming undone, followed suit. Violet hadn't joined them. With Ma gone and Fa's body already imitating Earth's deterioration, somebody had to be the tower.

She hadn't even cried at Fa's funeral.

They received an interruption in the form of their captain, who wasn't quite a captain as much as he was the person with the dreary job of ferrying researchers from Ashland to Helheim. The ferry was the only way to reach the island, and Ashland, Helheim's closest western neighbor by roughly two hundred miles, operated the service. No one had risked flying an airplane near Helheim since a disastrous crash in the 1980s. The fog was too thick, and no one wanted to get caught in a lightning storm.

The man, an Ashland Blacklander who spoke what Violet suspected was Kalaallisut, announced in broken English what she had already announced: They'd arrived. Oliver followed him into the cabin to help with the casket. Heaviness clogged the passenger deck as they pushed the coffin out.

Oliver hadn't cried at the funeral either.

It didn't matter if he approved. Violet was going to find the troll. Oliver's opinion hardly mattered. He'd given up his brotherly rights years ago.

Their captain turned the exit hatch. He'd prepped himself for Helheim with a face mask that made him look like a bandit, with goggles over the two eye holes.

The hatch squealed open. The captain motioned them into the gale outside.

CHAPTER TWO

"Ragnarök's far-reaching consequences were first discovered in Ashland in 1134, when an Inuit woman complained that the most fruitful portion of her fields were no longer producing. Her tribe called it 'That which curses the ocean black.'" - *Ragnarök: An Overview* by Dr. Mariemma Crawley

T HEY STOOD ON A black beach in a windstorm that savored of egg. Violet could taste it, despite the scarf that shielded her from the windblown sand. The goggles made it difficult to see, though she would've been hard-pressed to find light regardless. All the pictures hadn't prepared her for the darkness. It could have been dusk on a stormy evening; the sun made a bleak halo behind the perpetual clouds. Not even a seagull plunged through the fog. None would have survived if they'd tried.

Nothing did, other than the scientists, and it was a matter of opinion whether they were really living. Fa had known many, back in his prime. They rarely lasted longer than a few weeks before requesting a transfer. "*Helheim eats the life out of you,*" he'd said.

"This is a terrible idea," June shouted over the wind. "Fa couldn't have wanted this."

"This is exactly what he wanted." Through his goggles, Oliver surveyed the beach like it was a stain on his uniform.

The unforgiving wind cut through Violet's layers. She shivered. On a hot day, the temperature in Helheim barely reached fifteen degrees Fahrenheit.

Captain Napayok pointed his flashlight at the only life form on the beach. A man who seemed more clothes than person stood by a transport truck that, with its green canvas, looked requisitioned from the last war. That one had been over borders. Most wars were. In a race against Ragnarök, who got to decide when it was time to close the borders and send evacuees back to the Blacklands?

Violet could only observe as Captain Napayok explained on the Lyng's behalf. She'd researched Kalaallisut enough to say *Hello* and *Thanks,* but not much else. It had a warm and gentle flow, darkening the other man's Russian by comparison. The Russian was their guide, hired by Fa's former employer, G.E.O. Consulting.

This trip had been made possible due to G.E.O. Consulting, who had covered the expenses of transportation, lodgings, and even Fa's casket. The geotechnical company didn't fund the burial of every former employee, but Fa had been more than a name on a roster. He'd been the first man to dig up life in Helheim.

After shaking the Russian's hand, Captain Napayok tipped his cap in Oliver's direction, then left. The Russian wiped his palms on his trousers. Taking in the Lyngs, his thickly layered face furrowed. He aimed for the one in military fatigues.

"*Privyet*," Violet called, taking a step forward.

The man halted. "*Govoreetey pa-ruski?*"

"Not much," she answered. "Do you speak English?"

"Leetle."

"What did Captain Napayok tell you?"

"No idea." He ignored Violet's offered hand. "You ready?"

June's gaze yearned after the retreating Captain Napayok.

"*Da, spasiba*," Violet said.

"Let's get this over with," Oliver muttered.

The Russian and Oliver maneuvered Fa's casket into the truck. As there was no ramp, it proved a complicated process full of grunting and swearing. At last, the Russian called, "*Tak. We going now.*"

Oliver helped June climb into the truck and returned for Violet, but she had already boarded. Her brother shoved his outstretched hand into a pocket.

Standing in the back of the truck, with Fa's coffin between them like a bruise, no one seemed up for talking. They would have had a hard time; the truck bounced so much they had to balance the casket.

Violet hadn't stood this close to Fa since their final conversation in hospice. Unwittingly, her thoughts returned to that moment, when Fa had given each of his children a necklace. Once alone with Violet, he'd shared his last secret, pressing the flower pendant into her hand. Afterward, she had wondered whether it had been a secret at all and not the ramblings of a dying man.

"*I've always feared saying these words . . .*"

She was grateful when the truck came to a halt, booting that conversation from her mind. They disembarked. Once she saw the outpost, Violet understood why researchers didn't stick around for long.

The outpost, one of three on the island, comprised a series of squat concrete buildings that must have been clean at some point. Black snow covered the buildings and satellite dishes. Behind the buildings rose filth-crusted mountains. Mt. Rof's eruption had stretched its hand wide, smearing the tallest peaks.

A gale slammed into them. June toppled, and Violet and Oliver bumped heads on their way to help her up. June clutched hold of both their arms, a mischievous glint behind her goggles that Violet knew too well. She retreated, but Oliver missed the warning signs and was yanked down beside a cackling June.

Unfazed, Oliver helped himself to a handful of muck, which he smeared into June's hair. She shrieked. An unrelenting Oliver wiped one dirty finger on her nose, laughing again.

Violet observed their antics with a closed fist around her heart. Now that they were expected to be solemn, they forgot how to act. Yet Violet remained, without fail, composed.

Someone has to be.

The Russian watched. The bits of his expression that were visible beneath the scarf read disapproval. Violet felt obligated to defend her siblings—their father had just died, after all—but that would only strengthen the man's criticism.

"What's your name?" Violet asked instead, in Russian. June would tease her for testing a language when she only knew a handful of phrases, but Violet never missed an opportunity to practice.

"Utkin." He grunted. "Strange family. Come to dead land to bury dead man. Now you dance." He grunted again. "I giving you room now."

"Afterward, I'll look for the spot, if you wouldn't mind driving me."

Utkin's silence indicated he'd truly understood none of Captain Napayok's explanation.

"You know who our father was, right?" Violet said.

"*Bezumnyy.*"

"I'm not sure what that means. Twenty years ago, our father found some necklaces that—"

"Da, da." Utkin waved a hand, then scratched his chin. "Here is . . . *tak* . . . sign. I bring you."

Violet had assumed Utkin made a translation error when he'd offered to show them *the* room. The light bulbs hanging on rods said they'd find no comfort in the obvious storage shed. Wire racks held the sort of gear Violet recognized from Fa's old work: an auger drilling head, clinometers, empty spray bottles, and a variety of handheld digging tools.

"Excuse me," June said. "Sir? Where are our rooms?"

"Here," Utkin said.

She blinked. "And our beds?"

He rummaged around a shelf, retrieving a rolled-up exercise mat.

"And," she said, keeping her voice bravely level, "the bathroom?"

Utkin pointed outside.

"Nice," Oliver said.

Violet approached her brother. "I'm going to go look now, before it's totally dark. The sun sets around two."

"You're not going by yourself," Oliver said, warily eyeing Utkin.

"I'll be fine."

But Oliver was already readjusting his goggles.

"I'm coming too," June said.

This was becoming overly complicated. It only took one person to search, and Fa had asked for Violet. "Stay here," she told June.

"But—"

"Someone needs to bring in our luggage."

"*Hrofn*, I love grunt work," June muttered.

There wasn't time to argue. The meager sunlight would vanish soon. "Please," Violet said.

Her sister's face cycled through half a dozen emotions. Sitting somewhere between annoyance and fatigue was pain. When had that found June? She was the bubbly one, the dreamy one.

"*Góð*." June walked outside without a farewell.

Violet sighed. She hadn't meant to hurt June's pride. Later, she'd explain.

She, Oliver, and Utkin boarded the truck. There was no arguing with Oliver. He only wanted to come so he could gloat when she failed. Not that she intended to. The thought of failure was as outlandish as the Lykill.

Violet didn't believe in that either.

I N THE TRUCK, VIOLET and Oliver did their best to keep Fa's coffin stationary. At least the chore distracted from the discomfort of being alone together.

Despite Utkin's less-than-amiable mood, he'd agreed to drive them toward the coast. Violet had a strange feeling they were headed in the opposite direction of Fa's troll.

"The troll's imagined too," Oliver said, his palms flat on the coffin.

"Dr. Wiggins saw it," Violet said.

"Wiggins said that so Fa wouldn't get institutionalized."

Violet turned her head. June would've argued, but Violet didn't see the point. Oliver would only believe whatever made Fa look worse.

The truck groaned to a stop. The Lyngs disembarked. They stood on the edge of the cliffs, high enough to make breathing stiffer. Below spread the Atlantic in all its ghastly pallor, visible for twenty yards before consumed by the fog.

Utkin pointed to a metal sign jutting out of the sand. It was nothing fancy; only scientists would see it, and they already knew the story.

Violet and Oliver read it in silence. In English, German, and Russian, it detailed how, twenty years ago, a pedologist by the name of Quirin Lyng unearthed two necklaces in this spot. When he analyzed them, he found microorganisms thriving in the fragments of soil clinging to the necklace chain. This proved that something could survive in Helheim and represented a profound hope for the future of Earth.

Unfortunately for posterity, the sign had a few factual errors. Fa's research partner had designated this area as "the spot," since Fa couldn't satisfactorily explain where he'd found the necklaces. Fa hadn't even *found* them; a man dressed like a Viking had given them to him.

But the biggest mistake the sign presented was the idea that the necklaces said something about Helheim. Fa hadn't believed the necklaces came from Earth at all.

Violet should have taken a picture. It seemed the sort of thing to honor Fa. But he'd never wanted the fame. The scientific community had insisted upon a story he couldn't verify. Even Fa hadn't taken kindly to his own memory at first.

One thing was certain: This wasn't the spot where Fa's life had changed, no matter what history taught.

Oliver crossed his arms, angling away from the sign. "Well?"

They could go left or right. Something oddly magnetic prodded Violet left, but she distrusted it. The sign was already over a mile west of the outpost. If they kept going west, they'd get farther away. Fa had said the troll was near the outpost.

"That way," she said with a pointed finger back toward the outpost, bothered that her gut did not find that decision appealing. In fact, she noted a sense of betrayal as she directed her feet east. After a few paces, she successfully squashed the feeling.

They walked along the cliffs, searching the shoreline for anything the fog hadn't obscured. The cloud coverage on Helheim was so thick that researchers had learned to rope off the boiling geothermal springs whenever they'd accidentally discovered them. But Fa had told Violet you'd smell the springs before you stumbled into them.

Utkin crept the truck alongside them, probably not wishing to freeze. His tires squelched, adding clatter to the wind.

"Why did you tell June to stay?" Oliver said.

"I thought you didn't want either of us to go."

"I don't, but since you're determined, you might as well have an extra pair of eyes."

Violet didn't know how to explain her reasons, not to Oliver. June would think every formation looked like a troll, and she'd be disappointed when Violet said otherwise. "She'd regret coming," she said. June wanted Fa buried in a field of flowers, not this wasteland.

"Do you think tiny elves stole all the color?" Violet had asked Fa years earlier.

"Elves and trolls—that's the folklore." He'd pointed to his books. *"The real story's in here."*

"Ollie says the Lykill is folklore."

"Your brother doesn't know what he believes."

They searched until Violet's shoes were soaked through and her eyes ached from straining. Each time she spotted a rock formation on the beach, her hope lifted. But none bore any resemblance to a troll. Eventually, she forced herself to admit they'd gone too far.

"We done?" Oliver asked.

She squared her shoulders and retreated toward Utkin. "We'll pick up tomorrow morning. It'll be dark, but sunrise isn't until eleven so we don't have much choice."

"Violet, you need to prepare yourself."

"Fa wasn't crazy."

"The atmospheric conditions on Ground Zero—"

"How long have you been stationed here, Mr. Utkin?" She planted herself outside the man's open window.

Utkin, about to nibble on a sardine, warily held the fork. "Two month."

"Do you wear an oxygen mask every time you go outside?"

"No."

"Have you ever had hallucinations?" Noting his confusion, Violet added, "Seen something that wasn't there?"

"If I has, I would not know. Would I?"

Oliver snorted. "Have you ever seen evidence of a cure for the Outburst?"

Utkin, the dirtied scientist in his dirtied truck, looked wistfully at the sky. "I do not see green in long, long time. There is nothing in world but death."

He bit the tiny fish's head.

CHAPTER THREE

"Unless the Lykill is found and restored, Earth's fate is an abysmal one, with the tamest outlook projecting a complete ecological deterioration within the next thousand years." - *Ragnarök: An Overview* by Dr. Mariemma Crawley

V IOLET COULDN'T DECIDE WHAT made more noise: her alarm or June's complaining. She always sounded louder in Scandinavian.

After dressing, Violet set off for the rec room, where they'd shared a dinner of tinned fish and fruit with Utkin last night. Oliver was already sipping coffee at the table, having slept there. Their guide stirred sausage links on a skillet.

"*Kofye,*" he said, indicating a thermos on the counter.

"*Spasiba,*" Violet said.

"*Pojaluysta.*"

So that's how it was pronounced.

She took a sip, pressed her lips together, and forced down a gag. Had he used ocean water?

Oliver tossed her a sugar packet.

"No thanks," she said.

"It helps."

"It's not so bad, once you get used to it."

"Stop being stubborn." Oliver tore the paper slip open. White granules frosted the linoleum table.

Stubborn? Oliver hardly knew her.

"I drink it black," she said. To avoid Oliver's scowl, she assisted Utkin with the sausages. Utkin hummed. Violet couldn't say whether his humming indicated happiness or gloom, since the melody sounded like something the organist had played at Fa's funeral.

Breakfast ready, the three of them shared a table and noiselessly ate. The rec room held little in the form of recreation, other than a bookshelf of board games coated with dust. An attempt had been made to liven up the space with photos on a cork board. Scientists throughout the decades were featured, along with notes and reminders, one of them dated June 1987. Magnets, pins, and other knickknacks hung between papers.

Violet stopped cutting her sausage and stood. It couldn't be . . .

Dangling from nails, framed by scientists giving peace signs and a notice about a clogged toilet, were two necklaces. Both were identical but for the color of their triangular pendants, one purple and the other red.

She darted over. "Excuse me."

The clink of forks on plates continued behind her.

"Are these the necklaces my father found?"

Utkin glanced up, nodded, and returned to his plate.

"Are you sure?"

Utkin gave another, less patient, nod.

Gingerly, Violet took the necklaces. They were heavier than expected; her palm sagged from the metal chains' weight. Violet glanced around for a more appropriate way to display them. She'd known the necklaces in the national museum were copies, as the real ones were needed for testing—or so she'd thought. When had anyone last touched these?

She emptied a canister of tea bags. The necklaces looked absurd in the glass jar, like the odd collection of a scavenger. "Is there somewhere more appropriate I can put these?"

"Good is here," Utkin said.

"How long have they been hanging there?"

Utkin shrugged.

"They're just necklaces," Oliver said.

Just necklaces. They were the reason the news had broadcast Fa's death last week. The reason why the national museum was robbed a decade ago. If the thief had known the real necklaces were hanging on a bulletin board like someone's forgotten lanyard, he wouldn't have wasted his time.

Violet returned to her breakfast. They were on a schedule. Later, she'd find a more dignified spot for the necklaces.

Utkin drove them toward the cliffs and showed them a crumbling path down to the water. Yesterday, they'd searched the beach from the vantage point of the cliffs. Today, Violet wanted to walk along the shore itself, even if that did mean risking the random violent wave.

Headlights poked holes in morning's black shroud, until Violet and Oliver hiked far enough down and the truck's meager lights vanished.

Violet was reminded of the unexplored area west of the sign. *Too far away,* she reasoned. But that did give her an idea. "Why don't you go that way?" she told Oliver, pointing west. "If we split up, we'll cover more ground." *And I can search in peace.*

"I thought that was too far from the outpost. Dad said the troll was close."

Violet wished the wind was blowing harder so she could pretend she'd misheard him. He couldn't even say "Fa"? The word was too Scandinavian for him now? Bothered, she couldn't think of a reasonable excuse to send Oliver away. So she started walking east. Oliver followed.

By 8:00 a.m., the light hadn't increased, and Violet had a headache. The weather nipped at her skin, but she'd come prepared with hand warmers and two layers of socks.

Utkin said he'd pick them up at 12:00 p.m. That gave them time to return to the outpost, eat lunch, and freshen up. They had to bury Fa at one o'clock and be ready for the return ferry at two.

Each time Violet checked her watch and saw another half hour gone by, she walked faster. Discontentment nagged her every step. Even up close, none of these rock formations looked like trolls. They were searching the wrong area.

But there's nowhere else to look!

She turned around, facing west. The sign was probably three miles away by this point. Anything beyond that was too far from the outpost. But they were already farther than they should be.

Some of the internal tension unwound as Violet started walking toward the sign. But, with Oliver beside her, she couldn't relax.

Come noon, they'd passed the sign by half a mile. Still no troll. The side of her that thrived on deadlines warred with the side that had a lifetime of practice in defending Fa's name. Violet wanted to continue. If given the choice, she would stay in Helheim until she fulfilled her promise. The troll's absence suggested what Oliver had always said: Fa had been confused. Dr. Wiggins had made note of the troll but, as Oliver suggested, he could have done that out of loyalty, to spare his research partner some embarrassment. Wiggins certainly hadn't corroborated the *other* elements to Fa's story.

Fa made it up.

The treacherous thought slipped out. Violet had successfully ignored it this whole trip. It was harder to repress with the dark plain of nothingness before her. She was just as disloyal as Oliver.

She squeezed the hand warmer until her palm grew hot. Now was not the time to sit with these thoughts. There were plenty of practical reasons why she'd failed. It was dark; they hadn't had much time; the troll could have been weathered down into a different shape.

Oliver should have gone back to the truck. Yet he lingered, for the first time in years. "Look—"

"We need to leave. June's waiting on us."

He shook his head, gesturing at her like one pointing out a crack in the wall. "This is the problem with Fa. He put all this expectation on you, and now you feel guilty for not giving him the moon."

"I wanted to help him. I—" Her defense stalled. She couldn't explain this to Oliver, how she'd defended Fa with her lips but not with her heart. The troll was meant to be proof. For Oliver. For herself. Now, she had nothing.

"Can't you admit all this Order of the Lykill trash is pointless?" Oliver said. "We're not even Scandinavian. We're mutts. Our ancestors were living by the Caspian Sea until they got the insane idea to go back. Didn't you say that Scandinavian retained less than fifty percent of Old Norse?"

She *had* said that, years ago. He'd been listening? "That's not what this was about for him," Violet said. "He wasn't grasping at his own lost heritage. He and Ma left Scandinavia for a reason."

"Then why join the Order?"

"Again, you're conflating the two. It had nothing to do with our roots. He joined because he wanted the same thing the Order wants: Earth healed."

"By bringing back another lost heritage, except this one's got portals in space and magical monarchs and never actually existed."

"No. By bringing back sunlight and fertile—"

"There's no cure, Violet!" Oliver's angry arm sent the flashlight sinking into the muck. He scooped it up and smacked the glowing end into his palm. Orange light scattered oddly across the shoreline as he covered and uncovered it. "Everything's going to be dead in two hundred years," he said quietly.

"What do you mean?"

"It's speeding up. The Outburst. It used to spread at a constant rate, but something changed. New calculations estimate that the Outburst will cover one hundred percent of Earth's surface area by 2250."

Violet gripped her hand warmer, then forced her fingers to relax. "According to whom?"

"The military. It's classified. I'm not even supposed to know, but someone let it slip." He looked into the flashlight like he couldn't tell it was there. Weak light contorted his expression; Violet couldn't guess if he was bitter or just resigned. "Utkin knows. He and I talked about it. He doesn't even know what he's doing here. At least, I think that's what he was saying."

Like it had detached itself from the gloom and took on form, dread pushed against Violet's heart. Two centuries left. Fa had told her Earth had at least a thousand more years.

Fa said a lot of things that turned out false.

"Have you told this to June?" Violet finally managed.

"No. And I'm not going to."

That was a relief. June didn't need the additional burden.

"Listen." Oliver rotated the flashlight, watching it put bright patches on the sand. "I know I should have . . ." He looked up. Whatever he saw in her expression widened his eyes, like he'd just noticed her.

Self-conscious, Violet pulled her scarf up higher over her nose. "We'll bury him close to the outpost. It doesn't make sense to drive farther than necessary."

"Lettie…"

She walked away. Oliver hadn't called her that in years. The wind tugged her hair, and she focused on that, on fixing the tangles. But the wind was too fierce, her hair too matted.

There's a chance we missed it. We only had so much time. And Fa's directions were vague.

She couldn't help feeling irritated. Why couldn't he have mapped out a route? Why couldn't he have . . .

He wasn't crazy. She'd wanted to prove it, *had* to. Violet hadn't considered much else beyond that over the years. The fleeting time had not felt so very fleeting until now. Two hundred years, and Earth would be irreparably consumed.

And not a single person could stop it.

VIOLET FOUND JUNE ON the floor in their "room," thumbing through a book. She turned its pages with such disregard for the binding that Violet was relieved Mariemma wasn't here. "June, that's the Order's," she said.

"Fathka's the one who found it."

"And he wouldn't want it damaged." On her knees, Violet gently extricated the book.

June resisted. "Please. I've barely seen any of these."

Knowing June's stubbornness, and fearing for the book's safety, Violet let go. "Fine," she said, "but I'll turn the pages."

First, Violet exchanged her snow-damp gloves for June's dry ones. Then she relocated the book onto a pillow. Its weight sank the downy feathers. It was a hard cover, the width of an encyclopedia, but only because its pages were so thick. The cracked vellum showed drawings of royal dignitaries, castles, planets, and symbols.

Of course June had smuggled *this* book from home; it contained the least number of words.

This one was in "Ókunnigr," or "unknown speech" as the Order called the indecipherable language. No one alive spoke Ókunnigr. Violet had never been satisfied that an entire language existed with *no* guide for parsing it out, but Ókunnigr evaded logic. The runes weren't the Younger Futhark of

Old Norse, nor were they Anglo-Saxon. They simply existed, without reference, and the Order had to content itself with guessing based on pictures.

Although, there had been that one philologist from a few months ago . . . If only he'd given Fa his contact information.

"I'd live on the eagle world," June said, and Violet pushed her hand away before she could touch the rendering of a queen in white, wearing a chain necklace with an eagle pendant. "I bet they can fly. Earth's symbol is so lame. A sheep? What could we do—grow really long hair in the winter?"

"The pendants don't correspond to the magic. They have to do with the world's original monarchs."

"So Terlian's first monarchs were sheep?"

"It's allegorical, June."

According to the Order of the Lykill, whose aim was to preserve these long-abandoned legends, Earth had once been connected to eleven other worlds. Each of the worlds was represented by its own unique symbol, which the people wore on necklaces. One world wore knife pendants to honor the death of its first king, who'd been flayed alive. The Order hadn't deciphered the meaning behind every symbol, only some, like the world with the wheat grass pendant to signify how their first king had multiplied food during famine.

Violet hoped not every symbol was a callback to the first king's death. Otherwise, Earth's—or *Terlian*, as the Order called it—king had been somehow killed by a sheep.

These necklaces had indeed been worn on Earth before the 11th century. One of each pendant type, unearthed by archaeologists, hung on display in the Order's Chicago office. The twelve necklaces weren't ancient fashion statements; no, they were magical, according to the Order. But if that was the case, why weren't the vending machines in the headquarters overflowing with snacks? For as long as those necklaces had twinkled beneath glass cases, they'd done nothing. They certainly hadn't fixed Ragnarök.

June leaned on the wall. "I don't know any of this stuff."

That was Violet's doing. She hadn't wanted June's childhood to mirror hers. "That's okay," she said, closing the book. "I'm in the minority."

"Tell me the poem."

"You've heard it a thousand times."

"I know. Tell me again. Please?"

Carefully, Violet stored the heavy volume in her bag. Then she sat beside her sister, dusting off her lap so June could find no reason not to rest her head there. In another moment, she was picking fuzz out of June's ponytail.

Violet tried imagining the poem in Fa's reciting voice. He liked to sound melodramatic, to make the girls laugh. Toward the end, he'd lost control of his vocal cords. The result was a wispy croak that sounded nothing like Fa. That's the voice Violet heard now as she recited his favorite tale.

"In the beginning was Terlian,
And liryn abounded.
Some exercised their mind,
Where reason infers justice;
Others their spirit,
Where purity reigns;
Others their hands,
Where body meets purpose.
Until by pride was man divided.

Scattered they were
Across the heavens,
And as twelve worlds
They stood alone,
To temper man's pride.
For centuries man cried out
In longing imploration
To have, once again,
Unity.
Their cries were heard;
A high king was born.
He opened the gates,
That what was once whole
Could share its circle.
Twelve monarchs he assigned
To rule their lands.
He left the Lykill
To govern them all;
To root up
As well as to plant.
To purify
As well as to purge.
And liryn,
No longer divided,
Flourished."

The poem told the story of High King Eirìkr, of the scattering of the twelve worlds, and of the portals that later connected
them. Of course, no one had ever seen a portal. Writings from
the 12th century mentioned them, but either the portals were
invisible or they were simply an allusion to world unity.

And what of the Lykill? According to the Order, it had been the High King's relic. A thousand years ago, someone stole it from Earth. The result? One need only look outside the window. Until the Lykill was returned to Earth, the planet had no choice but to slowly deteriorate.

Were it not for the Order, these legends of the Lykill would have faded out of existence. No one could say for certain when the Order was formally founded, but the historical preservation society had been around for at least eight hundred years. People of the past had wanted an explanation for Ragnarök, and these stories were the result. They'd taken history and made something mysterious of it. For centuries, members of the Order had been hunting for the elusive Lykill, hoping to bring about Earth's healing.

Only two hundred years left . . . Mariemma doesn't know.

"You need to work on your delivery," June said. "Listen and learn, dear sister. *'In the beginning was Terlian!'*" And so, June continued, intoning the poem in a ridiculous voice that would have made any Order member cringe.

Violet smiled, twirling June's hair.

"Did you find the troll?" June asked once she finished.

Violet's smile faltered. "No. We didn't have time."

Time. To Violet, who'd be long dead in two hundred years, the time was irrelevant. But what about those who'd have to watch Ragnarök swallow Earth to the last green inch? Fa had been certain that someone would find the Lykill in his lifetime and reverse the devastation. How could he have been so utterly mistaken?

"Are you okay?" June said.

"Yes."

"I still believe Fathka."

"You should. Don't let Oliver influence you. Fa wasn't crazy." *He wasn't.*

"Even if he did belong to the Order and wear his scarf in the shower?" June said.

"You wear your necklace in the shower."

"Fair enough."

Their silence grew to a comfortable lull. Fatigue caught up to Violet. But she couldn't rest. With the issue of the troll moot, it was time for Violet to figure out her future. Mariemma wanted her to fill Fa's position in the Order. He'd been their top procurer of artifacts and an amateur linguist. Violet could pick up where he'd left off.

But she had no intention of saying yes. She'd planned to go to college—online, so she could be nearby when Fa needed her. But he'd spiraled so quickly that she hadn't had time to apply anywhere, especially since adjusting her work schedule. Though it paid the bills, an office assistant was far from Violet's ideal trajectory. She wasn't sure what was.

Following in Fa's earlier footsteps made sense. She could pursue environmental sciences and put her mind to the cure. But Violet couldn't deny her experience with historical research, her budding interest in discovering old words and parsing them to their roots. Linguistics appealed to her. But to what end? Words wouldn't undo Ragnarök.

"Think about it."

Perhaps she should apply for college so she could turn down Mariemma without offending her.

"Do you think it's a key?" June whispered.

Exhaustion pressed harder. Dozens of times, Violet had debated this with Fa and Mariemma. None of their speculations solved the question of what the Lykill actually was.

"I don't know," Violet said. "The vegvísir's a compass, which is a type of key." The vegvísir, what people called the Viking compass, showed up in some manuscripts mentioning the Lykill. But, as the vegvísir could only be certifiably dated to the 1800s, Fa had never believed it was the Lykill or had anything to do with the Vikings—much to the outrage of every Order member tattooed with the sigil. That opinion hadn't made him very popular.

Because of the meaning of the word "Lykill" in Old Norse, many Order members expected to find a key. A Norse-looking key was, after all, incorporated into the Order's branding. Some thought the Lykill was Harðgjǫrð, the sword of Earth's first king. Others thought it was a white pendant, to complete the other two necklace pendants Fa had found in Helheim: One white, one purple, and one red. Those three necklaces appeared in the oldest manuscript the Order possessed, so there was credence to that idea, but Fa had never supported it. Therefore, neither had Violet. She hadn't supported Fa's theory either, though. He'd spent most of his time hunting for two necklaces with key pendants. He'd reached his hypothesis after finding one solitary depiction of the key necklaces. But the Lykill was meant to be *one* source of power.

None of it mattered. They were empty discussions leading nowhere. "Maybe it's a syringe of fertilizer," Violet said dryly.

"I can't tell if you're joking."

"Yes. It was a joke."

"Okay good. A syringe would be lame."

"Very lame."

"Gasp!" June followed up with a sharp inhale. "You said it!"

She referenced Violet's typical refusal to use the word "lame" to imply something stupid. Violet preferred to stick to a word's technical meaning, a habit developed out of necessity.

"You're a bad influence on me," Violet said. "Come on. We need to get ready." She locked the door as June spilled her bag's contents into one chaotic pile. "Where's your Calculus book?" Violet said as she collected a pair of socks. "We can go over formulas on the flight back."

"I finished all my homework."

"Oh." Violet frowned. "Well, have you submitted your application essay?"

"I did that last week. Before . . . Fa."

Violet was stumped. "Oh." She couldn't deny the rapidly approaching sense of floundering. Surely June had some other incomplete task that Violet could fix.

"Violet?" June whispered. "Do you want to braid my hair, like you used to?"

Something nettled Violet. A pinch in her chest. A burn in her eyes. Sure signs of a reaction she didn't have time for. More than ever, she had to be steady for June.

"Turn around," she said.

Violet was out of practice. But the movements returned, as familiar as making a bed. June's dark hair soon formed a knotted rope.

"Do you remember," June said softly, "when I asked that kid—Jaxon, I think—to the dance? You went ballistic."

"I did not go *ballistic,* June. I just told him he was rude. There are polite ways to reject someone."

"We were twelve! What do you expect?"

Violet unraveled the imperfect braid and started over.

"Did you see Jeremy Stiggs at the funeral?"

Violet's fingers slipped. "I did."

"He's gotten tall."

"He's too old for you, June."

"First of all, only two years older. Second of all, I'm not the one interested in him."

"I'm not either, if that's what you're suggesting."

"Vi-o-let!" June spun around, notwithstanding Violet's braiding. "Why not?"

"I haven't seen him since eighth grade. I barely know him. Will you please stop daydreaming about me and every teenage male we come across? First the grocery clerk—"

"Okay, I didn't realize he was fifteen."

"—then the one at the farmer's market, and now Jeremy. You're ridiculous." Violet twisted June back around. June grumbled but complied.

Jeremy Stiggs *had* gotten tall. Violet had noticed.

"The Order has youths too," Mariemma had said.

Violet chewed on her tongue. There weren't any teenagers in the San Diego branch. Not that she would know how to talk to them. She felt much more at ease having a conversation with a seventy-year-old who believed in magic.

Once June was dressed to Violet's contentment, it was her turn to get ready. She buttoned her black dress, sank her stockings into ankle boots, then combed her hair. Finally, she fitted herself with gloves, a wool cap, and her coat. From head to toe, she wore black. Her necklace matched perfectly.

"Do you want me to braid yours?" June asked.

"My hair's fine. Let's go."

June's gaze dropped.

After eating sandwiches, they met Utkin at the truck. Everyone kept quiet, once again preoccupied with keeping the casket steady.

Since Fa couldn't have his troll, the least they could do was bury him by the sign. Utkin took the man-made ravine down the cliffs, parking the truck on the sand that had encrusted everything from his tires to his chin whiskers. When he and Oliver lowered the coffin out of the truck, it sank so deeply that, despite every effort, the coffin refused to budge.

At last, Oliver stepped back and scrubbed his face. "We'll have to bury him here."

June stood arm in arm with Violet as the men dug around the casket, shoveling slick heaps of muck that reminded Violet of manure. Fortunately, it only smelled of sulfur and salt. They watched Fa sink lower and lower, swallowed as if by quicksand. Another Helheim oddity—the ground should have been frozen.

His velvet scarf sank along with him. He hadn't cared what he'd be buried in, so long as he had his scarf. There would be no flowers; just crusts of ash. No dirges; just two men cursing their shovels and probably Fa for insisting on this inconvenient ceremony.

After fifteen minutes, the coffin had dropped a decent level. Oliver and Utkin had an easy time maneuvering the mud back into its hole. It moved like it wanted to return. Violet wondered if the tide would eventually draw Fa into the ocean. He would have liked that.

June cried on Violet's shoulder. Violet anchored her hand. She forced herself to think of their return-home itinerary and not the gnawing at her conscience. The Order knew that Fa had expected Violet to find the troll. They'd think she gave a halfhearted search. But they didn't know that she'd wanted to find it more than Mariemma.

Oliver wiped the slime off his fatigues. He'd worn his dress uniform at the funeral, but here, without an appearance to maintain, he'd returned to the faded clothes of his boot camp days.

The four of them stood in silence until Utkin said, "Sorry for dead." He removed his hat, shivered, then rammed it back on.

Violet appreciated the gesture. She made a mental note to contact G.E.O. Consulting and see about supplying Utkin with better coffee.

A wet cough from June summoned Violet to the present. Here she was, at her father's burial, and she was planning.

"Come here, Junie," Oliver called, arms open.

June didn't even hesitate. Soon, Oliver was holding her. Their hug looked so . . . natural. Like they'd never fallen out of practice.

Violet couldn't remember the last time Oliver had hugged her. The last time she'd hugged June.

Something iron-like dug inside her. It stuck out like a nail that had finally broken through plaster. "Would anyone like to say something?" she called, disrupting the twinge.

"We love you, Fathka," June said, muffled against Oliver's chest. "We hope you're with Mathka now."

Oliver and Violet shared a long gaze. Each understood the other's job: to ignore the rift between them, and to take care of

June. Though Violet did the parenting, Oliver had been faithful with his monthly checks. Those would continue, so long as June needed them.

That time is dwindling too, interjected an unpleasant thought. Soon, June wouldn't need Violet—no more than anyone else did.

A glint in the mud disrupted her pessimism. Violet, recognizing Oliver's pendant, retrieved it. "You dropped this," she said, holding out the wooden object. She had a violet, June a sun, and Oliver the vegvísir. Even though Fa hadn't believed it was the Lykill, he'd liked the idea of leaving Oliver a compass.

Oliver stared at the sigil. As the moment lingered, Violet connected his guilty expression with his lack of movement.

He'd thrown it away.

Her fingers curled around it. "He gave this to you specifically, Oliver."

"I . . ." He found June's gaze, and his defense lost momentum. Then, anger encased his expression, so familiar, even after all this time. "I can't take it."

"Why not?" Violet said.

"For the same reason we didn't find the troll. None of it is real—other worlds, portals, ancient kingdoms."

"You don't mean that," June whispered.

"Do you believe in magic?" he asked her.

"Believing in magic is better than throwing away something given to you out of love!"

"It wasn't love. It was obsession. If he loved us, why did he let Violet waste her life for him? Look at what he's done to her." He pointed with the shovel. "She's a robot."

"Leave her alone, Oliver!" June said.

He stabbed the shovel into the ground. Meanwhile, Utkin shuffled backward as if hoping to dissolve into the fog. "It's all one big sham." Oliver's voice cracked. "Nothing can stop the Outburst."

"The Lykill can!" June said.

Oliver swore. Then they were arguing. Arguing, with Fa's coffin buried hardly five minutes.

A knot grew in Violet's chest. She looked past Oliver, at the cliffs making a dark streak across the sky, as if competing for the title of most ominous. If she'd been the sort to succumb to calls of the wild, she might have thought the cliffs echoed with her name. They did look tempting. From up there, she could survey more of Helheim. She could give Fa's troll a final search.

And she could extricate herself from this conversation.

"I'm going for a walk," Violet said.

"You can't," June said. "The lightning storms. You could get electro—"

"Let her go." Oliver's nostrils flared. "Don't forget we ship out at two."

"I'll meet you at the outpost." Violet turned toward the endless strip of death.

CHAPTER FOUR

"Some conflate Harðgjǫrð with Thor's Hammer of the Gods, but Thor is a myth. King Borgfastr is not." - *The Reign of Terlian* by Dr. Mariemma Crawley

H ER FEET MOVED IN a paradox. Aimless, because she had no sense of direction. Purposeful, because Violet was walking. *Somewhere.*

She made for a path up the cliffs before deciding to trek along the rocky beach, farther from the sky. June was right; the clouds were roiling. The wind snuck inside her goggles and under her scarf, sending her hair up like a kite. She did nothing to stop it.

Oliver's pendant felt intrusive, even against her gloves. She pocketed it. Discarding it had been impulsive. He'd take it back. Especially if June berated him enough.

Her walking stalled, her path blocked by a narrow stream pattering against the stones, courtesy of a small waterfall that poured from the cliffs. Why was the water unfrozen? With her head ducked against the wind, she turned toward the cliffs. In a rare moment of unconcern, she sat on the black sand without caring how it would muss her clothes.

This was the land her father had cherished. The whole world knew his story, but only a few people knew the truth.

Fa had been G.E.O. Consulting's soil expert. He hadn't been hired to find any artifacts. That job was for the archaeologists. But they'd walked in the wrong direction that day—or Fa had walked in the right one. That's when he saw the gigantic rock formation shaped like a troll. Spying movement near the base of the formation, Fa drew closer and found a man closer to death than life.

G.E.O. Consulting had sent eight scientists to Helheim. This stranger was not one of them. He wore unusual clothing, like a medieval costume, and the rough beard and braids gave him the appearance of a Viking. But those details Fa only remembered later. He was distracted by the blood glistening on the Viking's stomach.

Fa tried communicating in English and got nowhere. Then he realized he could understand bits and pieces of the Viking's muffled speech. Another dialect of Scandinavian, he'd guessed. Oliver used to suggest that the Viking had been a Blacklander from northern Scandinavia, some crazy fanatic who'd snuck over to Helheim. That was before Fa had determined that the Viking had been speaking Old Norse. Before Oliver decided that Fa had hallucinated the whole event.

The Viking, regaining some strength, gripped Fa's forehead so intently that Fa felt it would have been rude to pry him off. After thumbing through a book he'd shielded under his arm, the man spoke, now in a language foreign to anything Fa had heard before—the indecipherable Ókunnigr. The Viking then slung his scarf over Fa's neck and drew a rough symbol in the sand. Finally, the Viking forced his book, along with two necklaces, into Fa's hands.

That had been his final effort; the man fell unconscious with his cheek in the dirt.

Fa ran for help. When he returned with his research partner and medical supplies, the Viking was gone, along with any evidence that he'd existed. Fa searched one way, his research partner another. They found nothing but the same emptiness scientists had explored for centuries. Neither the book nor necklaces convinced Dr. Wiggins of the Viking's existence, only that Fa had made some excellent archaeological finds. So they returned to the outpost, where Fa examined the necklaces under a microscope. And there it was: life. There was bacteria in the sand, and where there was bacteria, there was hope.

But Fa wasn't convinced. Maybe initially, during the whirl-wind of interviews and news appearances. Fa had wanted to believe the world was one step closer to the cure, even if that meant admitting that he'd hallucinated.

G.E.O. Consulting kept the necklaces and sold the book to the highest bidder, which happened to be the Order. Unfortu-nately, the book was later stolen, probably by some avid history buff. It wasn't as if the book had value to anyone other than a collector of antiques.

As for the Viking's scarf, Fa shoved it in a box and never touched it, not until after Ma's death, when he was forced to reconsider his supposed hallucination. The headstone next to Ma's had the Order of the Lykill's logo on it—the same key the Viking had etched in the sand.

When Fa realized that the Viking's symbol pointed to a group of historians known to cosplay, his first inclination was to remind himself that he'd hallucinated the entire encounter. But a month after Ma's death, Fa was on a plane to meet the historian who'd received the Viking's book. Whatever Dr. Mariemma Crawley said had been enough. When Fa returned home, he dug the scarf out of storage and wore it until he died.

Much to the dismay of G.E.O. Consulting, Fa gathered his scientific research into a cabinet he never bothered to open again. Books shifted from geology to anthropology. Fa quickly became the Order's keenest researcher, unearthing more history in a year than the Order had uncovered in decades. He'd just had a knack for finding things.

When he was diagnosed with amyotrophic lateral sclerosis, he turned to his children for help. Someone needed to fill in the gaps of his research, driving to any assortment of libraries or museums on his behest. But Oliver hadn't wanted the mantle of a fictional legacy, one that had cut Fa's salary in half and made him a laughingstock among his former peers. So Violet had volunteered.

"I've always feared saying these words," he'd said to her during that final hour, when the approach of death had stolen his color and left his face a marred war zone beyond repair. Then, managing to squeeze her fingers, he had smiled, the mischievous grin that reminded her of the man who'd once had the strength to toss his children in the air. *"But, worse, I've feared never saying them."*

And so he did.

She only remembered a snippet. But it wouldn't have mattered if she'd remembered every word. They'd meant nothing when he said them, and they meant nothing today.

Violet's insides were cold. She could hardly defend Fa's hopes when presented with the irrefutable evidence: Helheim was dead. There was no Viking, no Lykill, no cure. In two hundred years, the satellite images would show every colorful patch of green and blue swallowed by black.

A wave swept up the sand, almost touching her boots. The tide had crept closer while she'd sat, and the waves were growing violent. She looked out—and found herself staring at a troll.

Violet scrambled to her feet. About fifty yards out, the towering basalt stack stood in the ocean like some wide, hump-backed creature, the sole formation in every direction. It looked lonely in the sea of night.

Fa's troll. Not where she'd guessed, but here it was. *Real.*

As she debated whether he would have wanted his casket relocated, the wind swelled. She staggered, shielding her face. The sky had turned as black as the beach. Waves sloshed around her ankles. Thunder pounded as raindrops began to fall. She needed to find shelter. Once the storm passed, she would return to the outpost and discuss this with her siblings.

Violet turned, assessing the cliffs for some overhang in the basalt columns. A few feet above her was an opening in the rock wall like a small grotto. Could she reach it?

The first white spike of lightning crackled overhead. Violet got a leg-up on the rocks and hoisted herself into the hole. She crawled away from the rain, which still managed to splatter all over her as the wind threw it. The hollowed-out space wasn't deep, coming to a dead end a few feet in, though it turned sideways into a narrow tunnel. A dim glow flickered from within its depth.

Curious, she inched closer, then paused, thinking of cave bats. But this was Helheim. Animals were extinct.

The humid air clung to her nostrils as she crawled through the gradually quieting tunnel. The space grew brighter, the ceiling higher, until she could stand. The tunnel had taken her into a low-ceilinged cavern, cozy as a bear's den. At its center, a large ball of light pulsed, like a giant was pointing his flashlight at her. Its color fluctuated; yellow shades bled into browner hues, forming a spiral of gold, the hazy rays reminiscent of the sun.

Violet spied around for an extension cord—obviously, something was producing the light. Yet she couldn't find an outlet anywhere. There was no lamp, nor cord, nor machine, nor anything capable of producing the hovering, golden glow. She pocketed her protective goggles, scrutinizing the light. Something this big should have emanated heat, but she felt nothing coming from it. Violet waved her hand through the dusty brilliance.

Her hand disappeared.

Alarmed, she pulled her arm back, then chastised herself for letting her eyes deceive her and reached again. Her fingertips touched the light, which felt like the same cold patch of air she stood in. The brightness swallowed her fingers, then palm, then wrist as Violet continued extending her arm. She could very clearly see the absolute nonexistence of her limb, not merely clouded or obscured, but completely invisible, like the light formed a dense shield that hid anything beyond it. Now that she studied it, she could make out nothing of the cave on the other side either.

Violet was tempted to ignore the light's confusing existence. But curiosity was taking on substance, a needling in her gut, the sort of voice she'd typically disregard. Listening to gut feelings was June's prerogative. Yet Violet couldn't dismiss the nudge, even as she skirted past the light in favor of the cave's more reasonable side. At her back, the light tugged.

She faced it. Disembodied lights did not exist. There had to be a source. Resolute with scientific curiosity and *not* spontaneous whim, Violet walked through the light.

Her eyes took a moment to adjust. Violet moved forward and banged her knee. Odd. She'd come to a wall, when she'd thought she had more room. Running water trickled down the stone, which had been dry a moment ago. Perhaps it was the rain leaking in from above?

Wind fluttered her black dress, sounding haggard and thin. Its cold breath found her cheeks. Where had the breeze come from?

Violet moved toward the wind, her bearings confused. Everything felt so much smaller than before; the damp wall kept butting against her shoulder, and what she could see of the cave by the light looked barely wider than a modest bathroom. The cave even smelled different, like mud and wet grass.

She felt along the wall for whatever opening let the wind in, determined to find the source for at least *one* confusing aspect of this cave. She found it quickly, her fingers touching air and her face blasted by cold wind. The glow illuminated an exit she'd failed to notice before. Either Violet's observational skills were abysmal, or this opening had materialized out of nowhere.

"What on Earth is going on?" echoed a June-like voice of confusion in Violet's head. It was like she had walked into a completely different cave.

She edged through, keeping one hand over her forehead to shield her eyes from the rain. Outside, the sound of rushing water grew louder. Her boots slipped over stones that patterned the ground in an incline. Violet reached out for balance and found the outer cliff wall. She secured a grip. Long grass, stiff as straw, poked through her gloves.

Violet paused. Grass?

Creeping down the cliff wall—which was not as black as she remembered—was what *looked* like grass. But it couldn't have been. Not in Helheim.

Staring somewhat dumbly, Violet belatedly registered that it had stopped raining. Tentatively, she lowered her hand. The noise of moving water continued, and now she saw why: She was standing thirty feet above a river or lake that flowed past in all its dim, confusing vigor. Somehow, she'd exited the cave at a much higher elevation than when she'd entered.

She peered up. Instead of a heather sky puckering with lightning, she saw an inky blanket covered with twinkles. Stars? Helheim's constant cloud cover made stargazing impossible. And there were thousands, white and shimmering spots carpeting a darker, cloud-like streak, similar to the sparse views she'd seen of the Milky Way, if the Milky Way had such a curved arm. Stranger yet, the pink on the horizon indicated the coming of morning.

But none of that confused Violet as much as the *other* object hanging in the sky. A moon, plump and full and oddly pinkish—and then another one. Another moon. A yellowish crescent dangling between the stars as if it was supposed to be there.

She stared, telling her vision to adjust. It was afternoon. Helheim had no grass, and Earth had one moon.

Much clearer than June's imaginary voice, she heard Oliver's.

"Breathe the air in Ground Zero too long and you start seeing things."

Violet moved, determined to make the sky reshape itself into something sensible. Her foot slipped, and she stumbled down the dirt and rock path, managing to land painfully on her backside so she could skid the rest of the way down like someone on a sled, only without the preferred instrument. At the bottom, she rammed her palms into the dirt to keep from rolling into the water.

For a moment, she lay there and caught her breath. More brown grass grew beneath her.

None of this should be here.

Something growled.

Violet peered up. All remaining fragments of understanding fled when she saw a wolf twenty feet away, pawing at the dirt.

She froze, stubborn logic hammering *There are no animals in Helheim* into her skull, yet failing to override her fear.

The wolf's shoulder blades shifted like sharp peaks. It shook its snout with something like a sneeze. Dissatisfied, it lifted its head. Eyes like black almonds noticed Violet.

Neither moved, except for the wolf's ears. They flicked and pointed back. Then its tail twitched and its front legs bent. Back went its lips, baring its teeth and gums. Violet couldn't hear the snarling over the fearful pounding in her eardrums. She had to run. Yet she had to remain still. Quick movement would set it off.

The wolf snapped, spraying saliva. Sharp barks followed next.

She pushed herself up and ran.

CHAPTER FIVE

"The Lykill will be found, but not on Terlian." – *On the Lykill*
by Anonymous

V IOLET RACED PARALLEL TO the river. The ground was hilly, strewn with boulders, which made it easy to zigzag. That seemed the reasonable thing to do, making it harder for the wolf to lunge at her. Violet focused on her weaving pattern and nothing else, not the landscape nor the sky nor the time. She'd never understood the Old Norse fear of the horrid *ulfr,* but now she was ready to agree that even a Viking should run from a wolf.

Ahead and to her right, she spied a bridge. It looked narrow; perhaps the wolf wouldn't follow. Violet dashed for it, crossed over the water, and kept going on the other side. Only when her chest surpassed the point of aching did she consider slowing. She spotted a large boulder at the crest of the hill she hadn't realized she'd been climbing. Violet darted behind it. There, she collapsed onto the grass and gasped for air.

Had she outrun it? Had the wolf even chased her to begin with?

Violet peeked around the boulder and accidentally smacked her forehead on it. White splotches overtook the black ones, dotting her vision. When the haze passed, she blinked at the landscape now lit with morning colors. There was the river, and there were the cliffs—no, these were mountains—but no wolf. She watched for another half minute, just to be sure, and then leaned against the boulder and worked on calming her heart rate. The winter air made her damp legs cold, though the temperature felt milder than it had before. *Much* milder. She was probably just overheated from the physical exertion.

Her temple throbbed. Violet touched it, wincing. Her fingers came away red. Not a lot of blood, fortunately. Otherwise, she appeared fine, albeit uncomfortable, given that she was sprawled on the grass and her shoes soaked through.

Grass.

Smoothing down the rising concern as if it were a wrinkle, Violet stood. The scenery did nothing to alleviate her worry.

Healthy bunches of purple flowers followed the curves of the land. Across the water, mountains stood where the Atlantic should have been. One wispy cloud fluttered across a sky beginning to bud with blue, a seamless transition at the crack that indicated dawn. The scene looked picturesque, the mountains an inspiring backdrop, where charcoal streaks of rock bled beneath swaths of clean, white snow.

Violet clamped down on the cuffs of her jacket. The familiarity of her own clothes calmed her, so she focused on the rest of her outfit, shaking out her wet shoes, wringing out her socks, and patting her flower pendant to make sure it was secure.

Oliver's necklace.

Hurriedly, she investigated her pockets, relaxing when her fingers brushed the symbol. She removed the vegvísir from its chain and added it to her necklace. The wooden compass formed a cage door over her violet. She didn't like that at all. As soon as she returned, she would make Oliver take this back.

Violet mentally worked through the possibilities. Just one stuck: She'd somehow found an island off the coast of Helheim, one that hadn't been affected by Ragnarök. It was a weak theory, but her only working one. Rather, the only one she was willing to consider.

She could figure this out later. Her current priority was finding her way back to the outpost. The ferry service, government-operated, ran on a strict schedule. It wouldn't wait for her. Oliver and June would have to leave, and Violet would be stranded with Utkin until the next ferry came.

Unfortunately, she had no idea where the cave was.

The vast mountain range across the water stretched left and right like an upside down map, completely unhelpful. The bridge was her only sure landmark, though she couldn't even see it from here. How far had she run? Once she crossed the bridge, she'd have to climb. The mountains looked insurmountable to anyone without a walking stick.

Her eyes found the moon now starting to fade as daylight took over. And then the second moon.

She turned her head and exhaled. First, the cave. Every other thought could come afterward.

As Violet made to walk in the direction she'd run from, something nudged from the opposite direction, like a flutter in her peripheral. She looked, finding nothing but the need to search harder. Breaching the last few steps toward the top of the hill, she glanced below.

A man was fishing in the river.

Even if he hadn't been the only other human around, he would have stuck out for his ginger braids, which protruded from head and chin in Viking style.

Having the word *Viking* interrupt her thoughts as forcefully as this stranger, Violet hastened backward. There was a stranger in Helheim. Even worse, someone who looked like a Viking.

There are flowers and grass, too.

There was a logical explanation. Determined to find it, Violet marched downhill. "Excuse me," she called when he was a stone's throw away.

He tested the slack of his line without pause.

"I'm sorry to interrupt," she said louder, keeping her distance. "Do you speak English?"

He replied something indistinguishable, and her hope drooped.

"English?" she tried again.

His shoulders strained against his baggy tunic when he sighed. Then, the man turned. He was much younger than his broadness suggested, not a wrinkle on him. Exasperation morphed to surprise when he registered her, and he shifted closer to the water, stealing a furtive glance toward his shoes. He spoke quietly, though not low enough to conceal his caution. Was he intimidated by *her?* He could have tossed her like a pebble.

"Is this Helheim?" she said.

His furrowed brows were like copper bristles.

"Ground Zero? Or…" She gave up.

He looked stiffer than Oliver's frowns, eying a copse of trees upriver as if he longed to escape. "*Nerir indz*," he said slowly, and continued in a language she couldn't pinpoint. The manner in which he spoke was stilted, as if he found the words as foreign as she did.

"I'm sorry, I don't understand," Violet said. "Um. *Spekish þú Skandinavski?*"

He sighed. Of course he didn't speak Scandinavian.

Their confusion grew awkward. She mentally sorted her pitiful lexicon of foreign languages. A decade of research couldn't leave her *this* ill-prepared.

A soft wind tossed the beaded braids within his beard. He'd taken pains to style himself in such a fashion. She'd never seen anyone dressed like a Viking unless he or she belonged to the Order. Did he? It wasn't uncommon for Order members to daydream about sneaking onto Helheim, though none had actually undertaken such a dangerous journey. If this man were in the Order, Violet could ascertain it with the customary greeting, a line taken from *Hávamál*, a poem in the Elder Edda.

"*Gefendr heilir*," she said. "*Gestr er inn kominn; hvar skal sitja sjá?*"

Hail to the giver! A guest has come; where shall the stranger sit?

He stared at her. Down came the ginger eyebrows. Violet didn't understand his expression. Rather, she did, but it was the first time that the Order's friendly greeting had elicited dark suspicion.

"Who are you?" he asked.

In Old Norse.

An enthusiastic cry burst from the trees. Violet jumped and the stranger turned as another young man skipped over, waving a wriggling fish. The gangly, barefooted newcomer took no notice of Violet.

The newcomer showed off his catch to the Viking. They had a back-and-forth—or, more accurately, the newcomer rattled on and on, speaking over the Viking's every attempt to interrupt him.

Old Norse. They're speaking Old Norse.

His accent was unfamiliar, and she only recognized a few words, but her comprehension was enough to pick out things like *fish* and *water;* they were the same in Scandinavian.

Their conversation concluded when the Viking finally grabbed his friend's shoulder and rotated the young man toward Violet. The newcomer hopped back and dropped the fish. Bedlam radiated from him, from his disheveled ponytail all the way to his dirty feet. He looked younger than his friend, Violet's age, and nothing about *him* screamed "Viking." Violet felt slightly less concerned for her sanity.

"*Ov jes du?*" Ponytail demanded, taking a defensive stance in front of the Viking. This wasn't Old Norse, but the gist still came across: *And who do you think you are?*

Violet mutely stood there, regretting not learning all the languages Fa had.

The Viking nudged his friend. Ponytail stood fast, glowering as if Violet was waving a hatchet. But, after a few murmured words from the Viking, Ponytail relented. He jogged toward the trees.

Carefully, the Viking returned the fish to the water, his back to Violet. She waited. Now he was letting water trickle through his fingers. Ignoring her.

He wouldn't help. But Ponytail might. Violet started for the woods. The woods with fertile, green trees. Though no less confused, at least she had confirmation that she wasn't alone in the middle of nowhere.

But how did this place escape Ragnarök?

Evidently Violet's education had some holes.

She wasn't far from the trees when a girl, loosely veiled with a scarf, erupted out of them. At the sight of Violet, she halted abruptly and peered past, presumably searching for the Viking, whom everyone seemed overly protective of. The girl relaxed when she spotted that Violet had not, in fact, murdered him in cold blood. Her eyes were red-rimmed, and her cheeks bore evidence of a fading flush, as if she'd hastily finished crying.

Yet another stranger exited the trees, a man around Oliver's age. He eyed the girl with undisguised regret, but he shook the weight free and addressed Violet. "Sun above you," he said in accented English. He stood like a prince beneath a purple scarf draped over one shoulder, buckled by a gemstone. The colorfulness extended to his red waist sash. "I am . . ." His focus went taut, and he stopped, pain marring his politeness.

Violet leaned back. Was he reacting to her?

"Kelispar?" the girl said. The rest of her question was in another language.

"My shame," he said to Violet through a strained smile, "I—" He stopped again, now holding his heart. Kelispar—Violet guessed that was his name—panted heavily, vision glazed over with pain.

"Kelispar." The girl reached for him, retracted her arm, then lay it tentatively on his elbow and asked another indiscernible question.

He shied away, exhaling through his teeth. Next it seemed he apologized, offering her soft words. Violet guessed he was telling the girl to leave; she kept shaking her head, hand on his arm. But he won the argument. Reluctantly, the girl left them and settled by the Viking, who remained at the river's edge some thirty paces away.

"Are you okay?" Violet said.

Kelispar answered in his language. Then he cleared his throat and said, "My shame." Immediately, he winced and shut his eyes. When he opened them, they were wet, which made Violet distinctly uncomfortable. "I was not . . . expecting that. But I am fully . . . committed to . . . Advocating on your behalf."

Violet didn't understand what he meant, other than the fact that he was unwell. "Don't worry about it," she said. "I can talk to someone else. I only wanted to find out where I am."

"I am not . . . ill. And you cannot talk to the others without my aid, I'm afraid. I am . . . the only Advocate near."

Advocate?

"I'm terribly sorry. This must be alarming for you." Embarrassment hung in his voice.

"You don't have to apologize. Do you need water?" Not that she knew whether it was drinkable, but she focused on the river. It gave her something else to look at.

"You are kind. It is I who should . . . offer you." In her peripheral, he dried his cheeks on his scarf. "There. I believe I understand it now. I am quite ready for you."

Violet risked looking at him. Color had returned to his face, though the smile under his golden beard was sad.

"May I entreat you to conceal what you have just observed?" he said softly. "I don't wish to alarm my friends."

Surely the girl had already picked up on whatever it was Kelispar was suffering from. But Violet replied, "I won't say anything."

"I thank you. Now, how may I aid you?"

"Well . . . is this an island?"

"No, the closest island is Torkash."

"Torkash? What country is this?"

"We are in Arat."

Violet's heart gave a nervous stammer. Now that he was no longer flinching, she noticed something wrong with the way he spoke, something an accent couldn't explain. His words sounded after his mouth stopped, as if on a delay.

Maybe this was what a concussion felt like. She was also wearing wet socks in winter. Hypothermia? Violet moved toward a patch of sunlight and organized her thoughts. "I've never heard of Arat. Is it—"

"My shame, is that blood on your forehead?"

In another moment, Violet was boxed in. Kelispar loomed, waving over the girl, who joined him in examining Violet's forehead without any concept of personal space. With a shout toward the trees, the girl demanded a blanket. Ponytail, from the forest, answered.

"Steady her arm, Kelispar," she said, mistaking Violet's retreat for fatigue. Her accent differed from the others', reminiscent of Spanish or Italian. "Eliath—cousin, gather wood for flames," she called to the Viking. "Here, sit. There you are, Alikar. What took so long? You didn't tell us she was injured."

Violet was maneuvered onto the ground and wrapped in a blanket delivered by Ponytail, whose grumbling indicated that he spoke perfect English. So did the Viking, who obeyed his cousin's request for firewood without playing dumb like he had with Violet.

The girl adjusted Violet's blanket. It was odd to be mothered by someone roughly her age. But Violet was too polite to object, especially to a stranger, so she accepted the smothering and tried not to grimace.

"Should we send for a Balm?" The girl spoke strangely too, the way it looks when a movie is dubbed and the dialogue doesn't match the movement of the actor's mouth.

No one batted an eye at this. Violet's breathing quickened. She was alone and defenseless, surrounded by four strangers. She opened her mouth, but nothing spilled out.

Kelispar's expression wrinkled. He drew so near that Violet's only escape would have to be the river. "Are you in danger?" he murmured.

"No. It's only . . . your mouth isn't moving with your words."

Relief smoothed out Kelispar's concern. "I see," he said, leaning on the balls of his feet. "I am so accustomed to it that I do forget how it appears." He solemnly touched his chest as if that explained everything.

If Violet had been June, she would have run away by now. Had it not been for the fact that Violet desperately needed to know where she was, she might've taken June's course of action. At the same time, these strangers hadn't threatened her with anything but their unsettling way of speaking. Violet could ignore their mouths until she had information. Then, she could run.

"Thank you for the blanket," she said, returning it to Ponytail. "But I need to get home. Where am I in relation to Ground Zero?"

"I'm not familiar with that name," Kelispar said.

"All right, then. What continent is this?"

"Northern."

"City?"

"She's very thorough," Ponytail said. He had the same accent and blond hair as Kelispar, though he was nowhere near as tidy. "Perhaps the injury stole your memory. Don't you know where you are?"

"No, I don't," she said.

"Ha!" Ponytail pointed at her, grinning. Then, seeming to remember his manners, he lowered his arm. "My shame, I assumed that was a joke."

"I don't understand." Violet touched her forehead, flinching at the bruise. "I couldn't have traveled far."

"Perhaps I can ask the questions, and your answers may provide us with insight?" Kelispar's smile was friendly, though his eyes remained heavy.

Violet nodded.

"Ask her how she knows Faartunga," Ponytail said, hands on his hips again.

Faartunga?

Kelispar glanced at the Viking before returning to Violet. "Are you from Kvale?" he asked her.

"She looks like she's from Kvale," Ponytail added.

"No," Violet said, "I'm from San Diego. In the States."

"My shame, I'm not able to understand the local names. You are of Bar'Talian, are you not?" Kelispar asked.

She had to focus on his hair, rather than the odd movements of his speech. "No," she said, "I'm of America."

"America? What is the insignia of your realm?"

"The flag? It's red and white with stars."

"I do not know such an insignia," Kelispar said, frowning now.

"Aha!" Ponytail pointed up. "How many moons on your realm? That ought to narrow it down."

"By 'realm' do you mean planet?" Violet said.

"What else would I mean?"

Pushed into her memory like an unwanted letter through a mail slot, two moons shone above the mountains. "One," she firmly said.

"One what?" Ponytail said.

"You asked me how many moons."

"But no realm has only one moon."

"Vessels say Terlian does," the girl spoke.

Ponytail laughed. "Yes, but she's obviously not of Terlian."

No one else gave the girl's suggestion further thought. No one except Violet.

"We of Terlian are not for this world," Fa would say.

She swallowed. Something toyed at the brink of understanding. It threatened to expand, taking over. *Not yet.* She wasn't ready. For a dozen reasons, Violet had to rein in this conversation.

"I'm from Earth," she said, "the same as you, unless you're all of the opinion that there are multiple inhabited planets."

"But there are," Ponytail said.

"And on Earth"—her voice grew louder—"there's only one moon."

"By 'one' do you mean 'four'?"

"No. I mean one."

"She hit her head too hard," he told Kelispar.

That prompted more fussing. Kelispar insisted that Violet rest, so she sat. While Kelispar and the girl conversed over the best way to handle Violet—someone so injured she'd forgotten basic facts of reality—Violet blinked at the pale, morning sky. It *was* morning. She hadn't stumbled onto an inhabited, English-speaking island off the coast of Helheim. She was somewhere else altogether, and it was nowhere near home.

Her limbs shook. *I'm cold, that's why.* She closed her eyes, shutting off the sight of Kelispar and the others in their strange clothes, with their strange words, in this strange land where flowers bloomed and two moons hung in the sky.

This wasn't Earth.

Her brain allowed the thought. Violet didn't—*couldn't*—resist. Of course there wasn't a mysterious island flourishing by Helheim. She'd gone through that light in the cave and walked into another world. Fa had been right.

And Violet had never believed him.

The guilt pierced sharper than the shock. In the end, she hadn't been any better than Oliver.

The others continued chatting. Violet vaguely registered things like, "No, can't leave her here" and "ask Dag to watch her." Her thoughts swam through the muddle of doubt and resignation. And then they calmed.

Violet had come to Helheim determined to find the troll, to prove one element of Fa's story. Now she had an entire world of proof. Denying it now would be foolish. This was what she'd wanted for years, and she wasn't the only one who needed it. Oliver had to accept the truth, and June—Violet winced—deserved to be vindicated. Everyone in the Order did. Violet could be the one to drag Fa's name from the mud. She'd fought for him all her life; she'd continue in his death.

Her quivering ceased. She stood. With determination on her side, everything looked a bit less foreign. "Excuse me," she called. "It's true. I'm from Earth. I'm from . . . Terlian."

Ponytail shook his head and sighed as if Violet were insisting on a joke no one appreciated. The much more polite Kelispar hid his doubt with a sympathetic smile, the type people give children who believe they can fly. The girl's expression grew contemplative. The three of them seemed robbed of ideas, but the Viking rose. He'd kept his distance, a quiet force collecting bramble for a fire no one cared about anymore. Now he neared, and as he did, a palpable energy fell over the group, like he'd wrapped them in a cloak. Violet braced herself, though unsure why.

"Give us your proof," he said. Though he looked Oliver's age, his entire demeanor spoke of a well-aged shadow.

"Proof?" Ponytail's voice jarred Violet out of the moment. "What do you expect her—"

The Viking raised a palm.

Violet had no proof. Why did they need it? They hadn't expressed any shock about the possibility of her being from another planet. Aliens weren't unusual for them . . . unless that alien came from Earth. Doors worked both ways. People on Earth didn't know of any access to other planets, and these people didn't know of any access to Earth. There hadn't been one.

Until twenty years ago.

She studied the Viking. He fit the description of Fa's Viking, though that man had been in his thirties. His father? An uncle? "Twenty years ago," she said, "a man in your family went missing."

The others exchanged uneasy looks, but the Viking was inscrutable. "You know much of me and mine," he said, "but every citizen of the eleven realms knows of my father's misfortune."

"He was wearing a vest made of fox pelt and a maroon, velvet scarf."

The last comment tightened the Viking's eyes. "How do you know this?"

"Because he gave the scarf to my father."

He held his pose a few more breaths. Then, the Viking moved. His reach was swift and sure. Over to his waist, and suddenly he held a sword. One more breath and it was against Violet's throat.

She sorely wished she was still on Earth.

CHAPTER SIX

"The Great Rift resulted in Terlian's utter isolation and a six-year war that came to an end when the monarchs of Bar'Talian offered refuge to Terlian's royal family—those who had been separated from their homeland. Thus, the Rift Treaty was born." – Vessel Davit, recitation at Torkash Summit

T HOUGH INSTINCT ORDERED HER to retreat, fear told her he'd slice her in half if she budged.

"Put that away, Eliathor," Kelispar said. "This is a matter of diplomatic relations and falls under my purview." Though he hadn't lost his politeness, something crisp had fallen into it.

"We know nothing of Terlian's liryn," Eliathor said. "She could be a weapon, a spy."

If she'd been able to safely swallow, Violet would have done so in shock. *Liryn* had been another one of the Order's words—for magic.

"I'm not a weapon," she said. "I came here by mistake."

"Unlikely. How is it that you know the language of my family?" Eliathor held the blade so practiced and poised, Violet wondered how many people he'd sliced with it.

Her hands twitched. This was absurd. Earth had minded its own business for centuries. How could they possibly consider her a threat?

"Whatever your assumptions about Terlian, it isn't dangerous," she said. "We don't have liryn. No one believes in other worlds. I wasn't sent here. I took shelter in a cave and saw a light. When I walked through, I arrived here. It was an accident."

"Then why do you know of my father?" Eliathor said.

"My father met him. He was injured. Mine ran for help, but when he came back, yours was gone."

"Where did this meeting occur?"

"On Earth. On—on Terlian."

"That's impossible. Who kidnapped my father?"

Kidnapped?

"Speak." Though Eliathor's voice grew louder, he didn't shout.

"I don't know anything about a kidnapping," she said. The last word jumped out of her, garish. Fa had assumed the Viking injured himself while hiking, not that he'd been intentionally harmed.

"Where can I find your father," Eliathor said, "that I may hear his story?"

She counted the hairline fractures in the blade. "He recently died."

Eliathor said nothing. The sword shifted back a centimeter.

"We weep for your loss," came Kelispar, softer now. "May he who has fallen asleep rise again."

His kindness confused her. Everyone had consoled June, the youngest; or Oliver, the only son. No one had said sorry to her.

Suddenly, Violet ached. Just a flicker of sorrow. It pulsed like a weak flame, ready to vanish at the slightest sign of water. She finally swallowed, and it faded.

"When you say Terlian has no liryn," Eliathor's cousin spoke, "you mean it's scarce?"

"I mean no one practices magic," Violet told her. "Not *real* magic. There are some people who think it existed a thousand years ago, but they're a minority."

"A thousand years." The girl looked at Kelispar as if from habit, then flushed and focused on Eliathor. "What if our assumptions are wrong? What if Terlian doesn't have it? No Lykill, no monarchs . . . no liryn."

"The Terlion is lying," Eliathor said as Violet said, "The Lykill?"

"You have it, then?" the girl asked eagerly.

Violet floundered for a reply. If inhabited worlds existed, why shouldn't a cure for Ragnarök? "No, but I've heard of it. It's real?"

"What do you mean, 'It's real?'" Ponytail crossed his arms. "Do you live in a hole, or are you willfully deaf?"

"Alikar," Kelispar chided.

"She claims not to know of the Lykill! Eliathor's right. She's deceiving us."

"Or," the girl said, "perhaps we've all been deceived. We've always thought it odd, haven't we, that Terlian never made any attempt at reconciliation in all these centuries?"

Kelispar inhaled, as if bolstering himself to take charge of the conversation again. "Then," he said to Violet, "the Lykill is not in the hands of your realm leaders?"

"Everyone believes it's a myth. All of this. Other worlds, magic." Violet wanted to move, then remembered the blade. "What is the Lykill?"

"The High King's relic."

She tightened the fists she'd already formed. "King Eirìkr."

Like some strange wind had stifled their words, everyone fell silent, letting the High King's name drift in their quiet. For the first time, Violet sensed the barest hint of unity, that maybe these people weren't comfortable having Eliathor skewer her after all. Sure enough, his cousin stepped forward.

"Lower your sword," the girl said. "She's not a threat."

Eliathor looked prepared to interrogate Violet until nightfall, but he said, "Search her."

She sighed and Violet stiffened, but neither of them thwarted Eliathor's demand. The girl patted Violet's arms, awkwardly and without much precision. "I'm Meliora," she said as she turned out Violet's pockets. "I'm sorry for the precaution, but you must understand. Terlian is the most powerful of the twelve."

"Terlian isn't powerful at all. It's dying."

"Dying?" Meliora looked up from Violet's shoes.

"Your world isn't?"

Meliora shook her head.

Once she declared Violet's person devoid of any threats, Eliathor stepped back. Sweat dribbled onto Violet's collar as he stowed the weapon.

"Oh, thank the Welder." An expressive sigh came from ponytailed Alikar, whose name almost rhymed with *Oligarch.* "I feared I'd have to tell Lali that her uncle committed murder. And in his fishing clothes, to shame."

"Mind your tact," Kelispar said.

Murder. Violet's throat twinged. She almost touched it, then tugged on her beanie, scanning the distance toward the mountains. Though the need to escape had lessened, she'd still rather be on the other side of the river, where she could continue her search for the portal without Eliathor dogging her steps.

But the Lykill. *It existed.* She didn't bother outlining some alternative, an excuse for the fact that these people knew the same word.

Perhaps there was a reason the Order hadn't found it yet. It might have been on this world all along. Violet couldn't return home, not until she was certain.

She opened her mouth, but Kelispar had already begun speaking.

"You say the Lykill is not on Terlian. If that is the case, pray, how was your gate opened?"

She assumed Kelispar meant the glow. With reluctance, she addressed Eliathor. "Your father opened it."

It was the simplest solution. Scientists had been investigating Helheim since the 1200s, and no one had found a glowing portal until now.

Skepticism crept out again, in Kelispar's patient smile and the way Alikar elbowed Meliora. Eliathor remained a human-shaped pillar of suspicion.

"That simply isn't possible," Kelispar said.

"Why not?" Violet said.

In a gentle manner, like explaining long division to a tear-stained child, Kelispar said, "Supposing he found the gate pendant, Chief Halfdan would not have used it. He was not the rightful owner of the Lykill."

Gate pendant? Violet mentally tallied through the Viking's possessions. He'd had the scarf, the book, and the necklaces. If he'd had the Lykill, he'd hid it well.

"Is that all the Lykill does?" Violet asked Kelispar. "Opens portals—gates?"

"You really don't know!" Alikar said.

"It contains the power of the High King," Kelispar said. "Control of the gates is one aspect, yes. It also gives its wearer all liryn, as well as power to weld."

"Depending on which pendant you're wearing," Meliora said.

That made little sense to Violet, who was more concerned with whether it could bring a planet back to life. "Then it's a pendant," she said.

"Three, to be exact," Alikar said.

Violet's pulse began a strange, expectant patter.

"Allow me." Alikar patted Kelispar's arm as he edged around him. "You're terribly pedantic with explanations, brother."

Brothers? Violet recognized it now, in the blond hair and their strong noses. The similarities stopped there. Kelispar's outfit looked pulled from a cosplay magazine for the wealthy.

Alikar was barefoot, his shirt untucked, and hadn't rolled his trouser legs evenly.

He traced three triangles in the dirt. "The pendants are differently colored. One white, one purple, one—"

"Red," Violet said. "Yes, but those aren't the Lykill."

Alikar propped up one eyebrow—black, unlike his ponytail. "You, who know nothing of the Lykill, are not permitted to argue with my artistic rendering."

"The Lykill is a single source of the High King's power. It can't be three separate necklaces."

"When the pendants are united," Kelispar said, "they form the Lykill."

Alikar drew to demonstrate his brother's meaning, his finger digging one unending shape that resembled three interlocked triangles.

"The Valknut," Violet said. "But that's a Viking symbol." She looked to Eliathor. "Do all the realms reference the Lykill with the Valknut, or only this realm?"

"What in Barikad does that question mean?" Alikar said.

His politer brother answered slowly. "This is the official representation of the Lykill. As far as I am aware, the symbol is ubiquitous."

Violet stared at the Valknut. Alikar had drawn it well; many Order members struggled with the shape. For the sole fact that it was associated with Old Norse mythology, Order members tattooed themselves with the Valknut as often as they did with the vegvísir. But no one had considered it to be anything more than a symbol. Its origins were unclear—maybe it was Hrungnir's heart, or maybe it had to do with Odin.

"It's odd that the Viking association carried over from Earth," she said. "You even call it 'Lykill.'"

"Lykill is a dead word, without meaning," Kelispar said.

"But it's an Old Norse word." And the same in Scandinavian, too. Violet glanced again at Eliathor. "For 'key.'"

"I do not understand these terms, 'Old Norse' and 'Viking,'" Kelispar said. "But I have never heard anyone refer to the Lykill as a key. How do you call 'key' in Faartunga?" he asked Eliathor.

"*Vegaréttur*," Eliathor answered.

"Then . . ." Violet considered the necklaces she'd held just yesterday. "You are certain the Lykill is those three pendants?"

Kelispar, Meliora, and Alikar nodded in sync.

"There is no other explanation," Meliora said to Eliathor. "Your father found the gate pendant. That means it was here, on Bar'Talian, all this time!"

Eliathor resumed collecting wood scrap. Kelispar answered in his stead. "It was not his to use, Meliora."

"How else was the gate opened?"

"I—"

"Which color is the gate pendant?" Violet asked, knowing she was rude for interrupting but determined to prove Fa right.

"White," Kelispar said.

She nodded. "Then it must have been on Terlian at the same time as the other two pendants. Meaning the Lykill was on Terlian. But since Terlian wasn't healed, those pendants *can't* be the Lykill."

"I don't follow your points entirely," Kelispar said, "but the Lykill must be more than reunited. It must be restored to its proper place."

Violet fought to keep her shoulders from sinking. This meant Fa had given part of the Lykill to the government, and then wasted his life searching for something he'd already found. All those Order members over all those centuries, and not one of them had suspected that the three pendants formed the Valknut. Fa had been so confident that the answer lay ahead, not behind.

Well, Violet now knew what the Lykill was, and where to find two-thirds of it. The cure for Earth was sitting in a tea jar. Now she just had to find the white pendant.

Meliora and Kelispar were still debating. Eliathor worked on his wood pile, and Alikar patted down a dirt castle that was surprisingly fastidious. When he caught Violet admiring it, he grinned and said, "It certainly isn't my finest work, but not bad in a pinch. What do you say, the monarchs' summer home?"

He was certainly nothing like his brother.

She made a noncommittal noise before turning toward Eliathor. "Did your father ever talk about the white pendant?"

His fingers halted on mossy bark. In profile, he looked chiseled onto the scenery. "I've never spoken to my father. He was found washed upon the lake shore. Twenty years ago."

Violet's throat felt as wobbly as the log pile. She should have realized. Fa might have been the last person to see him alive.

"Alikar," Kelispar said.

Alikar blew dirt off a turret.

"Go gather our belongings."

"Am I of no use to you except in drudgery?" Alikar said.

"Quickly."

Sighing, Alikar stood and wiped his palms on his shirt. "At your command, Emissary," he said with a bow before ambling off.

"My brother did have a point," Kelispar said to Violet with an apologetic smile. "You said you did not know what the Lykill was, yet you knew the pendants' colors."

"Because I've seen them before." To Eliathor, she added, "Your father gave the purple and red ones to my father. His friends hunted for the white one but never found it. He didn't think they were the Lykill, but I . . ." *But I guess he was wrong,* she didn't say.

If Eliathor's father had the gate pendant, that would explain how he'd vanished despite his injury. But why would he bother leaving two pendants behind and taking the third with him?

The others hadn't responded yet; they were gaping. Kelispar and Meliora, at least. Eliathor's frown deepened with every word Violet said.

"He had the red and purple too?" Meliora whispered. "He . . . *he found the Lykill?*"

Violet had assumed that much was obvious. "I don't know how or where. My father didn't know what they were, so he gave them to a museum." She wouldn't admit they'd been neglected on a bulletin board. "There's a chance the white pendant is here. Your father probably came through the same gate I did. Maybe this is the lake—" She stopped.

Maybe this was the lake that had carried his dead body to shore.

"Well," she said in an unpleasantly loud voice, "thank you for the information. I should be going now. Goodbye." With a nod in their general direction, she turned. It was a terrible farewell, but a plan had evolved, and she wanted to enact it. And the sooner she left, the sooner she'd stop saying things that reminded Eliathor of his dead father.

"Where are you going?" Kelispar said.

"To look for the white pendant. Then to the portal. The gate. Terlian is dying. My father believed the Lykill would cure it. If I unite the three pendants, we can start healing."

"Apologies, but you cannot find the Lykill."

"I realize it's a long shot, but the least I can—"

Kelispar was shaking his head. "No. *You* cannot. Only someone of Eliathor's bloodline can restore the Lykill."

"Do not speak of the prophecy," Eliathor said.

"It's the key to your family's restoration, Eliathor."

He stood. Whatever logs hadn't yet scattered did so when his foot bumped them. "You do not appreciate what you are asking," Eliathor said. Since he was watching the lake, Violet didn't immediately realize he was addressing her. "Those who seek the Lykill do not succeed. If they are fortunate, they survive the humiliation of their failure." He paused, noticing Meliora's taut mouth. The braids woven into his beard sagged. Eliathor held out a hand. She took it. Together, they walked to the lake.

"Chief Halfdan and Meliora's father sought the Lykill together," Kelispar said quietly. "They died during their quest, before their children were born."

That made Meliora and Eliathor twenty. He seemed so much older. "Chief Halfdan found it," Violet said.

"But failed to restore it." Kelispar sighed. A breeze tousled his hair, though it immediately returned to its ordered waves.

"The Lykill can heal more than your realm. It is meant to unite us, to restore liryn to its former purity." He touched his chest.

"Then your world has lost magic too?"

"I'm afraid my liryn doesn't recognize this word, 'magic.'"

"Your liryn?"

"Yes. I am an Advocate. A translator, if you will allow the crudity." He tugged at something swallowed by his scarf. A braided purple cord hung over his chest, similar to graduation cords, though with a single tassel on the back; Violet knew it was there because she'd seen this necklace before, in a display case. Kelispar tilted the pinkie-sized knife pendant that hearkened back to the king who'd been flayed to death.

Violet gaped. Kelispar had magic. That explained why no one's mouths matched their words, and why they hadn't understood each other until he arrived.

"I see," she said before clearing her throat. What else could he do? She considered asking, then wondered if that was rude, like asking about his GPA.

"Eliathor was correct," he said. "If you seek the Lykill, you will not find it. You are not meant to. The remaining pendant must be found by Eliathor's family. The prophecy wills it. The Hastein bloodline will rule your realm again. They ruled until the Great Rift, when the Lykill was lost and the gate to Terlian closed. No one has encountered a Terlion since." His eyes widened. For a moment, it seemed he expected Violet to start levitating. "But," he said, "if a gate is now open, Eliathor's family can return to their throne."

Eliathor's ancestors had once ruled Earth. Thanks to the Order, Violet was already familiar with the concept of planetary rulers. However, hypothesizing about some ancient monarch was very different from meeting the descendant of one. She couldn't think of anything to say other than, "Oh." The long-lost prince of Earth had almost sliced off her head.

"The Hasteins will find the Lykill," Kelispar said. "But this cannot be done without knowing the location of the gate."

"I understand that his family ruled in the past, but if they come to Earth and claim to be its rulers, they'll probably be put in a mental institution."

"I hear your concerns, but we should not fret about what will come. The prophecy will unfold as it's meant to."

Unease pricked Violet's spine. So far, the Order had been right on all counts. This prophecy was probably true too.

"Are you saying . . ." She lowered her voice and said, "Eliathor's family will attempt to conquer Earth?"

Kelispar's expression, which had until now belonged to someone who could run for president, turned comically aghast. "Gracious!" he yelped. "Certainly not! I apologize if I conveyed any semblance of threat of war. Eliathor's mother is a peaceful woman. She only hopes to see her throne before her death."

Violet relaxed. "All right."

"Gracious." He gave an awkward laugh. "What a horrible idea. No, crossing through the gate to Terlian will be sufficient. Could you direct us to it?"

Across the lake, the homogenous mountains stretched, daunting as ever. Without that gate, Violet was stuck on this planet.

"Is it in the mountains?" Kelispar followed her gaze.

"Yes."

"But you don't know where."

"I'll find it," she said. "It can't be far past the bridge."

"Before you do, I beg you to meet Lady Basilia, Eliathor's mother. Tell her what happened to her husband. Answer her questions about Terlian. Give your testimony that a gate stands open."

Go with these strangers on their strange planet? Violet didn't have the time. The ferry . . .

She checked her watch, knowing the answer even as she read the verdict, dread sinking like an anvil. The ferry had already come and gone, taking her siblings with it. June would've protested, but Oliver would've made her go. They likely thought she'd gotten lost. Utkin was probably looking for her.

With any luck, she'd find the gate within a few hours. But there was a chance she'd fail. First, Violet had to find the bridge. Then, she had to hike a mountain. The *right* mountain. That could take all day. Night would fall, and then Violet would be stranded on some mountainside without food or water, on an unknown world with unknown predators. Or wolves. And all this would happen after she combed this area for the white pendant.

Violet *had* hit her head too hard. The pendant could be anywhere. Maybe Eliathor's father dropped it in Helheim, or maybe he'd lost it in the lake and it currently hid in a coral reef hundreds of miles away.

The truth was, Kelispar and the others could find the gate without Violet. They knew it was in this area; the mountains didn't go on forever. But she could use *their* help. They could safely guide her.

Violet didn't have much choice. Hiking an otherworldly mountaintop during winter was plain stupid.

"How long will it take to speak with her?" she asked Kelispar.

"We can meet her tonight and return you here tomorrow."

One day. Violet hated to cause June worry, but the sooner she spoke with Eliathor's mother, the sooner she could reassure her sister that her body wasn't in tiny, fried pieces.

Violet searched past Kelispar's golden head. Meliora, like an overprotective mother, supervised Eliathor as he reeled in his line. Unlike Kelispar, he wasn't enticed by the Lykill. The disinterest was all too familiar.

"All right," Violet said. "I'll talk to her."

Kelispar beamed. "Thank you." He grasped her elbows and dipped his head, then hugged her.

As Violet awkwardly stood there, smothered by a total stranger, she knew this was going to be a long day.

CHAPTER SEVEN

"Basilia's silence on the subject of her husband's mysterious death lets us assume he abandoned his family, unable to stomach the news that a third son would bear the infamous Hastein name."
– Vessel Magda, recitation at Kapor Academy

V IOLET EXPECTED ELIATHOR TO protest her coming along, but he simply adjusted the fishing rod over one shoulder while Meliora collected his belongings. They all entered the trees.

Once out of the sun, Violet grew colder. She discreetly adjusted her jacket. If the gentlemanly Kelispar realized she was cold, chances were he'd insist upon loaning his cloak. That, or Meliora would attack her with another blanket.

The trees put forth sweet scents. None were particularly tall; most resembled magnolia and cherry trees, others budding with waxy leaves. Shrubberies, some berry-laden, made the area feel more like a garden than a forest. The air twittered with birdsong. Butterflies hovered over purple ferns. She'd never strolled somewhere so decadent with flora. Curiosity tempted—she was walking on another planet, after all—but she didn't want to be caught gaping at every leaf. And she would certainly be caught; Kelispar kept inspecting her sidelong, and Meliora repeatedly turned to Violet, opened her mouth, then changed her mind. Eliathor, however, pretended she was invisible.

"My shame, asking you so belatedly," Kelispar said, coming so close that Violet almost hit a tree to avoid bumping elbows with him, "but what do they name you?"

She almost asked *Who?* "Violet."

"Ah, *Violet.*"

His lips didn't form anything that remotely resembled "Vi-o-let." She wondered if her name had translated into the flower's scientific name.

He continued beaming, like she was his smartest pupil. His smile, revealing immaculate teeth, reminded Violet that she was muddy and unkempt. She pulled down her beanie, wishing he'd look elsewhere and also give her space to walk. Perhaps smothering strangers was a custom in this country. Remembering how he'd hugged her, Violet's cheeks warmed. The last boy who'd hugged her was Jeremy Stiggs in eighth grade. She had stood awkwardly then, too.

Ahead, a massive figure lumbered in the shadows. Eliathor slowed, touching his hilt, until proper lighting illuminated Kelispar's brother. Alikar, now quadrupled in size by a backpack, staggered closer and paused to wipe his brow.

"You seem overburdened," Eliathor said.

"Oh no, I'm fine. Not at all weighed down by this behemoth luggage."

Eliathor chuckled. "We cannot have that," he said, relieving Alikar of the bag. His thoughtfulness jarred Violet as much as the laugh.

"I see you've kidnapped the Terlion," Alikar said.

"Of course not," Kelispar said with a sternness he probably reserved for his brother and wrinkled socks. "Gracious. Do be serious. This is a grave situation."

"Grave situations call for grave measures," Alikar airily replied.

Kelispar ignored him. "I'll find Dag. Take Violet to the docks," he told Eliathor.

"Dag might have other plans for his boat," Meliora said.

"No, he will pilot us."

Her brows rose.

"What doubt you show for our fearless leader!" Alikar cried. "Do you not realize, sweetest Meliora, that Kelispar is emissary to Her Ladyship Basilia? A graduate of Kapor Academy? I believe he's also an Advocate, but it's possible I'm mistaken. And let us not forget his handsome visage and overall eligibility—"

"Your loyalty is most endearing," Kelispar said loudly. He cleared his throat and avoided Meliora's gaze. "Violet, I'm afraid you'll be unable to understand anyone once I've left."

"Yes," Alikar said, "I don't know how anyone survives without you."

"Would you close that mouth for once in your blessed life?" Kelispar said, finally gaining a mote of exasperation.

"He doesn't know how," Meliora said, then covered Alikar's mouth. He raised his arms in surrender.

Kelispar returned to Violet. "Alikar, Eliathor, and Meliora hide their faces in public to avoid attracting attention. I don't want you to be alarmed."

"All right," Violet said slowly. She was definitely curious. *Emissary*, Alikar had called Kelispar. Perhaps he was a recognizable public figure. That didn't explain why the others hid themselves. Then again, Eliathor was Terlian's royal descendant and Meliora his cousin.

And Violet was the sole Terlion on the entire planet.

"*Gracious*, Kelispar," Meliora teased, "you're giving her the impression that we're fugitives."

"That's certainly not the case," Kelispar said. "It's all rather political, Violet. I don't wish to bore you. Rest assured that we're doing nothing illegal."

"Not that he cloaks himself," Alikar said, having pried Meliora's hand away. "He could never obscure such a face. Could he, Melly?"

Pink spotted Meliora's cheeks. "Violet should wear something over her clothes. They're not at all customary. Trust the men not to notice." She gave a jittery laugh before slipping off the green and red fabric she'd been using like a head wrap. Her dark braid spilled free.

"No thank you," Violet said, but Meliora was already guiding the shawl around Violet's shoulders.

"Now you will be cold," Eliathor said to Meliora.

"I won't." Meliora wore something reminiscent of the Middle Ages: a brown, strapless wrap over a long-sleeved shirt, all of coarse material, trimmed in yellow and green and belted at the waist. Violet caught swirls of Nordic knots embroidered at the cuffs, collar, and hem. A Viking's dress, for certain. "I hope—Eliathor, what are you doing?"

He'd put his cloak around Meliora. There was a minute of fussing and arguing. Meliora insisted Eliathor needed the cloak for disguise. Alikar fervently, with much poorly disguised winking, suggested Kelispar's cloak for Meliora, which both pretended not to hear. In the end, Meliora took back her shawl and Kelispar shed his scarf for Violet, a bright purple wrap, which, in her opinion, made her outfit more conspicuous.

"With that," Kelispar said, "may you find the road to me again."

"We shall do our best not to miss you," Alikar said.

Kelispar bowed to Violet and strode away.

Meliora slapped Alikar's arm. "Why must you be so obnoxious?"

"I consider it my sacred duty to vex him, lest he . . ." The rest was Old Norse.

Liryn. Though unnerved by its existence, Violet felt relieved that it was practical. She'd have a harder time relaxing if Kelispar started spewing fireballs or morphed into a toad.

Violet grew more curious about Kelispar's political position as Meliora withdrew additional accessories from the backpack. A puffy wool cap went to Eliathor, who tucked his hair away, then wrapped a scarf around *that* until only his eyes were visible. Meliora shrouded her head like some sort of desert hermit. Alikar just strapped a black beard over his face, which clashed with his hair but matched his thick brows. He looked so ridiculous that Violet thought it defeated the purpose.

But apparently, he wasn't done; Meliora bossed him about. Sighing, he fitted on knee-high purple boots, shrugged into a long coat, and donned a fur-lined hat as boxy as a fez. He spread his arms out, seeking Meliora's approval. She wrapped a red tasseled sash around his tunic.

Without any comparison but clothes on Earth, Violet guessed Alikar's outfit cost more, judging by the fur and intricate embroidery. He popped with reds and purples, while Meliora and Eliathor blended better with the forest. But then they finished their outfits with identical maroon jackets that matched Alikar's. Gone were any earthy Viking hints, everyone now thoroughly colorful.

Maybe Kelispar's shawl *was* fitting.

They set off. Violet fell behind, where no one would notice if she spent too long scrutinizing the forest. She awaited the arrival of some woodland unicorn or sprite. Fa hadn't believed in fairytale creatures, but she'd already been surprised a dozen times today.

If one didn't fully comprehend a language, was it still considered eavesdropping? Violet couldn't help leaning in to better hear the Old Norse conversation. If only she'd studied it more diligently, like Fa had. Many Order members were as dedicated to preserving Old Norse as Violet's own Blacklander grandparents were protective of Scandinavian—an ideal too progressive for some among her grandparents' community, who resisted Scandinavian's mutations and lobbied to make Old Norse their official tongue.

Yet, even those militant defenders of Old Norse cared nothing for the Lykill. Violet's own grandparents had believed their son was delusional. The Blacklanders fought for a bygone world but had no interest in what the Lykill truly represented, which had very little to do with Vikings and Norse mythology, and everything to do with a restoration far surpassing one specific culture. Earth's healing was meant for all.

Oliver had never understood that. He'd thought Fa's obsession was just about bringing back the Vikings.

The trees petered out. Eliathor paused at the top of a hill, which overlooked a village and the foggy harbor. Eliathor—the most authentic Viking she'd ever seen. She wondered if he had blue eyes.

A mist-shrouded sea spanned one wide carpet of greenish gray. They trudged downhill, battling against the wind.

If she'd had to guess what another planet looked like, Violet would've pictured flying motorcycles, robots, clothing made out of aluminum. So far, this realm seemed a healthier version of Earth.

The houses, varying shades of brown stone, satisfied the "otherworldly" feel. They resembled standalone turrets, each house cylindrical and tall, with arched windows and doors. The average house had a completely flat roof while the grandest featured domes like some Persian palace. The architecture looked like the renderings of the Ottoman Empire from June's history books.

Fishy scents swelled as the streets grew less residential, the houses replaced by taller, rounder buildings and the gardens by low walls. Well-bundled people populated the roads, the men wearing fezzes and the women warming their heads with colorful scarves. Pants were billowy, boots fur-lined, and coats either wool or something that resembled goat fur. No one had a waist sash like Alikar and Kelispar, nor their tall purple boots or otherwise ornate attire; these clothes were practical. Everyone was distinctly blond or black-haired, of Kelispar's shorter, stocky build and light skin. Alikar was easily the tallest person for miles.

At the marina, Eliathor scanned the boats. He said something to Meliora, and she shook her head. Both addressed Alikar, who shrugged. Violet guessed they couldn't find Dag's boat. Purple vessels swayed. Was everything here legally required to be purple?

They walked left. The breeze wasn't unbearable, but a gust made Violet stagger. She fought it, and the wind fought back, apparently intent on blowing her off the dock. Hoping the boats would shield her, she did what the wind wanted and shifted closer to the water. One step later, Violet walked into the stubby pole that anchored the nearest boat. Wincing, she limped forward, only to bump Alikar.

While he unintelligibly asked whether she was all right, she unintelligibly told him she was fine. Eliathor turned and noticed the boat. It was a squat tugboat with a two-tiered tower and colored like an eggplant. Eliathor nodded. Violet had rammed into the right pole.

Eliathor threw the backpack overboard, then guided Meliora onto the boat. Violet was surprised when he returned for her. An hour earlier, he'd held his sword to her throat. Now he held out a hand. She pretended not to see it.

"Stop being stubborn."

That was Oliver's voice, and there he was in her memory, offering sugar for her coffee. Then the memory split, and Oliver was lending a hand to help her board Utkin's truck. Violet drank her coffee black, and she knew how to climb.

Stubborn.

I'm not stubborn.

She took Eliathor's hand. The motion was awkward, and she let go as soon as her feet steadied, but something about it felt like victory.

Benches bordered the rim of the tugboat, which contained little furniture other than crates and barrels. Violet made room for Alikar, but he'd lingered on the dock, distracted by two boys kicking a ball around. While he joined them, Violet debated where to sit. Meliora and Eliathor's low conversation on the bench seemed exclusive. Meliora kept looking at Violet. Eliathor wouldn't.

Violet relaxed when Kelispar strode into view, accompanied by a man and woman. "I've found a Balm," he called, "who—"

"Who is injured?" The woman zipped past Kelispar—and the kickball match—and helped herself on board. Around her neck, she wore a liryn necklace. Her cord was red and the pendant a metal "X." Black hair showed beneath her scarf.

"Her forehead is wounded," Meliora said, indicating Violet.

"I'm fine—"

"Take off your hat," the doctor said.

"No, really, I—"

"The emissary has already paid me. Now, hurry up. I've got a woman in childbirth."

This realm was *really* not in favor of Violet's free will. She reluctantly pulled off her cap, accepting the woman's probing.

"Oy! Sir!" The younger of the boys on the dock ignored the incoming ball, engrossed by Kelispar. "Is that a real liryn cord?"

"It is," Kelispar said.

"And it's welded to you?"

"Verily."

"Can I see it?" He bounded forward.

Kelispar smiled. "Certainly." He knelt.

The doctor pursed her lips. "Foolish," she muttered, attacking Violet's head with a cloth like it was a dirty spot on the floor.

"It's heavier than I thought," the boy said, rubbing the knife pendant a little too freely. Kelispar didn't show offense.

Personal space doesn't exist here, Violet thought.

The boat creaked. Eliathor moved toward the edge, monitoring the exchange, hand near his hilt.

"You keep an eye on the emissary," the doctor told him as she pressed her fingers against Violet's wound. "Letting any fresh-faced urchin finger his cord. Now hold still, girl." She spoke rapidly. "*Coagulate and bind . . . coagulate and bind . . .*" The doctor's face twisted, like one in pain. Her hands went rigid.

An intense tingling tickled Violet's hairline. She was about to ask whether that was normal when she heard a *splash!* The boys took off running. Eliathor shouted after them, and Alikar shouted after Kelispar, who was currently spluttering in the lake.

Violet forgot about her forehead as Eliathor swung himself over the railing and chased after the boys. Alikar was on his stomach, reaching for Kelispar. Meliora hurried off the boat with a blanket, which she flung around Kelispar once Alikar finished hoisting him onto the dock. Beneath the sopping hair, it was hard to tell if Kelispar was angry, embarrassed, or simply winded. Alikar's ire was clear in his yelling. Kelispar wasn't translating anymore, which was probably for the best. Nothing that required such wild hand gestures could have been polite.

The doctor's head shook disapprovingly. She stepped away with a few unintelligible remarks, then clambered off the boat without a backward glance.

Violet was alarmed. Had she given instructions? Was her forehead supposed to be itchy?

Eliathor came thudding down the dock, dragging the boys by their scruff. The younger one had Kelispar's necklace wadded in his fist. Kelispar spoke firmly. The boys crossed their arms and ignored him. Eliathor rattled them, which made them angrier. The younger boy flung Kelispar's necklace into the water. Unperturbed, Kelispar held out his hand. The necklace floated back, traveling by invisible momentum, until it settled around his neck.

Violet was grateful no one was watching her ogle.

Kelispar motioned for Eliathor to release the boys. They tried to bolt but didn't make it far—Alikar shoved them straight off the dock. Kelispar looked ready to dive to their rescue, but Alikar restrained him. The boys swam as if pursued by sharks.

Kelispar reprimanded Alikar for a full minute before everyone boarded. "Ah, Violet," he said, smoothing his hair, "how is your forehead?"

"I'm fine," she said, knowing it was polite to reciprocate but thinking Kelispar might prefer if she pretended the whole thing never happened.

Monitoring from his squat tower, their captain called for them to sit. Eliathor obeyed first, and the others crowded around him, Alikar taking up six feet of bench by sprawling horizontally. Violet would've liked to sit alone on the other end but figured that might be rude. She took the spot closest to Meliora, readjusting her beanie. Her forehead felt normal. Liryn could heal too.

The boat vibrated. After another moment, it glided forward.

"I cannot believe you tried to help them after they robbed you." Alikar's arm hung over his eyes. "Actually, it's just the sort of thing you would do."

"Report them," Eliathor said.

"Mercy can be more effective than punishment," Kelispar said. "They're young. They can change. And I did not wish to draw any more attention to our party."

"Spoken like a true diplomat." Alikar yawned. "I should've pretended to be Yakiv Stefanos. That would've made the vultures fly."

"You look nothing like Yakiv Stefanos," Meliora said.

"Too skinny," Eliathor added.

Alikar cracked one eye open so he could glare.

"I hope those boys never have the misfortune of meeting Yakiv Stefanos." Kelispar, absently fingering his pendant, looked troubled.

Whatever that uncomfortable exchange on the dock had been, Kelispar's necklace was at the heart of it.

"Kelispar," Violet said, "is liryn not the same as magic?"

He smoothed his drenched hair. "It's possible your word 'magic' doesn't translate because it's dead. How do you define magic?"

"Something that allows you to do things you otherwise wouldn't be able to, like fix a broken dish, make objects float, or . . . fly around. Supernatural powers."

"That isn't liryn at all. It works through us as a natural force."

"So you're born with it."

"Of course not," he said.

"Then how do you use it?"

"With intention. My liryn is of *da'atan.*"

Violet had no idea what that meant, and Kelispar was missing her point. "But how do you obtain liryn?" she asked.

"Through the welding ritual," Meliora said. "Those who want liryn appeal to the monarchs. If the monarchs approve, they weld you."

Then liryn was something people applied for, like a permit. "Something is fused to you?" Violet said.

Kelispar shook his head. "We call it 'welding' when the monarchs bestow the cord upon the applicant."

"They use a sword," she said, remembering Fa's books, "while you kneel."

"We do kneel, but there's no sword."

She was certain of the sword. That must have depicted some other ceremony. "What else can you do, other than translate and heal?"

His face wrinkled with befuddlement. "I can only translate. I am an Advocate." He displayed the knife pendant.

"A person can only be welded once," Meliora said.

"With one ability," Violet said, remembering the doctor's "X" pendant. It came together now, why the people wore specific necklaces. There were twelve pendants, one per realm, representing twelve types of liryn. "What liryn comes from Terlian?"

"We don't know," Meliora said.

"Terlian has no monarchy installed," Kelispar said, "and we cannot be welded without them."

There was a perceptible shift as the others either looked at Eliathor or avoided him. Violet was in the latter category.

Eliathor's family had lost its throne. Without them, Earth's liryn didn't exist. But he'd suspected that Violet had dangerous liryn, which meant there was another way to obtain it. No Lykill, no liryn, Meliora had said. Did that mean that once Violet reunited the Lykill, people on Earth would start spontaneously spouting liryn?

She peeked at Eliathor, whom certain Blacklanders of her grandparents' community would have worshipped. He even spoke Old Norse. A *true* Scandinavian; though, after a thousand years, surely that gene pool had been diluted by marriages. And who knew how much his Faartunga resembled the tenth-century, patched-together Old Norse spoken by the Order and Violet's relatives?

"Excuse me," Violet said. "What do you call the name of your homeland on Terlian?"

He glanced her way, then toward the water.

"*Istlant*," Kelispar answered.

Iceland. What had Iceland looked like before Ragnarök destroyed it?

"How do they call it on Terlian?" Kelispar asked her.

"Helheim."

Eliathor laughed. The sound was dark.

"Does it mean something, Thor?" Alikar said. "*Heim*—that is 'home,' no? But what is *Hel*?"

"Death," Eliathor said.

"Hel is goddess of the underworld," Violet added.

"No," he said, "Hel is Death."

Quietly, she contemplated that. Some traditionalists of her grandparents' community had wanted to embrace Norse mythology, the same people who'd insisted that a true Scandinavian must speak Old Norse. The Order of the Lykill had let the Old Norse legends flow into their own ontology. Thor had once existed, so the Order said, but only as a mortal king of Earth. And he'd wielded Harðgjǫrð, not Mjölnir.

The boat left the village outskirts, traveling alongside the mountains. As morning lifted, so did the fog. Sunlight of a brighter yellow than Violet was used to dappled the snow-capped hills and glimmered on the occasional chunk of ice. Though frozen, the landscape spoke nothing of "Iceland's" gloominess. The sky was vibrant, not exactly blue; there were green tints, painting the celestial ceiling aquamarine. What gasses made up the atmosphere? How big was Bar'Talian's sun? Did—

"Hasn't the Terlion ever seen the sky?"

Alikar's voice interrupted Violet's reverie. He watched her with an undisguised smirk. She realized she was half-craning over the railing. Quickly, she settled back, not sure whether her annoyance lay with Alikar or herself for getting distracted—a very June-ish behavior.

After a moment, her attention crept overboard again. It was her scientific duty to document this. *Staring is a completely reasonable thing to do.*

Beneath an uninterrupted sun, she sweated. She removed Kelispar's scarf. The purple fabric moved like silk but warmed like wool.

"Do Terlions wear black as a rule?" Alikar, stroking his fake beard, asked.

"No," she said.

"Then why do you?"

She folded the scarf into a square. "Black is for mourning. We buried my father today."

No one spoke. Violet continued folding, wishing she'd sat elsewhere.

Kelispar rose. "I need to stand in the wind if I hope to dry off at any reasonable rate. Will you join me at the stern, Violet?"

"Okay." She lay the scarf on the bench and tried to walk at an easygoing pace.

They leaned on the railing. Birds cried overhead, and she intently examined them, feigning purpose. They were stocky, gray and white with maroon beaks. Violet couldn't say whether they were identical to birds on Earth or a completely foreign species.

"My father studied birds." Kelispar stared up. "He and Mother passed on two years ago. I miss them quite achingly." He smiled sidelong at her—a small, resigned expression.

Violet knew he was attempting to offer solidarity. She scraped at her fingertips, failing to think of anything to say other than, "What kind of birds?"

"Oh, any type, but he may have admitted partiality to seabirds." Kelispar began an essay on different species, giving so many specifics on bills and feathers that he must have shared his father's love.

Violet listened. Slowly, as if pulled with the current, the ache left. She grew aware of another ache, not hers. Kelispar squinted, though the sunlight was soft. In all the tumult of learning where she was, she'd forgotten about Kelispar's pained behavior when they first met. It lingered in his tight fists.

He quieted; his breathing turned thicker, like he couldn't get enough air.

"Are you all right?" Violet asked.

He dipped his head. His fingers unclenched. Clenched. "I'm well. Thank you."

She nodded. It wasn't her place to pry.

"Emissary," their captain called.

Kelispar stepped back. "Please excuse me."

Finally alone, she wondered about June, whose plane might have been airborne by now. Her sister would have yelled at Alikar for his bluntness.

A figure filled Violet's peripheral. She caught a glimpse of blond.

"May I, er, join you?" Alikar said.

Meliora stood behind him. Had she told Alikar to apologize? Violet wished she hadn't intervened. She'd rather move on.

With trepidation, Violet nodded. As he fidgeted next to her, dread grew in her stomach. He looked like someone bracing himself to say the worst.

"I wanted to apologize for my lack of tact. I did not mean to remind you of an unpleasant topic. I'm very sorry to hear of your father, may he sleep amid gold."

"Thank you," Violet said quickly. He'd obeyed Meliora. Now he could leave, and she could avoid discussing Fa for the rest of her time here.

But Alikar continued fidgeting. "Black is quite a nice color. I prefer it. *Dakni* is a favorite metal of Chisels. It's rare, mined only on Tolian. Dakni is the only metal considered truly black."

"Oh."

"Yes, I thought you might find that interesting. Very interesting, isn't it? Well, I'm sure you are quite preoccupied with your . . . er . . . preoccupations, so I will leave you to—*oooph*." Slinking backward, Alikar rammed into Meliora. They spent some seconds righting each other. Then, he dashed away.

Meliora's shawl shifted when she leaned on the railing, revealing skinny wrists. "Don't mind Alikar," she murmured. "He's known for being much more himself than the rest of us can afford."

Desperate for a change of topic, Violet asked, "Are you all speaking different languages?"

"It's complicated. Eliathor only speaks 'Faartunga,' though he knows conversational 'Arati'—that's the language of this country. I know Faartunga, but I like to speak my native tongue when someone's Advocating." She grinned. "I was born on Janlian, another realm. In my hometown, we speak what's called 'Greek.'"

That explained her accent. "Greek is on Earth too. There's a whole country called 'Greece.'" Violet held back that Greece was now part of the Blacklands.

Meliora's face was eager. "You know Greek?"

"Only the alphabet."

"Oh, say it. If you don't mind."

Violet didn't want to prattle on before a native speaker, but squashing Meliora's excitement seemed harsh. "Alpha, beta, gamma . . ." She gave the rote letters until "omega."

"I only speak Greek with Aunt Basilia. We're from the same city on Janlian. Eliathor knows a little, but he won't speak it, not since Princess Fila . . ." Meliora's tone darkened, and she let the sentence hang.

Sensing the mood shift, Violet searched for another distraction. "I . . . I guess no one studies languages here, not if people can communicate with liryn."

"Do they study them on Terlian?"

"Some people make a career out of it." She recalled the philologist she'd met at the last Order conference. He'd known seemingly every language, and he'd looked hardly older than twenty-five. "I know a smattering of several languages. My father was fluent in six."

"Six!" Meliora's eyes widened. "I'm an anomaly for knowing two. But it was out of necessity. I moved here when I was young, and Eliathor's family speaks Faartunga as a rule. Kelispar and Alikar were required to learn it because of their father's position, so they're anomalies too. It's the language the Terlion royal family spoke, before the Rift. Do you know it?"

Violet could parse it out; "faar" was used frequently in reference to Terlian. *Sheep tongue.* "A bit," she said, "but not enough to communicate."

Meliora wrapped a lock of hair around her thumb. "*Vessels* know multiple languages. They know nearly everything. They're scholars whose liryn enables them to . . . to memorize things after reading or hearing them just once. We rely on Vessels for learning."

Advocates, Vessels . . . Despite the obvious benefits, the idea of relying so heavily on liryn was unappealing. Violet would much rather study for fifty years than have to depend on some force outside her control.

"So when you came to this realm," she asked, "did you have to apply?"

Meliora nodded. "Naturalization is difficult and uncommon—not to mention expensive—but my emperors eased the process because I was young, with no other family."

An orphan. Like Violet.

"How does travel between realms operate? Does every city have a gate?"

"No, only the capital."

"Then there must be hundreds of gates per realm."

Meliora showed a brief flash of incredulity that she smothered with a patient smile. Still, Violet had the impression that she'd said something dumb.

"The realm capital," Meliora said.

The realm capital. As in . . . "There's only one gate per realm?"

"Well, no. The emperor's seat—their realm—has more. The emperors monitor realm travel, so we have to travel through their realms. I'm sorry, I've never had to explain this before. Alikar could draw you a picture."

"It's all right," Violet said hurriedly. "How many gates are there total?"

"Including your gate, twelve."

Then the realms weren't all connected to each other. That wasn't what Violet had expected for a society where gate travel was possible. "Is there a reason the realms aren't all connected?"

"Maybe they were, before we lost the Lykill. A Vessel would know."

Kelispar climbed down from the steering tower. The others drifted after him, like they'd needed his permission to move. Alikar sat on a barrel, tottering like a kid on a spinning top. Kelispar and Meliora shared a bench. Eliathor remained standing, exuding the role of watch guard. He'd removed the woolly cap, the wind snagging his ginger braids.

"How is your head?" Meliora asked Kelispar. "Have you ever Advocated for this long?"

"No."

Violet awaited an answer to the first question. Did using liryn cause him discomfort? Again, she recalled the pain he was trying so hard to hide.

"Take a break, Kelispar." Meliora touched his arm.

His gaze fell to her hand. She noticed, then curled her fingers and slid back her touch.

"Please don't Advocate if it's causing you pain," Violet said.

"The mental strain is . . . rather lessened today." Kelispar smiled. It looked as sad as all his other smiles. "I'm surprised too."

"You're certain?" Meliora said.

"There's almost no headache at all."

He normally experienced a headache? Had Violet known, she wouldn't have dared expect him to Advocate on her behalf.

"Well," Meliora said teasingly, "I do like not having to prattle on in horrible Faartunga."

"It's only horrible in your accent, Melly," Alikar said.

She threw a leaf at him, but it landed in Kelispar's hair. He and Meliora both reached to retrieve it. Their hands brushed. His fumbled, and hers retreated like a turtle in its shell.

Kelispar's beard failed to conceal his flush. He found Eliathor, whose squinted eyes conveyed a question. Kelispar shook his head. Eliathor frowned at Meliora, who avoided his accusatory gaze. The ensuing silence was so awkward that Violet wished

Alikar had noticed. But, as he was absently drumming on his barrel, he couldn't offer a diversion.

"Kelispar," Violet said, using the pause to gather her question, "if your necklace, or cord . . . Well, when that boy took it, you weren't translating anymore. Do you need the cord in order to use your liryn?" She hoped the answer was a long one.

"Yes," he said.

Meliora scooted another inch away.

"Then liryn is connected to your cord." Violet was determined to banish the discomfort. "Could that boy have used it?"

When he supplied another, "Yes," her hope sank. Then his beard shifted, and he added, "Cord theft is a despicable crime. A stolen cord can be used, but its liryn is perverse."

"You could make the cord fly back to you, though."

"What you witnessed is only possible over a short distance. That's why the boys ensured I was distracted in the water. Cord thieves take and don't linger."

"It's a shame Yakiv Stefanos lives so far from Arat," said Alikar, who'd apparently been listening after all.

"Let me remind you—for the dozenth time—that thief hunting is illegal," Kelispar said.

Violet's mental image of a man in camouflaged clothes, holding a rifle, was probably completely inaccurate.

"Yes," Alikar said, "but who else is going to fight cord thieves? Yakiv has done more in ten years than any Seer has done in . . . well, I can't remember when Seers stopped policing liryn."

Seers used to police liryn—Violet noted that for further study later, once she learned what a Seer was.

"It's not as simple as you make out, Alikar. Thieves should be policed by the proper authorities, not a vigilante. What we need, if we want order, is the Lykill." Kelispar eyed Eliathor.

"Yes, yes, I know." Alikar drummed his fingers, oblivious to the way Eliathor's entire body seemed to harden at the mention of the Lykill.

Silence grew heavy. So were Kelispar's eyes. He'd forgotten about Meliora, and the leaf in his hair.

CHAPTER EIGHT

"Urso Rosensverd moved to Arat, convinced that the Pretenders were being unfairly represented. Despite having no political experience, he appealed to the Bar'Talion monarchs and was welded. His descendants have fought for Terlion liberties since."
– Vessel Marciaretti, United Colonies Conservatory

T HEY'D TRAVELED AN HOUR when the boat slowed, a medieval-looking building with pointed purple domes coming into view. The stonework, which could have fit several Lyng houses, towered out of the water. It rested on the lake as if the building had come first, then the lake as an afterthought.

"The port of Vaspurakan," Kelispar said.

Cutting into the water were several docks that dumped travelers onto a covered terminal packed with pedestrians.

Kelispar frowned, somehow managing to look polite. "Crowded today," he said.

"Security check?" Meliora leaned over the railing.

"I hope not." Kelispar eyed Violet before calling up to Dag, "Can you see the source of it?"

Their ship's captain hadn't spoken two words to anyone other than Kelispar. But, given that everyone had removed their disguises, he must've been trustworthy. Dag adjusted the goggles that hung from his neck. On his face, they gave him the appearance of a mad scientist. He twisted the lenses like binoculars and frowned. "Separatists," he said.

Alikar shot off his barrel.

Eliathor moved to the railing and searched out. His face clouded. "There are Hands too." He shielded Kelispar. "We can't dock here."

"This is the closest port to your estate." Kelispar gave his beard a troubled rub, eying Violet again.

"Then we will disembark while you take a different route," Eliathor said.

"I cannot abandon Violet."

"I'll be fine," she said, guessing Separatists and Hands meant trouble for Kelispar's political position, whatever that was.

Dag suddenly made a noise like an uncorked cough. "It's a rally, sure and true." He peered down, worry huge in his goggled eyes. "For Yakiv Stefanos."

The name fell like coins, loud and clattering, before an equally weighted silence followed.

"In Arat?" Alikar surveyed the rally with unmistakable intrigue. "Are you sure? He's never come here."

"Would recognize that belly-aching anarchist anywhere," Dag said.

"But . . . why is he here?" Meliora gripped the railing like a towel she intended to wring out.

"Because the monarchs are out of the country," Eliathor said. "Coward."

"The timing *is* rather unfortunate." Alikar looked nervously at his brother. "Separatists and Hands never make for a happy party. And we've got two Terlions in tow."

This Yakiv Stefanos was someone who brought cord thieves to justice, though apparently not in a way that was legal. However, Violet couldn't guess what Earth had to do with him.

Kelispar's grave expression made the tension stifling. She unbuttoned her jacket.

"We will do what we always do," he said calmly. "Walk separately and reconvene at the park."

"You can't be seen here," Meliora said.

"I'll go with you," Eliathor said.

"Don't be a martyr," Alikar said.

They spoke over one another, a jumble of concern.

"Yakiv won't do anything rash on public property," Kelispar said.

"You're the Terlion emissary!" Meliora said. "And we already know he's not one for the law."

"My worry is for Violet." Kelispar watched her like Yakiv had already announced his intentions to murder her. "Your identity cannot be known," he said, quietly, so Dag wouldn't overhear. So, their captain wasn't privy to everything.

Eliathor had pulled a sword on her; what would an entire planet do if it became public knowledge that the first full-blooded Terlion in a thousand years was walking the streets?

"But it's not as if I'm recognizable," she said.

"Anyone accompanying me in a rally like this will suffer the strictest scrutiny."

"Which is why Violet will come with me," Meliora said firmly. "Kelispar, you'll go one way, Alikar another. Eliathor, you simply can't go with Kelispar. You know why. You'll come with Violet and me. Let's hurry."

Kelispar might have been the group's leader, but Meliora's suggestions carried the sound of finality.

Violet adjusted her borrowed purple scarf, mentally working her way through the politics. She didn't need a definition of Separatists or Hands to know why the others were concerned. If people distrusted Terlian, they probably distrusted the royal family that went along with it—and the emissary who publicly represented them.

Dag clambered down from his steering tower, a gold parcel tucked under his elbow. Rather than addressing Kelispar, he aimed for the figure standing apart. "For my Lady," he said to Eliathor.

He gazed at the package with the expression of a teacher presented with an incomplete assignment. "My mother appreciates your gifts, sir, but I cannot accept another."

Dag's head tilted. Pained confusion touched his eyes.

"Yes, he can." Kelispar swept to Dag's side, clasping the captain's shoulder. "Thank you, Dag, not only for your ship, but for your loyalty to Terlian."

"It's my heritage, true?" Dag beamed. "I love the good monarchs of Bar'Talian, but my blood's Terlion. Not ashamed to say so."

"And Lady Basilia treasures your loyalty."

With visible effort, Eliathor accepted the package and said, "Any man who honors my mother is counted as a friend."

Dag bowed, which affected Eliathor like a hot poker. He didn't acknowledge Dag until he stood straight again. Violet feared for the package, trapped in Eliathor's grip.

There were always loyalists whenever a monarchy was dethroned. However, these loyalists had no idea what Ragnarök had done. No ruler would want a dying planet. Supposing that planet wanted them back.

Their boat bumped against a dock. A man's voice, somehow magnified, carried over. Violet could see him now, a figure elevated over the heads of the attentive crowd. Yakiv Stefanos preached from a raised platform in the terminal, though she couldn't understand him. Presumably, Kelispar's Advocating range wasn't that far. To whatever Yakiv said, the crowd cheered.

They disembarked from Dag's boat. The energy of the crowd rattled the wooden planks of the dock.

"Make straight for the park." Eliathor rested a hand on Kelispar's shoulder, voice low. "No delays."

Kelispar nodded. He and Meliora met eyes. Then, Eliathor gave Meliora his arm, and they set off. Violet followed them into the crowd. Step after step, and suddenly, she could understand Yakiv.

" . . . not merely for the privileged few, but for all. Pure and untainted."

Violet searched for Advocate cords but saw only elbows and patches sewn on sleeves. Separatist logos? They were vibrant, not the stark symbol she'd expected from anarchists. Multicolored spheres formed a loop like beads on a bracelet. Several people wore masks too, black ovals decorated by a handprint. A red, white, and purple Valknut sat in the center of the palm.

Two of the fingertips cut eerily through the eyes. The overall effect was unsettling.

" . . . don't need their liryn," Yakiv was saying, "with its taint. You want it pure. But they can't give you that, see. Plenty a monarch can't do, or even an emperor. Because they're weak, scared of change, blind to . . ." He had a unique accent, one that pressed hard on R's and got lazy with vowels.

No one else barred the way to the terminal, the wide space supported by pillars strung with purple banners. A knife was embroidered on every flag. With the flapping purple material as his backdrop, Yakiv preached from a pedestal whose statues had been knocked off. Two stone figures sporting crowns lay broken apart on the ground.

He was in his forties, gray-streaked sideburns and scruffy beard. Yet his focus was sharp, his stance well-built. The collar of his jacket stood stiff, despite the wind. He spoke in a controlled voice, not so loud he could be accused of shouting. He cut a far more intimidating figure than some hunter in camouflage.

Violet searched his chest and found no cord.

A few with Separatist arm patches patrolled around his pedestal, their liryn cords swinging. One of them was an Advocate; Violet saw the knife pendant. None of them wore Hand masks.

Soon they were past Yakiv and under the terminal's high mural ceiling. Violet forgot Separatists and Hands for a moment, lured by the picturesque shopping square that drew visitors from the terminal. A road built of decorative tiles circled the water fountain in the center of the square. She'd never seen a bronze fountain, nor so many basins catching the water that gushed from a giant tulip.

The buildings were interconnected, a seamless flow of color. Red roofs adorned yellow shops; blue roofs covered purple shops. Every roof wore a dome crown. The buildings beneath were either cylindrical or square, with arched windows.

Violet blinked. Where to look? She longed for a closer examination, but Eliathor veered left, where pedestrians waited for the same thing everyone waited for at terminals: transportation. Violet had imagined this planet would have more magical vehicles, flying carpets or broomsticks. Though the parked, oddly-shaped contraptions looked otherworldly, they didn't steam or fly. The vehicles of crystal and copper resembled carriages without the horse. The Lykill Valknut was painted on every door.

Eliathor and Meliora broke into an argument, now unintelligible as they were out of range of Yakiv's Advocate. He was gesturing toward the rally; she was shaking her head. He won, backtracking into the crowd. She sighed and gave Violet a *He's impossible* sort of look.

Violet guessed he'd gone to find Kelispar. Eliathor might've been the most overprotective person she'd ever encountered. The trait was both admirable and inconvenient.

She studied the city square. The road gleamed, lacking potholes and oil stains. The monarchs had a strict cleaning crew. That, or liryn helped. Even the sky looked polished, the clouds whiter, with that overly yellow sun.

Dozens of people strolled outside the shops. Their animated gestures and awed pointing told Violet that she wasn't the only tourist here—and that perhaps not every building on the planet was this colorful. The variety of clothing choices, far different from the plain, homogeneous outfits back in the fishing village, hinted at Vaspurakan's popularity, as if the crowded port hadn't already done so. This was a place for visitors; no two outfits were the same, other than sharing a common winter theme. The tourists were diverse, too, of sundry builds, tones, and hair styles.

One such tourist came closer. He was college-aged, wearing a jacket that tangled his purple cord in the buttons. A tarnished Advocate's knife hung there. What drew Violet's notice was the pleased light in his face when he spotted Meliora. She, attuned to the rally, didn't notice. As the guy crept nearer, Violet figured she'd rather spoil his surprise than find out that he was a mugger.

"Meliora," she said.

Meliora glanced back. Her tense mouth morphed into a smile. "Jarek! What are you doing in Vaspurakan?" The words happily tumbled.

Violet could understand; that meant Jarek was Advocating. Did he and Meliora not speak the same language? She *had* admitted to knowing only Greek and Faartunga.

"Hoping to see you." Jarek caught her hand. "You always come back through the port. Thought I'd just steal a glimpse, but . . ." He swung her arm, grinning. "Here you are, without your paranoid cousin. Alone."

At that, Meliora glanced at Violet. She quickly withdrew her hand.

Jarek's eagerness fell flat, stoppered like a boy given an F instead of an A-plus. "Who's your friend?" he said.

"She's . . ."

The silence drew out. Violet wanted to be thirty feet away.

"I'll tell you later." Meliora searched the rally, then returned to Jarek. Her eyebrows had gotten more scrunched. "Did you know Yakiv is here?"

Yakiv's name darkened Jarek's face the same way mention of the Lykill clouded Eliathor's. "I heard," he said gruffly.

"I don't know what he's doing in Arat." Meliora absently fidgeted with a bracelet. "I understand if you say no, but . . . can you Advocate?"

Jarek pinched the back of his neck.

"Please, Jarek. I need to know what he's saying."

He exhaled. "Fine." His jaw clenched in concentration.

Then he could extend his range, like an antenna? Violet observed his furrowed features, wondering what exactly an Advocate had to do in order to translate. *"With intention,"* Kelispar had answered when Violet asked. Advocating was an act of the will, rather than something that automatically happened.

When some seconds passed and Yakiv's speech stayed just as unintelligible, Jarek's face grew more strained. He was tanner than the others in Vaspurakan, the hair that peeped out from his hat a coppery brown. A longer build, too. Not a native, perhaps.

"I know you can do it," Meliora said, touching his arm.

By the sharp twist of his mouth, Violet couldn't tell if he was embarrassed or just overworked. "I have to get closer," he said.

Meliora nodded. They followed him around the corner of the building, which put the rally in full view. Violet didn't like feeling so exposed, but everyone was far too preoccupied with Yakiv to notice them.

Slowly, like a radio station adjusted, Yakiv's speech grew intelligible. " . . . doing the work they stopped doing centuries ago."

"Thank you." Meliora squeezed Jarek's arm.

Jarek, leaning against the building, didn't watch the rally. His avoidance had the feel of defiance. In profile, he resembled a brown hawk. A ruffled one—a newsboy hat mussed his hair, and mud caked his boots. His clothes looked like third generation hand-me-downs. When he spied Violet's gaze, he shifted, smoothing down his hat, the picture of self-conscious.

Ashamed, Violet refocused. She couldn't help pitying Kelispar, who'd obviously lost the competition.

" . . . only way to get a realm without thieves," Yakiv was saying, "is to eliminate the need for them. No reason to steal if liryn's flowing, without crowns. Once I've taken the Lykill, even the emperors will come asking me to weld them."

The crowd erupted with applause that thundered uneasily in Violet's stomach. Yakiv was looking for the Lykill too.

She pictured two triangle pendants stuffed inside a tea canister. Utkin had no idea what sat on his kitchen counter next to a rusty coffee pot and stale bread.

Meliora's expression mirrored Violet's rising trepidation. "I didn't think he believed in the Lykill," she said, her voice barely audible over the commotion.

"He's been listening to Malokki," Jarek said.

"But Malokki doesn't—"

A new voice rose from within the cluster of those wearing masks. "The Lykill does not belong to you," a woman said. "It belongs to Malokki."

Some in the crowd jeered. Yakiv raised a palm for quiet. "You Hands and I, we've had our differences, but our goal's the same, see. I want what Malokki wants: liryn without pain."

Did he mean the headache?

"What's your plan?" someone else asked. "Send Terlian a letter, ask for the Lykill, please and thanks?"

A few laughed, but most booed the doubter. Violet thought the man made a fair point. Everyone believed the Lykill was on Terlian; how did Yakiv hope to get his hands on it when the only thing that opened the route—the gate pendant—was supposedly trapped on the realm in question?

Rather than ignore the doubter, Yakiv gave the man his full attention. His answer came so slowly, so measured, one could accuse him of making it up as he went along. Yet certainty brimmed in each accented syllable. "Malokki, he's been en-lightening us on the Lykill the past four, five years. Appeared like some crippled prophet on his boat, told us all the prophecy's fulfillment was nigh. I don't take to the prophecy, see, but Malokki . . . he knows a thing or two. Quite the filled Vessel. So I asked him. Asked him yesterday. Found his little palace in the forest and asked him how he expected to touch the Lykill if some Terlion didn't open a gate and hand it to him."

Violet hiked Kelispar's purple scarf up over her chin.

"You asked him, or your Goldentongue?" called the doubter. More chortles.

"My own two hands are just as effective as liryn," Yakiv said.

The man crossed his arms. "Well? What was Malokki's an-swer?"

"Tell us, Hands." Yakiv gestured at the masked woman who'd spoken.

She scanned the crowd in each direction. "Your ears are not ready."

"He that has ears, let him hear, yes?" Yakiv widened his stance, hands on his hips. Violet couldn't banish the image of a gunslinger ready to draw. His next words made her forget it entirely. "A gate to Terlian is open."

The crowd went still. Not even the doubter gave a dubious outcry.

Violet pulled the scarf even higher. How had this Malokki person found out about the gate? Were scores of Bar'Talions about to flood Helheim?

Jarek stopped feigning disinterest, letting his heel, previously propped on the building, smack down on the ground. "What did he say?" he hissed.

"Malokki's words?" The doubter found his voice. "And you trust it?"

"Not Malokki's," Yakiv said. "Halfdan Hastein's."

Meliora pressed the back of her hand against her lips.

Halfdan Hastein—Eliathor's father.

Yakiv did some digging in a pocket. "Water-stained, from his lake dive. But Malokki found what was left. I came here to Vaspurakan to search your archives, see Halfdan's hand for myself. The writing matches. It's in that Terlion tongue, but Malokki obliged a translation."

By the nature of Yakiv's controlled, unaffected tone, he'd arrested the crowd. Even Violet found herself breathing quieter, the better to hear.

Yakiv read from something she couldn't see. "'We walked through the gate. It touched me like a whisper. The sight here is dark and barren. The acrid tang of sulfur is on my tongue. I do not know where I am, only that it is Terlian. My home. Basilia, I long to see you here, standing on the soil of my fathers. That must please you. How I hated Terlian, that accursed name, and how I love it now, nearly as I love our sons. If I could take this land into my heart and carry it always there, I would. You were right, my holly. Terlian is my own. Let it be ours.'"

The gradually stirring crowd barely let Yakiv finish. Protests rang out even as he spoke, unsifted noise.

"Halfdan was mad!"

"You believe that rubbish?"

Jarek tugged Meliora around the building. Violet followed them, happy to be invisible again.

"Meliora?" He rubbed her shoulders, concerned.

Meliora squeezed the scarf that concealed her hair. "He called her 'my holly,'" she whispered. "For the holly oaks on Patmos."

"Then you think your uncle really saw it? Terlian?"

Meliora's answer was lost to Violet, who'd noticed two figures coming around the far end of the terminal. Kelispar spotted Violet too, but his attention swept past her, toward Meliora. Even at a distance, the pain in his tense face was palpable.

Eliathor shoved an angry footfall forward, but Kelispar stopped him. They argued until Eliathor gave a short nod and conceded to approaching without the flames of rage fanning his steps. Kelispar remained behind. With bated breath, Violet awaited Eliathor's arrival. It came uncomfortably fast, a sturdy build of poorly suppressed frustration suddenly at Meliora's side.

"We're leaving," Eliathor said.

Jarek let go of Meliora faster than waves during a hurricane.

"Did you hear what Yakiv said?" she asked Eliathor, though the wiser choice would have been to remove Eliathor from Jarek's proximity as soon as possible.

"Lies," Eliathor said.

"He called her 'my holly!'"

"What are your intentions with my cousin?" He rounded on Jarek, who bravely stood his ground.

"Stop." Meliora came between them. "This is not the place."

A swell of laughter from the crowd obscured Eliathor's reply.

"But all the monarchs will meet their end," Yakiv was saying. "I'm surprised ours haven't yet. Too old to handle a knife, I'm told. Someone has to cut up their food so they don't choke. And the Terlions, well . . . Halfdan died a fool. Fool king of a fool people."

That distracted Eliathor for a moment, but not as much as it should have. He returned to Jarek. "What is your answer?"

"Something for Meliora," Jarek said, "and not you."

"Please, stop . . ."

Violet tuned out Meliora's protests, intent on Yakiv. He wasn't done insulting Terlian.

" . . . Pretenders deserve their banishment. They prop up tainted legacy. Easy for them, living on Bar'Talian's backbone like a glutted flea. Oh, but they dole out humble gratitude to the Bar'Talion monarchs while pretending they've still got their throne. Parasites. But what else could we expect? They're Terlions. Filth breeds filth."

No one in the crowd rose to Terlian's defense. This was more than suspicion. This was hatred. But why? Terlian had done nothing for a thousand years.

"I cannot allow this." Kelispar had joined them. But he wasn't looking at Jarek; he faced the crowd.

Jarek, on the other hand, could not be accused of ignoring Kelispar. His expression held the conflict of one imagining strangling someone while contemplating the consequences.

"They're only words," Eliathor told Kelispar. "Let Yakiv vomit as he wills."

"Men do mad things for mere words." Kelispar took a step in Yakiv's direction.

Eliathor blocked him. "Leave it."

"I would ask you to stay, to defend your family's name, but the job is mine."

"Do not take this upon yourself."

"I already have. I am my father's son." Kelispar's tone was not cold, but it was steady as steel. "Let me go." He pushed Eliathor's protective arm—a losing battle. Eventually, Kelispar relented. "Would you have me be a coward?" he murmured. "More than Terlian's pride is at stake."

Quiet understanding passed between them. Eliathor lowered his arm.

Kelispar nodded his thanks and continued toward Yakiv.

"Kelispar."

Meliora's voice gave Kelispar pause. He waited.

She touched his elbow. "Be careful. Please."

Another nod. Then he braved the crowd.

Jarek's face indicated that he was thinking about strangling again.

"If you would speak ill of Terlian," Kelispar called out while he walked, "I ask that you speak to her directly."

The rally surged with renewed excitement before Yakiv could answer.

"Kelispar Muratsan!" someone shouted.

Two Separatists pinned Kelispar's arms and shoved him through shoulders and elbows. The people made sure he couldn't walk without tripping. At Yakiv's pedestal, the Separatists threw him forward. He stumbled but managed not to fall.

Meliora was squeezing Eliathor's wrist, avidly attune.

Jarek spoke near her ear. "I'm going. I'll hail you tonight."

She didn't hear him.

All the twists and conflict vanished on his face. Jarek went indifferent. He adjusted his hat and left.

"You're mighty young in person, Emissary," Yakiv said to Kelispar. Even with Jarek gone, Violet could still understand. Maybe Kelispar was Advocating, or someone else in the crowd. "You look like your old man. I met him once. Six, seven years ago. Spat in his hand. Did he mention it?"

"Yes, with pity," Kelispar said.

"Will your brother take up the cause when you're dead? Doubt he has a choice. The Pretenders have been stuck with your people for—what, four generations now? Migrated all that way across Bar'Talian, and not even a drop of Terlion blood in your veins. Don't know if that's admirable or just pathetic."

Separatists chortled.

Another figure appeared at Violet's left. She thought Jarek had returned until she recognized Alikar's gangly stature. "Why aren't you at the park?" he said. "Where is—" He caught sight of his brother at Yakiv's feet. Alikar lurched forward and met Eliathor's barricade.

"Wait," Eliathor said.

"What is he *doing*?" Alikar groaned, fisting his hair.

"And how do you like it, serving Terlian?" Yakiv said *Terlian* like one says *vermin*.

"I am happy to perform my duty," Kelispar said

"Duty toward whom? Who are you loyal to, Emissary: your own monarchs, or the leeches of Terlian?"

"Both."

"Both. And what will your Lady Basilia say when you tell her I'm going to find the Lykill?"

"Nothing."

"Why so?"

"Because she knows every generation produces at least one fool who thinks himself capable of bending laws he cannot comprehend. This generation has produced two." All gentility had fled Kelispar's voice.

Violet realized she was holding her breath. She couldn't see Yakiv's expression, but she could imagine it looked something like the way he said *Terlian*.

"Noble idiot," Alikar hissed.

Meliora's curled fingers dug into her cheeks.

But, with a roll of the shoulders, Yakiv's reply came out like oil. "The other fool being Malokki, I wager."

"Neither of you understand the Lykill," Kelispar said. "You won't find it. Even if you did, it isn't yours to use."

"Think the emperors deserve it? Think they won't reap its benefits while the rest of the welded suffer?"

"A crown is only a curse to someone who knows nothing of sacrifice."

This time, Violet could see that Kelispar had struck a nerve. Yakiv's shoulders went completely rigid.

The patrolling Separatists locked gazes. As one, they formed a fence around Kelispar.

"Eliathor." Alikar's eyes were wide. "Do something."

Eliathor seemed to be contemplating all manner of things he could do. He attempted none of them.

"I know nothing of sacrifice." Yakiv's cave-quiet voice would've made June shudder. "Is that right?"

Kelispar inhaled, searching beyond Yakiv. He found Meliora, and looked away.

"Those of you who got your cords back because of me," Yakiv called, "tell the little emissary your opinion of his wise words."

Dozens of cheers rang out. Red, purple, and white liryn cords dangled above heads as people fished them out.

"Who traveled countries, in cold and hunger and shipwreck, to enact justice? Not our monarchs. Not our emperors."

Kelispar's voice struggled to overpower the noisy frenzy. "Your definition of justice includes harassing the innocent who—"

"No, no. You can see it, when a man's welded and when he's not."

"And how can you tell a cord thief from a welded? You're not a Seer."

"I can see their crown. It's in the eyes." Yakiv commanded silence again. "You'll know the meaning of sacrifice soon, Emissary." The way his tone fell, quiet but rich, one might've thought he was advising a friend. "And you'll ask yourself, every day, if it's worth it."

Kelispar's jaw was set, though his focus strayed—toward Meliora again. "My yes will be the same as it was on the day I was welded."

Violet had only followed a quarter of the conversation. There was so little she understood, despite growing up under the Order. Their crown?

Yakiv resumed his easy stance, shoulders bendy and hands on his hips. "You see, friends? He's a product of the monarchs. We should pity him. He knows nothing but blind servitude. Wonder if—"

Sound, like the rushing of a highway, came from above. Violet glanced up, but the terminal roof blocked her view.

"Attention: one Yakiv Stefanos and party," echoed a voice, as smooth as if slipping from a car stereo. "You stand accused of vandalizing official property, of inciting civil unrest, of undue harassment of innocent citizens of the king and queen. How stand your pleas?"

Yakiv squinted at something Violet couldn't see. It made his hair whip, his jacket collar bend. The crowd saw it too, and they shook apart, scattering like criminals. The announcement repeated, with an additional request for Yakiv's cooperation. After a motion toward his allies, Yakiv hopped down. Then he and his Separatists dispersed.

Alikar made for Kelispar, but Eliathor prevented it.

"I'll get him," Eliathor said. "Stay with Meliora and—"

"She can survive ten seconds without a bodyguard." Alikar ducked under Eliathor's arms and took off into the frenzy.

Meanwhile, Eliathor visibly debated who needed his protection more: Meliora or the Muratsans.

"He has a point," Meliora said to Eliathor. "Go. We'll get a wagon. Come on, Violet."

They darted toward the carriages, now crowded by pedestrians fighting over them.

"Halt, in the name of the monarchs!" boomed a command.

Violet glanced back. Dipping into view were white canoes. Four of them descended as if lowered by ropes, except it wasn't ropes that carried them but two petal-shaped wings. The wings were purple, and the sides of the canoes bore the Valknut. A person piloted each. Others, wearing purple armor styled like a medieval knight and knee-length skirts, prowled the square, questioning anyone who'd yet to escape. The soldiers looked more ridiculous than menacing.

Meliora was arguing with a man who wanted the carriage for himself, despite having arrived second. She looked ready to give up when someone interrupted—Jarek. He shoved the man over and steered Meliora into the vehicle, then stepped aside to let Violet board. She sat on one of the two velvet-padded benches—purple, naturally—in a tight space that smelled of vanilla.

Slightly disappointing. It should have smelled of something purple.

"I thought you left," Meliora said to Jarek.

"Wanted to make sure you were safe. Talk to you tonight." Jarek closed the door.

Flush colored Meliora's face like jam on toast. She fiddled with her bracelet.

They waited for the others, safe in their carriage while the havoc raged outside. What a complicated mess. Hopefully,

Violet would never have the misfortune of meeting a Separatist again.

Symbols of the 12 Realms

CHAPTER NINE

"Man was not built to suffer. Leave any opposing theory to the ignorant, those who call a shackle a thing of glory." – Vessel Malokki, black pearl

T HE OTHERS FOUND THEM quickly. Alikar climbed in first. Meliora took Kelispar's hands and pulled him in. She made him sit next to her. Neither noticed when Eliathor entered and slammed the door shut; she was too busy smoothing Kelispar's tousled hair, and he was too busy staring at her. By the look in his eyes, she was dragging sandpaper across his skin.

He removed her hand from his hair and held it two centimeters from his lips. Then he let go and relocated to the opposite bench.

Meliora stared down at her empty fingers.

Without a rumble or any indication that an engine had turned over, the wagon sailed off. Violet wondered if the front contained some inner compartment where a man in goggles worked feverishly at the gears. Or did the vehicle run on liryn?

"I'm sorry you had to witness that, Violet," Kelispar spoke. "Men like Yakiv hate what they don't understand." He stared at the passing scenery, though his gaze didn't follow its movement.

"When can I set him ablaze?" Alikar said.

"When everyone who would stop you is dead."

"Good. I'm well-prepared to outlive you all."

"You are certain your mother never received any letters from your father?" Meliora asked Eliathor.

He crossed an ankle over his leg, consuming more horizontal space. "That letter is a farce."

"And if it isn't?"

"It doesn't change that he abandoned her."

"To find the Lykill, which he accomplished."

Eliathor's leg came back down. "And where has that left us?"

Meliora soundlessly fumbled for an answer before resting her head on the wall with a sigh.

"Was that Jarek Mieszko, Melly?" Alikar said. "I saw him bothering you while I was obediently waiting at the park for my negligent companions. What is he harassing you for?"

Meliora, Eliathor, and Kelispar shared the stony quiet. Violet heard passing clatter from the street. There was a reason no one had enlightened Alikar about Jarek. She wasn't keen on being present when they did.

"How far are we from our destination?" Violet asked no one in particular.

Kelispar cleared his throat. "The Hastein estate is one hour from Vaspurakan."

"Why the sudden muteness, Melly?" Alikar interjected.

Meliora fidgeted with her fingers. "He's a classmate."

"I know that. You shouldn't associate with him. Everyone at Kapor already gives you a difficult time."

"I can admire the compassion that draws someone to befriend an ," Kelispar said, staring at whatever scenery the window showed him.

Meliora's fingers stilled. Even her silence seemed to mournfully sigh.

"But not *that* outcast," Alikar said. "Jarek Mieszko is—"

"Let it rest," Eliathor said.

Alikar, though he rolled his eyes, obeyed.

When another awkwardly quiet beat followed, Violet threw out another inquiry, one certain to elicit a lengthy reply. "What exactly is a Separatist?"

"The distinction between Unionists and Separatists is fairly simple," Kelispar said. "Unionists, like ourselves, want to continue the practice of receiving liryn from monarchs. Separatists want to eliminate that dependency, find liryn from another source. That's one thing Yakiv wants from the Lykill."

"So everyone can be dependent on him instead of the monarchs," Meliora said. "Hypocritical to say the least."

"Not necessarily. Malokki has spoken of new welders," Kelispar said.

"It's just a theory."

"An attractive one for many."

"The Lykill can create welders other than the monarchs?" Violet asked.

"So Malokki posits." Kelispar's countenance grew weightier. Violet wondered when he'd remember how to smile. "You saw those wearing masks?"

She nodded.

"They call themselves 'Hands of the Lykill.' Malokki is their leader. He's a Vessel."

Vessels were historians with impeccable memory, Violet recalled.

"If he's even real," Alikar said. "He's never made an appearance at any of these Hands rallies."

"You've seen him on the shells," Meliora said. "And Yakiv met with him. Of course he's real."

"The Hands have a worshipful attitude toward the Lykill," Kelispar continued as if he hadn't been interrupted. "Yakiv used to scoff at them, but even he has become swept away by Malokki's theories. And, evidently, he's come to believe in the prophecy as well."

Meliora shook her head. "I don't think he does. He just wants the Lykill."

The prophecy that had convinced Malokki, that somehow applied to Eliathor's family too. "Would you mind explaining the prophecy?" Violet said.

"Which version would you like?" Alikar said. "There are eleven."

"There is only one official interpretation," Kelispar said. "Every other is merely tolerated. We don't have the original prophecy, Violet. One line was given to every realm. Including yours."

She followed his meaning. "You're saying that line is lost."

"What Vessels know is sufficient to discern its meaning. Even Malokki has acknowledged that the references to Eliathor's family are . The Hasteins—"

"That's enough," Eliathor said. His palms perched on his thighs, tense.

"The prophecy won't stop existing just because you don't like it," Meliora murmured.

"The prophecy turns men into zealots, driving them to abandon all obligation."

"Your father was obliged to follow it," Kelispar said.

Eliathor shook his head. "My father followed his guilt, dragging Meliora's father with him. If Yakiv wants to do the same, let him. He'll find his reward."

Kelispar started to speak; Alikar cut him off by stomping his toes. "No," Kelispar said, "don't stop me. It's my job to defend your family, Eliathor. That includes your father."

"And my ancestors? How will you defend them?" The sunny patch on Eliathor's knees vanished as his head moved, blocking the light. He looked right at Violet.

His eyes were a tense and fiery blue.

"She doesn't realize that theft and cowardice run in the Hastein bloodline," he said. "That to be of Terlian is to be despised. Tell her of the Rift Wars, Emissary."

Testy silence fell, as if Eliathor had shouted a curse. Violet held her breath. If she'd known her question about the prophecy would lead to more awkwardness, she wouldn't have asked. Yet she wanted to learn, needed to understand why anyone would despise her dying world that had peacefully kept to itself for a millennium.

Kelispar wasn't too shy to face her as directly as he could in the cramped wagon. "The Lykill consists of three parts. This, you know. They belong to the emperors. The twelve realms are divided among three empires: the Nehfey Empire, the Basareth Empire, and the Da'atan Empire. These correspond—"

Alikar coughed out, "*Pedantic.*"

Kelispar sighed. "The Lykill was stolen and locked inside Terlian. We'd always believed the thieves closed the gate from *outside* Terlian, that they'd sent the Lykill through before the gate finished sealing. Unfortunately for the thieves, they were captured before they could reenter Terlian. They died here, on Bar'Talian."

"Tell her who the thieves were," Eliathor said.

Kelispar rubbed his liryn cord. "King Leif and Queen Thorgunna." After a sidelong glance at Eliathor, he added, "The monarchs of Terlian."

Eliathor's ancestors. They were the ones who stole the Lykill, who closed Terlian's gate, who ensured that Terlian lost all access to liryn, the other realms, and its history.

"They wished for a stronger realm," Eliathor said. "It's the humor of fate that Terlian now stands weakest." He surveyed the road, which was a relief; Violet wasn't sure the wagon could handle his expression.

So that explained the lack of love for Terlian. Its monarchs were the reason the Lykill had been lost for a thousand years. But these people didn't understand that Terlian had suffered just as much for its rulers' mistakes, if not more.

"Are any other realms dying?" she asked.

Meliora shook her head.

"Then I don't see why anyone needs the Lykill that badly. Terlian is the only realm suffering."

"Terlian doesn't have cord thieves," Alikar said.

Kelispar nodded. "I suspect Yakiv's primary interest in the Lykill is for retribution. Against thieves, against corrupt monarchs who abuse their welding power. It's true that there is . .

. corruption involved in the welding process." He looked too reluctant to proceed.

"Most monarchs require payment for welding," Meliora said, "which, according to their own laws, is illegal. Many also show favoritism, or use welding as a tool for bribes."

"On Bar'Talian, we are fortunate to have just monarchs," Kelispar added. "Yakiv fails to acknowledge this. He's seen too many thieves."

Violet had to admit she was confused. As a Separatist, Yakiv wanted liryn without a monarch's involvement. The Lykill could give him that. She understood his motivation, and even his desire to undermine corrupt monarchs by distributing liryn behind their backs. But what did that have to do with Yakiv's vendetta against cord thieves?

"The Lykill will be able to stop cord thieves?" she said.

"Thieves only steal because they don't want a crown," Alikar said.

That response did absolutely nothing to clear away Violet's confusion.

Kelispar straightened with the air of one accepting a challenge. "Please bear with my pedantic answer, Violet. I don't know how else to explain." He drummed his fingers, gathering words. "Everyone welded suffers a headache. The strain is mild right after welding, but it intensifies as time passes, until using liryn can cause a headache that lingers long after one has stopped using liryn. Some experience such a severe headache that they go temporarily comatose. But the headache is inconsequential compared to a crown."

He found his knife pendant and gripped it tightly. "The headache is a universal pain, but crowns are unique. They look different for each of us, and it may be heavier for some and lighter for others, but one will recognize the crown when it comes. It's impossible to avoid. A crown isn't necessarily physical pain. It might be intellectual, or . . . emotional." Kelispar swallowed. "It's a pain that never vanishes entirely. The headache fades if we stop using liryn, but a crown remains. We might not feel it at every moment. It can come and go, like a painful memory made suddenly vibrant, or an old injury that flares up at random. But it *will* come."

He faced Violet, who wished he'd return to looking out the window. His emotions didn't manifest as easily as Alikar's, but their weight lived in his eyes like two squatters. Violet understood now why it was there, the pain Yakiv had been referring to. There was a cost to using liryn, more than a headache.

"Now," Kelispar said, "imagine a way to have liryn without a crown. Malokki first proposed the idea, saying liryn is not meant to come with a crown—that liryn has been *corrupted* by crowns. It seems Yakiv has subscribed to Malokki's theory: liryn without pain."

It was a simple motivation. Violet sought to bring cord thieves into the picture, considering Alikar's words: "*Thieves only steal because they don't want a crown.*" Finally, it clicked.

"When someone steals a cord," she said, "they don't feel the crown."

"Nor the headache. But the barren does." Kelispar's face, half in shadows, held a darkness that couldn't be blamed on lack of sunlight. "That's what one is called if one has been robbed: a barren. Empty. But still suffering."

The idea of stealing someone else's cord, while deplorable, hadn't seemed much different than taking someone's prized jewelry. But when Violet envisioned someone trembling with pain while a thief used their cord, her skin pricked with goose-bumps. It didn't matter if someone's cord was robbed; they still felt their headache and "crown" like the ghost of a limb. If those boys on the dock had escaped with Kelispar's cord, he would've suffered, and they would've felt nothing at all.

That's how Yakiv would eliminate cord thieves: by using the Lykill and giving people liryn without crowns. But she couldn't picture him as some benevolent leader. He'd make people grovel. And he certainly wouldn't let a Unionist or anyone affiliated with Terlian have liryn.

"I'm lucky you've escaped your crown thus far," Alikar said to his brother, grinning. "Seeing you with the headache is bad enough. What'll I do when you start groaning and whining, like Father did whenever his knee bothered him? Such a mild crown, really."

Kelispar returned the smile, or tried to. His eyes found Violet's.

She said nothing more, letting her questions make noise strictly in her head.

CHAPTER TEN

"High King Eirìkr left the Lykill to guide the twelve realms. Our emperors each held their respective share until the Great Rift, with the liryn pendant belonging to the Basareth Empire, the welding pendant to the Da'atan Empire, and the gate pendant to the Nehfey Empire." – *What the Lykill Doesn't Do*, essay by Vessel Davit

B Y THE TIME THEIR wagon slowed, Yakiv was far behind them. Violet had contented herself with examining Vaspurakan through the window, making her own guesses about the purposes of the buildings. She'd seen the palace—rather, the unending stone wall that barricaded it. To protect the gate, Kelispar told her, all the gates were concealed in the palaces of their respective realms.

"I wish we could have given you a tour of Bartholomew's Square," he said. "Tourists come from all over the realm to see it, and to shop. In Bartholomew's Square, you'll find traditional Vaspurakan wares."

Alikar cut in before Violet could voice her interest. "Those stores sell rubbish. None of it is handmade. Or useful, unless you require another painting of a pomegranate. You know, those costumes the shopkeepers wear, they're not even original to Vaspurakan. Made in Gutan, I've been told."

"Since when do you care about traditional Vaspurakan clothing?" Meliora playfully tugged on Alikar's waist sash.

"I don't, but if one is going to make oneself an authority on Vaspurakan culture, one ought to do it properly."

Kelispar smiled. "I agree with you, Alikar."

Alikar feigned dismay. "Gracious. What have I said wrong?"

Violet studied the clothing of the two brothers. It did look traditional. Why did they wear it? She hoped they weren't royalty, too. One royal family was enough. Though, if anyone in this wagon could claim the title of prince, Kelispar certainly fit the bill.

Miles from the port, nature was left to itself, the loping hills covered in wildflowers. The sky stretched over unending lowlands, one vivid shade of aquamarine.

Everything is so alive here. Earth could look like this again. It was odd, putting so much stock in something that only yesterday she'd considered fiction.

They drove until the light outside dimmed, courtesy of the forest shouldering the road. There, they disembarked.

"What a relief," Alikar said. "We're out of that depressing wagon. You're all far too somber. Especially you, Kelispar. Glum as a bear without honey. Not still upset about Yakiv, are you?"

No one said anything. Alikar was impossibly oblivious.

To cover the awkwardness, Violet returned Kelispar's scarf. She did this without speaking. Maybe he'd stop translating if she stopped talking.

"You may continue wearing it if you are cold," Kelispar said.

She shook her head.

"You're certain?"

She nodded.

"It seems I shall have to take everyone's minds off Yakiv," Alikar declared. "Terlion"—he bowed to Violet—"it is my greatest pleasure to introduce you to Barikad, the forest which separates the Hasteins from Vaspurakan. Perhaps you've noticed we're quite isolated. This is because no one wishes to associate with the Hasteins, other than the Muratsans, and that's because we're gluttons for punishment. Well, why are you all standing thus?" With that, he set off.

Beneath the great heights of firs and beeches, warmth vanished. She guessed the temperature was somewhere in the low forties, colder than the winters she was used to in San Diego.

"This forest is ancient," Alikar continued, and Violet, assuming he was talking to her, hurried to catch up. "It—"

"You don't have to explain," she said, even though she was interested.

"Of course I do," Alikar said, and Violet cast Kelispar an uneasy look. Kelispar's forehead wrinkled. "It's bordered Faargard since the Rift Treaty," Alikar said with a sweeping arm. "After Terlian's monarchs surrendered, they couldn't return to their realm. Not without the gate pendant. The emperors couldn't agree on where to put them, so the old monarchs of Bar'Talian offered the Hasteins a plot of land they call 'Faargard.' It—"

"Thanks," Violet said. "I don't need to know more. That is to say . . ." Should she claim to be tired?

"Violet," Kelispar said. "May I speak with you? Privately?"

She would rather speak to Yakiv Stefanos. Violet could see on Kelispar's face that he understood exactly what she was doing. Gathering air, she followed him to the base of a giant pine—was it a pine?—and waited.

"While I appreciate your courtesy," Kelispar said, "I accepted my crown when I accepted this cord."

He'd admitted it. Kelispar had received his crown. And only Violet realized.

She said nothing. How could he expect her to talk, knowing it caused him a headache?

Kelispar sighed. "Did you obey your father's wishes, even those that caused discomfort?"

A nod.

"As I should obey the monarchs who made me an Advocate."

Violet had never met anyone so firm in their convictions. Did Oliver have this attachment to the military?

"You loved your father, didn't you?" Kelispar asked.

She nodded again, this time unable to speak for a different reason.

"Then perhaps your discomfort was alleviated by the knowledge that your obedience made him happy."

Her commitment to the Order had caused discomfort. Violet had skipped untold social outings for Fa. Sometimes she complained, but most days she was relieved at the excuse to stay home. *Is that the same as Kelispar's pains?* She couldn't see how.

"It does seem like a lot to have a headache on top of a crown," she said quietly.

"I spoke truly, Violet. The headache is very light today, lighter than it has been in years." Kelispar's brows thoughtfully furrowed. "I can't understand it. My father told me that his headache was sometimes so intense that he would rest for an entire day afterward. Other times, he barely felt the strain at all. I have seen Advocates go completely senseless, their minds so taxed that they could not even stop Advocating. They had to be revived, so to speak. I've always dreaded coming to that point. A day like today gives me hope that my fate need not include drooling like a fool before an entire assemblage." Though he smiled, Violet still couldn't bring herself to excuse that he was suffering for her.

"You don't have to Advocate for me," she said. "I like listening to other languages."

"That's well and good, but I can't accept your offer. Men like Malokki and Yakiv call crowns unjust. If they loved their monarchs, they'd feel differently." When she remained quiet, Kelispar folded his arms. "Please talk. I don't think my brother will allow you to follow your conscience, at any regard."

He was stubborn, and he was right. Violet was confident Alikar would glue his lips shut if he thought Kelispar's headache was bothering him, but until then, he'd rely on Kelispar's liryn without qualms.

"Okay," she said.

He smiled that princely smile, and Violet remembered once again that she was wearing a bloodstained beanie. "Thank you for listening," he said. "You have a very quiet air that encourages conversation. You must have many friends on Terlian."

The absurdity of that statement almost made Violet gape.

He offered his arm and guided her back toward the others, all attentiveness and courtesy. That's exactly what his behavior was—courtesy, and nothing more. His "more" was reserved for Meliora.

No hope there, June, she thought, without disappointment. Kelispar was handsome and kind, but a bit too ceremonial.

"Well then," Alikar called, "are you two finished colluding? I've got about ninety-eight percent left of my historical analysis."

Alikar, on the other hand, could use some ceremony.

They continued deeper into the woods. Isolated, Alikar had called Faargard. He hadn't exaggerated.

Faargard. Sheep stronghold.

"Now," Alikar said, "someone remind me of my last remark."

"The Rift Treaty," Meliora said.

"Oh yes. Bar'Talian offered to house the Terlion refugees until Terlian reopened the gate. Of course they never did, and thus Terlion descendants have resided on Bar'Talian far longer than the monarchs planned. Mind you, most have died out. The rest are scattered around Janlian. Janlian and Bar'Talian are Terlian's only allies."

"I'm impressed you remember any of that, little sapling," Meliora said.

"Yes, I surprise even myself on most occasions."

Violet was intrigued. Segregated from the other citizens, trapped on another world, the Hasteins lived like political prisoners. "So there's no public access to Faargard?" she asked Kelispar.

"There is," he said.

"She's wondering why we aren't taking advantage of it," Alikar chimed in.

"You'll be found out," Meliora told Violet. "Any visitor to Faargard has to be judged by a *Chair*. Oh . . . their liryn tells them when someone is lying."

"Your existence must be kept quiet until the monarchs are informed," Kelispar said.

Violet nodded. Were Chairs mind readers? She longed for an encyclopedia. Advocates, Vessels, Chairs . . .

"We would have taken this route today anyway," Alikar said, "as this excursion wasn't quite approved. Eliathor is part sea serpent, you see, and grows cantankerous when away from the water for too long. Now that Meliora's university is on winter break, we snuck him out and— What?" he said, dodging his brother's swat.

"We are not 'sneaking,'" Kelispar said.

"'Any Pretender wishing to leave Faargard must receive explicit permission from the monarchs, under article fifty,' and so forth."

"It's article seventeen, which references article ninety-four, which states that the Terlion emissary reserves the right to take a member of the Hastein household anywhere within the established boundary. We're doing nothing illegal."

"Of course we aren't," Alikar replied, waiting until Kelispar passed before he eyed Violet in a way that said *We most definitely are.*

Eliathor's family wasn't even allowed to leave their house without a chaperone? Political prisoners indeed.

A quarter hour into their hike, Alikar paused by a wide-trunked tree, its gnarled roots exposed like knuckles. He stretched his arms and bounced from heel to toe.

"Do hurry," Meliora said. "It's cold."

"You cannot rush genius, my frightfully impatient Melly."

She rolled her eyes.

Violet, at a loss for why they were standing around, thought the group needed encouragement. "What—"

"Someone shush the Terlion," Alikar said, bending toward the trunk.

"She has a name," Meliora said.

"For all the pine in Barikad, Melly—*quiet.*" Alikar touched the bark. "Be open unto me," he murmured. A sheet of healthy vine peeled back, a layer undone. A deep hole appeared between the roots.

"Well," Kelispar said, "that did take you considerably less time than before."

"It's nice to know one is appreciated, brother."

They ducked into the tree. Its innards barely fit the five of them. Fortunately, their destination lay ahead, where a dirt-packed tunnel petered into darkness.

Eliathor sealed whatever Alikar had opened, putting them in a blackness so absolute that blinking made no difference.

"Your tool, little sapling," Meliora said.

After a pause, light flickered at the tip of a rod similar to a laser, only with a brighter and greener hue. Alikar pointed it down the tunnel. "Behold, oh gargantuan tree woman." He patted Meliora's head.

"Gargantuan tree woman?" she said.

"Do you not like your nickname? Do you find it highly annoying, not to mention inaccurate?"

"If you don't want me to call you 'little sapling,' you need only ask."

"Consider it asked."

"Fine." Meliora snatched his tool and took the lead, calling over her shoulder, "Oh tiny tree boy."

Alikar darted after and wrestled his tool back. Their squabbling caused light to bounce between wall and ceiling.

Violet followed, thinking of Oliver. They hadn't laughed together since she was ten.

He laughs with June.

A low voice from behind caused much-welcome distraction.

"I'm sorry," Eliathor murmured. "I thought she would say yes."

Violet walked faster.

"So did I," came Kelispar's reply.

"Did she state Jarek's intentions?"

"He hasn't told her."

"It won't last. He's not her equal."

"You've never cared about social status."

"I don't mean his father," Eliathor said. "She looks after Jarek like a hen with her crippled chick. No man wants to be coddled."

Violet stared determinedly ahead, trying not to hear Meliora's laughter.

"I'll talk to her," Eliathor said.

"You've talked to her enough."

"Then my mother will."

"No." Kelispar was firm. "Let it be."

"Don't relent so easily. Fight for her."

Kelispar sighed. "Some love isn't for this life, Eliathor. You know that better than most."

They quieted.

Discontentment shrouded Violet, an unexpected feeling of . . . she couldn't find the word, but it drove further into her consciousness as she considered the closeness between these friends. They had stronger bonds than anything Violet had with her siblings. She and June were close, but they'd never playfully fought over a pair of shoes. That was simply the nature of their relationship, Violet had always thought—she'd been too busy with Fa and the Order to have the energy left for fun.

But Oliver and June had found time to tease each other. Perhaps time wasn't the issue.

Straightening her beanie, Violet waited for Kelispar and Eliathor. "To open the tree," she said, loud enough to drown her memories, "was that liryn?"

"It was," Kelispar said.

"Then Alikar is welded too."

"You hear that?" Alikar swiveled, making them all squint at the onslaught of light. "She believes I'm as distinguished as you, Spar."

"And she," Meliora said, "is present and should be spoken *to*, not *about*, tree boy." She maneuvered him around.

"*Chisels* imbue objects with liryn," Kelispar said. "Anyone could have opened the tree with the proper ritual."

"But no one would have done so as elegantly," Alikar called.

Eventually, they came to a dead end. Using his laser like a staff, Alikar banged the ceiling. Dirt dusted his hair and cheeks as he cried, "Be open unto me, ye mystical roof!"

Nothing happened.

"You cannot create your own ritual," Kelispar said. "The words have meaning."

"And I said them."

"With your own flair."

"Very well, then." Alikar touched the ceiling again, this time politely telling it to open. The ceiling obeyed.

Alikar jumped. He dangled for a moment on the lip of the opening, kicking his legs around, before hoisting himself out of the hole. "Hurry, won't you?" he called down to Meliora. "I haven't got all day."

She grasped his outstretched hand. He tugged and groaned.

"What does Lady Basilia feed you, toast and stones?"

Meliora, half laughing and half rebuking Alikar, made no progress until Eliathor heaved her up. Kelispar climbed out next, and Eliathor took the rear. Violet was last. The three feet above her head seemed vast as a mountain range. Why was there no ladder? She did not want to be hoisted and heaved.

"There's a crate," Alikar called, "to your left."

As obvious as a smoke alarm, a metal box sat a couple feet away. In another moment she'd joined the others in an empty courtyard, beside a stone, weather-worn sheep balancing on a pillar. Green moss gave him a sickly pallor. Wind whipped halfheartedly, a quiet force against Violet's cheeks. The suddenly overcast sky painted gray and brown hues on a lonely, bedraggled tree that loomed over the cobblestone ground. It seemed the type of place where someone might find a peasant pushing a cart full of the deceased.

Alikar patted the sheep's head and told it to move. The pillar scooted over the tunnel's opening.

"Faargard." Kelispar gestured.

Violet conjured up scenes of a royal guard, servants, noble steeds, and elegant ladies strolling with umbrellas. She turned.

It *was* a castle, albeit a small one, straight out of the Middle Ages. A rounded turret on one side, and squared ridges everywhere else. The bare stone was cracked and chipped, and several spots looked painted over. Violet had expected more pomp, but the building seemed embarrassed of itself, giving up hope with a shrug of its stone shoulders. There was no flowering orchard; just a few scraggly trees. No trimmed bushes; just weeds. No flags boasting Terlian's sheep insignia; just a single turret that protruded like an awkward spare arm. The only decorations on the building were the vines growing up its side.

Beyond the forest, Bar'Talian shone of all the beauty Fa had wanted for Earth. In Faargard, Violet felt she'd returned to the Blacklands.

Kelispar motioned toward the arched entrance that swallowed the ascending steps. She followed him out of the gloom.

CHAPTER ELEVEN

"If Terlian is so bent on tradition, the Pretenders would speak the language of their *rex primus*. We can be sure King 'Borgfastr,' as the Terlions call him, wouldn't have recognized Faartunga in the slightest." – Vessel Yal, recitation at Darbinyun Manor

T HE SMELL OF INCENSE struck like a match. Violet wrinkled her nose as she crossed the threshold into a foyer, beyond which waited a great hall. Her feet padded over a rug, maroon with a gold border of checkerboard design.

There was no doorman, no butler, no one to greet them but a fire in the far wall. The fireplace was carved into a wood facade as wide as Violet was tall. Beams passed over ornately tiled designs in the high ceiling. Pillars supported the beams, giving everything the feeling of a forest. The room even glowed green, due to the stained glass. The overall impression was reminiscent of an empty museum.

Heavy stomping pulled Violet's attention toward a stone staircase. First came a little boy and girl in a game of chase. An older boy followed behind, shouting after them. In the rear came an older couple, she with a baby on her hip and he with black braids that put Eliathor's to shame. He stood taller than Eliathor too, though the suspicious eyes were familiar. Definitely Eliathor's brother.

The little girl bolted off the final step, closely tailed by the disappointed loser. Their older brother—Violet assumed—wrangled them apart. Meanwhile, the parents finished their descent as if all was calm. She was night as much as he was day. Dark where he was ruddy; midnight where he was fair. Violet couldn't decide whose braiding was more ornate, his or hers.

"Kar!" The little girl waved at Alikar.

He put a hand to his forehead as if searching the seas. "Excuse me, young maid. Have you seen Lali? I'm certain you are not her. You are too tall."

Lali giggled.

"Oh well. I suppose you'll do." Alikar knelt. Lali raced over and hopped onto his knee.

"You've outdone yourself today, Eliathor," his brother said, and pulled something from the pocket of his baggy linen trousers. A pearly compact opened like a clamshell, revealing an inlay of crystal. He traced his thumb over it. Out floated a grainy, purplish image, similar to something displayed from a projector. Eliathor in miniature form prowled through a crowd, his hood having slipped just enough to reveal the ginger hair that no one else in Vaspurakan seemed to have.

"Next time," Eliathor said, "I'll shave my head first."

His brother cursed.

"Mind the children, Karleif," his wife said.

"They've got to learn these words somehow," Karleif said.

"No, they don't."

"I heard you, Dada," called the eldest boy.

"Stop eavesdropping!" Karleif yelled.

"Yes, sir!"

"I heard you too, Dada," Lali said from Alikar's knee.

"Don't tell your mother," Karleif said in a far more affectionate tone.

Lali nodded solemnly. Her mother rolled her eyes.

Karleif returned to Eliathor. "Mother wants an explanation for your carelessness," he said.

"Give her this." Eliathor tried handing off Dag's gift, but Karleif shook his head.

"You'll want that to pacify her. First the shells"—Karleif snapped the compact shut—"and now this." He gestured to Violet. "If you're going to continue sneaking off, at least refrain from bringing strangers home."

"She is of Terlian," Eliathor said.

Karleif sighed. "I can't fathom why you're the favorite."

"Chief Karleif, Dame Gisa," Kelispar said, bowing to each, "your brother speaks truly. May I present Violet of Terlian. We found her near Borku. A gate has been opened."

"By your father," Meliora added. "The gate pendant was here on Bar'Talian all this time."

Even the children fell silent. Karleif swooped around his wife and towered over Violet. One eye grew beady. Maybe he hoped to find the word *Terlian* spelled on her forehead. Eventually, he barked, "Liam!"

The oldest boy glided over with the air of someone much more dignified than an eight-year-old whose vest buttons had popped open.

"Take her to the blue room," Karleif said, so sternly that Violet assumed "blue room" was a euphemism for "dungeon."

Liam gave Violet an elegant bow.

"Take her to my room," Meliora told Liam. "The blue room is too drafty."

Certainly a dungeon, one without windows.

"The blue room is for strangers," Karleif said.

"Violet is a Terlion," Meliora said. "Do you remember my sign, Liam?"

"Gaia!" he said proudly, and set off.

Violet moved after Liam. From behind her, she heard Karleif saying, "Have you been Advocating this whole day? Take a break, Kelispar . . ."

The conversation disintegrated into Faartunga when she climbed the stairs.

Liam, probably thinking he'd been subtle, went wide-eyed when Violet caught him staring. On the third floor landing, he stepped off. "*Ek heiti Liam*," he burst.

The Old Norse introduction was similar in Scandinavian. "*Ek heiti Violet*," she said.

He nobly dipped his head.

They passed through a hallway of parquet floors and papered walls, both peeling. Liam led her to a door and, with a gesture like a butler, said, "Gaia" to the closed door, which was mysteriously lacking a doorknob. It swept open.

Violet entered a room containing a bed that hung on ropes, a desk, and a wardrobe that too many children had treated like a canvas. The room was tidy and surprisingly ordinary. Violet pictured her room in San Diego, where an invisible line divided the neat from the chaos where June's side spilled onto hers.

Liam snapped at whoever was clopping along the hallway. In a moment, his younger siblings appeared, tottering under the same tray of food with as much apparent strength as the ancient wardrobe. They looked like twins, around five.

Violet relieved them of their burden; the boy cheered, earning a smack from Liam.

"*Þǫkk*," she thanked them. She'd never attempt Old Norse with the others, but children were less observant of mistakes.

Liam bowed. "*Gerðu svá vel.*"

The twins continued gawking until Liam dragged them away.

"*Far vel,*" Violet called.

"*Far vel.*" Liam beamed at her for a moment, then appeared to realize he was acting out of character and smartly closed the door with another "Gaia."

Violet's mouth twitched.

The tray held a bowl of broth, bread rolls, and a goblet of water, most of which had sloshed over the sides. Violet quickly ate. The edge of hunger gone, she noticed her aching limbs. According to her watch, it was after 5:00 p.m. on Helheim.

Her nerves churned. When Violet returned, she would have to convince Oliver that she'd stumbled through a portal to another planet.

He hadn't believed Fa. He'd never believe me.

Someone knocked. Meliora entered. Meanwhile, Kelispar shifted in the doorway.

"My shame," he said. "Normally I would not intrude upon Meliora's privacy—"

"It's all right. You and Alikar practically grew up in here." Meliora waved at the wardrobe.

His eyes alighted on the furniture, where faded stick figures marred the wood. "I forgot how poorly I draw," he murmured, touching a crooked shape that could have passed as a horse or a cat. "Alikar's, I assume." He found a well-defined dragon, complete with a burp of fire.

"I'm sure I can find a pencil if you'd like another attempt." Meliora smiled.

"No, that would only humiliate me further." Kelispar retreated to the doorway. "Eliathor and his brothers are explaining your situation to Lady Basilia. She will expect you in a half hour. In the meantime . . ." He rocked on his heels.

"You're underdressed," Meliora told Violet.

The people of Bar'Talian were wholeheartedly opposed to Violet's clothing.

"I think I have something that will fit you," Meliora added.

"Then I leave you ladies to it." Kelispar gripped the edge of the door, but Meliora held the opposite side. Their hands touched. Both jerked back, apologizing. When neither made a second attempt, Violet was tempted to close it for them. But Kelispar scooted into the hallway, allowing Meliora to finish the task.

She commanded it closed, then leaned on the frame. "He proposed this morning," she whispered in a rush. Kelispar's liryn worked through walls? "Alikar interrupted my horrible, confusing answer to tell us there was a strange girl harassing Eliathor. I've been waiting for him to ask since I was fifteen. I've been waiting to say yes. But then, I met Jarek at university, and . . . well, I don't know what Jarek is." Meliora's expression pleaded.

Violet didn't assume she'd earned the spot of confidant. Meliora needed to talk, and Violet was the only ear around. She fumbled for the right response. "Well," she said—stalled—before finally blurting, "I think Kelispar understands. He's not mad at you." That was the best she could offer without betraying Kelispar's confidence.

"I know." Meliora covered her face. "But he's so unhappy. I hate it. I do love him. I can't imagine any future in which I am not his wife. You must think I'm a . . ." The rest of her sentence was in Greek.

"Um. Meliora?"

"*Nai?*"

"I can't understand you."

The conversation dropped.

Meliora searched her wardrobe with the discernment of one choosing wall paint. Eventually, she handed Violet a yellow dress. Violet wouldn't have selected that one—a plain black dress caught her eye—but Meliora had a way of deciding things that didn't leave much room for argument.

While Meliora took another dress through a door off the bedroom, Violet inspected the yellow material. It was an apron dress, draped over a long-sleeved shirt embroidered with yellow thread at the cuffs. At least it would be warm.

Once Violet had the shirt and apron on, she realized this was a two-person endeavor. The back gaped, but Violet did her best to tie the fastening. A rectangular strip of wool hung vertically down the front, flapping awkwardly. Violet wanted a belt, both to secure the apron cloth and hike up the train.

Meliora emerged in white, looking like a bride. Nordic swirls were embroidered down her apron cloth. She gave Violet an approving smile, which was kind of her, given that Violet probably looked like she was wearing a sack. Meliora found a belt, which she tied around Violet's waist, as Violet slowly relinquished her dreams of personal space.

Meliora motioned to Violet's hair, then pointed to her own braid. Evidently straight hair was too mundane for Lady Basilia. At least Violet knew how to braid. That seemed to be the hairstyle of the Hasteins.

"Clip?" she said, pointing to the one twisting back Meliora's bangs.

Meliora retrieved some gold pins from her dresser. "*Fourke-ta*," she said.

"*Fourketa?*"

Meliora nodded.

Violet secured her braids so they formed a low bun. "Hair," she said.

"*Hi-er.*"

They continued this game. Meliora loaned Violet twine sandals that were *sandalia* and named other objects in her room, with Violet reciprocating in English. It cheered Meliora, who took to English with studious wonder. Violet enjoyed it too. The game was almost . . . well, like the sort of thing friends would do. If Violet was the sort of person who made friends.

Kelispar waited for them at the bottom of the stairwell, having changed into all manner of purple and silk, with a red sash around the waist, a sleeveless vest over his tunic, and a velvet fez. There must have been a dozen shades of purple, red, and gold in his clothes, making Violet's yellow positively bland by comparison.

He looked quickly at Meliora, then away. "Very lovely," he said, addressing neither of them. "Shall we?" He tucked Violet's fingers around his elbow.

Violet hadn't attended prom, but she imagined it was nothing like this—wearing a costume gown while on the arm of someone who walked, talked, and dressed like a prince. She chewed her cheek, longing for the aged, graying members of the Order.

They entered a hallway. Iron-wrought torches illuminated portraits of monarchs, each squared in a gold frame. The first painting depicted a bearded king cloaked in green, the draped toga suggesting a Greek philosopher rather than a Viking. Yet Younger Furthark runes spelled his name: *Borgfastr*. Terlian's first king. He held his sword, Harðgjǫrð, and wore a gold chain necklace whose pendant had been gouged out of the painting.

"An imperial punishment," Kelispar said, "after the Rift." He indicated the proceeding paintings.

They walked, Violet studying as many monarchs as she could without slowing. Only Borgfastr had ruled alone; his predecessors ruled alongside queens. The clothing styles changed with the rulers, togas replaced by capes, then armor. Harðgjǫrð disappeared from the paintings, reappearing later with King Björnson, who'd recovered the stolen weapon. His and Queen Solrun's clothing looked Celtic. But, come King Karlmikli and the garments turned more Germanic. Every single monarch's liryn pendants had been marred, paper and paint peeling, until King Leif and Queen Thorgunna, whose appearances were distinctly Viking. They were the last monarchs wearing liryn cords. The last crowned monarchs at all.

For as quick a moment as she could subtly manage, Violet scrutinized them. Helheim's historical records had been destroyed by Ragnarök; no historian on Earth knew who'd last been living on Helheim before the volcanic eruption. Violet was glimpsing forgotten history.

The Viking style lingered for the remaining monarchs: braided beards, helmets on both monarch's heads, the king holding Harðgjǫrð and the queen carrying a horn. Their clothes grew less ornate, but the same expression shone out of every man and woman: defeat. Once royal, now reduced to this ramshackle building, not even permitted to be painted wearing a liryn cord. Yet meeting Lady Basilia was an important moment. Violet had no idea how she should behave.

She must have slowed; Kelispar squeezed her hand. "Don't be nervous," he said. "Lady Basilia is a good woman, though her initial demeanor is one of . . ."

"Suspicion?"

"You have Eliathor pinned well," Meliora teased.

"I'm not nervous." Now faced with the even more intimidating prospect of unbarring herself, Violet came to a stop beside a couple whose unhappy faces seemed to lean out of the painting. "I don't know the etiquette for meeting royalty. Do I curtsy? Can I only speak when spoken to? Do I call her 'Your Majesty' or 'Queen'?"

Kelispar took it all in stride. "May I borrow you, Meliora?"

Their eyes met. Hesitance clashed between them. Meliora's cheeks colored. "Certainly!" she said with too much energy.

He pulled his hands close to his chest. "Hail, Venerable Lady," he said in a high-pitched voice, curtsying. "May the Great Welder's hand bring health and happiness to you."

A smile showed on Meliora's face like a reluctant sun. "We thank you for your graciousness," she replied in a deeper voice, inclining her head. "We now bestow upon thee the hand of justice"—she swatted Kelispar's cheek—"and await thy groveling."

Violet's heart skipped. A royal slap?

"And how, noble Lady, shall I abase myself?" Kelispar asked with perfect politeness.

"At our feet."

"Naturally." He got on his knees and pretended to grovel.

Meliora laughed. "Don't be ridiculous." She tugged him upright.

He rose, looking far too much like his brother with the silly grin. Meliora held on to his elbow.

"To be clear," Violet said, reminding them that she was present, "there is no cheek slap or groveling?"

Kelispar reclaimed his arm, and his solemnity. Meliora shifted, scratching her bracelet. "Only if you are Liam and have been torturing your cousins," she said. "Don't worry. My aunt is a firm woman. Especially in the throne room. She follows Terlion tradition. But she's the kindest woman I know."

They continued walking. "Upon first address, she is 'Venerable Lady,'" Kelispar said. "After, you may simply call her 'Lady.'"

"Okay," Violet said. "Thank you."

They reached a wooden door. Its cracked face would fit in well at a tavern.

The last painting in the gallery featured a man whose hair grew in auburn braids. "Chief Halfdan," Kelispar said quietly.

Violet scanned the man's face, searching for Eliathor and finding him in the jawline. This must have been painted decades ago; Chief Halfdan and Lady Basilia looked too young to have grandchildren. She stood a couple inches taller than him, and he wore the furs that Fa had described. And there was his velvet scarf, much less frayed than it had been at Fa's wake. Chief Halfdan couldn't have predicted that Fa would treasure the scarf like gold, wearing it beyond his dying day.

"Eliathor's family has Harðgjǫrð?" Violet homed in on the hilt in Halfdan's hand.

"Harðgjǫrð?" Kelispar said.

"The sword." She gestured.

Meliora shook her head. "That's been lost since the Rift, supposing it's real. But it's tradition to paint the king of Terlian with that sword."

Supposing it's real. Violet knew what Fa would have said.

Meliora spoke "Lykill" to the door, and it opened.

CHAPTER TWELVE

"When worn, the Lykill's purple pendant gave the Da'atan
Emperors the power to weld not only Vessels, but any liryn
whatsoever." – Vessel Magda, recitation at Kapor Academy

A HUSH DESCENDED AS soon as the door closed.

The throne room thrived where the rest of the estate
surrendered. The arched windows weren't missing a single
pane; the chandelier gleamed from every candle; the tile glistened; the statues looked polished; the rug didn't suffer a single
tatter, stretching from Violet to a dais. Lady Basilia waited at
the top.

Violet swallowed and stepped forward. She sensed gawking
from the onlookers, but she kept her sights fixed on Lady
Basilia. That proved both easy and challenging. Easy because
the woman's presence sucked focus like a magnet. Challenging
for the same reason.

When Violet reached the bottom of the dais, Kelispar touched her elbow. "Venerable Lady Basilia, may I present Violet of Terlian."

Those words made the silence palpable.

Violet curtsied. "May the Great Welder's hand bring health and happiness to you, Venerable Lady Basilia."

"You do us a great service, maiden," came the reply.

Lady Basilia seemed like a painting, with a tasseled curtain framing her. For a moment, Violet could imagine she was looking at an older Meliora; she favored her olive-complexioned niece more than her sons. Basilia's gray hair—braided, naturally—formed a crown, yet there was plenty left over to form a single braid over one shoulder. White skirts spilled around her ankles, as did the cape pinned beneath her furs.

Of all this regalia, nothing struck Violet so intensely as the woman's expression. It was proud, made bolder by the wrinkles and touch of red on her lips. Brown eyes pierced as beadily as an eagle's.

She stared at Violet. Of course—she was in the center of the room, the reason this meeting had been called. But Basilia's staring conveyed something more than curiosity. A note of yearning softened her gaze. Wonder, too. Maybe Violet was imagining it though, and the strange reciprocation that stirred inside her, something that made her want to draw closer.

She stepped back.

Lady Basilia winced. But she gathered air and spoke. "Our son tells us there is no trace of liryn upon our realm."

Violet took this as her cue to straighten. "Yes, Lady Basilia. Very few people believe that the other realms exist, or that liryn was ever on Terlian."

"What a sorrow, to have lost . . . so much." Trouble showed. Lady Basilia spoke through it. "Tell us of your father's encounter with Chief Halfdan."

Violet scanned the onlookers. Meliora had settled by Eliathor, who bordered Karleif and another presumed brother who took the most after Basilia. They stood by their respective wives, with the exception of Eliathor. Three sons total. Alikar and the children had been excluded from the meeting.

"My father was abroad for work in . . . Iceland." Violet quickly explained the rest.

Someone sniffed. Lady Basilia, for all appearances, was unmoved. "What items were in Chief Halfdan's possession?"

Violet explained that the pendants were in Helheim and the book stolen. More stiltedly, she added that the scarf had been buried with Fa.

"He bequeathed your father with his scarf?" Basilia asked.

"Perhaps he thought the man was cold," Eliathor's unnamed brother said dryly.

"Mother," Karleif said, "what book was this? And how did Father come by the pendants?"

Lady Basilia's attentiveness drifted, a ship deviating from its course. "Chief Halfdan was not the first to find a pendant." She glanced toward Meliora. "Niall Mykaois was."

This new silence brought attention to the sound of mouths popping open.

"My father?" Meliora whispered.

"This is true," Basilia said. "He found the liryn pendant. It, too, was not on Terlian."

"But . . . how?"

"You have heard of the cave on Janlian we call '*Sapila*'?"

Meliora nodded.

"The cave of decay. No Seer dares enter it. We know not what guided Niall into that darkness, only that he braved it and there found the red liryn pendant. Your father brought it to Janlian's monarchs, who believed the first stage of the prophecy had been fulfilled. *'The eagle must drop that which is tainted.'* The good monarchs wished it to be given to Chief Halfdan, that the line of Terlian might bind the wounds of the past. Chief Halfdan contacted our emperors and promised the pendant. Our emperors agreed to collect it. A dignitary was sent." Lady Basilia's eyes closed. "The dignitary informed us that Chief Halfdan and Niall never met him. We know not what befell them, that Chief Halfdan should wash upon Lake Vaspurakan one week later and our sister's husband should be discovered having taken his own life. But today, one of our own stands before us."

Violet had never felt so conspicuous.

The conversation contained a lot to unpack. Meliora's father found the liryn pendant and was told to give it to Halfdan. After agreeing to hand it over to some emperors, Halfdan broke his word and disappeared with Meliora's father. Somewhere along the way, they found the gate pendant and entered Terlian. Both died shortly after.

Violet wondered where they'd found the purple pendant. Had none of the Lykill been on Terlian at all? The ancient Terlion monarchs could hardly be blamed for a crime that was getting harder and harder to prove.

"Why did you not tell us that Uncle Niall found the liryn pendant?" Eliathor steadied Meliora's shoulder, wearing his usual concern.

"Why did you not tell us that the liryn pendant was on Janlian?" Karleif added. "And that, for the past twenty years, our emperors have believed Father absconded with it?"

"They probably think he lied about ever having it," spoke the third brother.

"That is no better!"

For the first time, Lady Basilia's composure cracked. "I did not wish you to bear a heavier burden," she told her niece softly.

Meliora nodded, though she looked no less dazed.

"Father deceived you." Eliathor's focus hadn't swayed, as if this conversation was for him and Basilia alone. "He made you believe he was meeting the dignitary, but he chose his own path and made Uncle follow him. Can you still defend him?"

"He knew I would have him follow any path to the Lykill," Basilia said.

Eliathor started forward. "You would not have—"

Meliora took his elbow. He stepped back.

"If I may interrupt," said Karleif, who looked as if he didn't care one way or another if Basilia minded his interruption, "I really must insist on knowing why you shielded me from this. I am the heir apparent."

"And what would you have done with this knowledge, Karleif?" Basilia asked him.

"Defended our name! Everyone believes Father abandoned us and fell in with robbers."

"And you believe people would forgive him sooner if they knew he had disobeyed our emperors and taken the liryn pendant for himself?"

"Well"—Karleif's lips flapped for air—"we would have given due blame to Janlian, of course. The Janlion monarchs are the reason the liryn pendant fell to Father in the first place."

"The realms do not need another reason to oppress Janlian."

"Nor another reason to oppress the Hasteins! We have been the blight of the realms these twenty years past—"

"Thousand years past," the middle brother said.

"—and our name might have been salvaged had the realms realized *Janlian* was involved." Karleif said *Janlian* like he was saying *those people,* despite the fact that *those people* were his mother and cousin's heritage.

"Janlian gave Father the pendant," Eliathor said. "Janlian did not tell him to steal it and abandon his family."

His words struck an invisible whip across Basilia. Yet her voice remained level. "Your father did not abandon you. He believed he'd been prompted to seek out the Lyk—"

"I beg you not to speak of the prophecy. It is only a charade to hide our family's mistakes."

"Respect your mother," Karleif snapped. "It's not our place to question her."

"No, it's only *your* place, Karleif," said the third brother, and Karleif spluttered.

"Silence," Lady Basilia called.

At this point, Violet felt thoroughly out of place. This had turned into a family disagreement. She wanted to slip backward through the exit.

"Why did Janlian's monarchs assume the pendant meant the prophecy's fulfillment?" the middle brother asked, and Violet appreciated his laid-back way of speaking, as if there was no tension. "You mentioned a tainted object. The Lykill can't be tainted, can it?"

"Janlian's monarchs believed otherwise," Basilia said.

"Yes, but Seers would say a lamb is tainted. Not exactly a trustworthy lot, are they?"

"My parents were Seers," Meliora said, a touch loud.

Eliathor shifted protectively closer to her.

"Only ignorance calls Seers deranged, Sweyn." Basilia's voice carried the sharpness of a dangling icicle.

"Fair," Sweyn said lightly. "Didn't mean to offend you, cousin Melly."

"You can't help being an ignorant toad, cousin Sweyn." Meliora smiled.

Sweyn chuckled.

"Let's return to the other two pendants." Karleif had recovered his voice. "How were they found? Who opened the gate, Father or Uncle? Where are the pendants now?"

"These questions remain a mystery, unless Dame Violet can solve them." Basilia returned to Violet.

"I can't answer the first two questions," she said, "but I can tell you where the pendants are." Violet detailed the outpost station, careful not to mention where she'd found the two sacred pendants.

"And nothing of your father's conversation with Chief Halfdan can be recalled?" Basilia asked.

"I've always feared saying these words . . ."

Fa hadn't been able to read the book Halfdan gave him, but that hadn't stopped him from obsessing over it. Namely, one page: the page Halfdan must have read from. Fa even copied it on countless scraps of paper, which proved useful after the book was stolen. Yet the Ókunnigr remained indecipherable until six months ago, when she and Fa met that young philologist at an annual Order conference. He hadn't been able to translate the Ókunnigr runes, but he could pronounce them. Fa had recorded their conversation and listened to it dozens of times. Those were the words he'd said to Violet on his deathbed.

"Before he . . . Recently, my father told me what Chief Halfdan said." She closed her eyes, bringing the conversation to focus. For a moment, she was there, right beside Fa as his breath wheezed and his eyes sunk into skin that had grown too loose. A thorn in her chest pricked, and she had to exercise all self-control not to wince. Forcing herself past that stage of the memory, Violet saw Fa's mouth form the words and heard them spill over in his broken voice.

"*Esh leydesh thul sílfar,*" she said. To her disappointment, the words remained in Ókunnigr. Had Kelispar stopped Advocating?

The room's silence told her the others were equally confused, until Karleif said, "Father tried welding!"

"How do you know?" Sweyn asked.

"What do you mean, how do I know? You heard the Terlion. But what is 'sílfar'?"

"You make a wide leap, Karleif," said his wife, Gisa. "Your father didn't have any power to weld."

"Yes he did," Meliora said. "He had the Lykill."

"And the ritual?" Gisa said.

"It must have been in that book."

Everyone looked to Violet. But how could she know? Fa hadn't possessed any special ability. Or had he? Had her father been welded, unknown to all, especially him?

"Well," Violet said, "welding involves a ritual, right? Where the person receives their . . ." She stopped. Looking up at Lady Basilia, Violet read the same conclusion on her face.

The scarf, which Fa never removed, which he had treated as his most prized possession without knowing why.

The volume in the room reached an unpleasant level. Kelispar fretted by Violet's side. Finally, Lady Basilia raised her hand. "Leave us," she called. "All but Violet and Emissary Kelispar."

Karleif protested the loudest, but his wife tugged him out. Once the door slammed shut, Basilia descended. Violet noted Kelispar tensing and wondered whether she should curtsy, stand rigid, or lay prostrate with her nose on the floor. By the time Basilia stopped before them, Violet had never felt shorter at five feet, three inches.

"When Chief Halfdan spake those words," Basilia said, "did he repeat them thrice?"

It was because of the repetition that Violet remembered Fa's deathbed words at all. "Yes," she said.

A chandelier could have fallen, clanged on the floor, and no one would have noticed. The power of Violet's answer tightened her chest, confirming something she hadn't known needed confirming. Kelispar's face locked in disbelief. Lady Basilia's head bowed.

"'*The child of silfar,*'" she whispered.

Kelispar looked slapped upside the head. The mood plummeted. Violet felt like an intruder on their grief, without any idea what had gone wrong.

"We charge you to speak of this to no one," Lady Basilia said. Her voice trembled. "Now . . . leave me."

Before Violet knew it, they'd been shooed out.

THEY WALKED BACK THROUGH the hallway of painted ancestors, who appeared even more depressing. Kelispar's mood resembled Eliathor's. He and Basilia found nothing pleasant about the idea of Fa having liryn. But it wasn't as if he had demanded to be welded.

"Why is it so upsetting if my father was welded?" Violet asked, hoping she didn't sound petulant.

He slowed. "Do you recall what I explained about cord thieves?"

"Yes."

"To use a cord not welded to you is a grave crime. The Lykill is the greatest of the cords. The High King created the three pendants for specific bloodlines, the royal families of the empires."

"Not for Chief Halfdan," Violet said. Kelispar and Lady Basilia weren't upset about Fa; they were upset about Chief Halfdan breaking the law. "But he was technically Terlian's rightful ruler, so he was allowed to weld Terlian's liryn. I assume that's what sílfar is."

"Terlian's monarchy was stripped of its power. When King Leif and Queen Thorgunna were brought before the emperors after the Rift, their welding cords were confiscated."

"Maybe Chief Halfdan found one."

Kelispar shook his head. "The emperors still have Terlian's cords. Besides, a monarch's cord has no effect unless he has been crowned. Even a prince cannot use his father's cord."

"But your cord can be used by someone else."

"The monarch cords are different. They were created by the High King himself. Even if Chief Halfdan found one of Terlian's monarch cords, he couldn't have used it."

That left the Lykill—its purple welding pendant.

"He must have thought it was necessary," she said.

"Wrong does not become right based on personal conviction."

"Maybe Chief Halfdan tried but it didn't work."

The way Kelispar paused, intently focused, made her scoot sideways. "Your father never removed the scarf, did he?"

She didn't have to answer.

He nodded. "It worked, Violet."

For some reason, Chief Halfdan welded Fa. It wasn't as improbable as the idea that Fa had been welded for twenty years without realizing it.

"You really don't know what Terlian's liryn is?" she said.

"Vessels don't speak of it, but we know that our greatest explorers were welded by Terlian. We assume it has something to do with traveling."

Violet wracked her mind. Fa definitely hadn't been able to teleport or fly, if that's what Kelispar meant.

Despite knowing that Chief Halfdan had used something he shouldn't have, Violet wasn't unhappy. Though she'd seen evidence of Fa's belief in the fantastical, meeting Lady Basilia had confirmed it. *Welded* it. And to hear that his parting words hadn't been nonsense gave her peace. In his final moments, Fa hadn't been crazy.

He'd just had liryn.

CHAPTER THIRTEEN

"The last Seer to apprehend a cord thief was Hedwig Madella. The thief was released after Madella was declared unsound due to her crown, which made her babble uncontrollably. No Seer has made an arrest attempt since. Madella died thirteen decades ago." – *Where Have the Seers Gone?* by Vessel Abina

KELISPAR SUGGESTED THEY CATCH some fresh air before dinner. The news of Halfdan had turned him so forlorn that Violet wished she knew how to cheer him.

They walked through a study. Wallpaper peeled where it wasn't stained with water damage. Windows let afternoon light dust the desks. Though the bookcases were as ancient as everything else, the books and scrolls filled the shelves in neat order. The Order would have wasted hours here.

Kelispar ushered her into a mudroom. Shovels and brooms were scattered like strewn twigs. Beyond the door, Violet heard happy shrieks.

A tangle of children played on the lawn. When she saw the lanky figure in the midst of the Hastein grandchildren, she thought the shrieks might have been coming from Alikar, who was currently being treated like a jungle gym. The children's mothers, each toting a baby, called a halfhearted "Be gentle, Lali" or "Leave poor Alikar's shoes alone." The more he protested, the more the children climbed him until, shaking, he succumbed to the ground, which only made him an easier target.

"Kelispar, come here," Gisa called.

The Hasteins would raise his spirits. Violet left him to Gisa and aimed for an orchard, but Kelispar followed.

"No, it's all right," Violet said. "I'd like to explore."

"Well, if you're sure . . ."

"I'm sure. Thank you." Violet strolled in the opposite direction.

She bypassed Alikar and his admirers. He called out, probably a plea for help, but without an Advocate around, she had no obligation to understand. She nodded at him, feeling a bit mischievous.

Mischievous? Mischief had never been on Violet's agenda, not since she was five, when she and Oliver used to play pranks on June. Then the three united in jest against their parents. But that had been before Ma's death. Before Oliver and Fa's first fight.

Suppressed emotions gathered steam and choked her. She touched her necklace, finding Oliver's compass covering hers. A violet in its cage.

Feeling as if the trees crept too closely, Violet left the orchard, letting herself meander. Yet, the more she gave in to wandering, the more she sensed her destination. Past the orchard, down the slope, edging alongside a garden of purple squash—yes, Violet was going somewhere.

Metal clanged metal. She rounded a trellis of grape vines and came across Eliathor's brothers fencing. Karleif didn't notice Violet as he vented his frustrations. Sweyn wearily parried, casting Violet a long-suffering look that indicated he'd rather be anywhere else. Before Karleif accidentally swung near her head, she scurried away.

Past the grape vines rose a stone hut. Eliathor leaned against a low wall, sitting at Meliora's feet as he sharpened his sword with a rock. As deftly as she could, Violet left them to their privacy.

They'd grown up together like siblings. Violet and Oliver might have grown so close had Fa not joined the Order.

She squeezed the vegvísir. Lately, everything reminded her of Oliver. She wished it didn't.

When she heard a plaintive *baaaa*, Violet figured she must have been subconsciously following the sound of sheep. She came upon a pasture enclosed by a cobblestone wall. Sheep, their fluff shorn off, grazed alongside spotted goats. The animals ignored her. Violet wasn't particularly interested either.

Something nudged, like someone was whispering her name. Violet's neck obeyed the tugging. Uphill, Lady Basilia strolled between trees, head bowed.

Carefully, Violet tread in the opposite direction. If she could slip away, unseen, then—

A twig snapped underfoot with all the vigor of a falling tree.

Lady Basilia caught her. Quickly, Violet curtsied, and Basilia waved her over.

So much for escape.

Basilia set off. Violet figured she ought to follow. They passed beneath dripping vines that sheltered a bridge. How long did Basilia intend to accompany her—all the way back to the estate? At least Violet couldn't be expected to converse. All the same, the silence was nerve-racking. This was the woman who'd married into a detested bloodline, who'd encouraged her husband to disobey the emperors, who'd raised three children under the shadow of her husband's shame. Meanwhile, Violet hadn't been certain Chief Halfdan had existed until today.

And then there was that strange force between them. Something pulled her toward Basilia, made her want to look at the woman's face or hear her voice. Basilia must've felt it too; she kept eyeing Violet sidelong, as if hoping she'd speak.

Violet wished she'd explored some other part of the grounds.

They rounded dead trees and came upon Kelispar, whose pacing and furrowed brow revealed that Eliathor's sisters-in-law hadn't cheered him up one bit.

He greeted them in Faartunga. By the time Basilia answered, he'd begun translating.

"I wish to speak privately with Dame Violet, Emissary," Basilia said.

Violet hid her discomfort.

"Of course." Wrinkling with concentration, he stepped aside, letting them pass.

"An Advocate may loan his ability without being privy to its usefulness," Basilia told Violet.

That was possible? Kelispar could Advocate for others while not understanding himself. Liryn benefited others as much as the person welded. The welded even had to endure suffering. Violet hoped the headaches were still sparing him.

The reality of Fa's welding returned. He would have had a crown. Or would he? He'd been welded by the Lykill. According to that Vessel, Malokki, that meant no crown. Yet Fa's life had held plenty of pain. Ma's death. ALS. Oliver. Even without a crown, he'd still suffered.

"I fear you have much to bear, my child," Lady Basilia spoke. Her gaze fell like sunlight, inviting yet intense. "To be of Terlian is to be despised. You have been told your history?"

That gaze—it hiked up Violet's nerves. The sooner she answered, the sooner Basilia might decide Violet made an uninteresting walking companion. At the same time, she felt that walking away would be like leaving behind her favorite book.

This was all so strange.

"Yes," Violet said. She sensed Basilia wanted her to elaborate, so she gathered her thoughts. "Terlian's monarchs ruled until the Rift, when they stole the Lykill and closed the gate to Terlian, hoping to make Terlian the most powerful."

"I see my son has spoken louder than Emissary Kelispar."

Violet felt awkward, but Lady Basilia continued without any sign that she was distressed.

"You must forgive Eliathor." Basilia took Violet's arm; Violet couldn't help flinching. Basilia's demeanor had softened shades from the throne room. She was a contradiction—tall and stern, yet graceful as a deer; formal and reserved, yet now intimate. "Eliathor's life has been one of sorrow. He was born under the shroud of his father's death. In his youth, he lost someone he dearly loved. Since that tragedy, he has not allowed any new affections. His friends find in him a most loyal protector. Strangers do not find the same, I fear." Basilia's tone was apologetic, but Violet wasn't offended by Eliathor's less-than-cheery welcome. "Tragedy follows my son whither he goes. Perhaps the fault is mine for giving him a Greek middle name." Something of a teasing smile curved Basilia's mouth.

Is she making a joke?

"Now," Basilia said, "have you discerned your purpose?"

"My purpose?"

"Eliathor tells me you, too, seek the Lykill."

"My father thought it could heal Ear—Terlian."

"And why does my realm require healing?"

Violet explained Ragnarök, how it had spread like poison in a wound, a shadow over land. Lady Basilia's expression grew sorrowful. Violet found herself trimming out the worst bits from her account. Basilia didn't need to know how far Ragnarök had spread, or the fact that Earth would be a wasteland in two hundred years.

Lady Basilia processed the information for heavy moments. "I do not understand," she finally said, her voice so mellow that Violet stepped quieter. "Why does Terlian alone suffer in this particular manner?"

Violet didn't understand, either. The Order believed Earth was dying without the Lykill, but hadn't *all* the realms been robbed of it?

Between rows of browned apple trees, Lady Basilia stopped. Violet did too. Her arm was still entwined with Basilia's. She'd forgotten.

A cloud of worry, the same that perpetually drifted over Eliathor, settled on Basilia. "I must hope in the prophecy, for all the realms need it. While they do not suffer the physical death of Terlian, they are decaying nonetheless. A Seer can see the unraveling, but when a Seer is called a madman, there are few who will heed him."

"What are Seers?"

"They see liryn, the corruption it brews on those who misuse it. In our history, Seers policed liryn, ensuring the guilty were brought to justice—both thieves and those who abused their liryn. Today, Seers do not fight. They have been oppressed, for those stewing in corruption do not wish to be corrected. Only the Lykill can restore order." She traced a finger along the browned spots on an apple.

"Because it will take crowns away from liryn?" Violet asked.

"That is the guesswork of a weak Vessel who fears suffering." Basilia's words were steely. "The Lykill will purify that which is tainted, yes, but these 'Hands of the Lykill' are mistaken. A crown is not a taint. The Lykill will strip liryn from the corrupt. It will render stolen cords useless. It will restore the purity of liryn. And it will heal my realm."

Remembering what Kelispar had told her about bar-rens—welded people who suffered while thieves used their liryn—Violet understood the need for the Lykill here too. She couldn't hoard it for Terlian, not unless she wanted to be like Eliathor's ancestors.

"Is it possible to share the Lykill between all the realms?" Violet asked.

"The Lykill will heal all when it is restored to its proper place."

Violet's next question was about where it needed to go, but Basilia continued.

"Vessels tell us the history of the accursed monarchs of Ter-lian, but the tradition of Janlian speaks another story. I am of

Janlian, and there my loyalty to Terlian was cultivated. I do not believe my husband's ancestors are to blame for the Rift. No loyalist does, but we are a minority—fools in the eyes of a society that mocks those who hope. Any mention of the prophecy incites disdain, for it was borne of a Seer and held fast by Janlian these thousand years." She lifted her chin, as if addressing the apples. "'*In the Lykill's golden time, the royal pair will cause calamity. A great breach will rupture the provinces. The sheep will be silenced. But what was muted can proclaim again. First, the thief must relinquish what he does not own. Second, the alien must die in his own land. Third, the mouth must breathe anew. Then one will come from the line of infamy, and of this line will the Lykill be restored. With the hard cleft, the Lykill will be found. Only then can peace abound. And the Lykill will converse with all.*'"

Wind stirred, swaying the apples. That did seem the appropriate response to an ancient prophecy.

"What do you make of this?" Lady Basilia asked.

"The first part is referencing the Rift. The royal pair are Terlian's monarchs—I think. The thief relinquishing is about Meliora's father giving the pendant to the monarchs. The alien dying in his own land is about Chief Halfdan, and the mouth is about the gate opening. The line of infamy is about someone from your family finding the Lykill."

"A prophecy is a living thing. Like liryn, it can be perverted by the wrong hands." Basilia stroked an apple. "Each realm was given one line of the prophecy. We do not have the line that was given to Terlian, nor do we have the original prophecy. Not even a Vessel can recite it, for the realms have fashioned it to their liking. I have given you Bar'Talian's version. It does seem evident that the seeker of the Lykill will descend from my husband's line. That was my belief, until now. For I know Janlian's prophecy also: '*Then will come the child of sílfar, and this child will seek out the Lykill.*'" She stopped, staring purposefully.

Violet pulled her arm free and stepped back.

"We have forgotten the liryn of Terlian. Yet I have heard the name 'sílfar' many times. It belongs to Janlian's prophecy—and it belongs to you, child of sílfar. You are of the infamous line. You will find the Lykill and restore it. Only then can Terlian heal."

Being bluntly informed of her role in the prophecy hadn't been on Violet's agenda. "Lady Basilia," she said, "I do want to find the Lykill. But I . . ." How could she say it? She'd planned on searching for the Lykill already, but that was before, when the Lykill was merely a matter of healing Earth and not of fulfilling a legendary prophecy. "I can't go on a long quest. I have obligations."

"What obligation could be greater than finding the remedy for our realm?"

Violet swallowed.

"The Lykill's proper place is with the emperors for whom it was made. Once restored, '*the realms will be tainted no more.*'"

Violet wanted to believe it could be that simple. It nearly was. Two-thirds of the Lykill were in a tea canister. "Does the prophecy say where the gate pendant will be found?" she asked. "You mentioned a cleft."

Basilia nodded. "*With the hard cleft.*' Janlian's version states that it will be found '*where water meets sand.*'"

"A beach?"

"Shepherd's Crag, a bluff two days hence. The prophecy of Meslian states that the Lykill will be found '*at the sheep's wall.*'" Basilia hesitated before saying, "Chief Halfdan's body was discovered on the sand beneath Shepherd's Crag. It is there that you will find the remaining pendant of the Lykill. The time is nigh. Even this Vessel Malokki senses it. The prophesied one has come. You and Sir Karleif will begin on the morrow. Emissary Kelispar will accompany you."

Before Violet could put forth an alternative plan, Lady Basilia suddenly drew Violet's hand between hers and whispered, "Why do you resist me?"

Violet stiffened.

"The bond between a monarch and her people is strong. I did not hope I could ever have the privilege of sharing it with a true Terlion. But you are here, my own subject. Yet I sense your reluctance."

Then that's what was happening—some magnetic pull based on the fact that Basilia was meant to be Violet's queen. Basilia *did* feel it. Violet wanted to explain that she didn't resist because she disliked Basilia, or Terlian, or the idea of having a queen. But words failed her.

Basilia curled a finger against Violet's cheek. "I wish to see you freed of these shackles. It is good to guard oneself, but a heart must have room to beat."

Violet couldn't move. She didn't know why she ached. Perhaps from the effort of constricting a torrent that had quietly invaded the moment Basilia took her hand. Even after such little interaction, Basilia had *seen* her—seen the iron inside, the carefully maintained heart. Composure, Violet called it, though sometimes she wondered if it was something else. After all, shackles were for broken things, bound together so they didn't fall apart.

"I . . ." she tried.

"You have suffered much on Terlian. But all will be restored. There is hope yet. Do not despair." Lady Basilia smiled, so warm and genuine that it dispersed the thoughts Violet couldn't say.

Violet exhaled. The tension flew out like a leaf. She found she could look Basilia in the eye and not feel like a flower under a microscope. Even the touch on her cheek was two shades closer to welcome.

Lady Basilia took Violet's arm again and resumed walking. Violet didn't recoil this time. "Once you have the Lykill, you will return to Vaspurakan. Bar'Talian's monarchs will present the Lykill to the emperors on behalf of Terlian. Then, you may return home. Do you accept your role?"

Find the gate pendant, unite it with the other two, and bring it back to Bar'Talian's monarchs. No one had succeeded in restoring the Lykill in a thousand years. Why would the answer be Violet?

She straightened. Lady Basilia believed in her. That hadn't mattered an hour ago, but it did now. And if the fate of Earth had to rest in someone's hands, she preferred her own. "Yes," she said. "I'll find the Lykill."

A great exhale, one Basilia must have held for twenty years, was carried away on the breeze that gently fluttered her braid. "Emissary Kelispar," she called.

But obedient Kelispar was so invested in not eavesdropping that he wasn't even looking. Violet had to tap his shoulder. Lady Basilia relayed the plan. He showed no surprise; he'd already guessed Violet's role.

"You and your brother must sleep here this eve," Basilia said. "I would not wish you to make the journey from Muratsan Manor so early."

Kelispar bowed.

"Do not be sorrowful any longer, Emissary. I cannot believe my husband did ill. Even supposing he had, good can always arise from evil."

Though he nodded, the shadows that tinged his face remained.

"You do not have much cheer today. Are you unwell?"

Violet pitied Kelispar, whose crown couldn't escape an observant eye.

His polite expression flaked apart, exposing the pain he'd shouldered all afternoon. "My crown . . . has come," he said, like one swallowing poison.

Lady Basilia glanced at Violet.

Kelispar shook his head. "Violet already knows. She's quite observant." He tried smiling.

"I can guess the cause," Basilia murmured. "I am most sorry."

"Please don't tell her, my lady."

"You have my silence, and my gratitude for treasuring my niece so tenderly. I wish this were not so. But your crown will mold you into who you must be. And for that reason, I cannot be saddened." She cupped his chin. "Take heart. Lady Muratsan would have been proud of her son, as I am."

This must have been too much to bear; Kelispar answered in Faartunga.

Violet walked away, her throat hard. Meliora did love Kelispar; he must have known that. But, more certainly, he knew they would never be together. His crown gave him a glimpse of a future Meliora didn't even realize.

She counted the apples on the trees and tried not to hear Kelispar's voice breaking.

He got her attention after a couple minutes. His nose was red, but the tension was gone from his eyes.

"I will see you both at dinner." Basilia patted Kelispar's cheek and nodded to Violet. "I hope you felt no particular attachment to our sheep, Violet, else you will find your dinner most distasteful." With the slightest hint of humor, Lady Basilia glided away.

Kelispar laughed. It was too airy, but he probably needed the release. "She does leave an impression," he said.

"I don't see how anyone could dislike her." Violet felt immediately vulnerable. Why had she said that?

"People who dislike her don't know her. But I suspect you like her more than most. It's the bond. Even Separatists feel bonded to their monarchs, though they resist."

That consoled Violet. She wasn't alone in this strange process. "You feel the same with the Bar'Talion monarchs?"

He nodded and gestured for her to walk. "Do you need anything before dinner?" He winced, quickly turning his cheek to hide it. So his head *was* hurting.

"No," Violet said. "Can you speak without Advocating, so I can learn your language? Arati, it's called?"

He donned his stern professor face.

"I like learning languages," she said.

"I'm sure you do."

"I'm not lying."

"Nor was I. I intend to Advocate, regardless of the discomfort." He touched his temple and quietly said, "I don't know why the strain has returned."

"You've been translating for hours. It's to be expected. But I really do want to learn Arati. Will you teach me?"

Kelispar studied her and eventually relented with a head-shaking chuckle. "As you say, child of sílfar." He loaned his arm. "You're a Terlion; you ought to know Faartunga. And so . . ." His face relaxed, and he spoke the familiar sounds of Old Norse, though in no accent any Order member had. Smiling freer now, Kelispar led her to the house.

CHAPTER FOURTEEN

"Tolian (current reigning: Cleophas the Ninth and Tabitha) can boast of war as easily as it can of stone. Within the past fifty years alone, it has endured the Barons' Conquest, the Winter Skirmish, the Battle of Lydia, the Spring Skirmish, the Second Battle of Lydia, the 748th Dakni War, the Cold War of Jagur, and Realm War 624." – *Chisel and Spear: The Survivalists* by Vessel Davit

T HE SUN HUNG LOW; Violet could barely see it over the horizon. Everyone had gone inside except the lone Alikar on a bench, arm slung over his forehead in exhaustion. Kelispar stared down at him, amused.

"You could have said no." Kelispar grimaced, automatically touching his temple before hiding his hand behind his back.

Internally, Violet sighed and wished he was less polite.

"Do you know what they do when I say no? They're terrifying." Alikar dragged himself upright. Dirt streaked his cheeks, his hair was a wild ponytail, and several buttons on his grass-stained shirt had popped off. "Where—" he began, then registered Violet. Surprise bolted across his face so swiftly it could have been nothing. Alikar smoothed down his hair, gave up, cleared his throat, and finally said, "In that dress, you remind me of yellow topaz."

Violet could think of nothing to say.

"I hope that was a compliment." Kelispar frowned.

"It was merely an observation of fact."

Kelispar hauled him up. "Go change. You're not remotely presentable."

Grinning, Alikar tried loping an arm around Kelispar, who skirted backward. "Can't I embrace my brother?" Alikar said.

"I know your aim." Kelispar pushed the swinging door to the mudroom, indicating for Violet to enter first.

"To hug my noble brother," Alikar said.

"And dirty his clothes."

"Of course."

They passed from the mudroom to the study. Violet stared, once again, at the rolled-up scrolls and wondered if she'd be able to read any of them. If only Dr. Mariemma could see this.

"What does it matter?" Alikar continued. "Melly's already seen you looking worse. Unless you believe she's forgotten your single day as a blacksmith. I assure you, she—"

His voice cut out with a strangled yelp. Kelispar had Alikar in a headlock. It was an odd sight, Kelispar behaving like a rambunctious schoolboy. Violet blamed Alikar.

"I regret the day I admitted loving you," Kelispar said, dragging Alikar along. "You've used it against me since."

"I'm not to be blamed for your—*ow*—sensitive heart." Alikar punched wildly at the space beside Kelispar's head. "Stop loving me if it's causing you this much distress."

"Believe me, I've tried."

They tumbled into the entrance hall, tripped toward the stairs—and nearly bowled over Meliora and Gisa.

Kelispar released Alikar, tugged his red sash around, and fixed his hat. "Ladies," he said breathlessly, bowing.

Alikar leaned on Kelispar's shoulder, mischief in his eyes. "Hello, Melly. We were just discussing—"

"You heard your brother, Alikar," Violet called. "Go change."

Kelispar offered her a grateful glance, which she returned with a nod.

Alikar ogled Violet. "Unbelievable. I can't escape you insufferable people, can I?"

"You could if you found something productive to do with your time," Gisa said.

Alikar took the insult with a smile. "Ah, but if I were productive, I would be dreadfully busy."

Eliathor's sister-in-law rolled her eyes and strolled away with Meliora, who paused long enough to wink at Alikar. He excused himself, leaving Violet and Kelispar at the bottom of the stairs.

"If you will excuse me," Kelispar said, "I have to make sure he actually changes. Oh—no, my shame. You need an escort to the dining hall. Allow me—"

"Just point me in the right direction," Violet said.

"Well—"

"Really."

Kelispar relented, motioning solemnly, as if giving directions to a prison.

If Violet had her way, she'd skip dinner and start off for Shepherd's Crag immediately. Dinner was sure to be a lengthy affair, during which she'd likely have to talk. To everyone.

She sighed. At least it was only for tonight. Tomorrow, she'd be back home.

After passing through a sitting room and an outdoor hallway, Violet smelled a gamey scent that brought to mind Lady Basilia's comment about sheep. Echoing string music drew her onward. She arrived in a banquet hall that made her feel right at home, like she was in the Order's Viking-themed headquarters.

The furniture was dark wood, each table edge carved with a sea serpent's head so it resembled the helm of a ship. With the candelabras, lanterns, and garland runners bedecking all three tables, Violet wasn't sure how there'd be room for plates. The antler chandelier could have carried Eliathor. White banners with sheep designs hung beside shields on the wood-paneled walls.

Unfortunately, there was nothing to obscure her; everyone noticed the exact moment she walked in. The music faltered. Eliathor's brothers stopped laughing over their tankards.

She wondered if she could retreat to Meliora's room until morning.

"Liam!" Karleif barked.

Karleif's young son strutted across the hall, gave his regal bow, then offered an arm.

The idea of being escorted by an eight-year-old made Violet cringe. But she obliged. Liam flushed as soon as she touched him and immediately forgot how to walk, tripping so much that she had to steady him. He yanked his arm free as soon as his parents allowed it.

A sister-in-law loped over. "Nazeli," she introduced herself, tapping her chest.

"Sweyn." Eliathor's tan, Basilia-like brother raised his tankard. Nazeli's husband.

"Karleif." The eldest brother bowed; Liam had obviously inherited that from him.

"Gisa," Karleif's wife called, waving her lyre.

Five children shouted their names in an indiscernible clamor of excitement.

"*Kom heil, Manishag,*" Karleif said to Violet.

"Manishag?" Liam tittered. But one look from his father and he screwed up his face. "*Hon er Manishag eigi. Hon er Violet.*"

"Violet?" Meliora stared at her.

Violet shifted, nodding. Did they . . . did they think her name was Manishag? "*Ek heiti Violet,*" she said.

"Violet!" Meliora looked aghast.

She longed to vanish. Violet could guess what had happened: Kelispar's liryn had translated her name literally. "Manishag" must've been Arati for "purple" or "violet."

Someone's chuckling cut through the discomfort. Violet looked to Sweyn, but it was Eliathor, standing apart with his tankard and slowly shaking his head. *Smiling.* He spoke, mentioning Kelispar. He'd realized it too.

Soon, everyone was grinning. Meliora's embarrassment gave way to an apologetic smile.

Violet kept envisioning her introduction before Lady Basilia. "*May I present Purple of Terlian.*"

Meliora took Violet's arm, steering her away from Sweyn, whose amusement was doubling into robust bellows.

It wasn't *that* funny.

The two wives resumed strumming their lyres, which successfully overshadowed Sweyn's howling. Meliora kept Violet company, swaying in rhythm. She gave Liam some command. He took off, returning a minute or two later with a crystal glass of bright yellow liquid, which he presented to Violet.

"Liam!" Meliora intercepted the glass before Violet could take it.

Liam defended himself, gradually drifting into English. " . . . a yellow drink to match her dress!"

Violet scanned the room. Kelispar and Alikar had arrived.

"I said water," Meliora said. "Do you know what this is?"

"Dada drinks it after he and Mami squabble. Mami says it makes him 'tolerable.'" Liam's face fell. "I thought 'tolerable' was a nice word. Is it bad?"

Violet was glad no one realized she understood.

Meliora pressed her lips together, failing to hide the quiver. "You've done very well, my lamb. Go get Uncle Eliathor."

As Liam shot off, Kelispar and Alikar neared, the latter much more presentable in a belted tunic. His red sash matched Kelispar's. He'd made an attempt to comb his hair too. It hung out of its ponytail, just touching his shoulders: straight, thick, and warm blond. Violet hadn't believed Alikar capable of looking like anything other than an overgrown boy.

"You remind me of a yellow topaz."

She wished she'd opted for the black dress. The yellow was causing quite the commotion.

"Red sun above you," Kelispar said.

"Liam nearly incapacitated her," Meliora answered. "And we must talk about Violet's name."

"Her name?"

Liam returned, dragging Eliathor by the sleeve.

"Liam thought Violet would enjoy an entire glass of *floki*," Meliora told Eliathor. Her poker face was commendable. "Evidently Karleif drinks this so that Gisa will find him tolerable."

Liam eagerly nodded.

Alikar turned his laugh into a cough and hacked into his elbow.

Eliathor took the glass, peering down. "He drinks this much?"

"Only a little," Liam said, "but I thought Dame Violet would like more."

"Thank you, Liam," Violet said, torn between pity and guilt.

Eliathor ruffled his nephew's hair. "Better you don't repeat everything your mami says. Yes? Take this back to the kitchen."

"We'll go together," Meliora said. They drifted away, Liam swinging Meliora's arm.

"I hope you paid attention." Alikar elbowed Kelispar. "Floki must work wonders for marital disputes."

Kelispar closed his eyes.

"Enough nagging from you," Eliathor said.

"Why? I assumed . . ."Alikar seemed to notice his brother's mood for the first time. His good humor vanished. "Kelispar? Did she say no?"

"I should send word to Dag and need my emissary's advice." Eliathor moved his head toward Violet in what might've liberally been called acknowledgment, then steered Kelispar away.

Alikar made to follow, then held himself back, despondent.

Violet examined the lines on her palms, wishing she didn't know as much as she did.

They stood in the tension until Meliora returned, empty-handed. "Our cook wouldn't allow me to bring you water," she told Violet. "She says we'll eat in five minutes, and if you die of thirst before then, it's your own fault." She laughed. "Such a Fabia response, isn't it?" she asked Alikar.

He was silent. Violet hoped he would stay that way, because the expression on his face made it very clear that anything he might have to say would be uncomfortable for everyone in the vicinity.

She was relieved when the music faded, robbing Meliora of the chance to ask Alikar why he looked like he wanted to smash the chandelier. Everyone stood at attention as Lady Basilia strode toward the center of the hall.

"Twenty years ago, my husband and beloved brother-in-law died in disgrace," she said, and the children ceased fidgeting. "My hope in the prophecy faltered. Violet Lyng has reignited that hope. She is the one who will restore the Lykill. The names of the great King Leif and Queen Thorgunna will be exonerated. I had prayed that this honor might belong to my sons. The will of the Great Welder is ever-humbling."

Violet wished there was another Violet in the room.

"I ask you to repeat?" Karleif spluttered. "You believe this *stranger* will fulfill the prophecy?"

"Yes," Lady Basilia said, "and you will accompany her, Karleif."

"But I—"

"Tomorrow morn you depart for Shepherd's Crag. Representatives of King Giannis shall join us in celebration."

"You contacted Janlian?" Karleif groaned.

"Certainly. The Bar'Talion monarchs have been informed as well. They have cut their journey short and will sleep here this eve upon their return, that they might join us in tomorrow's farewell breakfast."

More festivities, Violet bemoaned, with Janlian's royal representatives *and* the rulers of Bar'Talian. She'd have to practice curtsying.

"Mother," Eliathor said, "why have you brought Violet into our affairs? Let the prophecy and the Lykill die along with Father."

"I wish you did not feel this way, my son," Lady Basilia said. "Your father's quest was honorable."

He moved closer. "Mami," he whispered, "stop this madness."

"Will you not fight for your sheep, Eliathor?"

"Terlian has none. We lost our right to them a thousand years ago."

Lady Basilia passed a trembling hand over her forehead.

"I will not see this family fall into further disgrace. I pray your mind is changed, before the Lykill ruins us all." With that, Eliathor exited. The sound of the closing door echoed like a stranger that had lingered too long.

Lady Basilia winced.

"I'll talk to him." Meliora kissed her aunt and hurried after Eliathor.

"A hard slap should convince him," called Sweyn, who had somehow developed the ability to joke despite having Eliathor and Karleif for brothers. "He always was the gloomy one. Blame Karleif."

"Oh, shut up," Karleif said.

"Are you sure you trust Karleif with this quest, Mami? I'm a much better swordsman. More tolerable, too."

"Be seated." Lady Basilia drifted toward a table, limping, as if her spirit had caught up to her age. Her daughters-in-law hurried to assist her.

Fortunately, the children raced around and caused a commotion with their chairs, readjusting the mood. Violet wondered where she was supposed to sit. She searched, finding Alikar gaping at her.

"You are the prophesied one?" he said.

"Evidently. We should take our seats."

"Well, yes, but—you are a Terlion! Everyone believed . . . *anak*. One thousand years of study did not teach us anything, did it?"

"Those chairs over there are empty."

"All right then, oh impatient one. My shame for asking one simple question about the fate of the realms." Alikar was still shaking his head when they reached a table that could have held a dozen more people.

"Is this the right table?" Violet asked.

"Kelispar told me to keep you isolated so you may eat in peace."

Violet was relieved. She wouldn't have to talk to anyone else who thought she made a poor choice for the savior of the realms.

Alikar pulled out a chair for her—maybe he *was* a gentleman—and then another. Which he took.

"You're sitting here too?" Violet restrained the accusatory lilt.

"Kelispar appointed me as your escort."

Violet unfolded her sheep-shaped napkin and stared long-ingly at the children's table.

Neither of them spoke until the first course, served from rolling carts by a wrinkly couple. Alikar commented that the leek soup looked browner than usual. Violet examined her utensils. The fork had only two prongs, and the spoon was shaped like a ladle. Both were copper, sharply diagonal, and had a loop on the handle.

"Do you eat with your hands on Terlian?" Alikar asked.

"No, I'm just looking."

Discreetly, she observed how he slid his index finger into the loop and copied him.

After finishing, she sipped from her pint-sized goblet to occupy herself. The lukewarm water tasted bitter. How quickly could she leave without offending Lady Basilia?

"I cry your pardon," Alikar said, "but that's mine."

Coughing, she slammed down his cup, accidentally knock-ing it against her plate. The goblet tipped. Water sloshed on the table and onto the floor.

Her cheeks burned, but Violet collected a napkin as if noth-ing was wrong. Steadily, she dabbed at the stain as Alikar scurried out of the way. *The water is nowhere near him,* she thought, humiliation spurred into irritation when he dropped down on all fours. Was he crawling away? It was only water.

"Everything fair?" Sweyn called.

Violet wasn't going to lie. She opened her mouth.

"Oh yes!" Alikar replied. "I will forever be a klutz."

She peeked down. He had his own napkin out, mopping. Not escaping after all.

Confusion robbed Violet of speech. Why was he cleaning her mess? And why had he taken the blame? The second question grated her more.

She knelt beside him. Her drenched napkin smeared water over the stone. He had to wipe afterward, doing all the work while she only made things worse.

"Well"—Alikar balanced on the balls of his feet—"I say we ought to be thanked. I doubt the floor's been cleaned this thoroughly in years." He smiled a Kelispar smile, even if Alikar's teeth were crooked and not as white.

"Thank you," she said, "though you shouldn't have taken the blame."

"Nonsense. It's not you who should thank me, Terlion, but Mr. and Mrs. Sarkissan, who clean the floor." He stood. "Shall we?" Alikar's hand waited for hers. Evidently he was a gentleman as much as Kelispar, far more than Violet had given him credit for.

She gripped his fingers. He twitched, as if she'd passed him a fish, and pulled too hurriedly. She bumped into him, and he into the table, where he tried righting himself by grabbing the tallest thing—which happened to be the other goblet. Water doused the utensils and created a fresh puddle by their feet.

They stared at each other, Violet's humiliation mollified.

"I've always preferred the left," he said, motioning to the other, dryer side of the table.

They relocated after cleaning their mess. "If anyone asks," Alikar said, "we were sword-fighting. Unless you can think of a more compelling tale."

She could have shrugged, but Violet found herself thinking hard. The only tales she knew belonged to the Order. Once upon a time—no, it was probably true—a king had been served a poisoned chalice. After making a gesture over the drink, he consumed it. The poison left his cup and entered his enemy's. An eagle had been involved somehow. "Maybe . . . the water was poisoned," she said, "and we had to dump it out." It was pitiful; Alikar would prefer his own imagination.

But he nodded and said, "A satisfying excuse. I was the brave knight who knocked the dangerous brew from your hands, thus saving your life and earning the title 'Alikar, He of the Copper Chalice.'"

Violet almost smiled.

They ate in a pleasant silence after that. Alikar, sopping up his soup with bread, said, "I don't envy you, having to endure Janlions tomorrow. That means Seers. They're odd."

Violet was not looking forward to more ogling. "How so?"

"They see corruption everywhere. Even in the gates."

"They're coming because Lady Basilia is from Janlian?"

"Janlian and Terlian have always been allies. The royal family used to visit here frequently, but that was before Princess Fila di—" He paused. Broth dripped onto the tablecloth. Then, Alikar consumed his bread with intense concentration. "I intend to be a Chisel. What do you know of them?"

"Nothing."

"Behold."

He thrust a crumb-covered hand into a pocket. Out came what resembled a tin for mints, with gold metal plating and shaped like a diamond. Violet jumped when something shot out. A chortling Alikar grabbed the protruding shape, pulling until it stretched down the table. The thin stick, decorated by foreign characters, reminded her of measuring tape. Next, he unlocked a tool pointy as a scalpel. The diamond case, no bigger than his palm, also held a copper chisel, a cable that seemed to uncoil indefinitely, and an instrument to write with. Violet couldn't fathom how everything fit.

"It's a genetic malady," Alikar said. "Mother said I reminded her of her brother. Fascinated by puzzles and the like. I suspect he would have wanted to be a Chisel too."

"Chisels are builders," she said, thinking of his sandcastle.

"Craftsmen, of the natural elements."

"Fire and water?"

"No, no, no, no. Metal, stone, wood, fibers."

"Plants?"

"Plants! Anak, Terlion. I'm happy to leave plants to Sowers. What a boring liryn. Next you will be asking whether Chisels commune with animals."

"Is there a liryn that does?" Violet asked, alarmed.

"Not within *basareth*. Beneath the aspect of *basareth*, there are four types: Chisels, whom I have already explained; Sowers, who make things grow; Balms, whom you have experienced"— he gestured to her forehead—"and Pillars, who strengthen the body. All require knowledge of the appropriate rituals, unlike Advocates. Kelispar doesn't need a ritual; he only has to will to translate. *Da'atan* is of the intellect, *basareth* of the body. You see?" He continued before Violet could nod. "Chisels are the only ones capable of imbuing an object with liryn, like doors. Anyone may open them, provided they know the ritual. A rather generous liryn, isn't it?"

Violet's mind overflowed with words detached from meaning. Her curiosity was distracted by movement. Eliathor and Meliora entered the room. Though conversation and clinking continued, Lady Basilia noticed. She whispered something to Kelispar. He scooted over, freeing up his chair. Eliathor took it. He said nothing, only clasped his mother's hand.

"Are there laws prohibiting you from becoming a Chisel?" she asked, returning to Alikar.

Carefully stowing the tools, he said, "Technically, no. But Tolian is not only another realm, it is within another empire."

"Could you explain the difference between realms and empires?"

He groaned. "I had hoped Kelispar would tell you this. Then again, he'd likely still be explaining." Lips pursed in concentration, Alikar spied around the table. He ripped three white leaves off the garland centerpiece and arranged them in the shape of a triangle. "The realms are divided among three empires, designated by liryn. Da'atan Empire—pretend that's purple—Basareth Empire—pretend that's red—and Nehfey Empire. Already white, as you can see. Bar'Talian is within the Da'atan Empire because Advocates are of the mind. Ah, liryn is either of the mind, body, or spirit. Do you understand?"

"So it's a liryn distinction, but also geographical."

"Erm. What do you mean?"

"All the realms within the Da'atan Empire are close."

"Oh. No. The realms are scattered across the heavens."

Just like the Order's poem said. An emperor could be over a realm that was millions of light years away. "Which empire is Terlian in?" Violet asked.

"Nehfey."

So Terlian's liryn was of the spirit. Whatever that meant. "Do the emperors have more liryn than monarchs?"

"No. They *are* monarchs, like Asbed and Nora, only with greater political power."

"Where do they live?"

"In their seat."

Violet blinked.

Alikar gaped like he'd been asked to explain astrophysics. "The Da'atan emperors live on Matlian, where Vessels are welded. Matlian is their seat."

Violet finally understood. She likened emperors to state governors. California was the empire, Sacramento the emperor's "seat." It wasn't a perfect analogy, but it worked.

"I see," she said.

"Good." Alikar slumped back in his chair.

The Lykill was meant to be restored to the emperors. But then the Lykill wouldn't really be the Lykill, but three separate pendants across three separate empires. That contradicted the fundamentals of the Lykill: one source of power. Violet couldn't solve that dilemma, so she returned to Alikar's.

"If becoming a Chisel isn't illegal, you should try. Unless you don't think your parents will approve." As soon as she said it, she remembered that they'd died. Her mouth hung, failing to recapture the statement.

When Alikar sobered, he looked more like Kelispar. "They wouldn't, no. But they've passed on."

The quiet expanded. Violet had to disrupt it. "I'm sorry. I'm an orphan too," she said.

He fiddled with his tool kit. "Well, I suppose I can't qualify as an orphan when Kelispar has so rigorously assumed the role of both Father and Mother. He disciplines me, then soothes the sting afterward."

Violet was surprised he was willing to admit that. He had no obvious sense of embarrassment about anything.

"No one else in this country is interested in Chisels. But I'm used to being the cross-billed bird. My eyes aren't exactly Arati. Nor my height. I take after Father's ancestors." He grew thoughtful, as if just realizing he didn't fit in. Then he shrugged. "I'm Arati blond, though. Evidently the ancient Rosensverds were thoroughly brunette. My father's line, you know. Muratsan is my mother's. Her noble *azat* name superseded my father's, so Rosensverd became Muratsan. He was fully Arati, really, after so many generations of Rosensverds here. Blond as a willow warbler."

"You fit in with the Hasteins, with how tall you are," Violet said, thinking of Eliathor's height.

"That's not the Hastein blood; it's from Lady Basilia. Chief Halfdan was proper Arati height, like Kelispar, even if he was a clay head."

"Clay head?"

"Yes. The color of clay?"

"Oh. We call redheads 'ginger.'"

"Is that not yellow on Terlian?"

"It is." Violet paused. "I have no idea why we say 'ginger.'"

"Because you Terlions are mad." He smiled.

Dinner arrived: lamb chops with white sauce. Violet couldn't squelch a twinge when she remembered the sheep.

Between bites, she considered Alikar's career dilemma. It wasn't that different from the struggles of an ordinary teen. "You should put together a portfolio, then befriend a Chisel," she said. "If he thinks you're good, he might hire you. Once you have experience, you can petition the Tolion monarchs."

Alikar stared. Had she offended him? "That," he finally said, "is a very good idea." He snatched the napkin off his lap. In another moment, he'd pulled a pen out of his diamond tin. "I do have a concept for a hairbrush that oils while it combs," he mumbled, head bent over the table. "To prevent snags. Not that I'd ever use it." And he feverishly ruined his napkin, then hers when he ran out of space.

Despite his utter disregard for someone's linens, Violet couldn't deny that it was nice to see Alikar focused.

"Thank you for the inspiration." He glanced over. His eyes glinted, and he aimed his pen toward her mouth. "I see I've caught you smiling. Don't fret. I shan't tell." He returned to his drawings, smirking.

Violet bit her lip and stirred her sauce.

He worked quietly throughout the rest of dinner. She was just debating whether to excuse herself when Sweyn called out, "Purple flower!" as he marched over, swinging a tankard.

"Pretend you're ill," Alikar muttered. "He's going to force you to try his mead."

"His—"

"Happy eating?" Sweyn clunked the tankard on the table.

"Yes," she said. "It was very good. Thank you."

"Excellent. Have a taste of this." Sweyn pushed over the cup, decorated with unevenly carved antlers. "You know mead? Honey water?"

"I've heard of it, but I'm not twenty-one."

Sweyn stared at her. She sensed Alikar's confused head tilt.

That wasn't going to work.

"Don't make her drink that poison," Alikar said.

"Let the girl call it poison on her own terms." Sweyn gave the tankard another push. It bumped against Violet's plate.

She should have excused herself when she had the chance.

Tentatively, then quickly, she took a sip. The viscous, mildly carbonated liquid tasted nothing like honey; it burned her throat and gave her the sense that she was drinking rocket fuel. But, oddly enough, she enjoyed the flavor.

"It's nice," she said, taking another sip to prove her point.

"What in Barikad?" Alikar said. "You Terlions really are mad!"

Sweyn thudded his fists on the table. "She likes it! Come. We'll dance to that." He held out a hand.

A dance? That was hardly fair. "I don't know any of your dances," she blurted.

"My wife will show you. Nazeli!"

Violet's toes curled, gluing themselves to the floor. Absolutely nothing, not even politeness, could convince her to dance with Sweyn.

"Stop bellowing," Alikar said, scratching his ear, "and loom elsewhere. I'm busy."

"Since when is our little sapling busy?" Sweyn said. "Rude, too. A pretty maid sits by your side and you do not ask her to dance?"

Alikar's ear-scratching stopped. His wide stare suggested that his drawings had just burst into flames.

Violet wanted a gate to appear and return her to Helheim.

Fortunately, Nazeli arrived, breathless and carrying a baby. "What do you shout for?" she asked.

Sweyn slung his arm around her. "Teach this girl to dance."

She looked at Violet. "Do you want to dance?"

"No," she answered firmly.

Nazeli nodded. "Leave her be, Sweyn."

"She enjoys my mead!"

"No one enjoys your mead, my husband." Nazeli dragged him away.

Violet exhaled and took another sip.

Kelispar came over after Alikar had commandeered five more napkins. In the chandelier lighting, he looked spotty with age. He asked Violet whether she'd had plenty to eat, if she was too warm, if she'd prefer to sit in a more comfortable chair. Eventually, she convinced him she wasn't dying.

"Anak, you're haggard," Alikar said. "Go to bed, Spar, or stop Advocating."

"I will eventually." Kelispar's whole stance looked strained, as if he shouldered a backpack of bricks. His presence made Violet keenly aware that he was only translating for her benefit.

"I'd like to go to bed too," she said, standing.

He and Alikar escorted her to Lady Basilia. Eliathor had an arm draped across the back of Basilia's chair, giving him access to Meliora's braid, which he was tugging.

With her hundredth curtsy, Violet said goodnight.

"Until tomorrow morning." Basilia inclined her head.

Eliathor tweaked Meliora's hair more earnestly. She shot up. "I'll show you to my bedroom, Violet," she said.

"Her company is unnecessary," Alikar said stiffly. "I am the Terlion's escort."

"We'll all escort *the Terlion*," Eliathor said. He kissed Basilia's cheek. "Goodnight, Mami."

Alikar threw visual daggers that Eliathor ignored, so he pulled Kelispar ahead. "Hold these drawings. They're for my portfolio. It was the Terlion's idea."

Violet landed in the middle, trapped between Alikar, intentionally monopolizing Kelispar, and Eliathor, urging Meliora to talk to Kelispar—Violet could tell by the whispers behind her.

In the entrance hall, where the staircase climbed, the group stalled. Alikar piled napkin after napkin into Kelispar's hands, speaking so fast that Violet thought Kelispar had stopped Advocating.

"Kelispar," Meliora murmured.

Alikar rambled on, until Kelispar touched his elbow. The silence drew out.

Meliora inhaled. She stood there, fidgeting, as the discomfort multiplied more tangibly than Alikar's napkins.

"Will you join me in the study, Meliora?" Kelispar's smile was bittersweet but kind.

She nodded gratefully.

"What an excellent idea." Alikar started after them.

Eliathor stopped him. "Upstairs you get, little sapling."

"But I'd rather go with them."

"You have a guest to see to."

"And you?" Alikar folded his arms.

"I owe Lali a dance." Eliathor walked off, though not so quickly that he caught up to Kelispar and Meliora.

"She likes me better!" Alikar called. "His niece," he added to Violet. "We compete for her affections. I've had the lead for years."

"You can go with him," she said. "I know the way to Meliora's room."

"I am your escort and cannot *hrazharvel im* . . ." He drifted into Arati and held out his palm.

Ignoring the uptick of nerves, Violet took his hand. Alikar spewed out a phrase and moved her hand to his elbow.

Violet wanted to rip her hand away. Better yet, march up the stairs alone. But she forced herself to match Alikar's pace. If only Eliathor had stayed. His gloomy company would've ensured neither she nor Alikar had the chance to blush for long.

Outside Meliora's door, she slipped free. "Well. Goodnight. *Gaia,*" she told the door. She tried to shut herself in, but Alikar blocked the way. Exclaiming, he bounded toward the wardrobe. Like someone inspecting lost treasure, he ran his fingers over the drawings, cackling when he found Kelispar's lopsided figures.

While Alikar hopped around the furniture like a toad, Violet discovered the addition of a pallet on the floor, and on it a purple nightgown that reminded her of one June's baby doll had worn. A pair of socks was folded with it.

Alikar took out his writing utensil. After winking at Violet with a finger on his lips, he began sketching. A scene came to life under his strokes: two cartoon characters at a table. One, with Xs for eyes, grasped her throat. The other thrust his sword at a goblet. Fumes rose from the drink. Violet and He-of-the-Copper-Chalice were forever branded onto Meliora's furniture.

"Alikar," he said, tapping the swordsman, "*yev Terliona.*"
"Violet," she said.

"Fi-leet?" He laughed. "*Noch Manishag!*" Alikar added a flower over cartoon Violet. "*Manishag,*" he said, pointing at it.

So he *had* known her name. Well, her false name.

She yawned. Alikar had started drawing another figure. "Excuse me," she said.

He looked at her, confused. She pointed to the pallet. Immediately, he jumped upright and bowed. "*Barr-barr gishar,*" he said, and escaped.

Violet lingered by the wardrobe. There she was, included alongside decade-old sketches. Alikar had even included the swirls on her dress. He'd noticed.

Hot in the palms, Violet donned the nightgown, annoyed by all her blushing. Alikar had spent more time being ridiculous than charming, but he clearly felt awkward around her. Maybe he'd grown up around old people, too. Or maybe her social ineptitude was so potent that he felt awkward on her behalf.

Violet yanked on her socks. This was juvenile. She had more important things to worry about. The fact that she was featured in an ancient prophecy, for starters.

After rinsing her face and teeth in the attached bathroom—it contained a copper basin for a sink, which poured a constant stream of water like a fountain—she crawled onto the pallet, relieved that she didn't have to share a bed with Meliora. Not that Violet wasn't used to it. June treated her own bed like a hamper and wound up in Violet's bed most nights.

Thoughts of the prophecy pushed June out. But that was too daunting, so Violet thought of Fa. Because of his scientific accomplishments, she'd always held the unwavering belief that he was special. Every child surely thought that about their parents, but in her case, it would be proven—by her. She wouldn't be able to convince her family that Fa had possessed some magical ability that might've had to do with sheep herding; but, once Earth was healing, everyone would know that Fa had been right all along.

She didn't remember falling asleep until she awoke some time later. Meliora was tiptoeing around. A warm, rumbling weight on Violet's stomach suggested that a cat had made her its bed; she was too bleary to confirm.

Meliora whispered Jarek's name. She must have been on the phone.

Do they have phones on Bar'Talian? was Violet's last conscious thought before sleep returned.

The Empires

The 12 Realms

Ao'atan

Seat:
Mallian

Mallian~
Vessels
Bar'Talian~
Advocates
Silian ~
Goldentongues

Nehfey

Seat:
Thulian

Thulian~Choirs
Meslian~Sprites
Janlian~Seers
Julian~
Unravelers
Terlian~ [illegible]

Basareth

Seat:
Eslian

Eslian~
Pillars
Tolian ~
Chisels
Anlian~
Balms
Pilian~
Sowers

CHAPTER FIFTEEN

"The Lykill will only be restored by blood." – Vessel Malokki, black pearl

S HE HADN'T BEEN SLEEPING long when she awoke with a start, an eerie sensation along her skin. Seconds passed before she registered someone shaking her. Violet flinched.

"*Xypna!*" It was Meliora, her face half shadows and orange glow, bouncing from a window lamp.

Even in a haze, Violet registered one certain fact: Meliora was afraid. That pulled her fully awake. She sat up; the cat jumped off and dashed away. "What's wrong?" Violet whispered.

Meliora put a finger to her lips and pointed. She wanted Violet to get under the bed.

Violet's eyes expanded. What was—

A *thump thump thump* made them jump. A man shouted. A baby whined. Footfalls thudded like an avalanche outside the room.

Meliora all but wrenched Violet's arm off. They crawled under the bed. Hunched like watchful soldiers, they monitored the strip of light beneath the door frame. Violet's heart sprang every time a shadow passed. She wished she didn't understand what all the clamor meant.

Invasion.

When a wide shadow paused in front of the door, Meliora clasped Violet's wrist. Nails pinched her skin. Thunder beat so violently in Violet's ears, she couldn't hear when the door opened.

"Meliora," came a harsh whisper.

Meliora poked her head under the bed skirt. "Eliathor!"

Violet dipped her forehead on the floor and exhaled. Quickly, she shimmied out.

Eliathor wore a vest he hadn't buttoned. Violet homed in on his sword, pale with a point sharper than his gaze.

"*Kelispar kai Alikar?*" Meliora said, gathering Violet's jacket and shoes.

He nodded.

Violet took her coat. This seemed confirmation that they were fleeing, but to where? Wishing more than ever that they spoke the same language, she tugged on her boots, then found her beanie.

"Gaia?" Meliora peered under her bed. "*Edo, edo, Gaia!*"

Violet guessed she was looking for her cat.

Eliathor took Meliora's hand, shaking his head.

She bit her lip.

He leaned an ear against the door, then commanded it to open. Out tipped his sword. Satisfied, Eliathor guided Meliora into the hallway, then Violet, falling into step behind them.

Shadows and gloom marred the hallway; their creeping forms made crooked silhouettes on the wall. Violet trod as if on glass. For all that chaos, no one was around to catch them slinking by.

Eliathor's pace quickened. They stood outside another door now. "*Felagi*," he told it, and it opened. Eliathor didn't enter until both Violet and Meliora were inside.

An odd, disjointed sound came from the bed. Alikar snored on his stomach in absolute surrender to sleep.

Meliora shook him. He mumbled, stirring. She spoke over him, words pouring in a tumult. At the name of Kelispar, Alikar sat up. Panic overlaid his groggy features, a burst of cold smothering the lazy warmth of summer. He dashed to a door, which led into another bedroom. Signs of struggle showed in the tangled sheets, the broken vase, the discarded pillows.

The empty bed.

Alikar froze, clutching his hair, not registering when Meliora threw a shirt at him. Violet, wanting to be useful, found Alikar's boots. Eliathor moved to a full-length mirror. One palm on the glass, he spoke. Fog clouded the mirror—and then vanished. His entire reflection did, swallowed by a hole. The mirror had hidden a tunnel, a dark, dusty thing.

Alikar asked Eliathor about Kelispar. He replied by shoving Alikar into the opening. Next, he took Meliora and, much gentler, nudged her through. Violet tried moving on her own, but a distracted Eliathor pushed her in.

"*Finndu Dag*," he told Alikar.

Find Dag? The boat captain?

Alikar shook his head, waving Eliathor inside the tunnel.

"Eliathor!" Meliora said. "*Kom!*"

Sorrow and certainty made a heavy mixture across Eliathor's face. He pulled Meliora close and pressed his forehead against hers. She clutched his shirt, tugging, but he won the battle by disengaging her fingers. The floor creaked when he stepped back. His cheeks were wet.

"*Ek ann þér,*" he said.

Violet knew that one. *I love you.*

Meliora reached, almost making contact . . . and then he disappeared as the mirror reformed. Her fingers folded against the hard surface. She and Alikar shared a look of dread.

He retrieved his tool set from a pocket, finding the laser-tipped light. Then he snatched Meliora's hand and led the way, checking to make sure Violet was following.

Additional light within the tunnel came through iron grates set low along the walls. Each time they passed one, they listened. Nothing.

They would find Kelispar. And the children. Violet's stomach tightened as she pictured Liam. But the Hasteins knew about this escape tunnel. They would be safe. She told herself that repeatedly.

When distant voices echoed, Alikar covered the laser. They took quieter, slower steps. By unspoken agreement, they sidled along the wall and bent their knees. It was a tight squeeze; they had to touch shoulders.

". . . expect anything different from leeches," drifted a female voice.

Through the grate, Violet recognized the familiar decorations of the throne room, cast in orange hues from torchlight that painted everything with choppy shadows. A few figures stood. Some were on the floor.

Her breath caught. Karleif and Sweyn lay spread-eagle. She blinked and blinked. The effort did not make their chests rise and fall.

Karleif had welcomed her to the dining hall last night and told Liam to lend her his arm. Sweyn had wanted to dance with her.

Violet's heart twisted.

Meliora covered her face. A white-knuckled Alikar gripped the iron grate, mouth agape.

A college-aged girl loped around the room like a curious panther. A man with a red liryn cord knelt nearby, hunched as if in pain, while a third stranger effortlessly restrained Kelispar. His hair was glossy with sweat, his mouth bloody, and he glared at the fourth stranger. This one stood before Lady Basilia, who held her head high despite her disheveled night dress. Violet recognized the man's graying hair and the Separatist patch on his arm.

Yakiv Stefanos.

"Welder above," Alikar whispered.

" . . . my predicament," Yakiv was saying to Kelispar. "Your Pretenders killed my Advocate, see." His head jerked toward another body on the floor. "So I have to use you."

"I'll hook the lady," the girl said, "make sure she answers you straight." The girl tweaked the purple liryn cord that decorated her arm like a band and turned eagerly to Basilia.

"Kora, wait—" Yakiv said.

"Tell us *de Halfdani skhovav . . .*" The rest of Kora's inquiry drifted into her own tongue. Kelispar had stopped Advocating.

Yakiv appraised Kelispar's defiance with silent calculation. The inability to communicate made for a powerful weapon.

It seemed Yakiv wanted to interrogate Lady Basilia, but how would he be effective if he didn't speak Faartunga and she didn't understand his tongue?

Without visible consternation, Yakiv moved toward Basilia. In profile, he was unaffected. Matter-of-fact. Patient, even, as he withdrew something from his belt. A metal coil. He gripped Basilia's arm and kept walking, as if he'd picked up a book. Was he so strong despite her height, her resistance? Yakiv hauled her up the dais to her throne. With clipped, speedy movement, he tied her to the armrests. Then Yakiv took her hand, spread her fingers apart, and gripped her pinkie. He found a dagger inside his sleeve.

Bile filled Violet's mouth.

Kelispar quickly spoke. Basilia shook her head.

"*Ochi, ochi . . .*" Meliora moaned.

Yakiv slashed Basilia's pinkie away.

Basilia hissed, jerking. Kelispar cried out. Alikar shoved his knuckles against his teeth.

Coolly, Yakiv struck off Basilia's ring finger.

Violet turned away. But everything she heard was almost as horrible. Meliora whimpering. Alikar trying to comfort her. Basilia's hissing. Fear, pity, and anger made a mess of Violet's reasoning. Then that strange, unbidden loyalty rose, a clarity that steadied her. Violet had to defend Lady Basilia. She could sneak away, find help.

But half the help lay dead on the floor.

"Stop," came Kelispar's voice at last. He was panting. "I'll Advocate."

The throne was awash with red. Basilia's head dipped onto one shoulder.

Yakiv sheared off her remaining thumb.

"I said stop!" Kelispar shouted.

"I heard you," Yakiv said.

Eliathor's words came back to Violet: *The prophecy turns men into zealots.*

Basilia convulsed. Blood ruined her nightgown.

"Please, forgive me," Kelispar called out to her.

Alikar cursed Yakiv to places Violet had never heard of.

"We have to help them," she whispered.

Meliora watched the man with the red cord. "The Pillar," she said. Her teeth chattered. "Too strong."

The man who was doubled over, doing nothing?

"Please, Emissary." Basilia could not lift her head to push out the plea. "You must protect Terlian. No matter . . . the cost."

Kelispar's eyes passed from Basilia to Yakiv, then back. Violet could see him weighing it. He knew the exact cost. The cost of refusing to Advocate, and the cost of capitulating. Would he rather let Yakiv hurt Lady Basilia or the Hasteins' secrecy?

Perhaps it didn't matter what Kelispar wanted. Basilia had pleaded, and he was faithful.

His eyes narrowed. Obedience had won out.

"Now, Kora," Yakiv said.

The girl spoke to Kelispar. "Keep Advocating."

His eyes narrowed further.

"I said, keep Advocating." Kora dashed to Kelispar. Compared to Yakiv and the rest of his men, she was the youngest. Perhaps that explained her overexcited energy—and the way Yakiv monitored her like one who's awaiting a mistake. "Listen to me. Advocate. Don't stop."

Violet craned her head to glimpse Kelispar over Kora's shoulder. Defiance retreated from his jaw. He did nothing, said nothing, but stared blankly ahead. Docile.

Kora pressed her temples with a pinched expression. A headache. What power, exactly, did her liryn cord give her?

"Now we can talk," Yakiv said to Basilia, smooth as wood. "You're wondering why I'm here. Not to kill you, matter of fact. Your sons could have lived, too. But they chose to fight a Pillar. Nothing I can do against stupidity."

Basilia didn't even lift her head, but Violet found a whisper of oxygen. Yakiv wasn't here to kill anyone else. He'd make his point, and then he'd go.

He tapped his dagger on his thigh. "The gate pendant. Halfdan found it. You know where he left it. You're leaving in the morning to get it."

Violet and Meliora exchanged looks, Meliora's surprise showing through tears.

"I've heard the same prophecies as you, Basilia. Malokki spouts them like spittle. '*Sheep's wall*'—Shepherd's Crag, where Halfdan's bloated corpse landed. Could be there." Yakiv favored one foot on the dais. "But then there's the Amber Forest. Never heard of it until a few hours ago. It's there, in the archives, the ones I was searching to find Halfdan's handwriting. Your son tell you about the letter? I saw on the pearls that he was lurking at my speech."

Basilia gave no reply.

"The archives are glutted with gossip on the Pretenders," he went on. "They told me your brother-in-law died the same day as Halfdan, in that forest. Now, what was a Seer doing so far from the comfort of his Janlion nest?"

Violet couldn't guess Yakiv's point. He was certainly taking his time making it.

"They were together," he said, "Halfdan and the Seer. His letter mentions 'we.' But one drowned himself in the lake, and the other ate his own knife in the Amber Forest. Mighty far apart, from what your Arati maps tell me." He let that hang. "They were using the gate pendant," he concluded. "But who used it last? Is it at Shepherd's Crag, or is it in the forest?"

Basilia's head finally rose. Her pallor was ashy, her stare without warmth. "One who depends on the prophecy should not need an answer."

"You, Malokki, the rest—you make the prophecy a thing to worship. Now, I find it informative. Might even put some faith in it. But we don't need its permission, see. A man who follows a prophecy is stagnant. Unavailing. A wise man, he takes what the prophecy can give, and he puts the rest to himself."

Uncomfortably, Violet heard her own logic in that. Hadn't Fa simply expected the Lykill to appear, and hadn't Violet urged him a dozen times to do more than idly hope?

"I'll find the Lykill," Yakiv said. "But I don't want to waste my—time." For a blip of a moment, Yakiv's words got clipped. He grabbed at his elbow. Then his hand dropped. "So don't make me wait," he said, impatience now staining his un-flappable calm. "My friends are hurting." He motioned toward Kora, whose teeth were gritted, and the Pillar, who still crouched on the floor in apparent agony. Was it an intense headache causing his pain, or was this his crown?

"Their suffering need not be fruitless," Basilia said.

"How do you reckon?" Yakiv said.

Basilia's arms strained; her remaining fingers stretched out like someone beseeching. But it was in Violet's direction that her whisper went: "Surrender."

Yakiv took a moment before he hissed the word back to her. "Surrender." His shoulders rolled. He gripped his elbow again. "You would watch us all writhe, killed by our crowns. And still you would use—that—word!" His shout echoed inside stone walls.

Violet's sweaty hands slipped down the grate. She hadn't taken him for a shouter. Yakiv's patient indifference, hard and cold, had been intimidating enough. She didn't want to meet a Yakiv who lost his temper.

He jerked left, snatching a torch off the wall and tossing it at a curtain. The entire strip of fabric went up in flames, a wall of firelight. "Now you're going to tell me where Halfdan left the pendant," he said, a feverish energy stirring under the monotone that now sounded forced. "And you'll tell me while Terlian's legacy burns." His face was eerily cast in the twitchy light of shadow and flame.

A heady moment passed, during which Yakiv rapidly tapped his foot; Basilia watched the fire; Kelispar fought a useless struggle; Alikar whispered commands his brother couldn't hear; Meliora closed her eyes, seemingly praying; and Violet crouched, squished against Alikar, like one set apart. Like one whose world would not crumble if this ended poorly. She hadn't cried for Fa. No one would expect her to cry for this house.

The realization was an ugly one. She rested her forehead on the grate.

Flames jumped onto more curtains, on the Terlion flag, licking anything that would catch.

Yakiv gave an impatient *tsk.* Fervor hovered about him like an anxious energy. Where had his calm gone? His cool command? "The emissary only needs a heart and a brain to Advocate," he said. And then yanked a tool from his belt, a rod attached to a curved piece, tied together with a taut string that unmistakably identified the weapon as a crossbow. "How much will you let him suffer for your stubbornness?"

Alikar's grip on the grate smashed Violet's finger. Meliora clamped a hand over his mouth, dampening his cry.

Basilia's posture wilted. Without the bindings, she might've slid off her throne.

Kelispar watched Yakiv's approach, hair unkempt, nowhere near the polished man whose clothes never wrinkled. But he was every bit the Kelispar who'd told Violet he was glad he was welded, even though it cut his heart.

Violet wanted to close her eyes but couldn't. An earnest prodding in her gut, perhaps wishing to spare her the sight, pushed her attention to the other side of the room. Smoke clouded every corner; there was nothing to see in the haze. She searched anyway. For what, she didn't know.

Then, with a grunt, the Pillar collapsed.

"Slav's out!" Kora yelled.

"I can't . . . hold—" The man guarding Kelispar floundered. Kelispar broke free and ran to Basilia. Yakiv didn't bother swiping for him, too busy clutching his own arm.

As if making up for the painfully dragging moments of tension, everything turned chaotic. Kelispar worked feverishly at Basilia's bindings. Kora shook the unconscious Pillar's shoulder. Kelispar's captor sought answers from Yakiv, in their own language now. Without Kelispar blocking him, he showed as a short, pudgy man, pale with stringy hair.

Now that the Pillar was unresponsive, Kora and the short Separatist seemed to have lost their nerve. They fretted, but Yakiv had recaptured his poise, his shoulders relaxed again. He wasn't even paying attention to his Separatists, nor to Kelispar's futile attempts to free Basilia. Yakiv scrutinized one of the statues, some king no one but the Hasteins would care to remember.

Violet peered again into the smoke. Something stirred within it. A form. A figure. Eliathor emerged from behind the statue. Smoke drifted over his features like a warped mask, clinging to his sword.

Hope undid some of Violet's knots. He was outnumbered, but a person with an air that deadly wouldn't be easily deterred.

Yakiv aimed his crossbow at Eliathor and addressed Kora. She darted toward Basilia and Kelispar. The short Separatist took Kora's place by the unconscious Pillar and began slapping him.

Eliathor advanced, ignoring Yakiv's weapon. So Yakiv reversed its aim. It pointed to Lady Basilia.

Eliathor stopped.

Violet's hope vanished faster than smoke.

"You're outnumbered," Yakiv said in English; Kora had coaxed Kelispar again. She looked worse for wear, cupping her head.

"I have my sword," Eliathor said.

"I have my friends." Yakiv glanced at the now-upright Pillar with the red cord. The Pillar nodded, unnervingly eager, and spoke under his breath. Immediately he was on his knees again, unable to prop himself up. It must've been his headache. Yakiv and the short Separatist moved like identical blinks. Yakiv materialized by Basilia's side, crossbow at her temple. The short, unimpressive Separatist restrained Kelispar again like one wrangling straw.

Violet was beginning to understand. The Pillar made the others faster and stronger. That explained how Yakiv's small army had so easily infiltrated the estate.

"You want to preserve your mother's life, you'll answer my questions," Yakiv said.

A new dread rooted in Violet. Yakiv didn't need Kora to pry answers out of Eliathor. He'd say anything to protect Basilia, and he didn't care about keeping the Lykill's secrets.

"My son," Basilia murmured.

Eliathor could have been another statue. He held his sword pointed down. But, as he spoke, he took one step. "I have no answer."

"You don't care for her?" Yakiv said.

"I cannot tell you how to chase legends." Eliathor took another step.

"You don't believe in the Lykill." Yakiv eyed Basilia. "Your flesh and blood."

"My son," she whispered again.

During Yakiv's distraction, Eliathor gained more ground, but he wasn't any closer to Yakiv.

Violet realized what he was doing. Eliathor's goal was the Pillar.

Yakiv saw where Eliathor was. "Boh," he called to the short Separatist. "Watch Slav."

Eliathor gave up discretion and ran. Boh ran faster. He released Kelispar, bolted over, and formed a shield in front of Slav in two seconds. Eliathor swung, but Boh caught the blade like it was a broom.

Violet gaped. Was Boh invincible? No, blood colored the sword that Boh tossed aside. But he ignored the pain, laughing.

"Not smart, Pretender." Yakiv shot Basilia in the thigh.

It was fortunate Eliathor shouted—it covered the sound of Meliora's. She buried her sob in Alikar's arm.

Violet exhaled shakily. It seemed she'd crouched behind this grate for hours, but it was only minutes. Minutes of watching horror unfold, knowing it could only end in pain. Kora and the Pillar were crippled by their crowns, but the fire had caught the ceiling rafters now, and Yakiv still had the advantage.

"Tell me what you know of the gate pendant," he said.

Eliathor's chest heaved. He stood in the middle of the hall, weaponless, a man trapped. "You will step away from my mother. Then I will speak."

Yakiv debated. Then nodded, leaving Basilia doubled over on her throne.

Eliathor waited until Yakiv reached the edge of the dais. "My father found it," he said.

"Some Terlion come through and hand it over?"

"It wasn't on Terlian. It was on Bar'Talian."

"Bar'Talian." Yakiv tasted the word like he had all the time in the world.

"Kelispar, don't," Alikar whispered.

Violet's attention broke away from Eliathor. Kora was on her knees now, arms curled around her head—still coaxing, but unable to monitor Kelispar, who crept to a flaming curtain.

He stuck his arm in the orange. Metal glinted with a flash of purple.

"What did he do with it?" Yakiv asked Eliathor.

"He opened a gate."

"Where?"

"In the mountains. *Hjá . . .*" The rest was Faartunga.

Violet counted a tense beat before Yakiv searched for Kelispar and realized what he'd done.

Kelispar stepped away from the flames, satisfied. His hand was raw and red, and his cord was gone.

Yakiv spoke one cool word that raked Violet's nerves. Then he pointed his crossbow at Lady Basilia and fired. Her chin fell. Then Yakiv swiveled to Kelispar. The Terlion emissary didn't have time to blink before he dropped.

"*Voch!*" Alikar shouted, writhed, and yanked at the unyielding grate. "*Voch, voch, voch, khntrem . . .*"

A cold grip on Violet's spine kept her in place. She stared at Kelispar, that princely bearing now reduced to an awkward heap. Then Lady Basilia, handcuffed to her throne, head drooped like she might be sleeping. Strange longing tugged like a pebble attached to string, drawing Violet toward Basilia.

And then the pull snapped. Gone.

Violet's chest contracted until she grew numb.

Noise returned to her ears. Someone else was yelling. Eliathor. He ran to the nearby statue, gripped the king's hilt, and pulled. The sword scraped right out of the stone.

But Yakiv wasn't watching Eliathor. His focus was in Violet's direction. Alikar was loud, and this grate worked both ways.

Violet fell back. Alikar sobbed, his face against the grate. Meliora made the perfect statue, despair chiseled onto her face. Neither of them seemed capable of registering their imminent capture. They needed to run. Violet would have to lead them. She had to be the one who didn't cry.

Shackled.

It might as well be her.

She touched Alikar. "Come on," she urged. Then, knowing words would make no difference, she tugged, stumbling as he flailed. He accidentally whacked Meliora, bringing the statue to life. Her jaw trembled; her expression crumbled with unabashed, childlike pain. But when Meliora looked at Alikar, determination overrode the sorrow. She gripped Alikar's shoulder. With effort, Violet and Meliora lifted him. He kicked like a horse. His eyes shone bright and wild. Violet had never seen someone so unhinged, so flowing with chaos. That, more than Yakiv, frightened her.

They took one ungainly step before the air behind them shuddered. Meliora cried out, barreling forward. Alikar dug his heels, but they dragged him along. Violet didn't risk glancing back, even as she heard the wall cave in.

A battle cry rebounded. Violet ducked when the *ting* of something hitting metal erupted behind her, but she didn't turn around. On they raced.

They carted Alikar around a curve, the battle sounds growing faint. Violet wondered if they'd managed to gain ground. When no urgent footfalls thundered, she peeked behind. Nothing but their shadows.

Eliathor. He'd stalled Yakiv, who had a Pillar. Eliathor had a stone sword that would probably shatter at first blow. The truth sunk hollowly.

Lady Basilia. Her sons. Kelispar. Who would be left of the Hasteins now? Violet remembered the grandchildren. Blushing Liam. If she had found safety, they might have too. She conjured an imaginary escape route for them while she ran, seeing them safely through it. But Violet knew better than to trust wishful thinking. Death came when it chose and couldn't be deferred by hope.

They hit a dead end. Alikar's crying had turned into broken sobs, the kind that get caught in the throat. He stooped so low that Violet nearly met his height.

She inspected the impenetrable barrier before them. They couldn't go back toward Yakiv, and there was no way forward. They were trapped.

"Alikar," Meliora whispered.

He didn't react. Meliora prodded him until his head lifted. With a shudder, he patted the wall from top to bottom, then top again. He paused around the center. "*Eph . . . e-ph . . .*"

Meliora moved his hand, set hers in the same spot, and said, "*Ephpheta.*"

The wall disintegrated, revealing more hollow black. Meliora hefted Alikar forward. Violet followed last. She turned around, holding up a palm. Someone had to seal the wall. Kelispar had said Chisel liryn depended on the enchanted object and not the user.

"*Ephpheta,*" Violet said.

The hole in the wall didn't close. Had she mispronounced it?

"*Sawgar,*" Alikar croaked out behind her.

Violet repeated the word. A cracked stone face appeared over the mouth. Out of sight, out of memory.

The tunnel deposited them somewhere in the woods. Two moons really did change the look of nighttime. A bright glisten washed blades of grass shooting in every direction; the tree trunks; the pine cones that resembled silver crowns. The chilly air had a way of freezing the dark memories behind them, locking them in Violet's mind.

She turned, wanting to convey some sense of *We need to keep going.* But Alikar's face was buried in Meliora's shoulder. She squeezed him, shivering. Violet felt as much an intruder as Yakiv.

Too much.

Wind swam through branches, gentle as waves on a beach. All was deceptively peaceful. Yakiv and his Separatists would catch up. They had to move.

"This way," Violet said.

They didn't react. So Violet, resigning herself to practicing a new language, pulled them apart, took their wrists, and guided them to the trees.

Meliora snapped out of it first, slipping free with a nod. Alikar stumbled in a daze.

Roughly ten minutes passed when Violet thought they should veer east. Not that she knew where east was. She was well aware that following this inner tug was much like following instinct. Tonight, Violet had nothing else to rely on. It was either follow her gut or walk around indefinitely—which may have been the same thing. Her only certain goal was putting space between her and Yakiv.

When the trees widened out, Violet turned, squeezed around a bush, balanced over a log, and rounded a final cluster of brambles. Then, she stopped.

They stood before a mound of rocks, half the height of a tree. Moss and weeds climbed the stones. The structure reminded Violet of a cairn, something prehistoric people might've built as a burial mound.

"*Bravo,* Violet," Meliora said, without any apparent confusion at finding this random mound in the woods. She touched a rock and said, "*Ephpheta.*" As if they were molded together, a collection of stones separated from the rest of the cairn, so that a hole formed. Meliora waved them inside.

"Alikar." Violet shook his arm.

He lifted his head. She was grateful for the shadows, which marred his expression. His eyes, though, had plenty of shine to catch the moons' light. Her fingers clenched at the unfamiliar emptiness of them.

He let Violet guide him into another hole where, hopefully, horrible things never happened.

CHAPTER SIXTEEN

"Despite the fact that only one monarch is required, Bar'Talian still insists upon the tradition of both for welding." – *Liryn on a Mission* by Vessel Augustinia

Violet had exhausted every distraction in this one-roomed, dirt-floored cairn before accepting there was nothing left to occupy her. The lamp on the stool had been lit, thanks to the prods she'd given it with Alikar's tool; it had no electrical cord and simply glowed from a crystal source. She'd double-checked that there were no visible entry points. She'd even found a blanket inside a wooden hutch and draped it around Alikar. The kettle on the tiny stove had been tempting, but Violet wasn't about to boil water from an unknown source in a cairn that might explode into flames if she did something wrong. With nothing left to do, she forced herself to face her companions.

Alikar had immediately slumped to the floor and drawn his long legs to his chest. Meliora was staring at a bookshelf, letting tears hang off her chin.

Violet drew a chair out from the table, sat down, and set to planning. Their options were as followed: live indefinitely in this cairn, go search for the authorities, or bid these two farewell and find her way to Shepherd's Crag. She should have been leaving soon, with Kelispar and Karleif.

Her fingernails landed in the indentations in her palms that were probably permanent by now.

Option three held the most appeal. Considering her brush with the citizens of Bar'Talian, she was hesitant to rely on authorities who might detain her if they realized she was from Terlian. The sooner she left, the sooner she'd beat Yakiv to the pendant.

How had he known, not only that they'd planned on leaving in the morning but that their goal was the pendant? Maybe Iiryn had clued him in. The alternative, that someone in the Hastein family had leaked the news, was unthinkable. Regardless of how any of Lady Basilia's sons had felt about the prophecy, none of them would have run to Yakiv Stefanos.

She stood. She should go now, while there was some cover of night.

The sound of her chair scratching earth made no effect. Alikar continued staring into space. Meliora continued staring at the shelves. Would they notice if she left? Would they budge from their spots if she did? She couldn't abandon them.

Muffled voices clattered outside the cairn.

Violet stiffened. Meliora spun around and hunched protectively beside Alikar.

He registered nothing.

Outside, an elderly man's voice croaked in Arati, followed by a gentle, equally croaky female.

"*Oi monarches!*" Meliora said, and dashed to a wall.

Realization came as Meliora spoke the phrase to open the cairn. The monarchs had slept at the Hastein estate. Violet guessed Yakiv hadn't known that when he set the place ablaze. If he'd accidentally murdered the monarchs . . .

Stone rumbled open. Lali and her twin brother, soot on their cheeks, clung to the figures behind them. The monarchs of Bar'Talian were silver-haired and hardly taller than Violet. Her preconceived image of planetary rulers had been inspired by science fiction movies and included decadent vestments and gaudy crowns, not the haggard, ash-stained couple wearing nightcaps and purple bathrobes. First came King Asbed, guiding another Hastein granddaughter. Queen Nora entered next, steering a stooped, weeping woman—Nazeli, wife of Sweyn, who was unrecognizable from the carefree woman of last night. She carried Gisa's baby. There was no Gisa, no Eliathor . . . and no Liam.

Violet's throat constricted, but she called, "What about the others?"

The king paused, watery eyes concentrating. His Advocate's knife, twice the size of Kelispar's, hung from a gold chain. "You are the Terlion?" King Asbed said in a tired voice.

"Yes, Your Highness," she said with a curtsy, certain she'd called him the wrong title, but unable to feel any concern about it.

King Asbed didn't appear offended either way. "You come to us in evil times, young Terlion."

"Yet how lovely it is to meet a Terlion," Queen Nora said, her head bobbing in a rhythm she didn't seem aware of. Her voice was gentle, her gaze gentler.

"Thank you," Violet said.

"Are there not . . . more of you?" Meliora's hands rested on the shoulder of the eldest granddaughter.

"We encountered only young Eliathor," King Asbed answered, "who saw us to safety before he went after the brutes. I fear he perished alongside the poor souls trapped in the flames, for the brutes set fire—"

Nazeli broke into a wail and pressed herself against Queen Nora, who looked close to toppling.

Violet shrank against the counter and folded her arms tight. Meliora covered her face.

"Come now, come now," King Asbed said, patting Nazeli's shoulder. "The children have left this vale of tears. They suffer no more."

Nazeli wailed louder. Lali burrowed her face in the king's leg. Her twin brother moved to the couch, shivering. Violet pulled the blanket off Alikar and draped it over him.

"But weep, good mother," the king continued gently. "Yes, weep, that your heart may be relieved."

With his permission, Nazeli's cry grew all the more mournful. The eldest granddaughter slung her arms around her mother's waist.

Queen Nora was trying and failing to guide Nazeli to a chair. Hurriedly, Violet drew a chair out; there were only two seats, other than the couch. Violet moved the lamp off the stool and carried the extra seat over.

Lali was reluctant to release the king. It would be best to steer her away, though Violet didn't want to frighten her.

She knelt beside Alikar and murmured, "Alikar. Lali's here."

He raised his head. In this lighting, he couldn't hide the veins in his eyes. He glanced over Violet's shoulder. Something lighter tinged the sorrow. "Come here, lambie," he called.

Lali raced to Alikar, who made room for her on his lap. She tucked her head under his chin. His head rested on hers, and he held her tight.

"Young Terlion." King Asbed beckoned Violet over. "Prepare some tea for these weary souls."

Now given something to do, she set to her task with vigor. King Asbed must have trusted the tap, so she filled the kettle without concern. When it came to configuring the heating mechanism, however, Violet lost her momentum. She stared at the round, copper contraptions on the counter. There was a chance she wasn't even looking at the stove. Rather than bother anyone with questions, Violet tested the buttons and dials. When one of them turned red, she set the kettle on it and turned in search of tea—but the kettle was already steaming. Alarmed, Violet yanked the kettle off, though she had no idea where to set it down. So, holding the kettle an arm's distance away, she one-handedly searched the cabinets. A white canister was full to the brim of dried flowers that smelled minty. But what to steep them in?

Violet set the kettle back on the stove. It whistled—at least Bar'Talion kettles whistled—but she ignored it. Nothing in this kitchen was in a logical place. The utensils were in a cabinet and cups under the sink.

"The kettle, my dear," called Queen Nora.

"Yes, ma'am." Violet snatched a few cups and set them on a counter. She would have to steep the leaves directly in the water. Once this was finished, she returned the kettle to the stove, where she pressed more levers until the glow disappeared. Tentatively, she hovered her palm over the burner. Already, it had cooled.

While the tea steeped, she searched for honey. Finding only jars of unfamiliar things, she figured it would be better to serve black tea than tea flavored with something horrible. She returned to the steaming cups and spooned out the leaves. Feeling accomplished, Violet lifted a mug. Most likely, the king was expected to be served first.

"Thank you, thank you," he said.

By the time Violet was on her way to Meliora, the king had taken a sip. Violet froze when he coughed.

"Oh dear." He set down the mug and coughed again. "I believe you have served us mint milk, which works admirably against rodents but ought not to be consumed by anyone wishing to enjoy his tea."

Violet tipped the mug away from Meliora. "Oh." Her neck burned. She'd almost poisoned the king. "I apologize. I wasn't . . ."

"When in doubt, it is honorable to ask for help."

A rebuke like this would normally bolster Violet's determination to redeem herself. Given from the wrinkled king, who'd kindly not yelled at her, she felt her flush growing.

She collected everyone's cups, wishing she could be on her way to Terlian.

King Asbed cleared his throat. "Now, young ones, you must gather yourselves and come under our mantle. You will be safe in the palace."

"But Yakiv will attack you next," Meliora said, rocking Gisa's baby.

"He knew about our plan," Violet told him, "that we were looking for the pendant at Shepherd's Crag. He mentioned another place too. A forest."

"The Amber Forest," Meliora murmured.

Violet remembered what else Yakiv had said—that Meliora's father died in those woods.

The queen searched her husband with worry. "A spy in our midst. *Zarmanum yem . . .*" She drifted into Arati.

The king, gazing at his hands, didn't appear to hear. His fingers were arched, quivering. King Asbed made the picture of a frail old man. Had the horrors of the night caught up to him?

Queen Nora touched his shoulder. Her words cajoled. Eventually, King Asbed nodded, resigning himself to her wishes with closed eyes and a sigh. The queen kept her hand on him as she turned to Violet, translating now. "Most monarchs regard it as shameful to show their crown. Your good king honors you well by revealing his." She lay her knuckles on her chest with a sad smile. "Mine is of the heart. A lovely thing it is to suffer within the quiet of one's own sanctuary."

So King Asbed's crown had overwhelmed him, whatever it was. His head probably hurt too. Now, Queen Nora suffered—all so Violet could follow the conversation. Although, Meliora didn't speak Arati either.

"We thank you for the honor." Meliora kissed the queen's hand and received a stroke on the cheek.

Violet sought to cast her eyes toward a sight less tender, but nowhere else was any safer. The cousins held each other. Alikar stroked Lali's hair. Violet was out of place here. The Terlion who couldn't cry.

"Now," said the queen with a businesslike lilt, "you must have courage, my dears, for the journey before you is treacherous."

"Journey?" Meliora said.

King Asbed stood, revived. "Yes, you three must seek out the Lykill. The prophecy wishes it." He pursed his lips inward and outward, then said to Violet, "Terlion, with these companions, you will travel to Shepherd's Crag and there retrieve the gate pendant. In your absence, we will care for the surviving Hasteins."

Violet nodded. That had already been her plan, though she hadn't counted on Meliora and Alikar accompanying her. It seemed unfair. They deserved time to mourn. But Meliora didn't protest. Alikar's glassy eyes, on the other hand, indicated that he hadn't followed a word.

"We would send you with a convoy of our finest guard," Queen Nora said, "but until the horrible traitor is rooted out, I fear we cannot trust our own."

"You must undertake great caution," King Asbed said. "One within our royal household cooperates with Yakiv Stefanos and his Separatist guerrillas. Your survival will be of interest to them. We shall not speak of it outside this decrepit building."

"You'll tell everyone that we died?" Violet said.

"You accuse the king of weaving deception," he said with a bristle.

"No—I apologize, Your Majesty." She wondered if she needed to curtsy.

"The queen and I shall speak the truth of these events, and in doing so will reveal the survivors in our care: Dame Nazeli and the little ones. It is for the listener to decide the fate of any survivors *not* in our care." He tweaked his nose, then hobbled over to Alikar. "Rise, young Muratsan."

After easing Lali off his lap, Alikar stood, then bowed mechanically.

"You have no liryn?" the king asked him.

"I have not, Sire."

"Then we shall weld you. Kneel."

Some energy flashed in Alikar's eyes. They were the color of grass, not Arati brown. "I won't need liryn if I'm with you," he said.

"Your journey is not ours, my boy. You must go to Shepherd's Crag."

Alikar glanced down at Lali. "Sire, I wish to go with you, to help how I can."

"Your duty is to Flower. She is necessary to the prophecy."

Violet assumed she was Flower. Someone in her party had to be an Advocate so they could communicate. Because of her, Alikar would be deprived of something else he loved. If he became an Advocate, he couldn't be a Chisel.

"I can be welded instead," she said, dipping into a curtsy. "If that is possible, Your Majesty."

"Or I can," Meliora added.

"Alikar is one of our own," King Asbed said. "We wish this for him. But he must be willing."

"What of the ritual?" Panic made Alikar's voice higher. "I cannot be welded without it."

"The words of welding are written on our hearts."

"But, Sire, I've undergone none of the training."

"Your liryn will provide the aid. All that is required is a proper disposition." The king waited.

"I don't have the proper disposition," Alikar whispered.

"Emissary Kelispar spoke well of you," the king said warmly. "It is due to his faith that we deem you worthy."

Alikar rapidly blinked. His attention moved toward Violet, his expression no longer jovial. That spark had been stabbed out of him by Yakiv Stefanos. The betrayal he wore was dark. Raw. And directed entirely at her.

"Wait, please," Violet tried again. She knew enough Old Norse to get by. She couldn't have Alikar's life changed on account of her. "This really isn't necessary. I . . ."

But Alikar was already kneeling.

"In place of a cord," said King Asbed, "we will weld you with . . ." He inspected his outfit, then looked helplessly at his wife.

"This will be a lovely substitute." She tugged at his bathrobe's belt.

"Very good, very good." The king pulled the belt from its loops. It was purple, at least.

Queen Nora laid the rope over Alikar. He sucked in air, as if hoping that might keep the belt from touching him. The monarchs alighted their hands on his head. In unison, they spoke.

"What asketh thou of thy monarchs?"

"Welding," Alikar said after a moment.

"Durst thou seek us of thine own unencumbered will?"

Alikar closed his eyes. "I do."

"Wilt thou accept the liryn of *da'atan* as a gift, not to be tarnished, wasted, abused, concealed, nor maltreated?"

"I will."

"And wilt thou accept what suffering will come?"

His jaw was tight. But he opened his eyes, stared at nothing, and said, "I will."

The monarchs' next words were chanted, their voices surprisingly vigorous as they sang the minor melody.

"By the name of Li,
Three in one and one in three,
Kneel, O blood of Bar'Talian,
And receive thy knife,
Given that thou mayst rise
A rightful welded of da'atan.
May your lips speak truth
And your ears hear wisdom.
Take thy crown, then,
And let no man say
That thou hast not been proved.
Be thou faithful until death,
And thy crown shall be thy glory.
United as thy monarchs,
Nus leydesh thul femorlantri.
Nus leydesh thul femorlantri.
Nus leydesh thul femorlantri."

Violet half-expected a shower of purple. Nothing changed. Not even Alikar's expression. He stared dead ahead the entire time.

"Very good," said King Asbed, "very good." He and the queen bustled about, preparing Nazeli and the children for departure.

Alikar remained kneeling, oblivious to everything but the speck in the air he watched.

CHAPTER SEVENTEEN

"Kapor Academy's going to the pits. Apparently five percent of pupils and faculty dropped out after the Terlion emissary was admitted, and another ten when Kapor accepted Bartosz Mieszko's son. Then Meliora Mykaois? Kapor's going to send application letters to the whole Pretender bloodline next." - *Daily Converse*, gray pearl

S OON, THE MONARCHS AND Meliora's last remaining family had gone. Rather than have their guard retrieve them, the monarchs would meet them elsewhere, drawing attention away from the survivors who had not survived.

Once they'd gone, quiet descended over the cairn. Violet wanted to verify that the welding had worked. Could it really be as simple as a few words?

"We should leave while it's dark," she said.

Meliora stared at Alikar. His expression was resolute. She asked him a question—in Faartunga.

Then it hadn't worked.

Meliora pressed. He shook his head. Her voice got louder. Violet recognized her own name. Finally, as if removing a splinter, he touched the barest corner of the king's belt. His cheek muscle spasmed.

"Can you understand me?" Meliora asked Violet.

She hesitated. Alikar watched her with undisguised desperation. He wanted her to say no.

But Violet nodded.

He sank onto the sofa, face in his hands. Meliora's expression was pitying. "We can't go to Shepherd's Crag," she said, settling beside him. "Yakiv will probably go there next."

"The monarchs commanded us," Alikar said.

"Yes, but they wouldn't expect us to walk to our deaths. And they don't know what I know."

"Which is?" His tone, even muffled by his palms, rudely sharpened.

Meliora inspected him sidelong, receiving no verification for why he'd have an attitude with her.

Violet had an idea.

Meliora addressed her. "You say your father never saw the gate pendant. I think that's because my father had it. Yakiv's guess was smart. It's something I considered too, after Aunt Basilia—" Her voice choked. Meliora wasn't too embarrassed to sniff before she gathered strength and kept going. "Why didn't your father see mine on Terlian? And how did Pappa end up so far from Uncle Halfdan?"

"You think he made a gate," Violet said.

"Yes."

"He wasn't a descendant," Alikar said.

"I know. I think . . . I think that's why he died. But maybe my mother was a descendant." Meliora rubbed her bracelet. "She never knew her parents, only that she was born from scandal. The imperial families are infamous for scandals. She could have been one of theirs. The gate pendant belongs to the Nehfey Empire, which includes Janlian, where she was born. Descendants of the imperial bloodlines can rightfully use the Lykill pendants."

It was a stretch. Violet contemplated how to tell her that delicately.

Alikar lifted his head, revealing the scowl evident beneath pink finger smudges. "That's your theory? Maybe she was an illegitimate child born from the Nehfey imperials?"

Meliora's brows scrunched together. "Before she died, she told me I would find my purpose in the Amber Forest. She always repeated a certain phrase. It was in First Tongue, so it never translated around . . . around an Advocate."

First Tongue?

"And?" Alikar said. "What does that have to do with her being a descendant? You don't even know what the phrase means."

"Mama said Pappa appeared to her in a golden cloud and spoke those words." Meliora looked stubborn now. "It must have been a gate. He was telling her the ritual to open a gate."

"Wasn't lunacy her crown?"

Hurt left Meliora's mouth hanging open.

Alikar glared at the floor, appearing slightly contrite.

Nothing Meliora said had convinced Violet. Yet Fa's parting words had ended up being pretty significant. "Everyone thought my father was crazy because he believed in other realms," she said.

Meliora eagerly nodded. "Mama was a descendant of the Nehfey Empire. I know it. And if she was, so am I. I can rightfully use the gate pendant. Pappa had it, and he hid it in the Amber Forest. That's why he was found there. That's why Mama told me to go."

"But the prophecy says the pendant will be found at 'the sheep's wall.'"

"It says the *Lykill* will be found at the sheep's wall. The gate pendant is just part of the Lykill."

Meliora's theory ignored the prophecy, or at least Lady Basilia's interpretation of it. If the gate pendant was in that forest and Meliora could use it, then she could take Violet straight to Terlian to fetch the other pendants. But Meliora was right: Now that Violet scrutinized Lady Basilia's theory, it didn't make sense to look for the gate pendant at Shepherd's Crag. Maybe the sheep's wall had something to do with Terlian.

"This is all supposing you're correct about your mother," Alikar said. "If you're not a descendant, you can't use it."

"Of course I wouldn't use it," Meliora said, borrowing some of Alikar's irritation.

Chief Halfdan had. Both Eliathor's and Meliora's fathers had been desperate enough to die for their mistakes.

"How far is the Amber Forest from here?" Violet asked.

"On foot . . . three days?" Meliora guessed.

The same amount of time Violet had already planned for, though that didn't include the return journey to give the Lykill to the Bar'Talion monarchs. But Meliora could open a gate directly to King Asbed and Queen Nora. This plan was more straightforward than Lady Basilia's.

Violet nodded. Then they waited on Alikar.

He rose. Alikar was tall, but he'd never exuded the confidence of his brother nor the strength of Eliathor. He exuded something now, a bitter resolve that nevertheless made his six feet something worth acknowledging. "I'll accompany you to the Amber Forest," he said. "Then I will take my leave."

"Where will you go?" Meliora asked.

"The palace. I owe it to Eliathor to take care of his family." His voice broke on the last word. Alikar walked out. The door, clicking shut, was a final insult flung toward Meliora.

She was Eliathor's family too.

Meliora cleared her throat. "We should—can you still understand me?"

"Yes. How far is his range?"

"That's up to him." Her mouth trembled.

Violet leveraged her curiosity as a distraction. "Does every Advocate have the same range?"

"Liryn is stronger or weaker depending on the person. It enhances what's already there. Kelispar is—" She turned her head. "We should gather supplies."

They found a chest and dumped its contents on the table. Some trousers far too big, and several worn trench coats. Violet took one. She'd have to traipse around Bar'Talian in a purple nightgown, but no one had to see the twigs sticking out of it.

"He despises me now." Meliora fiddled with a belt that would wrap twice around her.

"No he doesn't. You've both had . . . It's been a terrible night. He's just upset."

Just—it was the wrong word. He had every reason to be upset.

"Last night, I told Kelispar I'd speak to Jarek. He said he would wait, but I could see in his face that he was already resigned. Do you think he knew? That he would . . . die?"

Violet had no idea how to begin answering that.

Fortunately, Meliora didn't seem to want a response. "I'm sorry," she whispered. "I know you're in pain too. I'll never forget the day the queen of Janlian died. I was fourteen, but I still feel . . ." Her expression conveyed so much sadness that Violet had to lower her gaze. "My aunt was your queen. You feel the loss, don't you?"

"I—"

"Yakiv Stefanos is a monster." The belt in Meliora's hands curled between her clenched fists. "But you'll find the Lykill first. And I'll help you. Jarek always talked about searching the Amber Forest, once I told him about my mother. I thought he was just being overzealous, but now I know. Finding the gate pendant is my purpose." She trembled with determination. "It's strange. Kelispar and Alikar are nobility. And Eliathor was heir to Terlian's throne. I was no one. But I was wrong. I'm a descendant."

To be no one, the daughter of someone who'd died as an outcast—those were the things she should share, to foster solidarity. But Violet couldn't talk about Fa here, where pain and regret already suffocated the room.

"I do want to find it, but I don't see how it can fix things, now that . . ." Violet swallowed. Lady Basilia had hoped to clear

Terlian's name. If the emperors forgave Terlian for stealing the Lykill, maybe the Hasteins could get their welding cords back, become monarchs again. But Terlian's future monarchs were reduced to a handful of children.

"She wanted the Lykill for every realm." Meliora touched Violet's hand. "Here. These gloves match."

They finalized their wardrobe in silence. Violet donned a coat that fell past her feet.

"May I wear that one?" Meliora asked. "It belonged to . . ."

"Here." Violet gave her Eliathor's coat and chose another.

"Silly, I know," Meliora whispered as she fingered the buttons.

"It's not silly."

Alikar returned once Violet and Meliora were adorned with baggy, drab accessories. Without a word, he pulled a cloak over his bedclothes. The king's bathrobe belt was obscured until Alikar tugged it free.

"Thank you for Advocating for us," Meliora murmured.

He rammed a wool hat over his hair.

Violet took out jars from the cabinets and sought Meliora's approval. Most of the copper canisters held unhelpful things—like pepper and clay and silver rocks Violet had no idea what to do with—but some provided dried fruit ("Ruby pits," Meliora said), nuts ("Kallumberries"), plant stems meant to be sucked on ("Waterleaf"), and plenty of jerky. While Meliora filled some canisters with water, Violet stored the others in a coat no one had taken, which she'd haul like a knapsack. But the jacket wouldn't tie properly, and the canisters fell out.

Alikar tossed her a gray, slippery fabric from the pile. "It's *layinthai*." Correctly interpreting Violet's hesitation, he added, "Elastic."

Violet doubtfully appraised the fabric, the size of a pencil bag, before inserting the canister. Her fingers met fabric, and then more fabric, which swallowed past her elbow. Alarmed, she yanked her arm free. The material was the same size, though lumpy, like she'd stuck an eraser in it. Her canisters fit without issue, as did Meliora's jars of water.

"Did a Chisel make this?" Violet asked Alikar, hoping for an ice breaker.

He ignored her.

She squeezed a canister and wished she'd said anything else, rather than stupidly remind him of another thing he'd just lost.

Soon they were ready, Violet with the magical pouch in her pocket, and Meliora looking tiny in Eliathor's coat. She fussed over Violet's clothes, straightening and smoothing. Violet accepted it. This was how Meliora coped. Then, she watched Alikar, nervously pinching her bracelet.

"Alikar, " Meliora began.

"*Shtapir*." He walked outside.

Meliora smoothed her braid, gave Violet's scarf another tweak, then followed.

Outside, the moons shone on leaves coated with dew. Everything that had felt so foreboding during their escape a few hours ago—the sense that their every footstep was stalked by Yakiv, the threat of wolves around every corner—had vanished, replaced by a quieter forest. The firs were only firs, the branches only branches. Violet took in the peaceful stillness and could finally breathe.

Then, Meliora spoke in Greek, and Violet remembered the reason she could no longer understand.

"Hold on," she said. "I can't understand you."

They waited for Alikar to consent. He did, after a few moments of scowling.

"I was saying we need to head east, toward Lake Vaspurakan," Meliora said.

They wended their way through the forest, Violet the only one slowing to scrutinize a leaf or double-check that the hedgehog scampering past wasn't some magical creature. She saw goats too, black as licorice. They never let her get close. Whatever time she lost by slowing, she made up by jogging.

Meliora and Alikar didn't notice. Neither of them spoke a word.

An hour into their journey, sunrise had stirred. Violet could make out the edge of the forest and the plain that lay beyond. Light grew, dapples of warmth that found their way into her coat.

A memory of Fa came, hotter than the sun and defter at slipping into Violet's skin: him, elbow-deep in the soil, planting lilacs. How he would have loved this forest, these hedgehogs, and the two moons of Bar'Talian.

At the cusp of the woods, they paused before endless lowlands that eventually piled into mountains. It fit the definition of exposed.

"We shouldn't walk somewhere this open," Violet said.

Once again, Meliora couldn't understand; but, after surveying Alikar's face, they let the matter drop. Meliora took the first stride. Feeling like someone about to cross a trip wire, Violet followed.

They reached the first roots of the mountains after a half hour. Thin paths of boulders crept up the slope, eventually connecting with a face of weathered black and brown. Violet had never seen mountains like these, so majestic and brown and snow-capped.

Before climbing, Violet and Meliora nibbled on jerky. It was tough, but Meliora insisted that Sowers had processed it for full nutritional value. Once again, Alikar had to be coaxed into Advocating for them.

"Yesterday," Violet said, "that woman who healed me was called a Balm?"

"Rumor says the monarchs of Anlian weld one thousand a day," Meliora said.

"They can heal anyone of anything?"

"They have greater power over man-made ailments and can't do as much for natural ones. Disease, for instance. But they can alleviate some suffering."

Then even liryn couldn't cure someone of ALS.

"Do you have a headache?" Meliora asked Alikar.

He was standing, arms crossed, having refused to eat. "It never hurts, not in the beginning."

But eventually, the headaches would come. And then Alikar's crown.

Violet brushed the crumbs off her cloak. "We should continue."

The mountain did not like to be hiked. Gravity pushed them continuously back. There were no trunks or branches to hold onto, only pitted slopes and rock. Hair stuck to Violet's jaw. She drew in air as if through a straw. The waterleaf did alleviate her thirst, though.

Further complicating their hike were the mountain goats—brown, pony-sized creatures with black beards, horns like scythes, and an alarming lack of skittishness. They refused to move, staring down the human strangers with such hostility that no one dared getting within ten feet of them.

Trying to avoid one such goat, Violet stumbled backward. Her fall was stopped by a grip on her waist and a grunt. Alikar shoved her forward. She tethered herself on a rock protrusion.

"Thank you," she panted.

An alarmed Meliora inquired unintelligibly.

"She's fine," Alikar answered, loping higher. "Everyone's dead, but she's content."

The comment stunned Violet into stillness. "That . . . that's not true," she said.

"Isn't it?" Alikar spun around. His cheeks were flushed, his eyes wild again. "You've yet to demonstrate otherwise." It was the most he'd spoken since the cairn. He'd cooperated with his liryn just to yell at her.

Violet stood there, gripping the rock, wishing she was any-where else. Alikar had finally realized she was a robot.

"Everyone processes things differently," Meliora said.

Alikar ignored her.

Meliora said something else, but it was Faartunga now. She gave Violet a pitying glance, then inched down and held out a hand. Somehow, Meliora found the space for warmth despite shouldering a mountain of suffering.

Why can't I be like her?

Together, they passed Alikar and the goats.

Aches had settled in Violet's limbs by the time they crested the mountain peaks. The sun was high now, much closer and bolder than Earth's. For a moment, the group caught its breath. Violet waited for her twitches to subside. Her thighs itched, her stomach ached, and the waterleaf stuck to her teeth. Several breathless moments passed before she could straighten to see how far they'd walked.

The plain below looked like brown carpet on a painted landscape. It touched Barikad Forest. Somewhere in there was the estate, burning.

A distant laugh floated from somewhere behind them. They spun around. The mountaintop was narrow, vanishing to a gap of air, beyond which grew another mountain. Violet's heart sank. Did they have to hike that too?

The laugh echoed again.

Meliora hissed an urgent word and pulled Violet and Alikar down. Violet felt the protests of her worn-out limbs as she shimmied over moss, crawling as close to the edge as she dared.

These two mountains bordered the lake, which weaved jaggedly between them, cutting out a ditch like a gully. The water wasn't too far down. Camped in the valley were some men, and docked in the lake was a boat, green and slim like a submarine. One of the men hammered at the bow. Another sat on a boulder, arms crossed, foot tapping. The remaining two stood at a distance.

Meliora spoke in Faartunga.

"It's docked for repairs," Alikar answered.

"But someone's fixing it." Meliora pointed toward the man hammering.

It seemed Meliora wanted a ride. "What if they're Separatists?" Violet said.

Alikar withdrew his toolkit, which concealed a device like a film canister. He adjusted it over his eye. "I don't see any patches," he said. "One of the men in white is a Seer."

"A Seer on Bar'Talian?" Meliora wondered. "Well, a Seer would never be a Separatist, and a Separatist would never befriend a Seer."

The two men keeping their distance wore clothes that contrasted with the vibrant colors of Vaspurakan. Over long-sleeved turtlenecks they had white tunics, cutting over one shoulder and cinched at the waist like a toga. They were knee-length, falling over boots that stretched to their thighs. What made the men the most conspicuous were the white turbans, concealing all but their eyes.

"Joining them is too risky," she said.

"Not as risky as walking in the open. And we'll save time." Meliora fumbled for a piece of her nightgown and tore it free. Soon she'd wrapped the gauzy square of black fabric over her face. It started below her eyes and fell over her chin, painting her stare a darker brown. "There," she said.

Violet wasn't convinced. "Is a veil like that normal?"

"For some women, yes. Hide your face," she told Alikar. "Walk poorly, with your shoulders hunched."

"I am an *azat*," he said with a scowl.

"Exactly. The more you show your nobility, the more you'll resemble . . ."

His scowl turned to grief.

"You can't use this either." Her fingers grazed the king's belt. "People will assume you're a cord thief."

"Because it doesn't look like a normal cord?" Violet asked.

Meliora nodded. "Many thieves convert them into other accessories. Bracelets, rings. Belts."

"The Seer will recognize it as a legitimate cord," Alikar said.

"You'll have to hide it. Concealing's not illegal if it's a necessity," she added quickly, but Alikar's scowl had already returned.

"I don't see that it is," he said.

"The Seer will wonder why the monarchs welded you with a non-regulation cord. You'll attract attention. Hide your cord, Alikar, and don't use it. Let the Seer think what he wants. No one else will realize you're an Advocate."

No one *else*.

"The Seer will know he's an Advocate," Violet said, "even if his cord is hidden?"

"Everyone welded has a 'luster' the color of their liryn," Meliora said. "Their cords glow too. That's how Seers detect thieves."

A thief's cord would glow, but not their bodies. The Seer below would see that Alikar's body glowed purple, along with the king's belt, and he'd wonder why Alikar had been welded with an unusual cord.

"So we won't be able to communicate," Violet said.

Meliora tilted her head, considering, then sheared away another square of her hem. "If our mouths are covered," she said, handing Violet the makeshift veil, "they won't notice we're not speaking Arati. With the veil on, we could be sisters."

She had a point; they shared brown hair and eyes, though Meliora's skin had warmer undertones. She was also taller, lither, but Violet doubted anyone would be that observant.

So, Alikar would secretly Advocate. The Seer would know Alikar was welded—maybe even that he was translating—but they'd have to hope he didn't care enough to point it out. Why *would* he care what some lone Advocate did?

Seers used to police liryn, Violet remembered.

She took the fabric, rubbing it between her fingertips. Meliora hadn't assuaged her doubts. While traveling by boat eliminated the possibility of Yakiv or some other Separatist spying them on the road, it meant they would be trapped with strangers for an indeterminate amount of time.

Meliora suddenly jerked forward, gripping the rocks. "Cord thief," she hissed.

"Where?" Violet searched.

"Look at the Seer, how he shies away."

The Seer stood the farthest back, angled more toward the mountain than the lake.

"The liryn of cord thieves is corrupt," Meliora told Violet. "Seers can't be around it without being in pain."

Alikar peered through his magnifying capsule. He spoke through gritted teeth. "The one on the boulder, wearing the bandanna. He has four."

"*Four?*" Meliora said.

"Advocate, Pillar, Chair . . . and Chisel." The last word pricked Alikar's throat. "He's a Separatist too. I see it now, his patch."

"We can't go down there," Violet said. "He might know Yakiv."

"Yakiv would have nothing to do with a cord thief," Alikar said.

"But he's still a Separatist."

Meliora leaned away from the edge. "We'll keep walking."

Relieved, Violet took the lead, pocketing the veil. They kept low, away from the edge, in case any of the men looked up. Violet had to concentrate on staying leftward; the slope kept veering her toward the men. Meliora and Alikar had an easier time following a straight line. Perhaps their path was smoother. Violet shifted their direction. A loose rock made her teeter toward the edge again, but Meliora caught her before she stumbled.

"Thanks," Violet said.

"Keep away from the ledge so they don't see you."

"I know, I—"

Something landed on Violet's head. She glanced up and had a brief glimpse of a bird right before it dropped grayish sludge on her eye. Frantically, she wiped at the stinging goo, which blurred her vision and smelled like fish. She gagged, vaguely aware of Meliora's whispered concerns. Another part of her registered the jolt of pain from a boulder around her shin. Violet did stumble now. Blinded by bird poop, revulsion, discomfort, and humiliation, she tripped right over the edge.

CHAPTER EIGHTEEN

"All Goldentongues must relinquish their cords prior to any negotiation, both formal and informal. Any Goldentongue who refuses to comply will be fined according to local levy custom, in addition to having their cord confiscated for no less than one year." – *Imperial Edict #288*

B Y SOME MIRACLE, VIOLET didn't break her neck. She staggered several steps in a chaotic dance of trying to catch her balance, managing to trip in such a way that she didn't go tumbling down the mountainside. Cheeks and palms burning for differing reasons, she watched in humiliation as two of the strangers scrambled up toward her, exclaiming. In a moment she was lifted upright and fussed over and carried the remainder of the way down. Finally, they were at the water bank, and Violet was free to reclaim her limbs.

One of her rescuers chastised her. He was the boat's repairman, sun-weathered as a date, sporting a head of scraggly black hair. *Scraggly* was the only way to describe him. Even his nose had a way of looking messy on his wrinkled face.

Her other rescuer, the Seer's friend, inspected her. His turban showed nothing but the outline of swarthy skin around his eyes.

They both questioned her; the Seer's friend pointed at her eye. "*Ayo,*" she said, Arati for "Yes." She vigorously scrubbed the gunk away, embarrassment fading as she grew more aware of the cord thief. He hadn't bothered helping.

"There you are!" she heard in English. Meliora and Alikar were picking their way downhill.

Violet wished she could communicate with her mind. But it was too late. What was Meliora thinking? Violet was certain it hadn't been Alikar's idea to come after her. Meliora must have convinced him to translate, too. His purple belt failed to swing into view as Alikar stomped down.

"Thank you for helping her," Meliora called. Her usual accent was gone; she was imitating Alikar's. "She doesn't speak Arati."

"I can help with that," said a voice coming from the direction Violet had determinedly avoided.

Someone wearing four liryn pendants should have boasted of obvious muscles, intimidating height, or countless weapons. The thief had none of that, the only interesting thing about him being the scar from mouth to jaw, and even that looked like something he could've acquired from shaving. His buzzed hair failed to cover bald patches, and his paleness gave him a sickly impression. But his smile held cold confidence.

"Your surplus of pendants has stopped up your hearing, my friend," the Seer's friend said amicably. His accent reminded Violet of Meliora's, though thicker. "I asked you not to use them in his sight." He inclined his head toward the Seer, who now clutched his temples in obvious discomfort.

"Liryn is for the people," the cord thief replied.

"Utilized by the welded. I'm afraid you don't qualify."

"If the Seer wants me to stop Advocating, he can beg me himself." The thief gave a crooked grin. "Once his eyes stop aching."

Alikar's spine was rigid. While Meliora's veiled expression remained a mystery, her stare was angry.

"I have asked politely," the Seer's friend said. "Now I must be rude. Stop Advocating, if you please."

"Words are useless without your cord, Goldentongue," the thief said.

The Seer's friend glanced at the scraggly repairman. "I admit, I'd allowed myself to forget you'd confiscated it, Captain."

The captain's boisterous beam contrasted with the tense mood. "You'll both be earning them hooks back once yer on yer merry ways."

Both? Then the thief had a fifth stolen pendant. Why hadn't the pendants flown back to their owners? Maybe a confiscated pendant wouldn't return to the thief, but it should return to the Goldentongue—whatever a "Goldentongue" was.

Since the thief was only Advocating on Violet's account, it was up to her to stop him. "I don't need your help," she said. Though matching his stare scraped her nerves, she did anyway. It might've been a useless attempt at bravery. She was no one. He was the victor of five pendants.

Irritation creased the thief's scar. He said nothing, did nothing. But the Goldentongue checked the Seer, who stopped gripping his head.

"Thank you for obliging," the Goldentongue said—still intelligibly, thanks to Alikar. He bowed to the thief. Violet couldn't imagine how he had the stomach to bow. Five people—no, six, including the Seer—suffered their headaches and crowns on the thief's behalf. He didn't care.

"Ye have important matters with this here lake?" spoke the captain with a businesslike clasping of hands that gave away his indifference to liryn politics.

"We do," Meliora said, clenching her fists behind her back. "Where are you traveling today?"

"The farthest I's going today is Sarken."

"Do you have room for three more?"

Violet focused on fixing her gloves so no one would notice her trepidation. Travel with a cord-thieving Separatist and a Seer who could observe that Alikar had hidden liryn?

The Seer, confirming Violet's unease, scrutinized Alikar.

"Aye, she's got space to spare," the captain told Meliora. "But she ain't a ship of charity. There'll be a fare, mind ye, and she takes mighty offense if it ain't paid."

"How much?" Meliora asked.

"Two hundred cottons, that's what."

"Is that the price before or after your conversation with the Fork-tongue?" Alikar demanded.

The captain's laugh shot out like gas escaping. "I ought to tack on fifty cottons for yon cheek. Captain Barome ain't be likes to the fools who let a Goldentongue charm 'em. Got them hooks hidden away." He snagged a hand comfortably on the flap of his shirt. "Only thief 'round us be this nasty laddie."

The thief smiled. "Can't steal what's already yours by rights."

"And what right have you to five pendants, my friend?" the Goldentongue asked.

"One right"—the thief flicked the knife pendant on his bandanna—"another"—he flicked the carpenter's square—"another"—the flame—"and another." A handsaw clinked against its neighbors.

"If I chose to wade through your artistic explanation, I'd guess your logic is, 'I see, therefore I take.'"

"If you offer, I won't refuse."

Captain Barome chortled.

Meliora squared her shoulders. "We don't have cottons, but we will gladly work off our debt."

The captain tipped his hat. "Enjoy yer swim, travelers." He grinned, turning toward his boat.

The Goldentongue swept in front of Captain Barome. "Surely one could make an exception for these young folk. We might pay their cottons. Yes?" He checked with his Seer friend.

"We don't need your charity, Fork-tongue," Alikar said, scrounging around his coat pockets. "Here, you swindler." He thrust his hand toward Captain Barome. Violet's heart gave an uncomfortable thump when she recognized his tool. "Will you take this? I assure you, it cost more than two hundred."

Barome gave the diamond tin a curious wink and whistled. "Donnat see much Chisel these sunshine days." He plucked the diamond from Alikar and turned it over in his much dirtier, stubbier fingers. He sniffed it, balanced it, held it up to his ear, and eventually said, "Three of ye? Aye, this'll satisfy her plenty." With a wicked grin, Barome plopped the diamond down his shirt.

"Lovely," Alikar muttered.

Unease worked up Violet's spine. Despite her better judgment, she followed the others to the ship.

T HEY HAD DIFFICULTY finding the space to keep themselves a comfortable distance apart. Captain Barome's *Vagabond* was well-aware of its name; the ship was not made for permanent living, nor large parties.

Its concave interior, narrower than the outside suggested, reminded Violet of a torpedo. Barome manned the steering by a viewing window, which she mistook for a large clock. Behind him, mismatched furniture indicated that, at some point, Barome had realized it would be wise to invest in seating. A rocking chair, stools, and pillows were scattered around a dining table. Chairs of varying sizes were squeezed everywhere else, shouldering bookcases and end tables. Nothing in the potted plants, stacked books, or vases full of unknown objects gave the impression that Violet was sitting in a boat and not a garage sale. It smelled just as stale and damp.

Captain Barome laughed when the Goldentongue asked for privacy for his friend. The Seer hadn't said one word, fidgeting by a window as if hoping to swim away. Violet couldn't blame him. The cord thief made her uncomfortable too.

He hadn't offered a name. No one had, other than Barome. The captain had said little since starting the boat, other than telling the Seer he was welcome to strap himself to the gunwale.

"How long will this take?" Violet murmured to Meliora, and still she worried she'd spoken too loudly. The thief seemed to breathe down her neck, even though they'd situated themselves at the farthest corner. Alikar was wedged between a bookcase and the sofa where Violet and Meliora sat.

"Less time than walking," Meliora said.

"Not necessarily," Alikar said, watching the viewing window controls. "We're going north."

Meliora's crinkled eyes told Violet north was the wrong direction. "He might need to drop the others off first. How fast are we going?"

"Slow. These ships gain speed exponentially."

"Meaning?"

"Barome is a smuggler."

Violet had no idea what exponential speed had to do with smuggling. "You're saying we'll pick up speed at the end?" she asked Alikar.

He nodded.

Then hopefully that made up for this detour.

For the first few minutes, all was quiet in that underwater, muted quality. The Goldentongue was busy trying to accommodate the Seer, and the cord thief busy watching with amusement.

"What exactly is a Goldentongue?" Violet whispered to Meliora.

"They can sway your thoughts, affect your reasoning. Like . . . like Kora did."

The girl who'd made Kelispar Advocate against his will. That was certainly an unnerving liryn. Was it possible to resist?

Meliora's gaze was trained on the two friends in white. "They're from Janlian," she said. "The capital."

"How do you know?"

"They're speaking Greek."

Violet listened harder to their unintelligible conversation; Alikar's Advocating range was limited, or else he was choosing to keep it on a short leash. "Is Janlian the only realm where Greek is spoken?" she asked.

Meliora shook her head.

"So they could be from anywhere."

"No. They're from Janlian. Seers don't live anywhere else. Every other realm has too many thieves. And if they're from Janlian, they're from the capital. Patmos is the only place we spoke Greek."

The odds were slim that two men from the same city as Meliora should be traveling this close to the Hastein estate. What were they doing here?

The answer came as soon as Violet thought to ask it. "The royal representatives," she whispered.

Meliora's furtive stare froze.

They were on their way to the estate for the sending-off party. They had no idea what they were sailing toward. "We have to tell them," Violet said.

"How?"

"If Alikar stops Advocating, you can tell them in Greek."

"But the cord thief."

"I'll know if he's Advocating because I'll be able to understand."

Meliora shook her head. "If he's skilled enough, he can Advocate so that only *he* understands them, and not you."

An Advocate was far more powerful—and dangerous—than a simple translator. Violet, Meliora, and Alikar were trapped by words they couldn't speak. Not with a Separatist nearby.

The Janlian representatives approached before Violet and Meliora settled on a discreet way to communicate. "May we join you?" the Goldentongue asked.

"Of course," Meliora said too quickly.

The thief lounged at the dining table, feet propped up—and eyes on the Seer.

There had to be a way. The thief would lose interest eventually. Surely he had no use for a Seer cord. In the meantime, Violet hoped Meliora's desperation to talk to a fellow Janlion wouldn't tempt her to say something rash.

The Goldentongue dusted off a chair for the Seer before choosing a pillow on the floor. The Seer sank hesitantly, like expecting the chair to restrain him. After sitting for five seconds without catastrophe, he relaxed. His eagle pendant, hanging from a white cord, gleamed as if polished this morning.

Violet swallowed. He was staring at Alikar's chest. The Seer knew exactly what hid there.

Her suspicion was confirmed when the Goldentongue spoke. "Bold, hiding your cord around a Seer," he said to Alikar, "but, given our fellow passenger, I don't fault you. Neither will the Seer report you."

Yet he'd managed to make his statement sound exactly like a threat.

Fortunately, Alikar didn't reply. Meliora took up the reins. "Where . . . What brings you to Bar'Talian?"

The Goldentongue rested one elbow on a propped-up knee. "A curious way to begin a conversation, accusing us of being foreigners."

"Excuse me." Meliora's hands retracted into her cloak. "I—you're from Bar'Talian, then?"

He took his time, adjusting a ring on his pinkie, never taking his penetrating gaze off Meliora. "Where are you from? Not far from home, at this early hour."

"No."

"Then you've recently begun your journey. To return your lady friend home?"

"Yes."

"And where is your sister from, that she has not learned Arati whereas you are wonderfully fluent?"

"The . . . south."

Violet winced. The man had changed his wording, referring to her as a friend and then a sister. Meliora hadn't noticed his mistake. It hadn't been one.

Violet regretted, again, not speaking Arati. The Golden-tongue had put them under the spotlight. She imagined he saw three young adults, one of them hiding beneath a veil and another dirty and scowling, and figured they were up to no good.

A staticky noise drew Violet's attention. The thief fiddled with a compact, scallop shell-shaped device that resembled the one Karleif had used to project the image of Eliathor at Yakiv's rally. A shell, Karleif had fittingly called it. Arati voices trickled from it.

Finally, he was distracted. Violet prodded Meliora's foot.

Meliora withdrew her hands, which she clasped with forced nonchalance. "What brings you into Vaspurakan today? Visiting friends?"

She was terrible at this. Meliora was better off asking outright.

Before the Goldentongue could reply, a soft voice drifted from the Seer like from someone sleep talking. "The sheep stands on a compass and the needle points north. Yet she follows south."

Violet stiffened as she pretended not to understand him.

Sheep.

Could he see that she was a Terlion?

The Goldentongue chuckled. "Do not be offended, please. These Seers have precious few ways of speaking that don't involve making everyone distinctly uncomfortable."

"I do not make people as uncomfortable as you make them." The Seer's voice was uncertain, timid, younger than Violet had guessed. "You make everyone blush. The gardener's daughter. The chef's daughter. The librarian's—"

"How observant you can be, Ez," the Goldentongue said, "when you choose to be. Now, what is that racket?" He turned, scanning the thief, who still relaxed at the table with his blaring device. "My friend, please lower the volume—" He faltered. In the lack of conversation, the voices issuing from the thief's shell grew distinct.

Meliora gasped. Alikar's chin jerked up. Even Barome turned from his steering to listen.

"Which pearl is that?" the Goldentongue demanded.

"Gray," the thief answered. He absently spun the shell with a pinkie.

"Separatist propaganda."

The thief shrugged. "It's the same on the monarch's pearl. Don't think it'd be smart of you to label that propaganda."

Alikar's liryn didn't extend to the shell, but Violet made do without liryn. Lady Basilia's name sounded the same in Arati.

Her tongue stuck to her teeth. The thief's shell was some sort of radio broadcast. The Hasteins' murders had made news.

The passengers listened without comment. The Seer bowed his head, missing Meliora's attempt to muffle her sob.

Alikar disappeared through the door Barome had indicated as the bathroom. No one noticed except Violet.

She counted to one hundred by fours. And then kept counting.

"Yakiv Stefanos?" the Goldentongue said. His next question was in Arati. Violet was surprised he knew this country's language.

Barome's reply was Advocated. "A long trail from home ye are, traveler, if ye've not heard the name Yakiv Stefanos."

Then the news had revealed the suspect. There might have been a warrant for his arrest. Maybe this would all be resolved by the end of the day.

"A pity Stefanos didn't stamp them out sooner," the thief said.

Violet stared. He'd said something else, surely. Nothing so blatantly cruel.

"Find your manners, thief," the Goldentongue said.

"Or what?" The thief grinned. "Your friend will arrest me? Like the Seers of old, before they turned tail and cowered away on Janlian?"

The Goldentongue patted his chest, but Barome had taken his cord.

"You'll be keeping yer fights off my ship," Captain Barome said, "or you'll be paying me all yer cottons to clean up the stain."

The thief and the Goldentongue settled their disagreement with a staring match interrupted by Barome moving between them. The thief, shrugging, adjusted the shell, finding another set of reporters.

Meliora's crying made noise. Violet crossed her legs. She could pat Meliora's hand. Would that be strange? Would it draw more attention to them?

Will Meliora realize how robotic I am?

Stiff with indecision, she did nothing.

The Goldentongue started forward. Even the Seer turned around. A projected image of a person rotated above the cord thief's shell.

Another Arati comment came from the Goldentongue. The thief replied in kind. Alikar, from behind the bathroom door, translated for the Goldentongue's next words.

"Because it's a fool's theory. A girl that size couldn't possibly be accused of conspiring with him. She . . ." The Goldentongue slowed as the figure finished spinning. She wore all black and Kelispar's purple scarf.

Silence hung in the air, though not as tangibly as the hand-drawn sketch of Violet. She held her breath, hearing the hungry pulse in her ears. *Why* and *How* danced in her thoughts.

Why was there a sketch of her in the news?

How had the artist known what she looked like?

Why do they think I'm working with Yakiv Stefanos?

She couldn't swallow, couldn't blink. She imagined standing, moving to the bathroom, not caring if Alikar wanted nothing to do with her. But she sat, feeling the eyes in the room fixate on her.

The Goldentongue reacted first. He closed in on Violet and spoke in a tone fully devoid of mirth. "Name yourself."

He was Violet's ally, but she couldn't tell him. To speak was to oust Alikar's liryn, to divulge Meliora's identity in front of a Separatist who thought Yakiv had taken too long to kill the Hasteins. To stay silent was to condemn herself. Violet's lips parted.

"She . . . she doesn't speak—" Meliora said.

"The Seer knows your Advocate is translating." The Goldentongue, not wavering from Violet, held out a hand. "My cord, Captain. I swear it will not be used against you."

Meliora stood, staggering on the hem of Eliathor's cloak. "A Goldentongue can't perform an interrogation without authorization!"

"The law stands with me." The Goldentongue's hand waited. He'd been nowhere near this firm with the cord thief.

"We'll talk to you privately." Meliora's tone rose in pitch.

"Captain Barome."

Meliora swiveled toward the Seer. "Please. We'll talk, just not in front of the thief."

"Don't answer her," the Goldentongue said. "She's a Separatist, sheltering a murderer."

"I'm not!"

The Seer showed furrowed eyebrows. "Her concern is just," he murmured.

"It's a tactic of delay," the Goldentongue said. "Captain! My cord."

Barome let his hand fall into a pocket. The thief had silenced his shell. Violet's image still floated. He studied it, and then her.

Meliora staggered toward the Seer, who shied back. She grasped his arms. "Please. You don't understand what we've been through—"

The Goldentongue wrenched her away. Their argument washed over Violet, who numbly sat like a lump on a log. She had to correct this horrifying mistake. The Goldentongue would fight *for* them if he realized who they were, but how could they tell him in front of the thief? There was no telling what he'd do—nor Captain Barome, who hadn't expressed any regret over the Hasteins' death.

"I can give you this here hook, aye," Barome was saying to the Goldentongue, "but I've got me some stipulations."

"Name them," the Goldentongue commanded.

"You hook the girly uphill and downhill. And Barome gets them reward cottons."

"So long as you report her to the appropriate authorities and not the smuggler's guild."

Barome's grin was toothy. "Aye," he said, the most obvious lie in the world.

But the Goldentongue didn't care. He wanted his cord.

Barome drew a wooden box from his pocket.

"Wait!" Meliora said, at the same time that the thief lurched upon Barome with the flash of a blade.

"It's not fair that the welded gets his hook back and not me." The thief hooked an arm around the captain's neck and stuck the tip of his knife on Barome's belly.

Barome cackled and stomped on the thief's foot. The thief grunted, dropping his knife, making himself the perfect target for Barome's backhanded slap. "Not getting the likes of Captain Barome!" he bellowed as he tussled the thief to the ground. The wooden box slipped free, and the thief dove for it. So did the Goldentongue, who got a kick to the face for his trouble.

Violet took Meliora's arm, steering her toward the stairs which led up-deck. What did she hope to do, jump into freezing water and swim to the Amber Forest? And they needed to get Alikar. He was still in the bathroom, not wholly oblivious, because he'd been consistently translating since Violet's image showed on the shell.

Switching gears, she motioned Meliora past the Seer, who'd curled himself into a ball, hiding his head in his arms. *Maybe Seers* are *cowards,* Violet had the space to think as she aimed for the bathroom. The door swung open. Alikar seized Violet and Meliora and yanked them in.

"Close the door!" he said.

Violet slammed it shut, fumbling for a lock. But, naturally, there wasn't even a knob. A metal handprint sat halfway up the door. She matched her palm over it and heard a click. Not a second too soon—someone banged from the other side.

"Open this door, girl," called one of the Janlion representatives, "lest it be opened on you."

He had a point. If he broke through, the heavy door would collapse on her head. It would be safer to avoid injury.

She reached for the handprint.

Someone snatched her elbow. "He's hooking you," Alikar said, and shoved her toward the sink. Where a mirror should have hung, a wide opening sat instead, which Meliora had just finished clambering through. She waited inside an ovular room of silver walls and ceiling, hardly bigger than the bathroom.

Violet's comprehension lagged. "What—"

Alikar pushed until she could either climb the sink or be climbed by Alikar. She hoisted herself up and over, into the hole, Alikar on her tail. He spun back, sealing the opening with a foreign phrase.

For a moment they breathed in utter darkness. Then, Alikar made some invisible motion. Meliora crashed against Violet as everything abruptly tilted.

CHAPTER NINETEEN

"If the High Seer's going to hide away on Janlian while thieves infect every realm, I warrant he got what he deserved. Plenty of men have lost wives and daughters to thieves. Why shouldn't King Giannis?" – Yakiv Stefanos, speech at Lake Winslow

As THE DARKNESS FAILED to abate, Violet's fear increased. They were trapped. The Goldentongue would break through, or the thief, who had no qualms about using his knife.

Then, lights flickered on around her ankles, chasing the shadows away. The hollow room, concave like an egg, was bathed in a silvery glow from the floor lights, revealing Alikar by one of the two rods sticking out of the wall. His head wasn't far from the ceiling: a domed window. The lights from the floor trickled out into an inky underwater world, so dark and full of unseen creatures that Violet chose not to stare too long.

Meliora said something in Faartunga. Alikar ignored her, frantically spying around. There was nothing to see, other than the rods, and not much space to explore. But he did, crouching and running his hands along every scrap of space. Violet had to shift out of his way.

It was just a matter of time before the Goldentongue found them. He'd convinced her to open the door. She hadn't even had the presence of mind to realize he was "hooking" her. No wonder Kelispar had burned his Advocate cord. Yakiv's Goldentongue could have pressed information out of Eliathor like water from a drenched rag.

With an exclamation, Alikar pried open a section of the wall. A rectangular panel swung out. Inside the tiny compartment sat something like a metal jewelry box. He yanked it out. The box was etched with red Aramaic script. Under the box's glass lid, Violet spied a black rock.

Alikar and Meliora chatted urgently. Violet longed to know what was happening. Was that rock a bomb?

Suddenly, the room jerked. They collapsed into each other. Alikar shoved the box into Violet's hands—she tensed, afraid to move—and jumped up, snatching at a rod. He tried turning it clockwise, grimacing. Meliora scrambled up to help. Meanwhile, Violet rooted herself to the floor, trying not to consider the fact that she was potentially holding an explosive.

Something under her shuddered. There was a groaning sound, like massive gears churning. Alikar and Meliora wrestled with the rod. Then, the room rocked again, like a magnet had sucked them back. Violet smacked her head on the wall but managed not to drop the box. In her center of gravity, she felt a tug-and-pull; some force drew the room one direction while another resisted.

Alikar dropped to his knees, pushing her feet aside. He found another Aramaic character on the floor and said, "*Ephpheta.*"

That spot of floor peeled back, showing another compartment. Alikar grabbed the box from her and tossed it into the hole.

Violet froze, awaiting an eruption.

"*Sawgar*," he said, and the floor reformed.

The room bounced again. They made another tangle of bodies. Alikar dragged himself up so he could turn the rod counterclockwise. It moved easily now. The rumbling rattled Violet's already confused bearings. Then it silenced. The room tilted into a gentle bob, and Alikar slid to the floor with his hands in his hair and a heaving sigh of relief.

No one spoke. Alikar continued exhaling. Meliora stared at the ceiling with apprehension. And Violet, who couldn't begin to piece together what catastrophe had just been averted, occupied herself with making sure she hadn't crushed any of the jars in the magical pouch.

Meliora spoke.

"*Ayo,*" Alikar said.

". . . all right?" she asked Violet.

"Yes. So no one can get into this room now?"

"This is a smuggler's pod," Alikar said.

For Captain Barome's stolen goods—or people. That meant they weren't on *The Vagabond* anymore but floating in a pod.

Violet exhaled too. "What was that black rock?"

"*Rav'aham,*" Alikar said unhelpfully.

"The strongest magnet in existence," Meliora said. "Barome was using his rav'aham stone to pull us back. That's why we dropped the anchor. Even that didn't stop it. But our rav'aham is gone now. He won't find us."

Violet eyed the Aramaic on the floor, doubtful. "That compartment cancels out the magnet?"

"It's a waste chute," Alikar said.

Then that rav'aham stone was currently floating somewhere in the lake.

"We can steer this to the Amber Forest," Meliora said.

"Do you see a wheel?" Alikar asked her.

A slip of irritation crossed Meliora's face. "I thought that might be one," she said calmly, pointing to the rod they hadn't touched yet.

"That's the water intake. Keeps us from being buoyant."

"Fine. How fast can this go?"

"These pods aren't designed for traveling. They're meant to be ejected, then pulled back once the inspections are over and the smuggler's safe. There's no propulsion. All it can do is follow the current."

"I never knew you were so up to date with smuggling practices." Meliora tried smiling.

"I'm up to date with basic information."

Her levity evaporated. "Stop being rude, Alikar."

He opened his mouth, then stood, swaying for a moment before balancing himself on the wall. Alikar searched out the window, trained on the black water.

Violet wondered what Kelispar would say if he saw this Alikar.

But that was just it. This Alikar only existed because Kelispar didn't.

She adjusted her position. "Does this have a navigation system, so we'll know when we've reached the Amber Forest?"

"No," Alikar answered.

Violet thought it unnecessary to point out the obvious problem: They could float past the forest and never realize until it was too late.

"We'll have to do some calculations." Meliora straightened. "We just need to determine how far we are from the forest."

She and Alikar talked it out in forcibly polite conversation. Evidently this lake ran alongside the forest; they could drop anchor at their destination, adjust the water intake, and rise to the surface to disembark. After several minutes, they determined that they'd be able to feel when they were near based on the uptick in the current, as this lake ended in a waterfall by the forest. Alikar guessed they had at least six more hours in this pod.

Violet wasn't a fan of the plan, especially the idea of hurtling toward a waterfall. But what alternative was there? All she could do was wait and try not to think about the uncomfortable reality that they were stuck in an underwater egg with no steering and no visual of land; in an eerie, dim lake swirling around them, in which shadowy shapes could occasionally be seen. At least they had food and water, thanks to the pouch in her pocket.

As the current dragged them along, Violet considered how much had happened in under twenty-four hours. Yesterday, everyone had been alive. Now, they fled from more than Yakiv. Even allies like the Janlion representatives were after Violet.

"That 'shell' the cord thief had," Violet said, "it's like a radio broadcast?"

"I don't know what that is." Alikar could have been talking to the lake. "Resonance shells bring us news. They hold pearls. Color denotes the source. Separatists use gray."

"The Separatist pearl had your image," Meliora said. "The monarch's pearl didn't mention you."

Then perhaps no one would believe the news that Violet had conspired with some infamous Separatist leader. The idea was absurd. She was eighteen. Hardly threatening.

"If only I could have spoken to the representatives," Meliora said.

"I'm sure they remember the shunning edict," Alikar said.

Shame colored Meliora's cheeks.

Violet looked purposefully outside. But the burden of the secret—or maybe the worry that Violet was imagining something horrible—must have been too heavy, because Meliora spoke after a moment.

"King Giannis issued an edict that prohibits any citizen of Janlian from associating with me."

"Because you left?" Violet said.

"Because I knew about Eliathor's betrothal to Princess Fila and kept it a secret."

The answer was nowhere in the proximity of Violet's expectations.

"Fila was betrothed to some earl from birth," Meliora said, "but she and Eliathor became close. It happened when they were young. We used to visit Janlian often. Alikar and Kelispar too."

The mention of his brother made Alikar flinch.

"They made a solemn pact when they were eleven," Meliora continued. "I was the witness. When King Giannis found out, he forbade Fila from seeing Eliathor—or me—ever again."

If anyone could have decided his future spouse at eleven years old, it was Eliathor.

"Then the princess will have to marry the earl?" Violet asked.

"No, because she's dead," Alikar spat.

It was her turn to flinch. The only noise was the soft *womp-womp* of the current.

At least Princess Fila wouldn't have to be told about Eliathor's death. But he'd been told about hers.

Memory met understanding. Lady Basilia had said Eliathor lost a friend and never recovered.

"She was fourteen," Meliora said, scraping at her bracelet. "It was a diplomatic mission. Their ship was attacked. Fila and the queen were kidnapped. Whoever did it sent King Giannis the queen's eyes and Fila's . . . tongue." Her fingers curled. "A message to Seers."

"I'm sorry," Violet murmured. Fourteen. That had been June two years ago. "The king never caught them?"

"It was rumored that the empires were behind it. Then the Da'atan emperors' son went missing. Everyone talked of High Prince Aurelius and forgot about Janlian. But King Giannis gave up long before that. He just . . . stopped looking. It drove Eliathor mad. Janlian isn't known for stamina these days." Meliora's words were flat, her eyes dry.

"Why would the empires have orchestrated it?" Violet asked.

"Janlian's royal line is ending. They only had two children. Fila was the heir. Now it's Prince Ezio and he's never been interested in marriage. After he dies, there'll be no heir."

"There's Nikos," Alikar said.

Meliora shook her head. "Nikos doesn't want it."

"He's next in line. He won't have a choice."

"What happens if Nikos says no?" Violet asked.

"A new royal family will be appointed by the emperors," Meliora said. "Who would love to stamp out Seers indefinitely."

"You shouldn't speak that way," Alikar said. "Only the uncivilized believed that rumor. The emperors would never cooperate in an assassination."

Trembling fingertips on her bracelet, Meliora murmured, "Even Kelispar could admit they aren't perfect."

They floated without much conversation after that, except to share food. Exhaustion struck Violet like a violent wind, but her mind worked, portioning out all she'd learned. Secret engagements, shunning edicts, assassinated royals, a missing prince—and still her understanding of these realms was woefully inadequate.

"Are you still going to leave us?" Meliora picked at a kallumberry.

"Yes," Alikar said.

"You can't walk to Vaspurakan, Alikar. It's too dangerous. You need to—"

"Stop telling me what to do!"

Meliora dropped the kallumberry, staring at Alikar's twitchy face.

"You used to dictate how we picnicked. You'd make me sit next to Ezio, and Ezio next to Fila, when I wanted to sit by Eliathor and Ezio by Nikos. You don't always know best. Just let us be." He glowered at the wall like it had told him where to sit too.

Violet did everything in her power to stopper a sneeze that had been building, working to remain both unseen and unheard.

More noticeable than Meliora's shock was her relief, the *ding* of a reached conclusion. She thought this was the reason Alikar was annoyed with her. "I'm sorry," she said warmly. "I know I can be bossy. It's because I want to help."

"You make everything worse," he said.

Meliora's relief faltered.

"Sometimes," Alikar added, but Meliora wiped at the kallumberry's sticky residue and didn't glance upward again.

Alikar watched her, frowning, then rested his head on the wall with a dull *thunk.*

Violet knew this squabble was tame compared to the one to come. Because Meliora was wrong: Alikar wasn't mad about her bossiness. The truth would come out. Violet could see it pushing against Alikar's last vestiges of self-control. And when it finally erupted, she doubted either one would bounce back.

Meliora fell asleep some minutes later, and Alikar's eyelids began staggering. Violet guessed they'd all be asleep soon. But what if they slept too long and missed the warning signs for the waterfall?

"We should lower the anchor." Her voice sounded dimmer without sunlight.

Alikar ignored her.

"Alikar."

He inhaled, fidgeting with his cord. "What?"

"We need to rest. We'll drop anchor and continue after we've slept."

She counted on him disregarding her advice and had already planned on waiting twenty seconds before she lowered it herself.

Sixteen . . . seventeen . . .

Alikar rotated the anchor rod. Violet felt the moment the anchor dug into the lake bed. Their pod reeled back. Meliora mumbled something in Greek. Then Alikar sat, arms crossed.

"Will it—"

"*Ayo.*"

"—hold?" Violet swallowed.

The three of them barely fit on the floor. There was no way to avoid touching feet. She pulled her legs to her chest and found Alikar watching her. The faint, yellowish lighting made him look ill. But the bloodshot veins in his eyes were vibrant.

"He would have cried, had it been you," he said quietly.

Violet's lips parted. Something tightened in her stomach, a knot she'd forgotten about. A question formed, several of them. She struggled to select the right one.

But he'd already turned his head. In another minute, his breathing thickened with sleep.

Crammed in a floating pod with people she'd touch no matter what way she turned, Violet might as well have been the only one for how alone she felt. She'd prepared herself for some cutting remark about her dependency on Alikar's liryn. That would have been easier to endure.

Alikar's and Meliora's breathing had long mingled into one rhythm before Violet managed to fall asleep.

S HE AWOKE RANDOMLY. VIOLET opened her eyes to the same dim room, not knowing if she'd slept for hours or minutes. Every nerve in her neck ached, and she felt sticky with sweat.

She shifted, bumping Meliora. The latter didn't wake. Neither did Alikar, who'd slumped against Meliora's shoulder. In sleep he was no longer bitter or angry, but just a boy.

His words wandered through her, seeking validation. How could he know whether or not Kelispar would have mourned her death? The confusion and frustration of it all brought her fully awake. Violet tried getting comfortable but failed. In all her scooting and adjusting, it took some time for her body to register that the rocking had increased. They shouldn't have been moving this much, even with the current flowing around them. Had the anchor disengaged?

Violet's muscles twinged as she stood. One-handedly balancing on the wall, she touched the anchor rod. Turning it clockwise lowered the anchor. But should she risk adjusting it if nothing was wrong? What if she broke it?

A croaky rebuke echoed in her memories like a grandfather's wisdom. *"When in doubt,"* King Asbed of Bar'Talian had told her, *"it is honorable to ask for help."*

Steeling herself, she prodded Alikar's elbow. His snoring continued. It took a full shoulder shaking before his head snapped up.

"*Ench?*" he mumbled.

"I think the anchor—"

The rest got shoved back into Violet's throat as the pod spun and flung her into him.

Meliora awoke with a cry. Violet fumbled to detach herself from Alikar. Fortunately, the pod swiveled again, scattering them. Alikar crawled along the floor and reached for the rod.

It snapped off.

He gaped at the useless tool in horror. Violet's inquiry was lost as the rocking spilled her to the opposite wall. This time, she braced her palms and heels on the floor and willed to stay still.

Alikar and Meliora had a rapid-fire conversation in Faartunga. Violet understood the words *water* and *swift*.

He glanced at Violet. "*Kann þú sundr?*"

She recognized "can" and "you." "*Ek skil þat eigi*," she said, admitting that she didn't understand.

Alikar rolled his eyes. "Can you swim?"

That didn't sound promising. "Yes," she said. "What's happening?"

"We're in the rapids." Meliora, hand to her forehead, looked one tumble away from vomiting. "The anchor didn't—" The pod lurched. She closed her eyes, exhaled, and wheezed, "Waterfall."

"I assume this pod can't survive the drop," Violet said, keeping her voice steady.

"You assume correctly." Alikar tossed the broken rod aside.

"Then we should use the buoyancy rod."

"Obviously. But disembarking from a moving boat is nothing like disembarking from an anchored one."

"Have you ever tried?" Meliora said.

"Can't say that I have, no."

"It might be as easy as spelling." She grinned at Alikar through her fingers.

Violet didn't think now was the time for humor, especially with Alikar. But, surprisingly, his lips twitched.

"You know I'm terrible at spelling," he said.

"Pretend it's drawing then."

A lightness overtook some of Alikar's gloom. Violet could almost imagine he was the Alikar from two days ago. Then he stood, regathering the storm clouds. "Fine," he said, and cranked the buoyancy rod.

Violet didn't feel the change as much as she saw it. The dark world outside began to brighten. Lumps became fish; waving shadows became seaweed; the haze became grains of dirt. The layers grew clearer, until she could make out bubbles and froth and chunks of ice. Their pod broke through the surface.

The rushing lake, clear in morning sunlight, couldn't be focused on for too long; their pod was spinning, blurring their surroundings, and giving Violet's stomach the unpleasant sensation that it was being compressed into a tube. She gritted her teeth as they smacked into a boulder and spun in the opposite direction. This was like being on a water park ride, only without a seatbelt—and with a deadly drop at the end.

Alikar staggered, hands on the ceiling.

"Sit down," Meliora told him.

"I need to open the roof."

"No, you need—" Meliora stopped, then turned to Violet. "Let's secure his legs," she said.

They gripped his ankles.

"*Ephpheta*," Alikar said.

The domed ceiling vanished. Wind and water sprayed Violet's face. The rushing roar overwhelmed her senses; she didn't notice Alikar was gone until she registered Meliora's shouting and the emptiness between her palms.

She opened her eyes to the chaotic water. Beyond the droplets and foam, she caught sight of Alikar clinging to a boulder. He was safe. Meanwhile, Violet had to plan her own escape. There were countless boulders within reach. She snatched at one and missed, then tried again. Her fingers gripped the wet and slimy stone. Their pod jerked to a halt, though Violet's hold was already weakening as the cold and the current fought her.

"Go!" she said.

Meliora clambered out and grabbed Violet's wrists. She hoisted herself onto the boulder just as the current whisked the pod away. Violet staggered to her feet and surveyed the lake.

Every peak in the water melted as soon as she spied it, blending with another. Endless churning stretched—until it didn't. She saw clouds and mist. The waterfall. It had already swallowed the pod.

Meliora called out, pointing. Up the bank, a wall of trees snagged the eye like a burst of color on a white canvas. Packed brown snow covered the bank and came to a stop before the forest. Golden plant life grew in clumps, dusting the tree trunks to form a landscape of amber. Violet hadn't realized the title of the forest was literal. Somewhere in all that yellow waited the gate pendant.

The path home.

They picked their way across the boulders and hopped onto the bank. There, they waited for Alikar to meet them. But he was still standing on his boulder, halfway across the lake.

"I will take my leave now," he called.

Though Violet had known he'd go, the reality came unexpectedly, like he'd announced his plans to become king. It'd be a relief to escape his moodiness, but communication would be harder. Yet that, too, would be a relief. Violet disliked being so dependent on him.

She'd thought Meliora had resigned herself to Alikar's leaving, but the crossed arms and defiant mouth said otherwise. "Say I'm bossy," she said, "but you aren't leaving."

"Yes I am."

"No you're not. You're nowhere near Muratsan Manor, with no means of affording a wagon."

"I'll walk," he said.

"That's absurd. Get over here, now."

With every command, Violet could see Alikar's face darkening, the way a storm cloud does before it unleashes.

"Stop controlling me," he said.

"Sometimes I *do* know best, Alikar."

"Do you?" he said through locked teeth.

Violet wanted to warn Meliora to quit before the lightning struck, but her throat felt dry, her tongue tacky.

"Yes," Meliora said. "We're days away from Vaspurakan, you're poorly dressed, and you're recognizable."

"I don't care."

"Well I do. Get off that boulder, Alikar, before I—"

"You were his crown!" Alikar's shout dissipated into the water's roar.

Violet wanted to vanish into the forest. By some horrible turn of events, she couldn't move.

Meliora sucked in. Her face was a statue's, shaped by horror.

"He told me as soon as you denied him that he knew. He wept. I never saw him cry, not since our parents' funeral. But he . . . He knew you loved him, that it didn't matter, that he would watch you love another. That the pain would never dull. Always raw. Always present. Inescapable. And do you know what his conclusion was?" Alikar's face twisted with a forced smile. "Peace."

Kelispar had told Violet as much. That knowledge gnawed on Violet's conscience. Meliora didn't deserve this attack.

"You're not being fair," Violet said. "Kelispar wouldn't want you to blame her."

Alikar's head swiveled so fast, his ponytail lashed his cheek. "How dare you speak his name? You, who cared nothing for him, for any of them, who watched them all die and didn't blink. Do you know what Tolian's prophecy calls you? *'Iron heart.'* I'm surprised it references a heart at all, as yours appears to be lacking."

Violet stood like a wall. She'd never felt such a tight, painful ache of shame. Of helplessness. Stuck inside a personality that refused to cooperate. Unconsciously, she squeezed her necklace. Oliver's pendant pricked her palm.

He thought she was a robot too.

Meliora stirred to life with two furled fists. "You cruel boy. I don't even recognize you. Kelispar would be ashamed."

Alikar flinched. An odd expression pinched his features. Maybe it was remorse. Or maybe he was too lost to his grief to care about anyone's feelings but his own.

"Go." Meliora's voice broke. "Violet and I will keep fighting for the cause your brother died for. You're welcome to join us when you finally realize that you're not the only person in this realm who matters." She turned around and walked away from the lake.

Violet turned too, catching up to Meliora. They left the lake behind and entered the Amber Forest. Violet didn't mentally argue with *what-ifs?* or *maybes*. Alikar wouldn't follow them.

A crackly crash made them jump. They spun around. A branch rolled on the ground, causing a flutter of fleeing critters. It had only been a tree. Not Alikar, hurrying to catch up.

Meliora stared at his empty boulder a long moment. Then continued on.

The Amber Forest, on a day that wasn't today, would've stunned Violet. The air smelled of syrup and incense, which calmed her nerves. Wind tossed gossamer golden vines—some leafy, others moist as dripping sap. Bright lichen smothered the trees, giving the bark the overall appearance of a fuzzy caterpillar. In every spot the sunlight reached, the amber growth turned hazy.

Fairy dust, June would've said.

Pollen, Violet would've argued.

Meliora's pace was chaotic, making it difficult to judge whether she knew where she was headed. She'd just learned she was the unintentional cause of Kelispar's suffering. That was almost its own crown. Violet wanted to say something comforting, but the language barrier kept her quiet. Why would Meliora appreciate the awkward attempts of a stranger, anyway?

Lifeless. Even the prophecy said so.

When they came to a wall of dried amber, Meliora paused. Fifteen feet away, a stag sniffed the ground. His coat must have been brown at some point, but yellow flecks covered him like shag. They crouched and waited for him to move on.

A twig behind them snapped. The stag sprinted off. Violet flinched, then froze when something cold prodded the back of her skull.

"*Nie ruszaj się*," a male voice spoke.

Even without any idea what he'd said, Violet knew they were in trouble.

CHAPTER TWENTY

"And we can't forget Yakiv's most infamous victim, that Piastan cord trader. Bartosz Mieszko stole something like 600 cords and supplied most of the Piast underworld. Yakiv had Mieszko publicly hung, then quartered. I heard his dame and boy were made to watch the whole bloody scene." – *Daily Converse*, gray pearl

"J AREK!" MELIORA ROSE.

"Go," Jarek said, in English now. "I'll find you."

Violet grimaced as he pressed the object firmer against her head.

"What are you doing?" Meliora said. "Where did you get that gauntlet?"

"Go," he repeated.

"Not until you stop pointing that at her."

"I can't. She's a Terlion spy."

Not this again. And how did he know she was from Terlian?

"You listened to the Separatist pearls." Meliora groaned. "You know those aren't trustworthy! It wasn't her. One of the monarch's attendants betrayed them."

Jarek wasn't convinced. Violet grimaced again.

"Put your arm down," Meliora said.

"I thought you were dead." His voice cracked, and he sounded less like the suspicious Jarek Violet was picturing and more like an uncertain boy. "The pearls said no survivors except some children and Nazeli."

"The monarchs didn't want whoever betrayed them to realize we're alive."

"Why didn't you contact me?"

"I had no means to."

Violet, still kneeling with that precarious feeling on her head, wished they would settle their disagreement soon.

"Look at me, Jarek," Meliora whispered.

The pause that followed was like a held breath. Then, the pressure disappeared, and Violet was free to move. She refrained, letting them have a private reunion. It was a good thing Alikar wasn't here. Kelispar's competition would have suffered a blow on the head, courtesy of the nearest heavy object.

Violet gave Meliora and Jarek ten seconds before turning around. They were still hugging, his Advocate cord sandwiched between them. The sight pulled Violet's loyalty in two opposing directions. After everything, Meliora deserved Jarek's comfort and care. But Jarek wasn't Kelispar.

Now you're being as ridiculously obstinate as Alikar.

"He killed them." Meliora clutched the front of Jarek's jacket. "The rest burned in the f–fire. Even the . . . children."

Jarek rubbed her back with one hand. The other was too busy clenching and curling.

"He wants the gate pendant," Meliora whispered. "So I thought, maybe you're right and that's what my purpose is. Is that why you're here?"

"I thought it would take me to her." Jarek scrutinized Violet. Dirt powdered his stubble. "How do you know she's not the traitor?"

"I told you," Meliora said. "Terlian is dying. There's no liryn."

"According to a Terlion."

"I trust her."

"You trust everyone."

"Have I made a poor choice yet?" Meliora's question lilted, and Jarek went quiet.

She must have told him about Violet's identity. Then she *had* been on the phone with him that night—or Bar'Talian's version of phones. He'd heard about the Hasteins' murders, and he'd suspected the Terlion.

Wait. Jarek had seen Violet before . . . wearing Kelispar's scarf, which she'd removed before any of the monarchs' attendants might have seen her. "You're the one who reported I had something to do with it," Violet said. "You gave the description of me."

"You didn't," Meliora said, and when he failed to defend himself, she added, "Jarek!"

"What was I supposed to do?" he said, and Violet bit her tongue to avoid informing him that he could have done any number of things other than broadcast to millions of people that she was a murderer.

"Violet was almost interrogated by a Goldentongue because of that," Meliora said, looking appropriately annoyed on Violet's behalf.

"That would've been useful. We know nothing about Terlian," he said with such Eliathor-like suspicion that Violet thought maybe they'd have gotten along after all.

Violet longed to build up her defense. The monarchs trusted her; Lady Basilia trusted her; Violet was sixty-three inches tall and more likely to knock over a cup than kill three sword-wielding Vikings.

"Next time," Meliora said, "trust me instead." She gave him a smile probably meant to look teasing, but her trembling mouth wouldn't cooperate.

Jarek's stoniness crumbled. He pulled her close again, chin on her hair. "I'm so sorry about your family." He absently squeezed the tip of her braid. "We'll find Stefanos and make him wish we hadn't. I swear it."

Meliora said nothing. Neither did Violet, watching Jarek's angry hand.

Finally, he eased her back, playing with her braid. "Tell us where to go," he said.

Meliora nodded. She dried her cheeks, letting composure overcome the remainder of her grief. "We need to find the tree where my parents first met," she said.

They set off, Violet clambering over the hedge first. The forest collected their crunching and cracking in a bubble; she couldn't hear much beyond it, not a bird or a squirrel. If there were even squirrels on Bar'Talian.

Jarek maintained a distance of no more than one foot from Meliora, like she'd vanish if he got too far away. "Sorry for reporting you." He glanced at Violet sidelong. "I thought it made sense."

She organized her opinions of him. Jarek was unpolished, but he wasn't unkind. Meliora liked him, and that counted for a lot. And ultimately, Jarek cared about Meliora. That was why he'd reported Violet. She couldn't blame him for being cautious.

"It's all right," she said.

"I know what it's like. To be wrongly accused, a notorious name over your head. It's a good thing you're going back to Terlian." He didn't offer more, and Violet didn't ask.

"I need a birds-eye view." Meliora halted. "We're looking for a field. My mother came here, to Bar'Talian, for Aunt Basilia's wedding. She'd always wanted to see the Amber Forest; Seers are drawn to gold. Pappa had the same idea. They met by this ancient, massive tree. Aunt Basilia showed me. Years ago. He would've hidden it there."

She wanted to climb for a better view. Jarek's Advocate range wasn't far; Meliora's English slipped into Greek a few branches up. When she called down her verdict from the topmost branch, Violet assumed she'd spotted the field. As Meliora descended, Violet awaited the invisible line that indicated Jarek's range. Was his shorter than Alikar's? If—

Something snapped. Meliora cried out. A branch plummeted, Meliora in its wake.

Violet's heart lurched with panic. Jarek, on the other hand, closed his eyes and muttered.

Adrenaline spiked throughout Violet, a sudden steadiness of legs and a clarity that slowed the world. Meliora's descent looked crisp; Violet saw where her skirts fluttered and curled in the wind. She could imagine Meliora's pulse, though maybe that was her own. Even her lungs drew in heartier breaths.

Just as Violet thought she had to try *something,* even if that meant attempting to catch her, Meliora landed on her feet, wide-eyed but uninjured. Violet hurried to her aid, moving too fast. Suddenly she was past Meliora, one hand extended to steady a tree instead. Violet turned, confused. The world was vivid, as if she wore binoculars. Too many sounds—leaves drifting, forest creatures scuttling, her own breathing—filled her ears, yet each was distinct, none of them overwhelming.

"Are you okay?" Violet asked, then winced. She hadn't intended to shout.

Meliora was studying Jarek. Violet could make out each bristle in his almost-stubble. Meliora spoke, Greek so clear Violet noted nuances in pronunciation she hadn't before.

Jarek trembled, tiny pulses along his jaw. How could she see that? He muttered again, and this time Violet could hear it. "*Oshapel.*"

Adrenaline seeped from her. Sounds hushed. The world muted and dulled. She moved, and her legs felt cumbersome.

"Are you hurt?" Jarek asked Meliora.

"Jarek," she whispered.

His eyes tightened, until Violet wondered how he could see. She shifted, snapping a pine cone. Her thoughts worked sluggishly; she couldn't understand why Meliora's expression had scrunched like a lonely child's.

"I landed on my feet," Meliora said. "It didn't even hurt."

Jarek said nothing.

"Please tell me there's another reason. Please."

The word made him shudder.

"Do you"—Meliora swallowed—"have a Pillar cord?"

A Pillar cord. That would explain Violet's adrenaline rush.

Slowly, she replayed the past minute. Jarek hadn't run to catch Meliora. Instead, he'd stood there, muttering. Pillar liryn was of *basareth*, of the body. It required a verbal ritual, like when the Balm healed Violet.

Jarek didn't defend himself. He'd have no success. Both Violet and Meliora had felt that invigoration, as if they could glide to the heights of the forest. He'd outed himself to protect Meliora. But a protective cord thief was still a thief.

"I don't understand." Meliora's lips barely moved. "How long?"

When he remained quiet, Violet figured he'd make Meliora do all the guesswork. Then, he sighed, answering in the direction of the branches. "A while."

"Where did you find it?"

Jarek returned to his stone-silence. He could have passed for a tree in a windless landscape, if trees could glare.

"You *stole* it?" Meliora staggered back.

Jarek's eyes blazed with sudden indignation. "He's in a coma. He can't feel anything."

"Maybe the coma is his crown!"

"Maybe liryn's not supposed to have crowns!"

"So you support Malokki."

"He makes more sense than the monarchs."

Meliora shook her head. "Liryn isn't a right. It's a sacrifice."

"It doesn't have to be," he said.

"I see. And are you a Separatist too, in addition to being a cord thief and a Hand?"

"I don't know."

Jarek let that hang like a tired vine. Violet suspected he'd forgotten she was there. They probably both had.

"Get rid of it," Meliora said, her words as unyielding as wind.

"You would've died."

"Get. Rid. Of. It."

He wouldn't blink.

"On second thought," Meliora said, "give it to me. It needs to be returned to its rightful owner." She splayed her upturned palm.

He touched his collar. A finger dipped beneath his jacket. He felt around, flinched, hesitated, pulled out his hand, lowered his arm. And did nothing.

"Jarek," Meliora said.

"I'll wear it for now. I won't use it."

"I don't trust you." Meliora stepped closer, hand waiting.

Relenting the cord was the simplest way to diffuse the situation. The damage had been done. But he stood there, unnecessarily stubborn. All it took was one reach beneath his shirt, one yank, and the guilty cord would be exposed. Meliora already knew it was there. Why was he holding on?

Violet could've kept her mouth shut. She nearly did. But Meliora deserved the truth.

"He has another cord," she said.

Not a hint of Jarek's expression changed. Violet was disappointed. She would've rather been wrong.

"Jarek." Meliora barely got the word out. Violet hated to see the betrayal overwhelming her face because, even after the past forty-eight hours, Meliora still had people to lose. "Are you even an Advocate?"

He gave up the defiance and spoke like a flattened tire. "I applied. They rejected me. Because of my pa. I had no choice."

"You always had a choice. You don't need liryn."

"I—" He faltered. "I needed to talk to you."

"Then you should have learned Greek. I defended you. Eliathor told me not to associate with you. He thought the students would bully me too. But I didn't care. I wanted to help."

Jarek reared up, ditching the guilt and letting anger foment. "I never asked to be your project. That's on you, Meliora. Always looking for someone to fix. Sorry to disappoint."

"I'm sorry too."

He turned his head, eyes brushing over Violet without any sign that he'd registered her.

A cord thief, and of multiple cords. Violet never would have accused him of it. He didn't seem the type, nothing like the cruel, unfeeling cord thief on *The Vagabond*.

"I was Kelispar's crown," Meliora said in a waif-like voice, competing with the air for stillness. "The last day of his life, he suffered—for me. He told me he would pray for my happiness with you. *You*, who walk around with someone else's pain and don't care. You disgust me." Her tone hardened.

So did Jarek's face. "You should have told him yes."

"I'll regret that all my life."

What seemed like every bit of Jarek's pent-up emotions came loose in an unbroken stream of bitterness. "You're just like every other Unionist, judgmental and proud, thinking yourself better because your political views have the favor of the monarchs. Open your pretty little eyes, Meliora. The monarchs hate you. Your own emperors would have left you an orphan if

Lord Muratsan hadn't intervened. Your skulking King Giannis is the reason hunters like Yakiv exist. If Seers would do their job, I wouldn't get the chance to steal." He kicked some leaves; they flared up and fluttered. "Everything's broken. The Lykill isn't going to fix it. Nothing can, not when our own leaders care more for their comfort than their clan. We're forsaken." Jarek's voice cracked. He glared at his second-hand shoes.

Meliora looked wholly unmoved, like she'd heard nothing. "You can have this back. You probably stole this too." She ripped off her bracelet and threw it at his face. He let it bounce off his chin. "Don't speak to me again, unless it's in Greek."

They stood there: Jarek seething, Meliora deflating.

Without a word, he turned. He walked into the afternoon haze, leaving Violet, Meliora, and a silver bracelet that not even the dirt wanted.

Violet waited for Meliora to inhale through it; to straighten her shoulders, tell Violet they had to keep going, and start walking. She'd treat Jarek's betrayal the same way she'd treated Alikar's farewell.

But determination was nonexistent in Meliora's gaze. She stared at nothing, said nothing. Perhaps she needed a moment. Violet could give her that.

Gold sunlight tinted the air, hugging branches and fogging the sparse patches of sky visible overhead. Not a breeze danced. The trees were frozen too. All felt melancholic and weary. Even the smell of sap took on a tired scent, like a candle meant to add cheer to a funeral parlor and failing horribly.

Meliora still didn't move.

"Meliora?" Violet said.

No reaction to that.

As the despondency lengthened, Violet realized she'd have to step in. They had to keep going. She had to remind Meliora that she still had to find her purpose here. Not that Violet could say much, with their Advocate gone. *Fake* Advocate. All she could do was the thing she was least comfortable doing.

Anxious to get this over with, Violet touched Meliora's shoulder. Awkwardly, she patted Meliora's back, trying not to think about all the times she'd comforted June this poorly.

Iron heart.

If only Alikar had never said that.

"Lykill," she said.

Meliora's head lifted. Slowly, resolution dripped into her stare. "Lykill," she said, nodding. "*Efcharisto.*"

Thank you. Violet recognized that. "Um," she said. "*Pojaluysta.*" Why was she speaking Russian? It had been the first language to react.

But Meliora's nose crinkled with effort. "*Uhmpojalusta?*" she dutifully repeated.

"Oh. No. That's, well—" She stopped, defeated.

Fortunately, Meliora didn't bother imitating Violet's spluttering. After adjusting her braid, she set off.

As Violet made to follow, something teased from behind, the sensation of forgetting. Her glance fell on Meliora's discarded bracelet. For good reason, Meliora wanted nothing to do with it. But she might not always feel that way.

After checking that Meliora wasn't paying attention, Violet pocketed the bracelet. Then she caught up.

The sun dipped with unpleasant swiftness; it couldn't have been that late. They had to slow, coordinating through a world of dusty light. Initially Violet relied on Meliora to lead, but either Meliora walked too slow or Violet too fast; every couple minutes Violet retook the lead. Trying not to became tricky, like fighting a current.

Jarek was long gone when the ground leveled out, meeting an invisible barrier where every tree and shrubbery stopped, making way for a clearing the size of half a football field. Its solitary tree was so vast and trailing that Violet wondered if it was several trees grafted together. Many of its dead branches touched the ground, creeping like the legs of an octopus. It must have been the branches propping the tree up; its trunk was so rotted, its bark so withered, that she was surprised it hadn't caved in.

Meliora's expression looked confused. She eyed the dead tree distastefully.

"This?" Violet gestured.

Meliora nodded.

Then the gate pendant was close, if Meliora's theory was correct. Violet sorely hoped it was, and not just because she cared about healing Earth. What would Meliora have if this plan let her down, too?

They gathered at the trunk. Violet went left, losing sight of Meliora as the tree's thick girth separated them. One could easily investigate it for an hour.

Meliora's father couldn't have hidden the pendant somewhere impossible to access. Yet he'd hidden it well enough that no one had found it in twenty years. Unless someone had and just didn't know how to use it. Violet dismissed that idea for now.

Fa had found Halfdan in February, a month from now. If Bar'Talian's seasons lasted the same duration as Earth's, she could assume the Amber Forest would still be in winter in another month. Meliora's father would've struggled to hide the pendant in a hard-packed earth. Of course, Violet didn't know if Arat lived in a perpetual winter or if spring would come next week. But for now, she assumed he hadn't buried it. It was probably somewhere in the trunk or in one of the branches.

Meliora spoke and pointed to the trunk. Then she moved toward a grounded branch and began patting it. The shadows made Meliora's eagerness harder to see, but Violet heard it in her quickened breaths.

Given the knuckled roots of the trunk, Violet progressed slowly. The dead tree put off a sickly sweet scent that made her nose burn. Soon her palms had collected residue, and her fingertips were cold, and she'd gotten over the eeriness of reaching into black orifices where Bar'Talion bugs lived.

A twig fell in Violet's hair. She used a knobby protrusion to scrub sap off her palms, then continued sideways. However, she was struck with the sensation of having given up a problem too soon. She was working too hastily.

No, I know I searched every crack.

Grasping the knot for balance, she scooted along the trunk. The unsatisfied feeling lingered. With a sigh, she surveyed the bark again. There was nothing unique about this section compared to the dozens of other holes and gnarls. Yet the knot caught her eye. Violet felt around it. The center was slightly indented and supple. It was possible that new bark had grown around what could have been a hollow knot twenty years ago.

New bark? This tree is dead.

Violet scratched at the softer bark. Her nails dug like a butter knife in tough steak. Soon the knot resembled a puckered wound. Violet wedged her fingers inside, not expecting much. So she was startled when her fingers brushed something stiff as cardboard. She tugged, and it resisted. Firmly, Violet yanked. Out came fabric that dirt, sap, and time had weathered. It was tied, keeping whatever it hid a secret. Two recognizable letters were embroidered in faded red: *N.M.*

Niall Mykaois.

"Meliora," Violet called over the tickle of nerves in her throat. It was here. Unless she was being overzealous, and someone had shoved a handkerchief full of rocks into a tree hole and forgotten about it.

Meliora was at Violet's side in a moment. They knocked heads as they pored over it. Meliora inquired in Greek.

"I don't know." Violet steadied her breathing. Perhaps this was nothing. Or perhaps this was what humanity had hunted for over a thousand years.

Meliora struggled to open the knot and eventually poked a hole in the material. She dug the hole open. Contrasted against the dirtied fabric was a triangle pendant, identical to the two in Helheim. It was stark white, imprinted with Ókunnigr runes.

One third of the Lykill lay in Violet's palm.

They shared a reverential silence. They had the pendant, the means of opening a gate to the other two. The means of Violet's return home, of Earth's healing. The solution had arrived easily.

But, when she thought of the Hasteins, she knew that finding this hadn't been an easy thing at all. People had died for this tiny triangle.

In the shadows of late afternoon, the pendant managed to shine, a clean mark on a blemished landscape. Meliora picked it up gingerly, the way one handles glass.

A rising sensation of dread dried out Violet's mouth. How, exactly, did the pendant open gates? Both Chief Halfdan and Meliora's father died shortly after using this. Meliora's father killed himself, but . . .

I'm being irrational. The pendant was part of the Lykill, and the Lykill meant healing. Just because Fa hadn't paid the pendants any mind didn't mean he shouldn't have.

"*Sto Terlian?*" Meliora said.

Violet nodded. Did Meliora merely have to think of Terlian as she opened the gate? It wasn't as if she could visualize somewhere she'd never seen.

Meliora's forehead wrinkled. Violet's nerves betrayed her unease. But this was what was supposed to happen.

"*Esh losa . . .*" Meliora mouthed the rest, then said, in a gentle cadence, the words her mother had given her, "*Esh losa thul, o maris, shema hach ull nad haeem fral.*" The words reminded Violet of Fa's deathbed poem, the sílfar welding ritual. It was Ókunnigr, beautifully ethereal in Meliora's accent.

A light the size of a fist materialized beside them, rapidly spiraling outward, collecting gold dust as it formed. The pulsing cloud grew to Meliora's height, a splash of brightness on the tree. The gate gently pulsed, silent and expectant, just like the one in Helheim.

It worked.

Meliora beamed at Violet. Her hopeful spirit had returned. She reached for the glow.

And the ground beneath them revolted.

Violet teetered. Meliora cried out. The tree cracked and shook, spewing splinters. Wind threw Violet and Meliora like two pebbles. Violet crashed onto a quaking ground, scoring her back on stiff earth. Her hat flew free. She clamped down on her skirt and breathed in cold, relentless wind.

The tree shed limbs as if an invisible giant hacked them off. In eerie, stilted animation, the trunk split open, sawed in half by that invisible hand. Golden leaves made chaotic whirlpools. Only the gate, hovering where the branch had been, kept its unmoving vigil.

The hurricane settled all at once. Violet's clothes went limp. Her hair rested on her cheeks. The ground stopped moving, and she could feel her aches and bruises.

Across the path of debris, the gate glowed by the carved-open trunk. The earth had swallowed several feet of the tree. Few branches remained intact. Dirt had been ripped up, as if an army of badgers had tunneled a circle around the gate, which stood in the epicenter of an eerily exact circumference of destruction. Outside the circle, the ground was untouched.

In the quiet, Violet's breathing wasn't the only rasp. She checked on Meliora, sprawled a few feet away. Her braid had collected splinters. A sliver of bark protruded from her forehead, causing a red dribble, but Meliora was preoccupied by her hand—by the white fingers, as if she'd dipped them in paint. She spit and vigorously scrubbed. The white remained, stark against her olive hue. The sight was even more disturbing than the dead tree. Using the pendant had stained Meliora's skin, which could only mean one thing.

Meliora wasn't a descendant.

Violet couldn't fight back a shiver. Stolen cords didn't punish thieves, but the Lykill did.

The gate beamed on them, unnaturally bright. What were they supposed to do now? They couldn't enter the gate; it might cause an earthquake on Terlian, or worse. Their only option was to deliver the pendant to the monarchs.

What was the point, then? Why had Meliora's mother given her daughter those cryptic words about finding her purpose here? Everything about this felt wrong, not a triumphant success but an unfortunate accident. Violet hadn't liked the idea of traveling to the Amber Forest against Lady Basilia's idea, but she'd trusted Meliora's plan. And indeed, it had worked. They had the gate pendant. But relief was hollow, and triumph nonexistent.

Violet rose, wincing. The bulky clothes had padded her fall, but she still ached. Her beanie lay in the circle of dead ground by the gate, which she'd rather avoid.

But it isn't as if the gate is evil. It was created by the Lykill.

Violet didn't know what to think.

"Meliora," she said.

In a crumbled posture, Meliora stared at her white hand. Violet called her name again. Meliora gave no sign she'd heard, so Violet crouched to her level. The grit, the spark of resolve after Jarek's betrayal, was absent from Meliora's face. Faint light from stars and moons showed her sagging shoulders, her limp braid, her vacant gaze.

"It's . . . it will be okay." Violet touched Meliora's elbow.

No answer.

This pendant had been Meliora's last grasp at hope. That had been killed, too.

"Meliora?" Violet tried again. "We need to go. Go. *Ire?*" She gave a stab at Latin. *"Imus. Nunc. Asbed et Nora. Intellegis?"*

None of it made an impression.

"Please," Violet whispered.

A tear, glinting in the gate's light, tread down Meliora's cheek.

Violet closed her eyes. She couldn't remember making a conscious decision, but she'd come to rely on Meliora. In truth, there wasn't anyone Violet relied on anymore—not carefree June, and certainly not Oliver. Once upon a time, she'd depended on Fa, but for years, Violet had trusted only herself. For a few days, she'd trusted Meliora. Had it been friendship?

If only Alikar were here. He would have dropped his frustration the moment he realized Meliora needed him. He'd make some joke, or annoy Meliora until she laughed. That had been his role in the quartet. Violet understood, now that it was gone.

The head was gone. The shield was gone. The soul had burnt itself out, and the heart had broken too many times. All that was left was Violet, the cold carcass.

She hoisted Meliora up, hating the doll-like compliance, and took Meliora with her as she scanned the ground for the pendant. It lay in the dead grass, near her hat. She moved, then stiffened when a male voice spoke out of the night.

"Seems I have business with one of you. That's what my pearls tell me, see."

Dread wrapped Violet like a straitjacket. Turning around to verify her suspicion was pointless. Violet knew who it was, as firmly as she knew they were trapped.

Yakiv Stefanos was here.

CHAPTER TWENTY-ONE

"In the time of great peace, the royal son and daughter will rebel. A rift will sever the unity. Terlian will be overthrown. But what was stirred can be stilled. First, the man who finds must hand over that which is not his to hold. Second, the man of peace must sow discord. Third, the seam must split. Then will come the child of bane to guide the Lykill to its resting place. The bane will find it between the trees. Only then can peace prevail. And Terlian will sail calm waters once more."

- Prophecy of Julian

P ERHAPS THEY WERE NAÏVE for not predicting he'd come here. Yakiv had wondered about the forest's connection to the gate pendant, which lay a foot from Violet, winking under two moons and the gate's light.

As twigs and dead leaves crackled, indicating multiple footsteps, Violet thumbed through their options. They could grab the pendant and run, but Yakiv had long-range weapons. That left staying put, because fighting wasn't an option. Not when she had no defenses, no strength, not even the ability to speak to Yakiv in his own language.

"I told us to come here," Meliora mumbled, slack-shouldered and vacant.

Violet could focus on nothing but Yakiv. He must have heard the earthquake. She slid one foot over the pendant.

When he neared, flanked by four allies, Violet could smell them. Musk mixed with dirt and some spicy scent that stung her nose. Kora the Goldentongue was there, along with an unfamiliar Advocate—the Hasteins had killed the other one—and the short man who wore a white cord, flame pendant. Then the man with a red cord, handsaw pendant. Yakiv's Pillar.

These were the people who'd killed the Hasteins.

Yakiv stopped at the gate. It glowed yellow on his front.

"Where's it go?" Kora called.

Had any of them ever seen a gate? Judging by their awe, Violet suspected not. She and Meliora might've been able to take advantage of their distraction. Gripping Meliora's arm, Violet inched toward the gap between Kora and the Advocate, scraping the pendant along the ground. They made it a couple feet before Yakiv noticed.

"Why has no one bound them?"

Violet pushed for Meliora to run, to no effect. Both their arms were yanked behind their backs by Kora and the Pillar. A cool, liquidy something enveloped Violet's wrists. She tried to shake it off, but her arms refused to move, bound together like roots. Arms pinned, Kora squeezing her elbows, Violet was going nowhere.

The short man—Boh, Violet remembered—watched the scuffle with the type of relish one finds on a bully. The Advocate, on the other hand, could've been mistaken for sleeping upright, his mouth hanging vacantly, his eyes glazed over. Violet remembered Kelispar's worry that the headache would one day turn him into this.

Yakiv reached a hand into the gate. It came out the other side.

"Is that supposed to happen?" Kora muttered.

"Never seen a gate, little girl?" Boh laughed.

Kora's hold on Violet tightened.

Yakiv walked into the glow. Violet held her breath. Meliora had intended to create a gate to Helheim. It was unclear whether she'd succeeded. Terlian was about to find out.

The tension was short-lived; Yakiv came through, just like his hand. The gate didn't lead anywhere.

"Broken," said Boh. Short and stubby, he looked too ordinary to belong to a band of Separatist murderers. But his appearance didn't matter so much as his liryn, whatever that was.

Yakiv turned. Shadowed, his stubble looked fuller, his eyes blacker, his wrinkles deeper. "Search them," he said.

"I'll do it!" Kora's hold loosened, but Yakiv shook his head.

"Let the men work, sweetmeat," Boh said.

The Pillar's guffaw had the unnatural pitch of someone trying too hard. It worked on Boh, whose face grew smug.

Kora's grip hardened again.

Violet and Meliora could do little but squirm as Boh emptied their pockets, rough and impolite. Focused on shielding the pendant, Violet tolerated his search distractedly. The pendant stood a chance.

Then, Boh knelt. He unzipped Violet's boots.

Violet held her balance as long as she could. In the end, it wasn't Boh who spotted the pendant. Yakiv came over and pushed Violet. She stumbled, dragging the pendant along. It gave her another second of ownership. Then Yakiv bent, grabbed Violet's ankle, and knocked her balance askance. Her awkwardly bound arms hit the earth. Yakiv scooped the pendant up.

Just like that.

"Can we see it?" Kora asked.

"Just don't touch it," Boh told her.

The others crowded Yakiv, except the Advocate, whose lackluster, comatose posture continued. Drool hung from his bottom lip.

As Kora *ooohed,* Boh greedily observed, the Pillar praised Yakiv as if congratulating a bruised and battered hero, and Yakiv emanated something uncomfortably close to pleasure, Violet measured the distance from here to the tree line. Yakiv had what he wanted. Violet and Meliora were of no use to him. He seemed more pragmatic than vengeful; he might simply walk away without further thought for his two captives.

Except Meliora was a cousin of the Hasteins. Not technically of Terlian's royal line, but her connection was enough to earn his hatred. And if he found out that Violet was one hundred percent Terlion . . .

"I'm no better than a cord thief," Meliora murmured to the air.

Violet forced herself to focus on Meliora. *I need to plan our escape*, the panic argued, while common sense replied that Yakiv would spot them running before they made it ten feet; that they were handcuffed and couldn't move quickly.

"We'll talk about it later," she whispered to Meliora. "How fast can—"

"I knew the truth. In my heart. I wanted to be useful. To help. But Alikar was right. I stain everything I touch, and it stains me."

Violet refrained from looking at Meliora's hand. "We need to run," she said, eying the Separatists.

"How's it work?" Boh was asking.

"A ritual," Yakiv said. So he understood that much. Did he know the words?

"Go, Violet." Meliora turned. Despair touched every vein in her eyes. "Please live. For your family. The prophecy. For Terlian." She finally moved, taking a stance in front of Violet, shielding her. "I'm so sorry," she whispered.

Violet stared at Meliora's shaking hands, captured behind her waist. She was trying to give Violet a chance. Violet was the one who had to fulfill the prophecy. Already, she'd done half her job.

But if she was meant to restore the Lykill, that meant she'd get the pendant from Yakiv. Somehow. Maybe that moment wasn't now. Now, she needed to escape, and she wasn't leaving Meliora behind.

She turned, groping behind for Meliora's arm. Once she had a hold, she ran. A whole scrap of treeless, open land divided them from the cover of the forest. But she'd try.

"Look," came Yakiv's calm voice. That's all he said.

Violet and Meliora were surrounded in seconds. Kora, Boh, and the Pillar dragged them back. Violet dug her heels to no avail. The Pillar wasn't even lending the Separatists his strength. Violet was just that pitiful, and Meliora wasn't resisting at all.

The Separatists threw them to the ground. Violet struggled to her feet, but Meliora stayed down.

Yakiv pocketed the pendant, nearing. Never had she met him face-to-face or felt those eyes on her. This close, he looked no older than forty, tan—though that was hard to gauge with the gate washing him out—wrinkled around the mouth, his beard more ash than charcoal. But his hair was fully black, as were the brows that came to points, putting a divot above his strong nose and giving him the expression of someone thinking. Calculating.

Violet could finally breathe when his attention moved to Meliora. "I recognize you. The niece." His head made a jab toward her hand. "That happen when you use it?"

Meliora's fluttering hair was the only response.

"Nothing to say." Yakiv gave her another beat to prove him wrong. His eyes were probing. Then indifferent. He shifted gears to Violet, weight relaxed on one leg, hand casual on the dagger at his belt. The one he'd used to slice off Lady Basilia's fingers. "And you," he said in that lazy accent. "Pearls say you're my accomplice, but I've never seen you a day. I want to know how it's come that you're mine."

Mine. The word carried a confidence that pricked Violet's own self-assurance.

"I'm not," she said.

"No. I don't think you are. But you're someone, see. I want to know who." He spoke so calmly, assuredly, as if he saw no reason why anyone would deny him. "I'll begin with first things. Your name."

Her name would mean nothing to him. Violet kept quiet, shifting closer to Meliora.

Yakiv would not blink. His unending patience rattled Violet. The sound of her silence grew obtrusively loud.

"Yakiv asked you to talk," Kora said.

", Kora. She will answer when she—" Yakiv stopped. His eyes went a little wide before they narrowed like lips locked tight. "How do they call you?" he said, and there was something less calm in his voice.

"I'll hook her." Kora came closer.

"Don't." Yakiv bit the word.

"I don't mind. Boh can judge."

"Orders don't come from you, sweetmeat," Boh said.

"I—"

"Enough." Yakiv rubbed his arm, exhaling.

Violet's gaze fell to his shifting feet. He seemed anxious all of a sudden.

"I'd rather you don't," he continued. "She's not worth the hurt."

"Haven't hooked since yesterday," Kora said.

"Brave girl." Boh smirked.

Kora stomped her foot.

"I'd hook her, if I could," the Pillar spoke up. Beneath his stringy, graying hair twitched a rabbit-like nervousness. "You know I would for you, Yakiv. You know it?"

"You'd let us gut you, Slav, wouldn't you?" Boh said.

Slav released his groveling laugh.

"Kora can hook, and I'll judge," Boh told Yakiv. "These loyalists rats aren't worth another centimeter, but I wanna know who she is, and I want the truth."

"Then do it," Yakiv said, sounding out every word with deliberate focus. "Quickly. Yank the girl and—and be done with it." He touched his brow, as if trying to push it into place.

Violet's mind stumbled over his last words. Did that mean . . . kill her?

"I'll do the Pretender first," Kora said.

"It won't work," Yakiv said. "Look at her eyes. Too much despair. Hook can't latch if there's nothing to grab." Now his speech was choppy and impatient. He twisted around and walked a few paces away. Violet wondered what had him rattled but didn't have the mental energy to care all that much.

Kora fiddled with the purple cord wrapping her arm as if rolling up her sleeves. She was going to make Violet talk. Foolishly, Violet tried covering her ears, but of course her bound hands didn't budge.

"Girl," Kora said, "look this way."

Violet focused on Kora's hook pendant, thinking hard. Liryn was stronger or weaker depending on the person. The Goldentongue on *The Vagabond* had been quick-witted and shrewd without the help of his cord, but nothing about Kora's manner was intimidating. Even the way she spoke was . . . well, she didn't boast of any obvious genius. Violet could outsmart her.

"Girl," Kora repeated. "Look at me."

"Goldentongue," Meliora spoke, her voice like one rising from a stupor. "Don't listen. She'll—"

"Someone gag the niece," Yakiv said, tossing something over his shoulder.

Violet moved in front of Meliora. The Pillar jostled her back while Boh scrounged through the little bag he'd caught. Out came what looked like plastic tongs, gripping a coin. Boh maneuvered the tongs until the coin touched Meliora's lips. The coin stuck, like he'd glued it there. Meliora contorted her mouth, but the coin didn't fall, and her lips refused to part.

"Tell Yakiv why your face showed up on the pearls," Kora said to Violet.

Kora's voice arrested Violet's attention. For a moment, she stared at the girl.

Tell Yakiv? Why would I do that?

Meliora made strained sounds that couldn't escape her lips.

There was something Violet was supposed to focus on. Her eyes returned to Kora's pendant. *She's a Goldentongue*, Violet remembered, like one recalling a snippet of a dream.

"It's a harmless question," Kora continued. Her voice grew smoother, less grating, reminiscent of a placid narrator. "There's no reason not to answer. Just tell us who you are, and we'll leave."

No, Yakiv would be far from content once he discovered Violet was a Terlion.

"If you don't answer," Kora said, "we'll be forced to hurt Meliora."

Violet's heart skipped, though Kora's tone had sounded far from menacing. She spoke conversationally, really. Almost pleasant. Violet didn't mind the sound of it so much.

"Think of it this way: The longer you hold out, the more desperate you'll become. You'll end up telling us more than you intend. You're better off giving less now than more later."

Kora made a valid point. If Violet answered on her own terms, before Yakiv set his Goldentongue on her, she stood a decent chance at giving Yakiv only the answers she wanted.

Something about that logic didn't sit right, but she found herself saying, "Jarek."

Meliora's unintelligible protests continued. She needn't have worried. Violet wouldn't reveal everything. She had this interrogation under control.

"Who?" Kora said, head politely tilted. Her left eye twitched.

"Meliora's friend. When he heard about the attack, he suspected me. So he described me to the . . . the people who make the pearls."

"Oh. I see." She nodded, then winced. "The one I followed. Are you aware he's a thief?" she asked Meliora as she massaged her own temples. "I saw three cords on him. That warrants a visit from Yakiv."

Meliora's straining quieted.

The one Kora followed?

"I'm curious why Jarek suspected you." Kora returned to Violet. "Are you a Separatist? Or a Hand?"

"No," Violet said.

"Then why?"

"Because of where I'm from."

"You need to tell us where that is, so Yakiv can understand."

Violet registered Kora's polite expression while simultaneously noting that Kora was gritting her teeth. In pain. The two images did not blend. Violet discarded the latter for the former.

Meliora called out again, muffled.

"Don't think about Meliora now," Kora said. "Tell us where you're from."

Violet's origin was her biggest secret, the one thing that could turn the tide in this conversation.

Kora inhaled, peeking at Violet through one squinted eye. A shrewd look, not a pained one. "Remember my advice. Give us a little at a time. You can be in control of this conversation. But you have to give just enough that we're placated."

Yes. Violet could answer indefinitely without giving Yakiv one hint. "California," she said.

"I haven't heard of 'California.' Is that in Arat?"

"No."

"Explain why Jarek associated you with Yakiv." Kora gripped her forehead with a trembling hand.

Violet's gaze slid to Kora's arm jewelry. Purple, almost like a liryn cord.

No. Kora wasn't wearing jewelry.

"Don't drag this out longer than necessary," Kora said. "We're nearly done. Where do you live?"

"California," Violet said.

"Where is that?"

"Near Mexico."

"And where is *that*?"

"Near Texas."

"Don't let her play with you," Boh said. "Let me—"

"Quiet. I got this." Kora's composure wavered. She was still clutching her head. Her voice sounded . . . strange.

Violet blinked. What was she—

"Which realm do you belong to?" Kara said.

The answer rose in Violet's throat. She swallowed it down. Then let it rise again. Her resistance was like putty, flattened out by resignation and doubt. She had to defend Terlian.

But that thought was hard to grasp; Violet's attention drifted toward Kora, a pine needle swept down a stream.

What if she *did* admit where she was from? Yakiv would never believe it. Maybe then he'd stop this interrogation. Violet wondered why he made Kora do it. He was certainly more intimidating. Though, at the moment, he wasn't even watching.

"Terlian," Violet said.

Yakiv's shoulders stiffened.

Kora gave a sympathetic smile. "Don't be absurd. Lying won't make this any easier."

Yakiv turned. His eyes were two fire flashes. "Boh," he said, the trembling in that one word foreign from his ordinarily dispassionate voice.

Boh tilted his head. "She's truthing. Make her say it again."

Violet noticed his white liryn cord. Flame pendant. Was he a Chair? Someone who could tell when people were lying—or honest?

Her stomach coiled.

Yakiv strode too-long strides, slipped his dagger free, and stuck it beneath Violet's jaw. "Say your realm. Now." His chest heaved. The gate light shone on his forehead sweat, though it was winter.

Violet bit her lip.

The dagger dug. Yakiv's hand was jittery, his breathing uneven. Because she was from Terlian? No, he'd been unsettled before she revealed that.

Why did I do that?

"Speak," Kora said smoothly.

"I . . . I already . . ."

"You will answer my next question with a yes or no. Are you from Terlian?"

Violet's lips pressed together. But her head betrayed her. The nod caused a prick against Yakiv's blade.

"Crazy loyalist rat," Boh said. "She believes it. I see it, sheep and all."

Violet was wondering how she ever thought she had the grit to stave off an interrogation. She'd performed horribly. Her only saving grace was the hope that Yakiv figured she was insane.

He scrutinized her from an unhitched gaze. The fervent energy that had overwhelmed Yakiv could have belonged to Alikar. She couldn't pin Yakiv down and that unnerved her. But even as Violet watched, the frenzy receded. His hand stopped trembling. Something in his eyes clicked, a certainty falling back into place. When he stepped away, pocketing the dagger, he was calm again.

"You used this," he said, that easy voice returned. Casually, he withdrew the gate pendant. "So. *Terlion.*" A bit of venom trickled back in. "Where's the gate?"

Kora repeated the question.

"It's at . . ." Violet's mind swirled for a vague answer. "In the mountains. Near Borku." She hadn't realized she'd remembered the name. "There's a cave. The lake. I fell . . ."

Why was she telling him this?

Kora was dubiously eyeing her. The Advocate was still drooling. Meliora—*Meliora.* She was in the dirt, that metal coin glued to her mouth. Violet had forgotten she was there.

"*At the sheep's wall,*" Yakiv said. "The rest of the Lykill is by the gate to Terlian."

Violet kept her mouth shut this time.

But Yakiv smiled. The sight was as welcome as poison in water. "And so a Terlion betrays its realm again." Framed by his team, he struck a hero's pose, the gate showering him in gold. "Get the Terlion," Yakiv told the Pillar. "We're leaving."

Numbly, Violet staggered as Slav, the sycophantic Pillar, wrangled her by her tied-together wrists. Yakiv wasn't going to kill her—he was kidnapping her.

"It's possible she's welded with Terlian's liryn," Kora said. A duplicate voice, overlaying or echoing Kora's, said something similar, though in a loud, coarse way that sounded nothing like her.

Slav skittered away from Violet. Even Yakiv showed some uncertainty.

"What's your liryn?" Kora asked. "Tell me what you can do."

As tempting as it might've been to fake having some threatening power, Boh would see right through it. "I'm . . ."

"Just tell me!" Kora cried out then, cradling her head. "I can't—" Her knees gave. She crouched, rocking back and forth.

"She's done." Boh snickered.

Done.

Violet blinked, feeling the wind again, smelling sweat and salt and metal, and wondering why she'd answered every single one of Kora's questions.

Goldentongue.

Yakiv stepped toward Violet. She backed up, but he gripped her shoulders and yanked her closer. Securing her one-handedly, he got a hold on her pendants. "Are these liryn?" he said.

Their chests were touching. She could smell his musk, feel his fingertips on her collarbone. Panic shook the answer out of Violet. She wanted him gone.

"No."

All heads swiveled toward Boh. "Truthing," he said.

Yakiv released her. She inhaled, giving another fruitless tug against her wrist cuffs. Slav captured her once more.

"I've got her, Yakiv," came his shuddering voice. "I've got her for you."

"Where we taking her?" Boh asked Yakiv.

"You and Kora, rest," Yakiv said. He kept talking, but Violet couldn't follow it. The past five minutes now lived in her memories like an old dream.

Someone else had interrogated her, someone shrewd and well-spoken and polite—not the Kora who was currently arguing with Boh about whose crown weighed more.

I just told Yakiv everything.

"What about the Pretender?" Boh's question was engorged with blood lust. "I'll do it."

Dread's hot finger made Violet warm despite the weather. Not someone else.

Yakiv surveyed Meliora, then squatted to her level. "Look at me," he said.

Meliora wouldn't.

"You're not a Hastein. You're just a lost, little Janlion who doesn't know more than what she's been taught." Yakiv pulled the coin off her mouth and stood. "Next time we meet, I kill you. I don't tolerate loyalists any more than thieves." He busied himself, checking his pocket for the gate pendant and telling

Boh to take Meliora's cuffs away because he needed the spare material.

Violet squirmed. If only she could get into Meliora's line of visual, she could convey something encouraging. At least Yakiv had no interest in killing her. She could run out of the Amber Forest, send word to the monarchs, alert Bar'Talian that Yakiv Stefanos was in possession of the gate pendant.

But Meliora sat, her shoulders low, her arms still behind her even though they'd been freed. The gate light showed her ghost-white fingers.

Violet saw that painted hand, then darkness as Yakiv pushed her toward the woods.

CHAPTER TWENTY-TWO

"The Hands of the Lykill serve one master: the Lykill, immutable and everlasting." – Vessel Malokki, black pearl

Y AKIV'S SEPARATISTS ILLUMINATED THE path with pencil-like flashlights similar to the one Alikar had in his tool set. He'd probably returned to the monarchs by now. Violet was relieved he'd gone. Yakiv might not have left him alive.

She couldn't erase the image of Meliora alone in the forest, thinking she'd fallen as low as a cord thief. Meliora had admitted to suspecting that she wouldn't have been able to use the pendant. Even so, she hadn't wittingly wreaked havoc on the ground.

The gate pendant had done that much damage in an innocent person's hand. What would it do in Yakiv's?

"How long have you been on Bar'Talian?"

Kora's voice twisted Violet's nerves while capturing her interest all the same. She eyed the Separatist, whose mistrustful gaze cut through her—a doubt worthy of Eliathor, with an additional layer of disdain.

No, Violet was misreading the expression. She should answer. They might treat her with less suspicion if they understood she hadn't been plotting and scheming for weeks.

But that logic wasn't right . . .

"No, Kora," Yakiv spoke. He steered Violet around bramble. "You've done enough."

Kora gripped her head and stumbled into a tree. Boh laughed.

Violet's compliance vanished. Clarity brushed against her consciousness, reminding her that Kora was a Goldentongue.

A Goldentongue's liryn wasn't a magnet, conducting Violet against her will. It worked more subtly than that, actually affecting what she perceived. The others must have heard Kora's real coaxing, while Violet experienced a fabrication.

"We need to know why she's here," Kora said. "There's probably more of them."

"Remember what I've told you. There's plenty ways to make someone talk. Depend on liryn so much, you forget how to breathe."

"Now that we know she's a Terlion," Slav said, "makes sense why that cord thief was talking so much about Terlian."

"What cord thief?" Kora said.

"Jarek." Slav jerked his head in Meliora's direction. "The one Kora heard the Pretenders' cousin talking to. Good snooping, that was, since Basilia snitched nothing. Or . . . or was it bad snooping, Yakiv?" He looked to his leader for permission to have an opinion.

"Basilia couldn't say what she didn't know," Yakiv said.

"Yes, yes, you're right. Smart on Kora to follow Jarek into that tavern, is what I'm saying. Never would've heard about the Amber Forest otherwise."

"All Kora did smart was get a drink," Boh said. "Don't praise her for accidentally eavesdropping."

"No, no, you're right. Stupid Kora. Stupid Kora."

Ugly, ruthless meaning formed from the snippets Violet webbed together. They were talking about Jarek's late-night conversation with Meliora, hours before Yakiv invaded the estate. He and Meliora had been discussing the gate pendant and the Amber Forest. Kora had eavesdropped. *That* was how Yakiv made the connection between the pendant and what he'd read in the archives about Meliora's father dying in the forest.

The monarchs' attendants hadn't betrayed them. Meliora had. Unintentionally, but the fact remained that Meliora's conversation with Jarek had led to the murders of almost everyone she loved.

Solving the mystery left Violet cold. She could never tell Meliora. But the monarchs needed the truth, that way they stopped suspecting their own household.

Talking to the monarchs is the least of my concerns right now.

"We taking her to the hammock?" Boh asked.

"You're going back," Yakiv said. "Rest. I'll take the Terlion."

"What are you gonna do with her, boss?" Slav said.

"What anyone does with a Terlion."

Slav's fawning laugh lasted long enough to make Violet miss mirthless Alikar.

"Someone help Denys," Yakiv said.

"I'll help him, Yakiv. I will." Slav slapped the comatose Advocate's face.

"Harder," Boh said.

"Not so rough," Yakiv said.

Slav, given two opposing commands, froze.

"I'll do it." Kora shook the Advocate by the shoulders. His head lolled about.

"Enough, Kora." Yakiv hitched Violet toward the Advocate. He pinched the man's nose. Slow seconds passed.

"At least he can't feel it when he's . . ." Kora began.

Violet understood nothing after the Advocate came-to with a violent gasp. He swiveled around, hacking.

They conversed for a few minutes. Even with the language barrier, Violet got the gist: Kora wanted to give the interrogation another go. But Yakiv won out.

Yakiv's team dispersed. Only the Advocate stayed. Denys was dark and thin, reed-like, and hadn't said one word.

Yakiv questioned him. His speech was lilting, reluctant. It made Denys tighten up like stretched elastic. But after one look at Violet, with a hatred so forceful that she stepped back, Denys nodded. The next moment, the Advocate's vision went vacant again.

Kelispar had dreaded that fate; and yet, he'd Advocated for hours without even a headache. Denys slipped immediately into mental lethargy, and Kora couldn't go five minutes without succumbing to the pain. What had made Kelispar stronger? Was it a matter of endurance? Why, on the day he'd received his crown, had he been able to Advocate longer than he ever had?

"They know what suffering is." Yakiv adjusted the cold rope on Violet's wrist. It lengthened, giving him the slack to tie the other end around his belt loop. "Agony every time they use their liryn. And that's not even their crown. Do you know pain, Terlion?" Easing Denys forward, Yakiv walked, dragging Violet by the rope.

She stumbled along. Being dragged like a dog burned her pride. When she dug her heels, testing the rope's strength, the leash just cut into her skin and made her shoulder twinge.

"You know about barrens?" Yakiv swerved right so Violet's leash didn't get caught on a tree. "Here, you get a name if you're robbed. They were all barrens—Kora, Boh, Slav. Denys here. I found them in a chattel house. Found out who was wearing their cords. I got them back, paid justice to the thieves. That's the part I play, see. I've always been limited to Bar'Talian. Gate travel is difficult when you're branded a vigilante. But I think I'll go to Terlian next. Show them my gratitude."

Reasoning with someone this deep in a grudge was pointless, but Violet couldn't say nothing. "You can't blame an entire planet for something that happened a thousand years ago."

"A thousand years. That's how long Terlian had to make it right."

Was it worth explaining that Terlian hadn't actually had the Lykill? But that would mean informing Yakiv that Terlian had no liryn—that it was completely vulnerable to attack.

"Pretenders tell you about scapegoats?" Yakiv's light fell on a snake that slithered into darkness.

Violet focused on her path, hiding a grimace from the rope.

He jerked the leash. She tripped. "Answer," he said.

"They didn't."

"No, they think too highly of the emperors, of their would-be fellow monarchs. Wouldn't cross a faithful servant's mind to suspect their master of cheating the other servants when no one's looking. And they're looking, Terlion. The emperors, the monarchs—they all know. And they do nothing."

Yakiv had a point somewhere; he was just strolling his way toward it.

"My grandfather was a scapegoat. Welded by the emperors of Matlian. They needed a Vessel cord for a new prime minister, and my great-grandmother needed *zloto*. They gave her fifteen. It afforded her one week of needles. Just enough to kill her. They didn't care that she died, likely never thought about her again. It runs in our rulers' blood, see. Not caring about the people they make.

"I'll tell you how my grandfather carried his crown: cut off his own arm. Apparently thought death was better than fear. Unfortunately, a Balm reattached it. Couldn't even die without liryn interfering." Yakiv's voice was a winter wind. "I can't say he loved his crown. Don't think he understood it. The fear came and went, there some days and gone the next. Never knowing when it was coming—that's what made it worse. Fear of living, of dying, of breathing, of suffocating. Fear warps the mind. Makes you stop thinking. A man can do a brave thing when he's afraid. But the people who call him a hero, they don't know he was half-mad when he cut it off, not even certain his two hands were his."

Yakiv stopped. He lifted the light so its glare dashed against Violet's face. She winced, but couldn't turn her head as Yakiv said, "They welded him when he was three days old. Branded him between the shoulder blades so they'd know he was one of theirs."

She turned away now, mouth thin, wishing Yakiv would keep walking.

"You can't even recognize it, can you? The horror? Welding's not legal until you're twelve, and the subject's got to be willing. No one wants to hear a boy scream until his throat's red because his crown makes him forget there's light outside his own darkness."

It couldn't be true. No monarch would be cruel enough to weld someone just to have a liryn cord.

Yakiv was probably lying. This might've been the story he told at every rally, something to rile citizens.

He nudged Denys forward, urged Violet none-too-gently. They continued trekking over dirt and leaves that had been amber in daylight.

"Bar'Talion monarchs have probably welded a scapegoat or two in their time," Yakiv said.

Violet pictured kindly Asbed and gentle Nora. "They wouldn't."

"Don't waste the breath. They're not your monarchs."

"No, you killed mine," she said, just as matter-of-fact.

Yakiv eyed her sidelong. "You felt it, the moment she was gone."

Violet's confidence disappeared. To speak of Lady Basilia with her murderer felt wrong. She redirected the attention to him. "If you use the gate pendant, you're no better than a cord thief."

"No. I'll tell you why you're wrong. A thief makes someone else suffer. The Lykill's the opposite. It makes the *thief* suffer, like the Pretender niece." Yakiv waggled a few fingers. "The gate pendant's not mine, true. But I'll bear the hurt if that's what it takes."

"In exchange for what?"

"Watching the monarchs fall."

The monarchs would quickly lose influence if Yakiv could offer liryn without crowns. All he needed was the welding pendant, which was so far out of his reach that Violet almost relaxed.

"You'll never find the rest of the Lykill," she said.

"Twice wrong, Terlion. Even your blessed prophecy says I will."

"No, just your interpretation of it."

"This doesn't look like interpretation to me." He rotated the gate pendant between dirty fingers.

And Violet, dread sinking her assurance, understood. Yakiv didn't need a map to Helheim. He held one already.

It felt close to an hour of walking when Yakiv slowed. They hadn't left the Amber Forest, though they'd come to a tamer area, by what Violet could see. The path was cleared of bramble, and there weren't chaotic branches sticking out of tree trunks.

"You have *rav'aham* on Terlian?" Yakiv withdrew something from his belt—the same bag he'd tossed to Boh. Out came the tongs, gripping that unusually sticky coin that had kept Meliora quiet. "This is only five percent." He let the tongs hover by Violet's face while she wondered if it was about to shock her.

The coin jumped to her lips, sticking to her flesh with a painful pinch. Violet's necklace chain flew too, cutting into her neck as it attached itself to the magnet. Her pendants dangled at weird angles as the chain grew comfortable, glued to the rav'aham coin.

"It's the iron in your blood," Yakiv said. "Metal to metal."

Already, Violet's cheeks and lips were beginning to tingle, like she'd grown overheated. She jerked her head. The magnet wouldn't dislodge. So she reached to remove it.

Yakiv bound her other wrist too.

Following a curve, they came in sight of a house as randomly placed as an elephant on a highway. It was small, not much bigger than a backyard shed, yet what it lacked in size, it quadrupled in attractiveness. Rather than an overgrown, wood-rotted shack one would expect to find in the middle of the woods, the cottage looked transplanted from some second-century German village. The neat roof tapered like an A over the wooden frame, complete with lattice work and shutters. Stubby candles glowed in the front two windows.

Was this Yakiv's house? She wouldn't have guessed he'd live anywhere so quaint.

He forced Violet onward. The light from the window candles flickered on a flag that hung near the threshold. Violet glimpsed Terlian's familiar sheep. A loyalist's sign. Not Yakiv's house, then.

He pounded on the door. Her brain sorted through ideas. If a loyalist lived here, he or she surely wouldn't be in favor of Yakiv capturing a Terlion. This loyalist could be an ally. Should she call out a warning?

No, Yakiv had stoppered that opportunity with the rav'aham. It felt sickly warm now, hanging on her mouth like a miniature plate.

Yakiv knocked a full ten seconds, until an unintelligible male voice inquired from indoors.

"Yakiv Stefanos," Yakiv answered. "I have something that will interest you."

The loyalist opened the door. Light from inside gave color to the sheep on Terlian's flag and the red mat under Violet's feet. The loyalist was leaning on a cane, hooded like a monk, and wearing a mask. A familiar mask, black and painted with a handprint and the tri-colored Valknut.

"I doubt you hold anything of interest to me," the man said. His voice was young, disdainful, and strangely familiar. He wore a purple liryn cord with a book pendant.

Violet didn't know much about the Hands of the Lykill, other than the fact that their leader was the one who'd come up with the idea that the Lykill could eliminate crowns. A loyalist who was also a Hand? Were the two not opposed to each other? Violet didn't understand the politics; she just knew that Kelispar and the others didn't think highly of Malokki and his Hands.

"Don't drop the ax before the tree," Yakiv said. "Might miss your firewood."

"—" The loyalist stopped. That eerie, masked face moved Violet's way. Window candlelight made the slits for his eyes glint like a possum in the night. He stepped over the threshold, gripped her chin, and turned her face toward the light.

The movement strained Violet's necklace chain, trapped by the rav'aham and unwilling to offer any slack. She dug her toes and wriggled back. His hold wasn't firm; she freed herself without difficulty. Her pulse hammered from that unwelcome touch.

"So you do listen to gray pearls," Yakiv said. "They're missing some information. Like where she's from."

The loyalist kept quiet, staring at Violet from that invisible face. She wished the candlelight would stop making his eyes glitter. "Why are you here?" he asked her softly.

Yakiv answered. "Information."

"Your exchange?"

"A Terlion."

The mask obscured the loyalist's reaction. He said nothing.

"Imagine what she knows, Malokki. She could tell you more than any other Vessel, satiate your obsession with a single conversation."

As Malokki pondered the offer, Violet pondered his name. This was the Hands' leader, the Vessel whose ideas had planted their seed in Yakiv. Was he really so young?

That must have been why something in his voice tugged at familiarity; she'd likely heard it before, projected through that cord thief's resonance shell.

The idea of being handed over to Malokki sounded marginally less awful than being trapped with Yakiv. He was a loyalist; perhaps he'd let her go, send her on her way once he'd sated his curiosity. She had no reason to think ill of him, other than an irrational doubt spurred on by the fact that Kelispar and Lady Basilia hadn't cared for him. But it was his ideas they hadn't liked. Just because someone was misguided didn't mean they had bad intentions.

Malokki limped inside without a word.

Yakiv shoved Violet forward and guided Denys with his other hand. Malokki's foyer was long and opulent and brimming with the scent of rosemary. Following them on the walls were ink etchings of Old Norse runes; tapestries of the realms; glass display cases of scrolls and manuscripts; paintings of kings and queens. Violet had seen artifacts and decorations like this before, in Dr. Mariemma's office.

They met Malokki in a sitting area, where there was more decoration than wall. Votive candles shimmered underneath more paintings. Where there weren't tapestries, there were bookshelves, enough to content a neighborhood. One open book sat at the center of attention on a podium; Violet spied familiarly indecipherable Ókunnigr runes.

Malokki waited by an unlit fireplace, his unbalanced weight sagging leftward, toward his cane. Above the mantle hung a painting. A king stood at a ship's helm, holding his sword taut. From his other hand flowed gold dust that swirled into a gate. Half the landscape was a stormy ocean. Beyond the gate, it morphed into a horse-covered plain.

"I require assurance," he told Yakiv.

"I have no war with you." Yakiv's voice was dull compared to the extravagance of the room.

"Assurance that the Terlion will stay with me when you leave."

"I'm not interested in extra weight."

"But you are very interested in Terlion blood."

Yakiv shifted. Violet was grateful Malokki asked the questions she couldn't. She needed assurance, too.

"The Pretenders chose to die," Yakiv said.

If Malokki was riled by that, the mask hid it. "I will accept the Advocate," he said.

"Will you, now?"

"I'll release him when you leave. An exchange."

Yakiv made a slow study of Denys, Violet, and the armchair Malokki had pointed to. "Sounds like one of us is giving more."

"The information I hold is far more valuable than this man's oppressive life."

Yakiv didn't appear to like it; he kept scrutinizing the lackluster Advocate, then Violet, weighing their costs. But Denys was just a guarantee, a temporary measure. He'd get Denys back.

He steered the man toward the armchair; Violet had to accompany them to avoid being dragged. All in all, Denys got the better end of the deal. The chair was cushioned, and the wooden board Malokki laid across the armrests didn't even touch him.

"Deaden," Malokki said over the board.

Its Aramaic script didn't magically glow, but something must have happened, because when Malokki tried lifting the board, it refused to budge. Denys couldn't get easily out of the chair. In his current state, he was trapped, regardless.

"And the Terlion?" Malokki said.

Yakiv pulled on Violet's leash. "She stays with me."

Malokki's masked face followed their movements. Then he turned toward the painting, slowly, his movements stiff with pain. "Your first question," he said.

"The Lykill." Yakiv crossed his arms, getting comfortable. Violet wished he'd chosen a spot closer to that book on the podium.

But no, she needed to focus.

"Each pendant," Yakiv continued. "How do they work? Start with the purple."

"You want to know about the three Clefts?" Malokki said.

"I'm asking about the Lykill. Call it what you like."

Violet watched wax drip down a candle and harden before Malokki answered.

"The Purple Cleft turns the wearer into a *lira*," he said.

"A what?" Yakiv said.

"One who welds, who is not of royal blood. Liras walked every realm before the Great Rift."

"They could distribute any liryn?"

"No. Liras were given just one liryn to bestow. An Advocate lira, a Vessel lira. But he who wears the Purple Cleft can bestow all liryn."

Yakiv nodded. "How's it done?"

"The same way it is always done." Malokki's tone seemed to roll its eyes.

"Then the wearer would need to learn all twelve welding rituals." Yakiv surveyed Malokki's vast library.

"There is only one book which contains the fullness of the welding rituals," Malokki said.

Violet wondered what motivated him to supply answers so readily, without sign of discomfort or hesitation. He wasn't afraid of Yakiv, nor did he show offense at the late-night interruption.

"The Tome of Rites is far beyond any simple man's comprehension," he added.

"They—" Yakiv began.

Denys gave a dog-like whimper. He was almost pitiable with his hanging jaw.

The concern knitting Yakiv's brows was as uncomfortable a sight as a weeping snake. He returned to Malokki, speaking quicker. "They don't have to comprehend. They just have to read."

Finally, Malokki turned. Violet had forgotten about the mask; she stepped back. The leash bit her tender wrists.

"No one can read First Tongue," Malokki said. "That power is reserved for the Lykill alone."

Yakiv took that in silence.

First Tongue. Meliora had mentioned that.

The Ókunnigr runes on the podium grabbed Violet's attention again. Was First Tongue the same as Ókunnigr?

"You have seen it before," Malokki spoke. He was watching her.

"The liryn pendant next," Yakiv said.

Violet still had Malokki's attention. With a tiny twitch that rattled her necklace, she shook her head. The less Yakiv knew about the Lykill, the safer Terlian was.

"The Red Cleft imbues the wearer with all liryn," Malokki answered. His Vessel pendant swung when he moved from the candlelight's reach. Violet could no longer make out his eyes.

"Simple enough. And the gate pendant?" Yakiv's deadpan showed only scientific interest. "Could there be a gate that leads nowhere?"

"If its destination has not been set," Malokki said.

"How is it set?"

"By the will of the first who enters it."

Comprehension crawled, like it had to get through all the candle smoke. Yakiv had walked through the gate and nothing happened.

He evidently understood more than Violet, nodding. "You have to *mean* it when you go in," he said. "And the ritual for opening and closing gates, it'll be in that Tome of Rites."

"Yes."

"And if you know it, you'll oblige my curiosity."

Don't, Violet wanted to say. She strained against her leash, made a noise in her throat.

"I know why you seek the Lykill." Malokki, relying on his cane, fit the image of some wizened prophet. But Violet couldn't shake the idea that, beneath the mask, Malokki was surveying Yakiv like a star pupil might survey the class idiot.

"Good," Yakiv said. "You've listened."

"I listen to what you withhold."

Yakiv's left arm twitched. "Well, if we're exchanging frankness, I've got an inkling who's under that mask. I know a jot or two about Matlion politics, *Malokki.* Sorry I don't feel inclined to bow. Matlian's left a rotted taste on my tongue, see."

That evoked no reaction from Malokki.

What might have made interesting food for thought was lost on Violet, who honestly didn't care who Malokki was, not when Yakiv might get everything he needed to show Terlian his "gratitude."

"You won't find the Lykill," Malokki said.

"Don't want me to have your role?"

"That role is not mine. Nor yours. '*Then the Compass will come and find the Lykill in shadow and smoke.*'"

The vegvísir hanging from her neck seemed to increase in size. What if she'd never noticed it in the muck? Would that line in the prophecy have never existed?

"Yes," Yakiv said, "I've heard. But you see, Malokki, I don't care about the prophecy. Just words, isn't it?"

"Then why do you follow?"

"I don't follow. I take." Yakiv shifted his weight to his other leg. "The ritual for gates. Write it. I'll find someone who can read your Matlion Latin."

Malokki paused, so long that Violet worried he'd refuse, forcing Yakiv to use violent force. If only he'd remove the mask and she could guess what he was thinking—or see where he was looking. She had an uncomfortable feeling he'd spent most of the conversation studying her.

He finally moved toward a bookshelf and gripped the frame for balance. "Your tongue. Ryurik?"

"Yes," Yakiv said.

"I know it." Malokki withdrew a feathered pen from a rose-colored vase. "Your Advocate suffers unnecessarily."

While Malokki wrote in careful, steady strokes in a hide-bound notebook, Yakiv inspected Denys. Translating and comatose, even though Malokki knew Yakiv's language, in addition to everything else. How deep was Malokki's knowledge?

Again, Violet shifted in the podium's direction. If Ókunnigr *was* First Tongue, Malokki wouldn't have been able to read it either, not without the Lykill.

Malokki gingerly ripped out the paper he'd decorated and handed it to Yakiv. Violet could make out the neat black writing. It resembled the Cyrillic alphabet.

"Your Ryurik's faulty," Yakiv said. "These aren't words."

"Phonetics," Malokki answered. "The ritual must be spoken in First Tongue. You understand, Terlion?"

She did, though she couldn't guess how Malokki had assumed she'd comprehend. Transliteration, from First Tongue to Ryurik.

Yakiv's brows dipped as he silently mouthed.

Violet could study modern Cyrillic. If First Tongue was Ókunnigr, that scrap of paper could give her a clue—

Yakiv pocketed it. Violet turned, disappointed, mostly in herself for her lack of priorities. What did it matter if she cracked Ókunnigr if she was still tied to Yakiv?

But he was almost done with her, ready for the trade-off. And then what? Did she want to be stuck with Malokki instead?

He could tell me about First Tongue.

No—no he couldn't. Not in English. He might've been a Vessel, but even liryn couldn't enable someone to learn a language that had developed after the Rift.

"Just a few more questions," Yakiv said. "The gate pendant—any limitations? Emperor's bedroom, by chance?"

"It can only take the wearer to destinations previously known and seen. Otherwise, one needs a Compass."

"Known and seen." Yakiv leaned on one leg, thinking.

So was Violet, relief softening the rawness in her arms. The gate pendant wasn't omniscient. He'd never seen Terlian, so he couldn't get there.

Then how did Halfdan get to Helheim?

"What kind of compass?" Yakiv asked. "Chisel-made?"

"True sheep follow north."

"Meaning?"

"Only a welded of Terlian can guide the White Cleft," Malokki said.

The room stilled but for the shadows from bubbling candles. A welded of Terlian. There hadn't been one of those until twenty years ago.

"How?" Yakiv said.

"There are many paths," Malokki said. "The true path is sílfar. The Compass knows."

"Even if the Compass hasn't seen it?"

"Yes."

That's what sílfar was? Violet supposed that did relate to traveling, as Kelispar had said. Then Fa had been a Compass, the first and last one in a thousand years. Had he understood, in some subtle way, or was the liryn completely useless if one was ignorant of it? Fa had certainly asked for directions more than once. He'd lost his keys and phone countless times.

"I have one more question." Yakiv scratched his chin. "You've said the Lykill can unweld. Remove crowns. Is that true?"

"Don't you already believe that?" Malokki returned coolly.

Nothing more was said.

If Fa had been a Compass, someone who sensed the true path, why did he give up the Lykill pendants as if they didn't matter? Could a Compass be faulty? Even Kelispar had mistranslated Violet's name.

"Release my Advocate," Yakiv spoke.

"The Terlion first," Malokki answered with equal composure.

Violet expected Yakiv to put his foot down, but Malokki's command failed to shake Yakiv's air of control. Few things did. Yakiv took his time as he reeled in Violet's leash. Slowly, he pinched the cool, wire-thin rope where it cut into her wrists. The material loosened. Immediately, she snatched at the rav'aham coin. It sucked in her fingers.

"Now let Denys go," Yakiv said.

Violet was still trying to unglue her fingers from the rav'aham. Finally, with a great wrench, she got it away from her mouth. Her lips tingled and throbbed, and her teeth clacked. Her necklace chain snapped, clinging to the coin. Trying to shake the rav'aham off her hand, Violet accidentally flung her two pendants across Malokki's carpeted floor. Oliver's compass landed close by, but her violet disappeared somewhere underneath Denys' chair.

No, no . . . Did she dare start digging under Malokki's furniture? She stepped forward, uncertain.

Out from under the chair shot a tiny black violet. It lifted off the carpet, floated through the air, and came to rest directly in front of Violet's face, hanging before her like a faithful bird.

She flinched, shooting back, elbow banging Malokki's bookshelf. The pendant hovered in place, a black flower waiting for her to take it.

Her pulse escalated. The room grew hotter. Malokki had too many candles, too much incense clouding Violet's thinking.

"I see," Yakiv said quietly. His voice jarred Violet from her confusion, from the leery sensation that she and her pendant were alone.

It seemed she was an X on a map; a star on a black night. Unable to grow any less conspicuous in a room with dozens of things that should've been more interesting.

Malokki moved. Kneeling slowly, gingerly, he picked up Oliver's compass. His head lifted, and she knew those two eyes, disguised as slits, were directly on her. "*Then the shackled flower will bud,*'" he murmured, "'*and the flower will find the Lykill blooming where the ground has been upturned.*'"

Violet stared at her airborne pendant. She replayed Vessel's remark. And she shook her head, finally registering the jolt in her funny bone. When she finished counting through the pain, her flower pendant was still on its invisible ledge, a perched bug.

How?

"You tricked Kora." Yakiv struck a casual pose, his gunslinger stance. But his eyes were sharp. "You another Golden-tongue? You welded with all twelve?"

"I . . ."

"Answer."

Violet shifted. The flower pendant followed her movement. She closed her eyes, then forced them open, searching for the exit. Her hands were free; now was her chance to escape.

"Can you not see she doesn't understand?" Malokki said.

"What do you know of her?" Yakiv asked him.

"What I know is of the Lykill. The rest, I deduce. The Lykill creates liras. Liras were lost. But the Tome of Rites was unearthed. A lira of Terlian was created. He welded a Compass."

Malokki had it all backwards. *Fa* was the Compass, which made Chief Halfdan the "lira." *Fa would've needed the ritual in order to weld me,* she thought, even as she heard Fa's echoing voice on his deathbed.

Chief Halfdan had given Fa a book. The Tome of Rites? Fa had obsessed over that one page, had copied it exactly. He'd assumed it had contained the words Chief Halfdan said on the beach. But what if that paper hadn't contained Halfdan's words to Fa, but the ritual for welding Compasses? It would have made sense for Halfdan to give Fa the ritual if he was going to make him the tool for performing it.

As layer upon layer of supposed evidence buried her, she reasoned out the remainder of her argument. Her pendant might be currently levitating, but nothing about her felt more unique than it had before Fa gave her the necklace. She'd know if she had liryn.

Fa hadn't known.

Yakiv kept quiet, and Malokki kept staring. It made Violet feel like an artifact on display. She focused on something else. But his books reminded her of the one Chief Halfdan had carried, his candles gave the whole room a reverential tone, and his paintings made everything about the prophecy seem all the more profound. The one behind Malokki was the most dramatic, that king opening a gate. The shape of his sword hilt caught her eye: rounded at the top with the Order's symbol, a key. The king was holding Harðgjǫrð, the famous stone sword—famous to anyone in the Order, that is. Of course it was depicted here, in Malokki's house.

"*This one will find it aided by the blade,*" Malokki said. He tossed Oliver's compass toward her feet.

Violet finally looked at her flower. After a tiny hesitation, she grabbed it out of the air and pocketed it. Then she bent, scooping up the vegvísir.

"Interesting," Yakiv spoke, sounding marginally more invested than utter boredom. He scratched his jaw. "My Advocate." He gestured to Denys. Yakiv stood so easily, his whole air seemingly uninvolved.

But Violet had watched his calculating eyes rest on her pocket, right as he touched his own. He'd just learned that he couldn't use the gate pendant, not without a Compass. Even if this was all some confusing misunderstanding, Yakiv was already convinced Violet could be his navigator.

The flower in her pocket seemed to burn. She hoped she was imagining it. Because if Violet was a Compass, then Terlian was doomed. In Yakiv's hands, she was more than a tool. She was a weapon.

Violet took a surreptitious glance toward the hallway. A plan as bare-bones and rash as escaping into a pitch-black forest made her uncomfortable, but not as uncomfortable as breathing the same air as Yakiv for another moment.

She edged toward the hallway.

A black, slim projectile launched before her path and tore a hole through Malokki's papered wall.

"Don't move," Yakiv said.

Violet froze.

Yakiv stood, calm as ever, the crossbow in his hand pointed at her. The same crossbow that had killed Kelispar and Lady Basilia.

"You gave me your assurance," Malokki said.

"That was before I realized what the Terlion is."

"He has the gate pendant," Violet spilled out. "He's going to use it to attack Terlian."

Malokki's masked face centered on Violet, rather than Yakiv. "You found it," he whispered. "Here, in the forest."

"I—I won't help you," Violet told Yakiv. "Even if I am welded, I don't know how to use sílfar."

"Liryn likes to be acknowledged. This Compass in you, it'll make itself known." Yakiv waved the crossbow. "Back this way, Terlion."

Violet hesitated, scrutinizing the sharp-tipped arrow pointed at her chest. It was a bluff. He needed her alive.

"The White Cleft isn't yours," Malokki said.

Yakiv didn't see a small, white triangle slip out of his pocket and drift toward Malokki like nothing more than seeds on the wind. Malokki caught the gate pendant and held it toward the candlelight. Ókunnigr runes shimmered.

Had Violet's pendant not just made a similar journey, she would've taken longer to comprehend. Malokki was a descendant of the Nehfey Empire. The pendant was his to use.

Yakiv's leg jerked. He'd felt the pendant leave him. His needle-sharp scrutiny switched to Malokki, though the crossbow still watched Violet. "You're born of Da'atan. But that's Nehfey."

"Yes," Malokki said simply. "As was my blood father."

"Imperial gluttons."

"You've lost, Separatist. Leave my house." Malokki closed his fist around the pendant.

Yakiv just chuckled. "You know the difference between you and every other spoiled welded who lets liryn make him brave?"

Malokki waited. Naïve of him. He should have run.

"Nothing." Yakiv spun the crossbow around and fired.

The Vessel stumbled back, arrow in his chest. As his cane fell and his knees caved, he cried out, *"Esh losa thul, o maris, shema hach ull nad haeem fral."*

A golden bubble materialized in time to catch him. Malokki vanished, in his place a gate to mirror the one in his painting. It pulsed a moment longer before beginning to dissolve into dusty shafts. Not quickly enough.

Yakiv dove into the light. Violet saw the flash of his boots before they, too, drifted into nothing.

Gone. Both of them. All without eruption, without an earth-quake.

Finally, she was free of Yakiv. Denys, still open-mouthed in the chair, was trapped by the wooden board regardless. She could escape.

Yet Malokki's house held so much history. It seemed a shame to leave this treasure trove without learning something more.

For the sparest moment, she entertained the temptation to rifle through the book on the podium. It hoarded her attention like a greedy dragon. But Violet wasn't a thief, and she wasn't suicidal. If she dawdled, it would be her own fault if Denys awoke and captured her. She moved toward the hallway. She'd pass the book on her way out. Maybe she could—

Light flared on Malokki's walls. Violet spun around. Yakiv tumbled onto the rug. *"Esh ligo thul, o maris,"* he yelled, clinging to the paper Malokki had given him, *"shema hach ull nad haeem fral!"*

The gate spiraled out of existence.

Violet held her breath, waiting. He'd just used the pendant. But he wasn't a descendant.

Malokki's living room exploded.

Unrestrained force threw Violet at the ceiling, then back down. She shielded her head as object after object bruised her. The entire house sounded like a groan, the shattering of glass mixing with the splitting of wood.

Once the wind died, the house took its time settling. Pages rustled. Glass tinkled. Gingerly, she dragged herself forward. Items slipped off her torso. Although her body ached, nothing felt too excruciating.

She climbed to her feet. Splinters and wallpaper sloughed off. The candles had been extinguished, painting the room in a dimness barely punctuated by whatever gray, ghostly hue the moons and stars offered—for there was a hole in Malokki's roof. Pieces of it were strewn on the floor.

All that decor, all that careful curating—ruined. Malokki's home had been destroyed by one sentence.

Violet searched for Yakiv. An arm peeked out from under a bookcase. Its owner's hand was pure white. Denys was slumped in another corner, his chair tipped back.

She tiptoed around the bookcase. Yakiv lay beside it, un-conscious, one arm pinned. With her lungs pinched tight, she searched the rubble. A needle in a haystack would've been easier to find. Among the shards of glass and other broken objects, the gate pendant could be anywhere.

A noise came from Denys' direction. Violet's head shot up. He'd risen, peering around in confusion.

"*Prei!*"

Alarm sounded the same in every language.

Foregoing the pendant, Violet dashed toward the hallway, tripped over a book, and heard it rip. Hopefully that hadn't been the Ókunnigr book.

Outside, she ran, her thoughts uneven like the forest ground, threatening to slow her with roots and slippery leaves. A branch pricked her cheek. Denys might've stopped to revive Yakiv, or he might've been ten steps behind. She chanced a look back and spotted nothing but trees.

Beyond her current focus on escape, a new determination formed. Yakiv had the gate pendant. Violet had to warn King Asbed and Queen Nora. But they were in Vaspurakan, days away.

The sound of rushing water coaxed her to a stop. She slowed at a bank, panting. A stream gurgled from a one-foot drop. It wasn't tremendously wide. Beyond it, a healthy thicket of trees offered more cover than her current position. There, she could hide.

No, what was she thinking? She couldn't jump through a stream in the middle of winter. And she had no way of guessing how deep the water went.

A shout echoed. Then another. Yakiv's voice.

Violet had to keep moving.

She raced along the bank, almost falling in countless times. Momentum kept tugging, as if hoping she'd take the plunge. Prodding her.

Her head shook out the thought, but it climbed back in. Violet was welded with Terlian's liryn. Her pendant had float-ed—she couldn't argue that. A Compass, someone who knew where to go.

Like into the water?

It churned parallel to her, endless white noise that failed to smear out the sound of another shout. Yakiv was closer.

She appraised the stream. Liryn couldn't tempt her into diving into a foreign body of water. That was—

The muddy bank gave. Violet slipped. She didn't have time to yelp as her legs plunged into an icy bath.

CHAPTER TWENTY-THREE

"The scarcity of information on Terlian's liryn cannot be blamed on Vessels. Knowledge is only passed down if someone cares to remember it." – Vessel Magda, recitation at Kapor Academy

THE WATER CHILLED HER bones, the way winter bites when the winds dip below zero. The stream wasn't deep, sloshing around her knees, but the cold was worse than lack of oxygen.

Male voices called out. Violet waded her frozen legs toward land. Her coat dragged, slowing her. She quickly wriggled out of it and let the water steal it. Maybe it would throw Yakiv off her scent. Freer now, she stumbled toward land, boulders smacking her shins until she hiked out of the water and found muddy ice. Though she desperately needed to catch her breath, Violet ran toward the cover of trees.

Once hidden by foliage, she slowed. She'd reached an edge of the Amber Forest. Not far past the trees ahead, she could make out a large body of water, silently slipping under the watch of two moons. Lake Vaspurakan.

Besides the sound of her chattering teeth, she didn't hear anything, including her pursuers. But Violet was hardly what one would call "secure." She was filthy, shivering, all alone on a foreign planet where no one spoke English. After her bouts with the gates and the lake, Violet had been deprived of her beanie, gloves, and cloak, with only a sodden nightgown as a shield against the bitter wind. If she didn't get warm soon, she needn't worry about Yakiv.

But where am I supposed to go now?

Meliora was somewhere in the Amber Forest, but backtracking risked running into Yakiv. The highest priority was warning the monarchs. However, Violet couldn't guess where Vaspurakan was any more than she could point to Terlian.

She withdrew her flower pendant. Terlian's liryn lay in her palm, seemingly smug, now that she was giving it attention.

Examining the past few days, she could see how someone might suggest that sílfar had intervened. It had led her toward Fa's troll.

No, Fa gave me some idea of where it was, she thought.

The gate in Helheim?

I only entered the cave because the storm.

What about finding Eliathor, Kelispar, and the others?

I just followed the lake.

And the gate pendant in the tree?

Violet had a headache.

She could scoff at Malokki, or she could accept that she was wrong. And if she was wrong, and her flower pendant was indeed welded with liryn, then she had to use it. Sílfar could lead her to the monarchs.

But Violet didn't want an invisible ability prodding her. She'd had her own path long before sílfar. And it wasn't as if she needed sílfar *now*. Vaspurakan was north. She could follow Lake Vaspurakan. Comforted by that, she pocketed her pendant and set off.

In order to avoid blindly stumbling, Violet had to walk along the lake. But staying in the moons' light made her nervous, and wind made the journey harder. She grew so cold that her jaw ached from all the chattering.

Ten minutes in, she had to take a break from the coast. She angled toward the trees. At every ominous rustle of needles or crunch of twig, she told herself to plow ahead. Pausing would only make her colder.

Creeping past her worry of hypothermia were thoughts of Malokki, whoever he was. Or, had been. Had Yakiv's arrow made a fatal wound?

Yakiv shot him, after saying he had no quarrel with him. His cruelty shouldn't have alarmed her. And now Yakiv knew how to use one of the most powerful tools in existence.

Violet was thoroughly lost, only faintly aware of her surroundings as she fought a useless struggle against the elements, when an angry woman's voice drifted along the wind. When Violet squinted, she detected faint light and smoke. That meant there was a fire. Warmth. The temptation was so strong that she almost moved in that direction, but she couldn't trespass on someone's property—or, worse, knock on a stranger's door and beg. She pressed on.

An equally irritable male voice replied to the woman. Violet stopped. That voice . . . it couldn't be . . .

A third voice shouted amid scuffling, and Violet hurried toward the chaos. Some outdoor fire lamps illuminated a cottage, shabbier yet brighter than Malokki's. It made for the backdrop of a scene that would have been humorous if it wasn't so horrible. An older man had a younger man in a headlock and was yanking at blond tufts of hair as if plucking a chicken. Egging on the brawl was a woman wearing a bathrobe and hairnet.

"Excuse me," Violet called.

The woman jumped. The man glared from a bearded face and yelled at her in Arati.

Violet was rooted by the man's victim—by the boy who'd abandoned her and Meliora outside the Amber Forest. Of all the people, in all the places, she'd run into Alikar.

He noticed her, eyes widening on a purpling face. When he fumbled for his cord, Violet guessed he was activating his liryn.

"Let him go," Violet said.

"Caught this cord thief stealing my fire too!" bellowed the man.

"He's not a c-cord thief, s-sir," she said, marching directly to the tangled persons. "He's an Ad-Advocate."

The man, who evidently believed Alikar's head was a bowling ball, adjusted his hold. "Ya think I don't know what a proper cord is? This chump claims that our blessed King Asbed used his—"

"Bathrobe sash, yes. I was th-there when he was welded, as was Queen N-Nora, who suggested the cord."

"Now that's sacrilege," the man said.

"No it isn't. Do you r-realize who you're harassing?" If these people respected the monarchs, they'd respect Kelispar too. "This is Emissary Kelispar's brother."

"Lord Alikar Muratsan," Alikar wheezed.

"I'm sure you can con-conclude the rest," Violet said.

The man stared at the face tucked under his armpit, then at his wife's horror. He jumped back. He and his wife stooped, faces in the dirt.

"Lord Muratsan!" they chanted.

Alikar straightened, loosening his liryn belt, which the man had tightened like a noose. His hair was disastrously tangled and his clothes filthy, but a glimmer of familiar Alikar peeked out of the gloom. "Simply 'Lord Alikar' for now," he said in a scratchy voice, then coughed.

"Please forgive us, Lord Alikar. Meant no disrespect to your personage nor your good brother. We aren't Separatists, swears. We're Unionists, happy to kiss the sacred boots of a welded."

"No such formality is required, good sir and gentle madam. I will be on my way, then?" Alikar, despite their groveling, seemed unsure that he'd escaped.

"Not without helping yourself to our stores, Lord!" squeaked the woman. "We have chickens and . . . and a goat for your lady friend there."

Alikar looked at Violet. "Would you like a goat?"

"No, thank you," she said. "But . . ." Her attention turned to the flame torches. "I would like to use your fire." Before they could tell her no, Violet settled beside one of the shoulder-high poles that supported a bowl of fire. Ordinarily, she wouldn't have thrust herself on a stranger's hospitality like this, but there was a line between courtesy and desperation, and Violet had discovered it. Her raw fingers wrapped the pole, and she set her face inches from the orange sparks.

"Well, there it is," Alikar said. "She wants a torch."

"No I don't," Violet said. "I just need a moment and then I'll be on my way."

"In that case, I will take advantage of the other one." Alikar towered over the neighboring pole.

Whatever the couple's reaction, it was lost in the smoke, and Violet to her thawing. Once she warmed, she would be mortified. For the time being, she closed her eyes against the gray sting and let her face heat.

This was too much. Had Violet *really* decided to walk in this direction, or had sílfar decided that for her? It didn't matter. She'd be on her way soon, without Alikar.

"Lady Muratsan?" came a timid voice.

"No, I'm . . ." Violet faced the woman. "Yes?"

"It's a cold night. Storm'll be coming 'fore ya knows it. These was my daughter's, Lady, and I think they'll fit you right." The woman displayed a bundle of clothes.

Violet hesitated. It was one thing to barge in on someone's yard fire, and quite another to take their children's clothes. But she was wearing a nightgown, and the woman had mentioned a storm.

In a stone outhouse, Violet stripped off her purple night-gown. The daughter's clothes included leggings that pinched together Violet's cold thighs, knee-high socks, a maroon, flannel dress ruffled at the wrists and neck, a bonnet, gloves, and a coat that Violet had to cinch to keep from trailing. She couldn't bring herself to wear the bonnet, but she did don the hood.

Outside, Alikar had been outfitted with a cap and a long jacket whose shoulders the husband brushed, as if Alikar were a horse. The wife reluctantly took back the bonnet. Her gaze strayed toward Meliora's nightgown. She fingered a sleeve.

"Such a pretty fabric, this," she murmured.

"Here you go," Violet said, but the wife stepped back.

"I couldn't, Lady!"

"Please, take it. It's the least I can do."

With a strange mixture of hesitation and eagerness, the woman accepted the nightgown. Giving it away filled Violet with guilt; it hadn't been hers to offer. But she didn't think Meliora would mind.

The couple would not hear of them leaving without a bowl of food. While they scurried inside, Violet and Alikar kept to their respective torches. Alikar spoke once the shutting door indicated they were alone.

"Where's Meliora?"

Violet's memory conjured that despondent face. "We got separated in the Amber Forest," she said. "We found the gate pendant, but Yakiv captured it, and me. I escaped."

Alikar's mouth opened. What was he doing here, wandering around strangers' backyards? Violet wouldn't ask. They'd be on their separate paths soon.

"Is there a way to contact the monarchs long-distance?" she asked.

He swallowed. "There is, but I haven't any cottons, and the process is lengthy. Your request for an audience might take days before it's approved."

But surely the process could be expedited in an emergency? Supposing Violet found the money. She might have to walk to the palace after all.

"Is she hurt?" Alikar searched the far-off darkness.

"No," Violet said, the word quiet as she remembered what Meliora's conversation with Jarek had unwittingly instigated. Alikar could never know. His feelings toward Meliora were already complicated enough.

The couple returned. Silently, Violet and Alikar ate bowls of bean stew. It tasted of comfort and warmth.

"You're rightly bent on leaving?" The woman nervously eyed the sky.

"Yes," Violet said. "I'm in a hurry." She handed over her empty bowl. "Thank you very much for the food and clothing. Goodbye." Violet nodded at the husband, gave Alikar half an acknowledgment, and then started for the trees.

A minute into her walk, noise stirred behind her. *Just a branch falling.* She didn't turn around. But soon she became aware of a presence on her right.

"Wait, will you?" Alikar jogged alongside her, panting.

Violet stopped. "What are you doing?"

"Joining you."

"I would rather you didn't." Violet hadn't intended to sound rude. Even if she had, Alikar would sooner be annoyed with her than have his feelings hurt. But when he slouched, she second-guessed herself.

"Yes." His voice hung lower than his posture. "I suppose I deserve that. But you see . . ." Alikar glanced up, and Violet was grateful for the dimness of night that concealed his expression. "I have nowhere else to go."

She shifted.

"As fate would have it, I got horribly lost. Then, while I was sitting against a tree so I could think, I fell asleep, only to awaken to a nest of mice that evidently mistook my hair for grass upon which to relieve themselves. My just punishment for neglecting my liryn."

Violet grew conscious of the flower in her pocket.

"And so you see, Terlion, I can say with all sincerity that I was wrong to leave you, against the express commands of the monarchs who gave me this liryn for your benefit. I had not hoped to find you so easily, but here you are. Please allow me to fulfill my monarchs' desires and accept me as your Advocate." He spoke formally, reminding her that he was a nobleman. But the hesitance reminded her that he was a boy who'd just lost everyone he loved.

They stood in awkward silence, Alikar staring at everything but her.

He hadn't apologized for his iron heart comment, but what did Violet expect? It wasn't as if he'd said something untrue. He was simply quoting a prophecy. Having Alikar *would* be useful, and the monarchs had requested it.

"Well," she said, "I suppose we're both headed in the same direction."

"Are we?"

"You wanted to return to the monarchs."

"Ah. Yes, I did. Before. Now, I intend to aid you on your path."

"I don't need aid. I—" She was speaking too quickly. "Are there any other ways to contact them?"

He took his time thinking. The wind picked up, as if impatient. "It would be faster to find Dag. We're not far from Borku."

The loyalist captain who brought them to Vaspurakan? "He has a way to contact the monarchs?"

"He has cottons. And if Melly's lost, she'll go there. It's what Eliathor told us to do. Besides, we can't contact the monarchs, can we? That would involve working through their attendants. One of them is a harpy owl."

"A what?"

Alikar, contemplating toward some unseen sight, took a moment to process Violet's question. "Oh." He pocketed his hands. "It's a bird. A sneaky one."

He was referring to the attendant who'd supposedly betrayed the monarchs. To that false supposition, she said nothing.

Regrouping at Dag's house would be easier than navigating through Vaspurakan and convincing a royal guard to let her have an audience. And Violet liked the idea of finding Meliora.

"How far is it?" she asked.

"I suppose we have to walk, without the cottons for a wagon." He considered. "One day. But we had best seek shelter for the night."

"I don't have time." A gust floated from the water, making her shiver.

"Here." Alikar unclasped his new cloak.

She stared at the proof that Alikar was capable of observing more than he let on. "I have a coat," she said, "and you'll be cold."

"I'm already cold." His voice was subdued.

She tweaked a crooked button and ignored his offering.

"Well," he said, "we had better start before the storm begins. Oughtn't we?"

Violet wasn't a fan of the word *we,* but she nodded.

"Thank you, Terlion," he said.

"Vi-let," she reminded him.

"Ah. Yes. Fileet."

Keeping a measurable distance between them, she continued on.

CHAPTER TWENTY-FOUR

"Dear Ollie, I wish you could come back home. Fa says the army won't let you. Maybe you can tell them you have to help him find the Lykill. They'll say yes if they know it's important."

THE PROMISED STORM STARTED soon. Snow nibbled Violet's nose. Soon she was squinting, the hood useless at keeping snowflakes from finding her eyes.

"I can't see a thing," Alikar said, stumbling.

Violet pressed on. The storm would pass, and they were short on time.

"Listen, we really ought to find shelter."

"I've told you, we don't have time." Violet sped up and rammed into a tree.

"Anak!" Alikar said as she staggered back. "Are you all right?"

Violet straightened her cloak. "Let's head toward the lake. There's more light there."

"Is that the right way?"

I don't know, but I'm sure sílfar does, she thought irritably. Her irritation was directed at a variety of sources. Herself, for not knowing the way; sílfar, for having sat within her, unnoticed, for days; and Alikar, for being a gentleman when, one day earlier, he was a toad.

Violet strode for the coastline—at least, where she assumed it was. The forest was a whirl of white dots. Continuing was foolish. She couldn't outrun the storm. It was unavoidable, like a liryn crown.

Violet slowed. A liryn crown. Relevant to Kelispar, Alikar, and every other welded, but not applicable to her. Fa had welded her, and he'd been welded by the Lykill. It was a strange idea. Not that Violet wanted a crown, but she was the only welded person alive without one.

"That man," Alikar called over the storm, "you know, the peasant who nearly strangled me, he gave me this before we parted. It's crude, but it will provide us some protection." From a pocket he withdrew a scrap of fabric that didn't look capable of protecting a mouse. Alikar crouched, pulling on the material, which stretched as he tugged, pliable as taffy. It grew a foot long, and then a yard. In a minute, Alikar was drowning in fabric.

Violet helped him unfurl it. Once flattened, it grew taut as plastic. She assumed it grew stiff on contact with the cold ground, but as they lifted the other corners, forming something of a tepee, those sides hardened too. It took Violet a moment to realize they were forming it into a tent. The final edge remained open so they could enter. Violet went first, immediately more comfortable out of the wind. Alikar stooped in, and together they lifted the last pliant section of the fabric. It stiffened into a wall. The seal wasn't perfect—cold air whistled through the cracks where the edges met—but the tent was far warmer than outside.

"Will this hold?" Violet tested the ground, which felt strangely firm. She couldn't see much of Alikar except some shadow of his form.

"Yes, barring hail." His voice sounded muted and close.

"And it's waterproof?"

"Certainly."

"All right." She sat, drawing her knees to her chest for warmth. What was this tent made of? Material created by a Chisel, no doubt. Alikar could have told her every minute detail. She would have found it interesting. But he wouldn't explain, not to her—the reason he'd never be a Chisel.

"Where is the satchel?" Alikar said.

"Satchel?"

"The purse with our provisions. There should be a lamp stone."

Violet fidgeted, relieved it was dark. "I lost it in the lake."

"I see."

Time dragged on. It had to be around midnight now. Without the distraction of looming hypothermia, Violet found it harder to ignore sílfar. She wasn't blind to the holes in her logic. She'd set off knowing she'd have to rely on sílfar at some point. However, she wasn't fully certain her liryn could be trusted. If only she could use it as Alikar had his tool, twisting and tweaking until it did what she commanded.

She frowned at the formless walls. "We can't travel in this. We might as well get some rest."

"Yes. I agree."

She lay on her side, hearing him do the same.

"Goodnight, Fileet," Alikar said.

Well, that was better than "Terlion."

Try as she did to appreciate Alikar's determination to obey his monarchs, he was only helping her out of obligation. But why did that matter? They didn't have to be friends.

By the time she said "Goodnight" back, he was already snoring.

S HE AWOKE WITH A crick in her shoulder. Pale light bled through the tarp. It was navy blue, of a waxy texture.

Alikar slumbered on the other side of the tent. Violet wouldn't wake him. She just had to use the bathroom.

She struggled to peel the stiff material apart and finally managed to create an opening. Snow and white light poured in, momentarily blinding. The sight outside made her pause in wonder.

Icicles hung from branches, catching rainbows where their points dripped. Beyond that stretched a postcard-worthy scene of winter. Snow clung like decorative ribbons from the unfamiliar trees, painting a vivid contrast between white and forest green. The whirring wind from last night had calmed, allowing birds to chirp. Crisp air left a spicy taste on her tongue. It was the most beautiful view she'd ever seen.

Unfortunately, it was also inaccessible.

She couldn't take a step outside without sinking past her shins. Her leggings were soaked by the time she shifted back inside.

"Anak." Alikar had awoken, face blemished with sleep smudges as he peered outside.

"There might be a shallow spot farther out," Violet said.

"Perhaps, but we would be very uncomfortable in our pursuit of it." He inspected the tent, running his palm over a wall. Then, he gripped one of the edges Violet had peeled back. "I can make sleds."

"Out of the tarp?"

"It's the only further use we'll manage out of it. Once it's been stretched, it can't return to its former size."

Violet tested the material, which felt closer to cardboard than fabric. "It's thin," she said.

He didn't reply, focused on his task.

It was a shame to dismantle the magical tent that had turned from a handkerchief to a shield against a snowstorm, but, as Alikar said, they couldn't reuse it. Breaking it into smaller pieces was difficult, like tearing jerky. Alikar succeeded faster, cutting out a long rectangle for himself in the time Violet got one edge free. In another five minutes, the floor of the tent was coated in snow.

When they were finished and Violet's fingers ached, Alikar tested his sled. It floated on the ground, sinking when he stepped on it, but only a few inches. He took one of the poles he'd fashioned from the tarp and pushed himself forward. The sled moved easily.

"A success," he said. His grin was bright and his cheeks pink. "What a relief. It's not often my ideas meet my expectations."

She handed him his second pole, then clambered onto her own sled. His hand was on her elbow, then gone before she could tell him she didn't need help.

They pushed off, strangely skiing. Violet still needed to use the restroom, but that would slow them, so she ignored the urge.

"Which way is Borku?" she asked.

Alikar pointed with his head. "I must say, this is the most absurd thing I've ever done." He smiled at her. Then, not finding reciprocation, he cleared his throat and turned his head.

Violet pushed harder. He was trying to be friendly. In fact, since last night, he'd been far more pleasant than her. Currently, she was being just as iron-hearted as he believed.

"Yes," she said, confused, "it's very absurd. But it was a smart idea, so . . . thank you." Then she took the lead, leaving him to trudge along behind her.

All the snow in Alaska couldn't match this spotless blanket, which no one had marred with dirty footprints, cigarette butts, or evidence that they'd walked their dog. The temptation to brush snow off branches needled almost as insistently as sílfar.

"Not that way," Alikar called.

She slowed. He was pointing left, whereas her sled was aimed decidedly right.

"Oh," she said, pretending this information didn't alarm her.

They continued left. Two minutes later, Alikar had to correct her again after she'd put an entire line of trees between her and their preferred direction.

She was doing it again. With a discomfited jolt, she remembered having the same difficulty along the mountainside with Alikar and Meliora, drifting toward the edge when they were trying to avoid being seen. Had sílfar caused the seagull to soil Violet's eye? Could sílfar even do that?

She readjusted her sled toward the way Alikar had pointed. And then hit an invisible bump, which flung her face-first into the snow.

"Fileet!"

Her nose was immediately frozen. Violet gasped, inhaling ice crystals, and tried pushing herself up. Snow swallowed her arms. This had to be the most humiliating thing ever to occur, and that included nearly poisoning King Asbed. If this was sílfar, it was entirely intrusive.

"Here." Alikar was nearby, holding out a pole.

She grabbed it, and he tugged. By the time she was stable, he was panting.

"Are you all right?" he said, looking down, but Violet noticed his twitching lips.

Violet commanded her flush to subside. That hadn't been sílfar; it had been a boulder, covered by the snow. Perfectly reasonable, given the landscape. Their goal was Dag's house, and she would stick to it.

The internal resistance increased as Violet moved in Dag's direction. Whether due to having been acknowledged or the fact that sílfar truly loathed this path, its tug was as potent as a vacuum. And she was a feather, fighting the wind.

Dag's house made sense. It was the quickest way to notify the monarchs. What was sílfar's motivation? Did it want her walking back to Yakiv?

No. It doesn't want anything, because it doesn't have a brain.

All was white and glistening until they came to a narrow assortment of trees, which followed them to a hedge barricade. Violet brushed snow off the leaves, finding impenetrable branches.

"It will take work," Alikar said, already holding his pole like an ax, "but these should hold."

They hacked for thirty seconds. Twigs and splinters dirtied the snow. Violet peered for any break in the barrier and found more hedges in either direction. This way was blocked. Violet knew it, because everything within her reached backward.

She closed her eyes, exhaling. She couldn't wander around Bar'Talian following a formless nudge. At the same time, she couldn't afford to stumble off another cliff just because sílfar didn't like where she was going.

With as much self-control as she could muster, Violet finally said, "We can't go this way."

"It's the most direct path."

"But we can't get through."

Perhaps he'd agree if she told him. Alikar understood the ways of liryn better than she did. But this was personal, and she didn't trust Alikar enough to brainstorm with him.

How nice it would be to have someone *with* her, and not merely beside her.

They turned back the way they'd come. Sílfar quieted. Violet imagined triumph from within.

"Before we continue," Alikar said, "would you enjoy something to eat? I could forage."

"If you're hungry, don't let me stop you."

"I was asking for you."

She stared back at him. His expression read as one conglomerate of guilt and hesitation. Violet didn't understand why. She didn't understand a lot about Alikar, and he knew even less of her. It shouldn't have bothered her. She hadn't asked for Alikar's company, and she didn't particularly want it.

Or did she? On her own, Violet could walk, but she had to admit she hadn't minded the snatches of solidarity she'd felt recently.

"A heart must have room to beat."

Suddenly, Violet's chest was much too small for a heart, let alone the one currently expanding and shrinking like a pitiful creature. She didn't know what to do with it, how to adjust it. But she wasn't a robot. Alikar had to know. At once, her mouth opened.

"My heart isn't iron. Just because I don't show my emotions doesn't mean I feel nothing. I did—I *do*—but we had to escape Yakiv. Someone had to hold themselves together. I've gotten used to doing that, and now it's hard for me to do anything else. I haven't even cried over Fa." She pursed her lips, succumbing to a blend of relief and embarrassment. What would Alikar think of her now—someone who couldn't mourn her own father?

He'd stiffened. Violet was too mortified to look at him. If only sílfar could extract words.

A bird sang a dirge, so minor and sorrowful it must have been mocking her. Its melody repeated several times before Alikar spoke.

"I'd forgotten I'd said that." He sighed, forehead in his palm. "My immense shame. Please forgive me."

The tip of her tongue was firmly pressed between her teeth. She nodded. She hadn't been trying to elicit an apology, but there it was.

"My brother often accused me of being insensitive. And selfish. And immature. And too liberal with my feelings. He told me all that, but kindly, because that was his way. I never did appreciate him as he deserved. Now I wish I'd studied his character more, that I might emulate it. Oh—I see that I am at fault even now, talking of myself when you have, rightly so, pointed out an injustice on my part." Alikar's shoulders drooped.

"Kelispar was a good man. He was kind to me too. I'm . . . I'm sorry for your loss," Violet whispered. As soon as she said it, something dull and weary sloughed off her heart.

"Thank you," Alikar murmured. He straightened, dashing tears away. "And I'm sorry for yours. Your father would be proud to know that you will bring the Lykill home."

Yes, he probably would have been.

Violet considered Alikar's words, allowing for a lengthening quiet that wasn't awkward or forced, but content. She kept waiting for the humiliation to return. Another moment stretched on, and Violet didn't flush.

"I have a proposal," Alikar said, not in his nobleman's voice but with the lightness of the boy who'd teased Meliora. "I think we ought to be friends."

Her fingers, picking dirt off her cloak, faltered. Violet mentally turned over the word, the one she'd never attached to anyone outside her sister. After her confession, Alikar's response was to draw closer, not pull back in horror.

"If you don't accept my proposal, I shall be forced to follow regardless, as my monarchs have tasked me with helping you. I might be an insensitive goat, but my sense of patriotic duty has been fortified of late. I blame you."

"I don't have much experience with friendship," she said, unable to let him continue under false pretenses.

"From what I've observed, you make a ready student." He smiled. "Do you accept?"

His invitation hung, an offer on the lowest branch, easy to take. Easy for anyone but Violet, who always checked for thorns, and after that preferred a higher limb because the lower one hadn't owed her anything and at least she'd know she'd worked for it.

Alikar was too open and unassuming to offer friendship with an agenda. Maybe she *did* understand him, a little bit.

Violet met his eyes. Then, finding that too much, she answered to the king's bathrobe belt. "All right," she said. She adjusted her clothes, wishing to be five minutes into the future.

"Oh, good. I was certain you'd say no." He leaned against a ski pole like easing up on a heavy weight. "Well then. Which direction should we pursue now?"

Violet wished she knew. They'd have to discover that together.

Together. What an unfamiliar concept.

"This way," she said, and glided her sled across the snow.

CHAPTER TWENTY-FIVE

"The supposed 'Tome of Rites' is held in reverence by the same lot espousing hope in the Lykill and the unending reign of Terlian. Need we give it any further consideration?" – Vessel Magda, recitation at Kapor Academy

*F*RIENDS. IT WAS ONLY seven letters. Violet tried not to overthink them.

Their sleds proved particularly handy when they came to a bridge, below which stuttered a stream of water and ice. Uphill made a challenge, but Violet and Alikar coasted downhill and had enough momentum to keep going until, finally, the snowfall ended. They left the contraptions behind, Alikar with a disappointed sigh.

The path sloped into highlands, swells of barren brown hills. Mountains rose in the distance. Should they stay the course alongside the lake, they'd keep to the Amber Forest.

"Dag is that way?" Violet pointed to the highlands, and Alikar nodded. She lifted her foot, then hesitated. But her face-plant had been an accident. Liryn couldn't produce boulders out of thin air.

She set her foot down. Nothing happened. Relieved, she took another step—and landed in a hole the perfect size for her foot.

"Anak," Alikar said as she freed herself, "these lands are unkind to you."

Violet rubbed her ankle, grimacing. She was going to have to tell him. They couldn't go in that direction. The ground would probably catch fire, or a horse would appear out of nowhere and trample her. Straightening, she spilled the truth. "I'm welded."

"I beg your pardon?"

"Chief Halfdan used the Lykill and made my father a 'lira,' which is someone who can weld, though only one type of liryn. Terlian's liryn, in this case. Right before Fa died, he welded me. It must have been an accident." Then, because incredulity was growing on Alikar's face faster than clouds on a humid day, Violet explained all Malokki had told her.

While Alikar acquainted himself with the fact that she'd been in the Hand's leader's house—something evidently more shocking than her liryn—Violet once again pondered the Vessel who sported a loyalist's flag while simultaneously spreading ideas that every other loyalist vehemently opposed. And Malokki was a descendant, to boot.

"Yakiv knows who he is," Violet said. "Royalty, from the Da'atan Empire. But he can use the gate pendant, so he's Nehfey too. On his father's side."

"Product of some imperial dalliance, then. And now leading the Hands. Hmm. Well, the Tome of Rites has been lost since the Rift." Alikar's sudden jump in topic made Violet's thinking stumble. "Supposing Chief Halfdan found it, he couldn't have read it. No one can read First Tongue, not even Advocates. Some Advocates can translate texts."

Violet hoped Halfdan *hadn't* given Fa the Tome of Rites, because whatever that book had been, it was long gone. The idea that someone had stolen a thousand-year-old book, probably to sell on the black market, made her cringe. "What is First Tongue?" she asked.

"Our first tongue."

"More specificity, please."

"I don't know much. The language of our ancestors, I suppose."

"*Whose* ancestors?"

Alikar waved his arms around. "Certainly not the trees' ancestors."

"You mean First Tongue is the first language ever spoken by humans?"

"Is that not obvious by the name?"

Violet ignored that.

No linguist on Earth had settled on Ókunnigr's roots. Scholars still debated on whether or not it was even Indo-European. None had ever been so bold as to claim that it was the first language ever spoken.

"Well," Alikar said, jolting her before the theories began to flow, "to your other suspicion, one cannot be welded accidentally. Monarchs must have the proper intent."

Then Fa knew what he was doing?

Perhaps it did make sense, now that Violet understood sílfar. Fa might've been prodded into welding her.

"This sheds light on that Seer's remark," Alikar said. "The one from our slimy smuggler's ship. Something about a compass, he said."

"If he could see I was welded, why didn't he say so?"

"He did. It's not your fault you don't comprehend the gibberish of Seers." With a yawn, Alikar shifted, temple against his walking stick. He looked as casual as if she'd mentioned that she knew how to knit. "This eliminates an enormous burden. Where do we walk, Compass? I suggest you listen, lest you wind up in a hornet's nest."

Violet moved farther from the hole. She could hardly admit that she had no idea where to go, so she gave a vague point and said, "That direction."

Alikar put an arm out. "I should go first."

"Don't be ridiculous."

"Are you certain?"

"Yes."

He consented. "I suppose if a whirlpool swallows you, we'll know whether you've ignored your liryn."

"That won't happen." Still, she hesitated, then grew annoyed for hesitating. Firmly and sure-footed, Violet walked forward.

No whirlpools. Not even a raindrop.

Alikar peeked at the sky. "Carry on."

The forest eventually thinned out. They found themselves in a valley somewhere within the highlands.

"We've always speculated about Terlian's liryn," Alikar said. He balanced his walking stick on one shoulder like a knapsack.

"Kelispar thought . . . Well, we knew it dealt with traveling. I'd hoped it involved flying. You haven't tried, have you?"

"Tried to fly?"

"That's the first thing I would have done."

"That sounds dangerous."

"It's not as if I would have experimented from the palace wall. A small ledge would have sufficed." Alikar eyed her meaningfully. "Have you tried?"

"I don't think I can fly, Alikar."

"You have, haven't you? And you failed." He sighed.

"No, I haven't, and I'm not going to."

"Why ever not? I'll push you if necessity demands it."

Violet imagined Alikar throwing her off a roof. "No you won't," she said.

"I might." He watched her sidelong, and she realized he was teasing.

That's what friends do.

Violet could try teasing in return. It couldn't be worse than trying to fly. "If you do that," she said, "sílfar will drop a hornet's nest on your head."

"No, sílfar will thank me for proving you wrong."

"We'll see."

"I look forward to it."

Violet chewed her cheek, not sure whether she was biting back a smile or a sigh.

The landscape was aglow with late morning sun when they encountered other life forms. First cows, then the occasional farmer or child running around, and finally goats.

"Have you heard of 'scapegoats?'" Violet asked.

Alikar jumped. "Fileet!" He peered at the nearest black-bearded animal as if making sure he wasn't eavesdropping.

"What?"

"Don't mention . . . *that*. It's indecent. Did the Separatists call you that?"

"No. Yakiv said his grandfather was one. They're real?"

"When schoolboys are trading insults, yes. We don't discuss . . . scapegoats." He whispered it. "It's a slur. Like calling someone a—well, I shouldn't say that either."

"But the monarchs actually do that? Weld someone, and then give their cord to someone else?"

"No. It's illegal, and immoral, and—" He stopped. The trouble in his brows showed his exhaustion. "I don't know," he said quietly. "Maybe some have. I certainly hope not."

Violet did too. She'd wanted Alikar to adamantly refute it, but even he, a staunch Unionist, couldn't.

"Yakiv said his grandfather was a baby when he was welded. Then, the ceremony"—Violet only dared mentioning that much, lest she remind Alikar even more of the welding ritual he'd unhappily participated in—"isn't necessary? The back-and-forth?"

"Every time you ask questions, you make me realize all the things I never think about. Hmm, he's not going to move, is he?" Alikar slowed, scrutinizing the black goat who was standing directly in their path. Its insolent stare unnerved Violet, who couldn't stop mentally measuring the length of its horns. "Get!" Alikar flapped his arms.

The goat's stare was certainly imperious.

Alikar sighed and picked up a rock.

"Are you sure that's a good—"

He threw it. The rock bounced off the goat's flank. Violet braced herself for a charge, but the goat evidently didn't think the pebble was worth his notice.

"Fine, we'll go around you." Alikar mock-bowed before escorting Violet widely around the creature, muttering under his breath the whole time.

"Returning to my question," Violet said.

"What question?"

"The welding ceremony?"

"Oh. Welding has always had a tumultuous history. There was a time when it was a sign of the monarchs' favor. Noble families would bring their children forward at a very young age. That was centuries ago, mind you. There's since been a law, which says the supplicant must be twelve before he can be welded."

Violet refrained from pointing out that his answer was just as pedantic as Kelispar's had always been. "But the ceremony isn't necessary?"

"No, I suppose not. All that's really required are monarchs, the supplicant, the words of welding, and some form of liryn cord."

"Then . . . Yakiv's story could be true. The emperors welded a baby."

Alikar's face was one heavy cloud. "We need the Lykill," he said. "Let's carry on, Compass."

They crossed another bridge, which led into a town quaint as a fairytale village. It smelled of sugar.

"Borku?" Violet said.

"I have no idea where we are, thanks to you."

That was encouraging. But sílfar was content as they entered the purple-bricked street.

"You should mask yourself," Alikar said, peering nervously about.

Violet wasn't used to being a wanted fugitive. "Only Separatists will recognize me, right?"

"Even Unionists listen to Separatist pearls. Gives them something to complain about." Alikar yanked off his scarf and dumped it on her head.

She wrapped her face like a mummy's as they strolled closer to civilization.

"Not the most prosperous land." Alikar inspected a house, finding something different than Violet, who saw the typical Arati turret home. What would he say of San Diego?

As they entered a city square, where stands and awnings indicated wares and people shopped with leisurely gaits, Violet's uncertainty grew into irritation. What were they doing here? Yakiv had owned the pendant for twelve hours. If he hadn't crafted a plan last night, he certainly had one by now.

She stopped by a hedge boxing in a park. "Let's ask for directions."

"*Directions?*" Alikar repeated the word like she'd asked what grass was. "You have sílfar!" He rapped her skull.

Violet winced and shooed his hand. "Sílfar isn't—"

"Lord Muratsan!"

The stranger's shout jarred them both. They turned toward a thick-set man whose fingers gripped an equally thick-handled ax.

"Step away from her, Lord!" the man said.

"I beg your pardon?" Alikar said.

Violet gaped at the crowd beginning to form. Faces were fearful, stances defensive—women hurried away their children, men held assortments of makeshift weapons, and everyone eyed Violet as if she were Yakiv Stefanos himself.

She'd hidden her face too late.

"She's working with that Separatist who killed your brother, Merciful Welder rest his soul," the man said.

"Anak," Alikar mumbled unhelpfully.

"That's Separatist propaganda," Violet said.

"And so?" The man, though defiant, took a step back, like Violet was diseased. "Stefanos has got a reward out for you. Thousand cottons. Says you're a Terlion spy."

"I see." Violet took in the group of five or six men crowding the speaker. "So this is about money. Otherwise, you wouldn't accuse Lord Alikar of being stupid enough to walk around with someone who got his brother killed."

"Well, I . . ." The man's face screwed up. Then he burst out, "Last warning, Lord! I'm doing you a favor. Serving justice and all. And you—" He spun, pointed his ax at the others. "I found her first. Stefanos wants her alive, so don't you be interfering."

"Was me who pointed her out," a man argued.

"And was me who did something about it first!"

Violet swatted the frozen Alikar's arm. Now was their chance to escape.

Was this why sílfar had guided her here—to be captured as a bounty? Why couldn't Chief Halfdan have made Fa a Vessel?

"Alikar," she whispered. "We need to run."

A wind chime sang, and a door slammed shut. A man dressed all in white strode outside, carrying a piece of toast and the breezy air of someone unalarmed to find a mob of angry men pointing weapons at a girl.

"You've interrupted my breakfast," he said, and Violet would have recognized him by the conversational voice if not by the turban hiding all but his eyes. "But I admit," the Goldentongue from *The Vagabond* said, "my curiosity is piqued."

She met Alikar's gaze and agreed with the apprehension in it.

"You again," the mob leader said.

"Yes. And you are?" The Goldentongue lounged on a windowsill, picking crumbs off his hook pendant.

"You can't hook me. I ain't in court. King's law."

"I obey a different king, and his law is clear: A Goldentongue may act in any way to serve the common good." He set down his toast and stood. Some invisible something fell over him like a snap of energy. It affected his eyes, drawing the twinkle from them. "Now, the preliminaries," he said, still casual yet undeniably authoritative. "You with the ax will introduce yourself first."

"Kalusd," the man said. He didn't blink. The ax remained fixed like he'd forgotten he was pointing it.

Violet had expected the Goldentongue to join the mob, but he wasn't paying her any mind. Was he eliminating his competition?

"Come on," she whispered to Alikar, edging back.

Alikar moved, though morbid curiosity slowed him.

"Kalusd," the Goldentongue said. "A strong name in your country, I'm sure. And you, with the—is that a spatula? Name yourself."

"Torkom," the man replied.

The remaining men didn't scatter, didn't warn their fellow bounty hunters that a Goldentongue was hooking them. They stood transfixed and docile.

"He can't manipulate them all at the same time, can he?" Violet said to Alikar.

"If he's powerful enough. Which he evidently is."

That was a good reason to flee. She prodded Alikar until he relented. They hurried back the way they'd come. What a waste of a trip. But perhaps it was *somewhat* useful to have learned that Yakiv had a bounty on her head. That meant he was active, that he hadn't forgotten her.

As they dashed toward the pastureland edging in the town, a fuzzy spot appeared twenty yards ahead. It grew in form and color—gold.

Violet shoved Alikar left. "That way!"

The brick ground quaked as they sped between turret-towering houses. The rumbling lasted until Violet and Alikar hopped over a low fence, landing in a splat of cold mud. There they knelt and panted.

"Yakiv's here," she said, vaguely aware of the black-spotted pigs sharing space with them. "We should separate. Those people saw us together. Can you find your way to Borku?"

"We're not separating."

"If Yakiv sees us—"

"We're *not* separating." Alikar's frown was secure.

Violet exhaled stinky air out of her nose. Before her counterargument formed, she heard footsteps. Alikar heard them too—he went stiff as the fence slats. They waited, watching pigs rub their noses in the mud, listening to the approach of potential doom.

"You can't hide," called the Goldentongue. "Quite the glow from the two of you, my friend tells me."

"Her luster is strange," came the Seer's voice.

Alikar shot up. "Before you hook us—"

"She's innocent, yes," the Goldentongue said. "Your monarchs informed me of my mistake."

Violet's shoulders unwound. Only then did she notice the bugs on the mound of manure beside her.

Alikar helped her stand. She did so cautiously, noting the lack of obvious concealment. If Yakiv searched behind the houses, he'd see them.

The Janlian representatives, faces as swathed as Violet's, stopped at the fence. The Seer's dark gaze found the pendant in Violet's pocket.

"Stop staring," the Goldentongue told him. "I'll interrogate her for you when we're not fifty paces from Yakiv Stefanos." He surveyed Alikar from hat to shoes. "You've grown tall, Muratsan."

Alikar frowned. "Who are you?"

"No one so interesting as a Terlion." The cloth moving around the Goldentongue's mouth hinted at a grin. "We've spoken to your monarchs. They sent us to meet you at Shepherd's Crag. What a shame they cannot trust their own subjects for a fetching job."

"And I suppose King Giannis is blessed with only perfect subjects," Alikar said.

"Yes, he is, may eagles guard him."

The force of Alikar's eye-rolling inspired Violet to interrupt. "Why are you here and not Shepherd's Crag?" she asked.

"How unkind, robbing me of the opportunity to ask you first. But, alas, we should not tarry." The Goldentongue eyed the Seer. "No?"

"Three of *da'atan,* one of *nehfey,* one of *basareth,*" the Seer spoke, looking at a house—or through it. Without warning, he jumped, his hands doing miniature flaps. "They're coming this way!"

Violet and Alikar glanced at each other, nodding in sync.

"We're going," Alikar said, stepping back. "May you find the path, and so forth."

"Follow us." The Goldentongue swept over the fence, stopping only to wave the Seer on.

Alikar bristled. "I think not. We will take our chances with—"

"Yakiv Stefanos is going to find you," the Janlion said calmly, exuding nothing but steadiness as he matched their stares. "I was sent by the Bar'Talion monarchs to aid you. Follow me."

His relationship with the monarchs was enough for Violet, who hoped Alikar could see reason past his distaste for the man. Fortunately, Alikar put forth not one objection. They darted after him, Violet intent on copying his path exactly. Perhaps this had been sílfar's purpose, guiding her to this Janlion representative, who could help her contact the monarchs. It all sounded perfectly logical to her.

"You've forgotten me!" came a cry from behind.

The other man, seeing that the Seer was stuck by the fence, called out, "What is the purpose of the healthy limbs attached to your torso?"

"You know Father has forbidden me from climbing."

"Ah, truth. I forgot. Go help him, Muratsan."

Alikar was surprisingly obedient. He hauled the Seer over the fence, causing the Seer to squeak out a plea for help.

"What a hornbill," Alikar muttered to Violet once he reached her again.

The three of them dashed after the other Janlion, who led them through some backyards, onto a narrow road, and eventually into a fruit tree grove with rotted citrus underfoot and an unoccupied wagon waiting like an overgrown pumpkin. The Janlion withdrew a pouch from the folds of his clothes and fished out tiny metal pieces, sculpted pods of cotton in bunches. These were fed to the wagon.

Then money really *was* cotton, at least in appearance.

As they hurried into the wagon, Violet couldn't shake the uneasy feeling one has in a nightmare where no hiding spot is clever enough. Yakiv had found them so quickly. Someone from the mob must have contacted him, hoping for payment. As long as he had the pendant, how could anyone slow him?

Their wagon, despite rolling over scores of purple citrus—had the monarchs commissioned specifically purple fruit?—glided smoothly out of the orchard. Soon they were on the road, the town behind them, with Violet suddenly recollecting that she had no idea why she'd so obligingly followed these two strangers into a vehicle traveling in an unknown direction.

Her eyes fell on the man's hook pendant.

Goldentongue.

She'd forgotten. And now she was trapped with him.

CHAPTER TWENTY-SIX

"Each hooked victim interprets the Goldentongue uniquely. Constantius Rigal's hooking was said to appear as a man in the throes of a most empathetic appeal, while those with stronger resistance found him merely whining." – *The Hook and the Claw* by Vessel Cicily

"PLEASE REFRAIN FROM THROWING yourself out of the wagon," the Goldentongue said to Violet, grinning with his eyes. He twirled his purple cord.

Alikar shot upright and smacked his head. "Anak!" He rubbed the spot. "You wriggling, muculent Goldentongue!"

"Muculent?" The Goldentongue's laugh had the ease of one who chuckles hourly. "Your cord fails you, Muratsan."

"Release us."

"And deprive myself of this enjoyment? Today has been duller than a moonless summer eve with no grape wine."

"Show him your face, Nikos," murmured the Seer.

The Goldentongue sighed. "Prudence must always spoil pleasure." He began unwrapping the turban.

Nikos . . . The name scraped the edges of Violet's memory.

"Nikos?" Alikar said. "Not Nikos of—oh. It's you."

The fabric fell away. Nikos was younger than Violet had suspected, not any older than Kelispar yet equally trim and princely, down to the dark goatee and his cloud-white teeth. He was tan, like Meliora, and possibly the most handsome man Violet had ever seen—a title she felt he did not deserve.

"A joy to see you well, Lord Alikar," he said, evidently resigning himself to behaving like a royal representative now. "Janlian's heart mourns with yours. Emissary Kelispar's legacy will be treasured."

"Your charity is a comfort." Alikar did not look comforted at all. "A Fork-tongue, Nikos? King Giannis allowed it?"

Nikos smiled. "He's my uncle, not my father."

Violet remembered now. Nikos was a childhood friend. Heir to Janlian's throne, after his cousin, Prince Ezio.

"You have no qualms over obeying his other commands." As Alikar slumped back to his seat, he showed none of the enthusiasm expected for a reunion between old friends.

"If you are referring to the shunning edict—" Nikos began.

"I am."

"Then be forthright. I tire of these starless conversations, covered like statues."

Alikar blinked. "Does he speak like this now?" he asked the Seer, continuing on as the Seer blanched at having been directly addressed. "Yes, Nikos, the shunning edict. I was never given the chance to express my concern, as the Muratsans were invited back to Janlian but once in seven years, and that was for the funeral."

Violet remembered the rest. Meliora and Eliathor had been shunned because of his secret engagement with the deceased princess. Alikar's loyalty knew no bounds; naturally, he chose a small, inescapable contraption in which to express his feelings.

Nikos' composure was laudable, given the clouds gathering force over Alikar's expression. "Now that you and Dame Violeta have arrived, we can—"

"A funeral from which Meliora and Eliathor were excluded," Alikar added.

"You know the reason."

The Seer withdrew a scroll from his boot and hid his face behind it.

"Yes, I know it," Alikar said. "Tell me, did King Giannis rejoice when he heard of Eliathor's death? His just comeuppance, I suppose."

The Seer went rigid. Nervously, Violet awaited Nikos' reaction, but he remained smooth-faced.

"I'll only explain this once," he said. "I loathe disharmony among friends."

"Don't hook me—"

"The late princess was already betrothed to the Earl of—"

"That betrothal was not contractually binding. At any rate, the Earl of Wherever was a thousand years old, and Fila loved Eliathor of her own free will—"

"Mind how you use the princess' name, may she sleep among the saints."

"—and I find it very disconcerting that the king should decree a shunning edict when *Princess* Fila protested it. I'm sure

Prince Ezio does. For all his oddities, he hasn't an unkind bone in his strange self."

"Your charity toward my cousin saves you from feeling the sharp edge of my hook." As if tired of holding itself, Nikos' formality relaxed. He sighed toward the ceiling. "I am but a silver brooch upon the altar of myrrh."

Alikar's incredulous, out-shooting arm almost whacked Violet's face. "Stop speaking like that! It's horrendous."

"The ladies find it quite rousing."

"Have any of them agreed to marry you?"

"None of them have received the honor of my invitation." He winked at Violet.

When Alikar's disgusted huff ran out of oxygen, he said, "Still such a peacock. Never worked on Meliora."

Her name made the Seer flinch. The Greek on his scroll was upside down.

"Her only flaw," Nikos said.

"Then you *do* protest the edict," Alikar replied.

Nikos rested an elbow on the back of his bench and let one leg sit on the other, ignoring the fact that his pointed foot nearly stabbed Alikar's knee. "He is a king," he said.

"You could have hooked him."

Violet eyed the Seer. Alikar shouldn't speak so boldly in front of a royal representative who might report that a nobleman from Bar'Talian was encouraging a Goldentongue to manipulate the king of Janlian.

"The walls of the palace prison are not to my tastes," Nikos said.

"No one there to flirt with?"

"I bear no ill thought toward she-who-is-shunned. Nor did I him. The news of his death was . . ." Nikos shrugged. "I should have liked to see the edict lifted before he flew on."

If that didn't appease Alikar's indignation, Violet worried nothing would. These preliminaries had lasted too long. Where was Nikos taking them?

"Perhaps it's for the better that Eliathor's not here," Alikar said, sounding weary now. "He'd have been dismayed to see you so syrupy. And a Fork-tongue to boot."

Nikos stroked his goatee. "Dismay is often the mask for jealousy."

Violet thought they might reach their destination before Alikar's eyes stopped rolling. It was her turn to steer the conversation. "Where are we going?" she asked.

"Ah, Dame Violeta." Nikos leaned forward to take her hand. His fingers were soft and his kiss softer. "Do pardon our most enigmatic quarrel. I am Nikos of the White Eagle. Before we begin, may I venture to explore a question of a most sensitive nature?"

She stole back her hand. "Um. No."

Alikar chortled. "You'll find she's not like the ladies of Patmos."

"Few are," Nikos said. "With nothing but flattery meant by that, Dame Violeta, for who can compare a dianthus to a peony?"

Violet preferred Nikos when he was trying to interrogate her. "I need to contact the monarchs," she said.

He repositioned himself on the bench, surveying Violet in the manner of one who's chewing a piece of straw. "We go to a loyalist whose name I've forgotten—"

"Dag," the Seer said.

"Yes, thank you, who lives in a town likewise forgettably named. Seer?"

"Borku," the Seer supplied.

"But we are traveling there too," Alikar said. "And will you not name the Seer, Nikos? Awfully rude of you."

"One cannot study my character and find rudeness. I chose not to introduce him. Shall I now?" Nikos asked his friend.

The Seer nodded.

Nikos gave his reclining arm a lazy flourish. "Please pay homage to Ezio Nikolaos Ambrosia of the White Eagle, son of the regent of Patmos, fledgling of the High Seer, prince of Janlian."

An odd thrill of intrigue roused Violet's joints. She eyed the Seer. Surely not the prince himself, when someone of a lower profile would suffice?

Alikar evidently agreed. "Don't insult me more than you already have." To the Seer, he added, "Ezio could scarcely leave his room without holding his sister's hand. You know better than I that he could not be paid to leave the realm."

"I was not paid," the Seer answered.

Alikar shook his head, incredulous. But Violet's misgivings cleared, because Alikar's comment had reminded her how the Seer had cowered on Captain Barome's ship—and how Nikos had called him "Ez."

She opened her mouth. Alikar should be made aware, before he continued ridiculing the prince to his face.

"Don't," Nikos said to her. "This amuses me. And was there not some message you wished to tell to me, Dame Violeta?"

She eyed his pendant, making sure she still remembered he was a Goldentongue. "Um," she said, torn between vying concerns: relaying information to the monarchs, paying the appropriate respect to a prince, and informing Alikar of his ignorance. Perhaps all three could be accomplished, in that order of priority. "Yakiv Stefanos has the gate pendant," she said, "which you've probably realized. The monarchs need to be warned."

"They already know, as even their purple pearls are advertising his accomplishment. Though I learned—through rigorous eavesdropping and no flash of the hook—that the bounty for your midnight-haired head is only being propagated on the Separatist pearls. If you find yourself bored one lonely night, I recommend listening to the recordings of each eyewitness convinced that you have stolen their children or eaten from their cupboards. Your efficiency is most impressive, as you have been sighted in no less than eleven countries, and have ransacked all manner of buildings. You gave one poor couple quite the scare when you made off with their daughter's clothes."

"Those beaks!" Alikar said. "They said they were Unionists!"

"And for that reason they feared that you had been duped by Stefanos' lovely accomplice. I am sure the promised sum of cottons was far removed from their altruism."

Nikos meant that couple in the woods. They'd contacted the news? No wonder the townspeople had immediately recognized her.

At long last, Nikos provided the explanation Violet had wanted, though she had to pluck out the relevant information from his flowery narrative, which spanned all the way from leaving Janlian to now. He detailed how he and Prince

Ezio—whom Alikar remained in denial of—disembarked from Captain Barome's *Vagabond;* how they met with the monarchs and realized the identities of the passengers they'd accused; how the monarchs requested that Nikos and the prince go to Shepherd's Crag; and, lastly, how they found the Crag empty of any Terlions and decided to make for Dag's house, Ezio having remembered the loyalist's relationship with Alikar and "she-who-is-shunned." The two Janlions so happened to stop for a meal in the very town that Violet and Alikar stumbled into.

Silfar, Violet thought.

"The prince hoped to find you in this loyalist's home," Nikos concluded. His entire explanation had ignored the fact that said prince sat beside him. "He worried for your safety."

"Solely mine," Alikar asked, "or was Meliora's included?"

The prince flinched again, and Nikos turned his cheek as if Meliora's name had lashed him. "Ezio does protest the edict, in his own way," Nikos said.

That made Alikar's frown diminish. "Kind Ezio, kind as he is odd. Has he changed much? I remember he used to dive under tables at any mention of bumblebees."

The pangs from Violet's conscience were not enough to breach her silence, not after a remark like that.

Poor Alikar.

Nikos' innocent deadpan told Violet he'd had the personality of a Goldentongue long before he was welded. "He's since tackled heartier fears, such as bathtubs and cheese."

"I still don't like cheese," Ezio said seriously.

"But you nibbled some last year," Nikos told him.

"Only because you hooked me."

"Yes, but you liked it."

"I *didn't* like it, cousin."

"Can't you name me as a friend?"

"No. I don't have any friends. If I did, I would not choose you. I would choose someone who does not annoy me."

"This wounds me, Ez. It is a scythe through a porcelain heart."

"I don't believe you."

By this point, Alikar was kneeling in the cramped space meant for feet, his mortified expression not as comical as it would've been had Violet not contributed to it. Did that make her a terrible friend?

"Your Reverence!" Alikar gasped. "Blessings upon you! I pray you are well?"

Fearing that sitting was horribly offensive, Violet quickly joined Alikar on the swaying floor, forced to grip his elbow for balance, as the alternative was toppling into Nikos' knees.

Prince Ezio answered to his upside-down scroll. "Hello, Lord Alikar. I have not seen you since two days past. Before then, I had not seen you since my sister and mother's funeral. Your hair was not so long then, and you were short. You are kneeling on my toes."

Alikar sprang upright, and Violet toppled into Nikos' knees.

Once all were seated again, and Violet was fully invested in pretending Nikos had not swooped her up like someone drowning, Nikos spoke, his voice swollen with amusement.

"May this be a lesson to mind your tongue, Muratsan. You never know at whom it's wagging."

NOON'S LIGHT BLARED WHEN their wagon reached Borku. Alikar parked them on a hill; the cliff paths were too narrow to accommodate the vehicle. Then he sprang outside. He'd said little since Ezio's identity was outed.

What now? The monarchs already knew Yakiv had the gate pendant. All that remained to be done was catch him, which was a job for the royal army and not a solitary Terlion.

The wind, barreling in from the coast, grew pungent. Sunlight shone on the sprawling seaside town that reminded Violet of a sandstone Mediterranean. Across the lake rose snowy peaks. One of those mountains hid her way home. She was right where she'd started. Maybe she ought to begin her journey back to Terlian.

The prophecy hadn't provided a timeline. Maybe a stooped-over, white-haired Violet would one day hobble back to Earth with the gate pendant. The mental picture was far from enticing, but did it matter, so long as Terlian healed?

"You know the way to this loyalist's home?" Nikos exited the wagon, wrinkling his nose as the wind found him.

"Yes," Alikar said, "but I don't see that your company is necessary, given that we are going to Dag's with the sole purpose of finding *Meliora*." Alikar looked satisfied when they flinched.

"Shall we return to the Bar'Talion monarchs?" Nikos asked Ezio.

The prince stood in the wind, still turbaned, still clutching his scroll. "What do you want?"

"I cannot be so bold as to advise the crown prince."

"Yes you can. You advise me daily, when you are not hooking me."

"Ezio, the speed at which you neglect the art of subtlety flies faster than—"

"Are you coming or are you not?" Alikar demanded.

Nikos missed not one beat as he refastened his head garment and swept toward Violet. "We cannot go where we are not led. Dame Violeta, the honor of your arm? I should hate to see you at the mercy of another hill."

"Enough syrup, Nikos. Go." Alikar pushed him downhill with all the joy of a shepherd and his stubborn goat.

Violet remained, surveying the far-off mountains wherein the way home hid. *So close.* Yet she was worse off than when she'd arrived.

"It should be worn," spoke Ezio in that demure voice that made it hard to believe he was royalty. His penetrating stare, drilling a hole in her pocket, was no less uncomfortable than Nikos' charm.

"The chain broke," she said.

"Stop ogling, Ez!" Nikos called.

The prince ran after his cousin.

They walked behind Borku's narrow, cylindrical houses, their footsteps too loud on streets that should've bustled with activity. There were no children playing in the streets; no one walking to work or coming home from the store. Violet saw not a few curtains moving behind windows. The atmosphere held the hushed sort of fear too wary of making noise.

"Here," Alikar said. They stopped before an unlit turret of yellow stone, capped by a flat roof. The loyalist flag hung somewhere in the jungle of vines ornamenting the front.

Alikar waited fifteen seconds after knocking before he gave Dag's door password: *Basilia*. The name plugged Violet's throat and caused both Janlions to dip their heads.

"Melly?" Alikar shoved the door open.

Nikos gave an elegant wave, gesturing for Violet to enter.

She came into a dim, cool home that smelled of coffee and cardamom. The familiar scents disoriented her; she hadn't expected to find nostalgia on another planet. While Alikar roamed into rooms out of sight, Violet and the Janlions lingered in the foyer, lit only by the sunlight that the drawn curtains allowed. Shapes off the foyer indicated a divan, a wooden table balancing on four crooked legs, floral wallpaper, and an expansive, Persian-style rug with one missing tassel. A decorative metal partition cordoned off the rest of the house, allowing her only dark glimpses through the gaps in the screen. One shadowed blob moving on the opposite side of the partition came around it.

"She isn't here," Alikar said, the paltry lighting adding more worry to his face.

"How long would it take her to walk from the forest?" Violet asked.

"A few days."

"Then of course she's not here. She's still on her way."

"I need to find her." Alikar barreled toward the exit, causing Ezio to jump aside. Then, Alikar spun around with all the frenzy of a swerving car. "No, *you* can find her, Compass! Let's go."

Violet, suddenly expected to perform, did the opposite of go.

"A Compass," Nikos said. "You did say there was something navigation-like to her liryn, yes?" he asked Ezio.

The prince, fully invested in staring at the curtain which covered a presumed coat closet, didn't reply.

"Terlian's liryn," Alikar answered. "It's how she found the gate pendant. Her liryn draws her toward things, and punishes her when she disobeys."

Violet didn't think that part was strictly necessary to the conversation.

Nikos moved into the sitting room and made himself at home on the divan, ignoring the round, velvet pillow flattened by his elbow.

"Shoes off," Alikar said.

They all removed theirs, Violet feeling silly in purple socks.

"Ezio," Nikos said.

The prince maintained his sidelong observation of the curtain.

"How does her liryn work?"

Ezio backed up, found himself against the metal partition, and then faced it, his answer projected toward the unexplored areas of Dag's house. "I do not understand the liryn of Terlian."

"But it's *nehfey*, the same as yours," Nikos said. "It must follow the same principles."

"I don't know!" He dropped his scroll.

"Ezio," Nikos said, an edge to his usual charisma. "Focus."

"Don't hook me!"

"I'm not."

"Your luster is glowing more violet than Dame Violeta."

"By the beak, was that a joke?"

"No!"

Nikos shifted. Dag's pillow would soon resemble a hash brown. "You can't even see me, Ezio."

"Can a Seer truly be hooked?" Alikar interrupted.

Nikos ignored him. "If you can't provide me with answers, I'll have no choice but to beseech the High Seer. Must your father be brought into this?"

"I don't like you at all!" The prince's arms gave a chicken-like flap as he, with equal squawky bearing, flurried around the partition and escaped.

Alikar let the racket of doors opening and closing fade before he spoke. "He hasn't changed much."

"To the unobservant." Nikos took in Violet, gazing somewhere around her neck, probably hunting for the pendant. "You could lead us to Stefanos."

She shook her head; she'd already thought this through. "He could be in another country, days away. Besides, if he sees us coming, he'll just create a new gate and escape."

Nikos leaned forward, elbows on his knees. Dag's pillow was free to expand to its former size. Violet nearly moved it, in case Nikos decided to recline again. Instead, she rescued Ezio's scroll. The parchment felt thick as hide. Was it old, or did the citizens of Patmos currently write on vellum?

"That's a dangerous look you're wearing, Nik," Alikar said slowly. "Usually followed by worms in Meliora's hair."

Nikos forgot to wince at Meliora's name. His eyes, already dark without the room's shadows, found Violet. "There's a fat sum of cottons for your capture, yes, Dame Violeta?"

"I beg your pardon?" Alikar said.

"You witnessed the Separatist's punctuality. He'll come for her."

That hung in the foyer like an additional tapestry.

"Turn her over?" Alikar *tsked*. "Fork-tongues really are an idiotic lot."

Nikos shook his head. "We will put no flowers in Separatist vases. When Stefanos comes, we'll be waiting. She'll be bait, but uncaught."

Violet, whose fingers had found a button as soon as Nikos mentioned handing her over to Yakiv, relaxed. "A ruse," she said. "But won't he suspect something like that? Or that we're lying just to get the reward? As you've said, there have already been false witnesses."

"Yes, I'm sure there will be some verification process. He'll need to see that it's truly you. Which means providing him with a visual." Nikos' expression grew harder with thought. It *did* appear somewhat dangerous, an odd look for the syrupy charmer.

"But how can we pretend we've captured her when any Separatist would recognize our faces?" Alikar said as a distant door squeaked.

"Don't be a hasty vintner," Nikos said. "Let the plan age."

Ezio came around the partition, his feet shuffling and scooting like a child about to be punished. Though they had privacy, he'd yet to remove his turban. The closet curtain stole his attention again. "Nikos," he mumbled.

Nikos paid him no mind.

"I need to tell you something," Ezio added. He adjusted himself so that he could eye the curtain without facing it directly. The way he angled his head, like someone avoiding the glare of an afternoon sun, reminded Violet of his skittish behavior around the cord thief on *The Vagabond.*

"Does this village have a mirrorgraph?" Nikos asked Alikar.

"This is a town, not a village. And every town has a mirrorgraph."

Nikos chuckled. "You have not ventured much from the luxury of Vaspurakan."

"And I suppose a Janlion has?"

"You'll find that poverty and insufficiency coexist much the same on every realm."

"Meaning?" Alikar said.

Meaning this small fishing town might not have whatever a "mirrorgraph" was.

"We may have to travel in order to send word to Stefanos," Nikos answered. "You'll help, Muratsan. I'm afraid my Arati vocabulary was stored in a cracked vase."

"I'm sure you only bothered remembering words like 'beautiful' and 'goddess' and 'Where is your husband?' and 'Your hand is like a dove's wing,'" Alikar said. "And we're not sending word to Yakiv. You're insane."

"Dove wings are prickly. 'A dew-touched sage petal' makes for a better compliment." Nikos paused, finally noticing his cousin. "Is there a cord thief behind the curtain?"

"That is what I wanted to tell you," Ezio said.

Violet's eyes widened. So did Nikos', though he was quicker at exchanging his shock for calculation. He strode over. The curtain innocently hung, a still and purple veil.

Nikos reached out, and Alikar stepped closer to Violet. Protectively? The idea was confusing. Intriguing. She almost smiled.

Before Nikos could yank the curtain aside, it flapped and shifted. And out spilled Jarek.

CHAPTER TWENTY-SEVEN

"Seers were to confiscate the contraband cord and bring the thief before the local magistrate. Cords were then returned to the appropriate monarchs, who reserved them for the annual Restoration Day, in which any welded who'd lost a cord could come and summon back their own." – *Where Have the Seers Gone?* by Vessel Abina

"Y OU!" ALIKAR'S SCISSOR-SHARP EXCLAMATION could've cut the curtain in two.

Violet needed several seconds before her brain confirmed what her eyes registered.

"You know him?" Nikos asked Alikar.

"I was not told he's a cord thief, as well as a . . ." Alikar miraculously kept the rest to himself.

Jarek's demeanor was not as guilty as one would expect from a person who'd been hiding in a stranger's closet. "I don't have any cords," he said, his scowl thick and his gaze on Violet, like she'd made the accusation.

"Ah, yes," Nikos said, "the light here is shy, and the eye perceives little. The pendant hanging from his cord is an eagle, my friend." He gestured toward Ezio. "There's no use in lying. Some Seers have been known to spot a stolen cord through steel and stone."

Jarek's scowl faded. "A Seer? Outside Janlian?"

"It's written that the Seers of old could outsmart a thief and summon back the wrongful cord." Nikos studied his cousin like waiting for such a thing to happen, but Ezio was treating Jarek like a painful spotlight.

"I'm not lying. I don't have any cords." Jarek addressed Violet again. The same defeat from earlier tugged down his shoulders and somehow made the wear and tear of his clothes more noticeable. "I sent them back," he muttered.

She met his stare, for some reason intended for her. Shame outlived his other emotions. Jarek wanted Violet to see it. He'd lied to Meliora, and he'd interrupted Kelispar's happiness—although, she couldn't blame him for that, even if Alikar did. But Jarek was sorry.

"All three?" Ezio spoke.

Jarek nodded.

"How did you know that?" Nikos appraised his cousin with something unmistakably close to wonder. "That he previously had cords, and the number of them?"

Ezio pivoted fully away from Jarek now. "He is three-times stained," he said. Though he delivered that without any drama or gloom, its effect was like another shade over the window.

Jarek's forehead creased, and Nikos glanced toward an unlit candle on Dag's table.

Alikar, on the other hand, had likely registered "Jarek" and "thief" and would let nothing more penetrate until he'd finished glowering.

"Why are you hiding in this man's home?" Nikos asked Jarek.

"I'm waiting for Meliora."

"She-who-is-shunned has garnered no shortage of interest."

Violet thought she detected a gleam of jealousy, or something more complicated, but whatever it was vanished as Nikos' air suddenly hardened like cold wax. Two eyes devoid of their usual levity hooked themselves onto Jarek's person.

"Sit," he said sharply.

Jarek sat right there on the floor, obedient as anyone under a Goldentongue's sway. Violet shuddered to think how foolish she'd looked, doling out every scrap of information Kora requested.

"You could have chosen the couch. But this will suffice. Dirt for dirt." Nikos wasn't glaring like Alikar, but his countenance could have suited a magistrate. "Were this Seer like the Seers of old, you would not presently feel the comfort of the ground beneath your bottom, but the pain of cold bindings around your wrists. Perhaps your neck and legs would feel pain too, a binding for every stolen cord. You would then know a Janlion cell and the taste of rat dung. A familiar taste to you, filth that you are, the very lowest dreg upon human society and all that beauty enshrines. It is no wonder the Seer marks you as stained. I cannot see it, but one recognizes vermin even without an eagle's eye."

The tight and measured defiance in Jarek's stare told Violet this wasn't the first time he'd looked up as someone else looked down. Nikos' disgust was too harsh for someone who'd never done him personal harm. Violet swallowed, thinking of Jarek's broken voice in the forest. Of the fact that he'd walked away—but mostly the fact that he'd come searching for Meliora, after returning the cords he'd stolen.

"You forget that every Seer has two hands."

Had Violet not heard the quiet voice from Ezio's direction, she would've wondered if there was a second person hiding in Dag's closet.

"That hasn't escaped me," Nikos answered.

"You speak only of the hand of justice," Ezio added. "There is also the hand of mercy."

"Mercy is for those who deserve it."

"I think . . . he does." Ezio dipped his head, scuffing his toes on the rug.

Jarek took in Ezio with nothing short of confusion.

The light of cordiality had yet to reenter Nikos' face, but he didn't spit on Jarek's hair, at least. "You are the Seer," he told Ezio. "You have the authority to rule on this matter. Does he stay, or do we banish him to a sunless void of wind and broken glass?"

Jarek didn't give Ezio the chance to decide. "I can help you," he said. "I heard your plan."

"Eavesdropped, you mean," Alikar muttered.

"Hear me out. Muratsan's right: None of you can hand the Terlion over. Two Janlions and the emissary's brother? Yakiv will know it's a trap."

"Who said anything about her being a Terlion?" Alikar's foot reared back, like one who's found a soccer ball.

"We met," Violet said quickly. "In the Amber Forest."

Alikar's head swiveling could have flattened a line-up of bowling pins. "I see Nikos' memory isn't the only cracked vase," he said, folding his arms.

"There's a mirrorgraph here," Jarek continued. "That's how people are contacting Yakiv for the reward, through the shells. I can shine a message. And I can bring her with me."

The heat of nervous energy warmed Violet's hands. This plan might actually work.

Nikos evidently thought so too; he gazed down on Jarek less like someone punishing a bad dog, and more like someone pondering how far the dog could run. "Are you a loyalist?" he asked.

"I'm loyal to Meliora." Then, beneath all the many panels that concealed Jarek's inner workings, the slow wheel of anger churned. "And I want Yakiv Stefanos dead."

Shadows dropped across the foyer as the invisible sun shifted. The stale, cold air in Dag's home didn't invigorate Violet like the brittle winds of Helheim. She tugged her sleeve down, shielding her fingertips.

"Well," Nikos said, "even Electra might have accepted Clytemnestra's aid if the outcome was the same."

Now Jarek just looked dubious, but Violet understood the reference, with somewhat of a thrill. Sophocles had traveled all the way to Janlian.

Or had his works traveled all the way to Earth?

Nikos turned to Ezio. "Let the Seer decide."

Ezio, upon finding all eyes on him, snatched Dag's purple curtain. Violet thought he might dive into the closet, notwithstanding the fact that Jarek was blocking the way. But he stayed put, clenching the fabric. There'd be wrinkles by the time he let go.

"There is no such thing as a sunless void of wind and broken glass," Ezio said. "And Janlion prisons do not have rats."

Nikos waved Jarek up. "You may stay. Now, where is the mirrorgraph?"

Dag's divan was likely more comfortable than standing crammed between the lamp and the wall, but the Janlions were taking up the couch, Alikar the floor (flattening Dag's pillow beneath him), Jarek the foyer, and Violet was not about to sit that close to Nikos. She wished Meliora were here. Meliora had a way of keeping everyone in check. There might as well have been poisonous fumes pouring from Jarek's body with the way Alikar avoided him.

Nikos was doing all the talking, drawing information from Jarek like he didn't know how to communicate except by interrogating. Soon Violet had some understanding of the "mirrorgraph," a small stand or structure that facilitated communication with the radio-like resonance shells. Violet would see a mirrorgraph up close, when Jarek pretended to turn her over to Yakiv.

Her fingers tightened around the black flower in her pocket, then released. Unlike June, she hadn't developed the habit of treating her pendant like a good luck charm. But June's pendant didn't hold sílfar, which was currently like a flickering flame blocking Violet's sight, following the movements of her head each time she tried peering past it.

Those are nerves. Violet shifted, failing to get more comfortable. Her eyes touched Ezio.

He was staring at her pocket.

She wished she could hide the pendant in another room. But Ezio would see it there, too.

Nikos' next order of business was rallying allies. The idea of the monarchs' royal guard was briefly entertained, but even Ezio didn't have a way to facilitate instant communication with Bar'Talian's king and queen, and neither Nikos nor Alikar were eager to send word through the monarchs' attendants, still under the false impression that one of them was working for Yakiv. Especially now that Jarek was here, Violet wasn't going to correct their assumption.

Once the prospect of the royal army swooping in to capture Yakiv was defeated, the conversation reached a standstill. Who could they trust? Ezio and Nikos had allies, but they were on another planet. Jarek's friends were in a different country—not that anyone was eager to accept *more* help from him.

"Where are you from?" Nikos asked him.

Jarek stared at the foyer curtain. "Piast."

"And where is Piast?"

"East of Arat," Alikar said. "Few thousand leagues."

"It's a country, then," Nikos said.

"One of the filthiest. The hub of cord trading for all of the eastern quarter. Or it was, until Yakiv hung the crook running it. The crook who happens to be—"

Jarek flung the curtain awry and took one step into the sitting room. "We don't need allies. We tell Yakiv to meet us somewhere with cover. Then we'll—"

"Stop." Nikos held up a hand. "Air is precious, and this room is already stifling."

"What?"

"Allies are a necessity."

"Fine. Who? Loyalists aren't exactly pears on a tree."

"Do they have to be loyalists?" Violet asked.

Nikos propped an ankle on his knee. How could he look so comfortable at a time like this? "Currently, there are two branches of people who would risk fighting Yakiv: those interested in his bounty, or those convinced he must be brought to justice. Given that he's publicly announced that he's in possession of the gate pendant, few would be brave enough to challenge him unless they're confident they can capture the pendant for themselves. That leaves us with loyalists. They want to see the Hasteins' murderer dead." He glanced toward Alikar. "The Muratsans must have some connections."

Though the word *dead* had fallen into the room like a storm's shadow, no one addressed it.

Alikar toyed with the pillow tassel. "I barely recall any names. Kelispar . . . handled that." He took a breath. "I suppose we could go to the manor and explore our social records. I should alert the staff of my well-being, anyway. They likely believe I'm dead."

Violet rubbed a dirty spot on her knuckle, wondering when "dead" and "murder" would just be words.

"How far is your manor?" Nikos asked.

"It's back in Vaspurakan."

At that rate, they might as well go with their original plan of contacting the monarchs. Violet was beginning to appreciate the inconveniences that came with having a high profile. Every single one of them would attract attention, excluding Jarek. If only they knew—

She almost flinched at her own blindness. "What about Dag?" she said.

"He's one man," Alikar said.

"But he might have friends here. Other loyalists."

"Well . . . yes. He might."

"I like your thinking, Dame Violeta." Nikos stood; the cushion re-inflated as if relieved. "Muratsan, you and I will find this man. Former cord thief—what is your name?"

"Doesn't matter," Jarek said.

"Then you will be '*Prospheta*.' It's a particularly moldy cheese. Rotten, but still useful."

"It's Jarek."

Nikos smiled. "Jarek, go explore the mirrorgraph and learn of Stefanos' latest movements. Ezio, stay."

The prince needed no permission before he fled into the unseen area behind the iron screen.

"Ezio?" Jarek stared after him. "As in—"

"Let the sun never fade and the moon find us idle." Nikos opened the door and gestured for Jarek to take his leave.

"I'll go with you," Violet told Nikos, adjusting her coat.

"We go toward no exciting purpose, Dame Violeta. I beg you to remain here, in safety. If you would, keep my cousin away from flowers. Excluding yourself, of course. He's allergic."

With that, the door closed, and Violet was alone in a stranger's house with the prince of Janlian.

The divan was free, but she paced instead. Hunger prodded, enough to make her wonder what sort of items stocked Dag's pantry, but she wasn't the sort to go digging.

It was too early to tell if this plan would succeed. Perhaps Dag was off on his boat somewhere, unreachable. Or perhaps he had no friends who'd be willing to help. Even if he did, no one could ward off a hurricane. Yakiv could blow them back and disappear.

We need something else. An advantage, something to catch Yakiv off-guard.

Finally, she sat, after scooping up the pillow Alikar had left discarded on the floor. He'd braided the tassels into intricate knots. She worked her fingers through the threads. Did none of these people respect personal property?

As she loosened thread by thread, Violet wondered if Meliora had gotten lost in the Amber Forest. She wondered if June had settled back in San Diego; if Yakiv had destroyed any more landscapes; if the entire Lykill would be in her hands in a few short hours; if Earth would be healed by midnight. Violet didn't waste time worrying that it wouldn't work. Fa had believed in the Lykill. He'd been right about everything else.

Had he been right about me?

She shook out the wrinkled tassels, smoothed down the pillow, and set it aside. Then she withdrew her pendants. Oliver's vegvísir weighed less than her violet, though it took up more space. A compass, according to some. Yet the vegvísir was just an empty symbol. Violet was the real compass. A Compass guided, but, according to Malokki, sílfar did all the work. *She* hadn't found Fa's troll. *She* hadn't known the gate pendant was hidden in the tree.

A jangle came from the screen's direction. Violet guessed Ezio was nearby. Sure enough, as she tried ignoring the sensation of being watched, she caught sight of two fingers sticking through the gaps in the screen. For another minute, Violet worked on the already-untangled tassels and pretended not to notice. Then, she couldn't bear it anymore.

"Prince Ezio?"

Another jangle.

Violet knew that, as a Terlion, she held some intrigue. But the prince wasn't spying on her because of her realm.

She stood, eager to get this over with. "Do you . . . want to hold it?" Hopefully, he'd understand her outstretched gesture.

The shape of Ezio's form passed alongside the grate until he emerged. There, straddling the division between the foyer and the rest of the house, he remained. Violet's flower pendant was like a pair of snake eyes for all Ezio's reverie. How did it appear to him? How did *Violet* appear?

Slowly, Ezio crept into the sitting room. He hovered near the divan for some moments before he turned toward the table.

She quietly exhaled her relief, and then sucked it back when Ezio returned her way. He was holding something, a figurine, which he placed on Dag's rug as he knelt. It was a little lamb. In its mouth it carried a flagpole.

Ezio extended his palm.

Does he want me to help him up?

Then she realized he wanted her pendant. She dropped it onto his hand.

"Lykill," he said, placing her pendant on the rug. Then he turned the lamb so its eyes looked away from her pendant. *"Kyria Violeta."*

Her pendant was the Lykill, and she was the lamb. She was facing the wrong direction. But how could he tell?

"Yakiv has the pendant," she said.

Ezio shook his head. "Lykill." He pointed to her pendant. *"Kyria Violeta."* He made the animal run away from the Lykill. The lamb lost its balance.

Violet stared at the toppled version of herself. "I'm not running away," she said. "I'm willing to face Yakiv."

Ezio was shaking his head harder. *"Ochi, ochi."* He fetched his shoe, a seamless ankle boot whose white fabric was mud stained. "Yakiv Stefanos," he said, waving the boot. "Lykill." He indicated her pendant. Two separate things.

Violet understood that. Yakiv only had a fraction. The rest was on Terlian.

Ezio dropped his shoe and reached for his liryn cord. "Liryn," he said, *"kai Ezio."* He patted his chest. Then he collected the lamb and Violet's pendant. "Liryn." He displayed the pendant in his left hand. *"Kyria Violeta."* He held the lamb in his other hand, stretching his arms far apart.

The implication stung with the bitterness of shame. She couldn't feign ignorance of his point. Seer as he was, he could tell that sílfar was in one hand while Violet was in another. Apart.

"I don't want . . ." She swallowed. Whatever had been about to come out would have sounded just like Oliver.

She bent over, but no sooner had she thought to retrieve her pendant than it floated up to meet her. The black flower brushed her fingers like a cat seeking attention. Violet closed her fist around it and stood, turning toward the window so Ezio wouldn't read more of her than he already was.

Yes, Violet and sílfar were at odds. She'd only known about her liryn for a couple days; could she be blamed for some hesitance? When she returned to Terlian, she could sort through this new discovery. For now, capturing Yakiv was only tangentially related to the fact that she had liryn.

The pendant went to her pocket, where it could be dealt with later. Violet would forge ahead on her own terms, as she'd always done. Stiff and coiled, but at least bound together.

The iron heart of Terlian.

CHAPTER TWENTY-EIGHT

"When the golden age is flourishing, the avaricious pair will rise. A rift will rupture the provinces. Terlian will be condemned. But out of oppression, hope can stir. First, the man of white must give up his desire. Second, the man of peace must sow discord. Third, the opening must be made. Then will the child come to carry the Lykill to restoration. This will come about after the Lykill is found in shadow and smoke. Only then can unity conjoin the provinces. And Terlian will not be oppressed." – Prophecy of Silian

JAREK RETURNED FIRST. VIOLET answered his knock, groping around the door for a moment before she remembered to give the password. As soon as he realized the others hadn't returned, he plopped onto the divan.

Ezio flinched. So Jarek got up and walked back outside.

Violet straightened Dag's pillows and wished humans weren't so complicated.

Alikar and Nikos eventually returned, Jarek trailing behind. Nikos immediately unwrapped his turban and opened his mouth, rattling off in Greek for some seconds before Jarek interrupted in whatever language he spoke. Nikos looked to Alikar.

He fingered his Advocate cord and leaned against the screen. "I'm tired."

"And I just wasted my breath. But we overcome." Nikos faced Violet. "Dag and his friends will confer in this house within the hour."

"Is that all?" Jarek said after a beat.

"Yes."

"Took you much longer the first time," Alikar said.

"The first time, I was under the impression that I had a captivated audience. Jarek? Were you successful?"

Jarek shoved his hands into his dirt-crusted pockets. "Yakiv is monitoring the pearls, but he says he'll ignore anything that doesn't include an image. Costs fifty cottons to shine one."

Nikos waved a flippant hand.

"Some people have duplicated her image and shined it out, pretending they've got her, so now he wants moving proof."

"Yes, we already assumed she would accompany you to the mirrorgraph."

"Don't know how we'll do that discreetly," Jarek said. "Might have to pay off the one running it."

"Money doesn't pose an issue," Nikos answered.

"Right. Access to Janlian's treasury, have you?"

"Not in recent years. My uncle has a strong prejudice against Goldentongues. It wounds me to my spirit."

Jarek's eyes narrowed, slinking across Nikos and Ezio, who was still on the floor, arms around his knees like a kid listening to a campfire story. "I knew it. You're the prince, and you're his cousin."

Alikar clapped.

"What a clever cord thief we have recruited," Nikos said, "one who knows how to use his eyes and ears."

The oozing sarcasm, all in that cheery tone, made Jarek's eyes go thinner. "Meliora told me about you. Very friendly with her, before the edict."

"Yes, she-who-is-shunned has always had poor taste in friends."

Violet watched Jarek's wall rebuild itself across a blank face. For the dozenth time, she wished Meliora were here. She changed the subject. "How is Yakiv planning to contact whoever's supposedly captured me? You show him you have me, but then what? Isn't all of this communication taking place publicly? Or are there private . . . pearls?"

"Yakiv knows you're somewhere nearby," Jarek said, "so he's set up a network. You're to be brought to designated Separatist venues. He's given the list. Once you're there, his people will signal him through the pipeways. They'll arrange the meet."

"So, after we go to the mirrorgraph, we'll have to find one of the designated spots."

"No," Nikos said. "You'll tell Stefanos where to meet you. We can't pass Dame Violeta through any other hands."

"Publicly broadcasting our location is risky too," Violet said.

Everyone mulled over that.

"Have you shared words with Stefanos?" Nikos asked her.

"Yes."

"Can you imagine a veiled hint that would be known only by you and him?"

She'd told him the gate was near Borku. Yakiv wouldn't have forgotten that. He might even already be nearby, scouring the mountains.

"Yes," she said slowly. "Jarek could say something to the effect of, 'I've got her in that town she told you of.' Yakiv would know what it meant." But there was another obstacle in the way of this plan. "Does he speak your language?" she asked Jarek.

"He has an Advocate," he said.

"I thought Advocates couldn't translate pearl messages."

"That depends on their strength," Nikos answered. "Some can, some cannot. If Stefanos' Advocate cannot, he will find one who can."

Violet almost reminded him that hunting down another Advocate would take time. Then she remembered Yakiv could instantaneously transport himself.

"Then the first stage of our plan is solidified. Here, we will wait for Dag and his friends." Nikos tossed his turban onto the divan before sprawling out on the cushion. "And then we wait for Stefanos."

WAITING FOR THE PROMISE of allies was like waiting for a winter storm. They'd done all the preparation they could; now all that was left was putting it into action.

Alikar helped himself to Dag's kitchen, bringing rose water, bread, and cheese into the sitting room. Violet ate with scientific detachment, a body satisfying a need. She forgot to study the nutty flat bread, or compare the tangy, crumbly cheese to the cheese of Terlian. Even the water's soapiness failed to draw her interest.

She needed space. In this room, there were too many hostilities. Too many strangers. Too many heavy loads no one was shouldering. And, for her, too many doubts that this plan could succeed. What could Dag and his friends—what could anyone—do against the power of the gate pendant? The longing for freedom, for some mental pondering that might give her the perfect idea to nail this plan together, pulled her so earnestly it might as well have been sílfar.

When noises like the stomping of feet thumped outside Dag's front door, everyone rose. Congenial Nikos, weary Alikar, flat Jarek, fidgety Ezio. And then there was Violet.

"Divulge the prince's identity and you'll never see the end of my hook," Nikos said lightly as Dag's door swept open. "Ah, may eagles wing you, good sirs!" He bowed to the ship captain's entrance.

Dag closed the door. "Lord Alikar," he said. "Kindly a word, please."

Alikar answered in Arati. For a moment, Dag was unsatisfied; his purple-hatted head tipped in Nikos' direction. But Alikar continued on, likely explaining that no one understood Arati. As the two talked, it became increasingly apparent that the subject of their conversation was Nikos, given Dag's not remotely subtle glances in the Goldentongue's direction. Nikos watched the whole exchange without change of friendly expression. Finally, Dag and Alikar took Ezio into another room. They returned a minute later. The prince maintained the rear like one being led to his own execution.

Nikos spoke in Greek, Alikar held up a hand, and then Nikos spoke again, cutting off Alikar's now-translated reply.

"It has been requested that I remove my cord, yes?" he said.

"Nobody likes a Fork-tongue," Alikar said.

"Begging your pardon," Dag murmured, not meeting Nikos' eye.

"The Seer will hold it for you," Alikar added.

Nikos chewed on this. Violet hoped he wouldn't put up a fight. She couldn't blame Dag's friends for their reservations.

"Very well." Nikos removed his purple cord. "The good men of Arat need not say that Linus of Janlian is difficult."

"I'm sure they'll find that out in other ways, *Linus*," Alikar said as Ezio draped the purple cord over his white one.

Satisfied, Dag opened the door. Four men stomped in, figures made bulky by their cloaks, tattered at the hems, and their snow-caked boots. Dag's foyer seemed to shrink, taken over by equipment: a row of removed boots; long, silver poles with prongs at the end; and a bundle of nets, seaweed trapped in their knots. With the men's entrance came the inevitable stench of fish.

There was an unspoken competition for obscurity between Violet, Jarek, and Ezio, who bumped into one another as they attempted to attach themselves to Dag's iron screen, as out of sight as they could be. Ezio capitulated first, fleeing to the kitchen, leaving Violet and Jarek to awkwardly shift beside each other as Dag's friends finished processing in. Including Dag, there were five in total, men sharing the stocky, medium builds of the Arati people. Alikar really was an anomaly with his tall and wiry frame, though his blond hair matched three of the men; Dag and one other had black.

"Lord Muratsan," spoke a man, and then each proceeded to clasp Alikar's hand and offer their condolences. The names given were Kristapor, Arek, Hazar, and Nareg; Violet could not track which belonged to who.

Throughout the formalities, Alikar carried himself graciously, giving Violet a glimpse of the nobleman who lived in Alikar when he wasn't being—well, his other self.

"Brave men of Arat," Nikos cut in when a half second of silence passed, "I am called Linus. My traveling companion, Heracles, has excused himself and will return momentarily."

Dag's friends ignored the introduction, surveying Violet. "I hear rumors you are Terlion," one of them said. Nareg? His tone was not unfriendly, holding cautious wonder.

"Ah," Nikos jumped in, "rumors are the fat of our consumption. How salty they taste! Yet how cruelly they treat us."

Dag's friends didn't bother acknowledging that. They were fixated on Violet, five men whom the sun and lake had wrinkled, their hair gone bristly, and their clothes made up of crooked patches. Simple men, with arms hefty enough to prove they earned their keep. And yet they ignored Jarek, the only other one in the room who looked like he'd gotten his hands dirty more than once. They seemed unimpressed by Nikos, and their interest in Alikar had ended with their condolences.

These men were loyalists. Their eyes were for Terlian. Would it be imprudent to tell them the truth? But could Violet disappoint them with a lie? Why did she care? She didn't know these men, wouldn't have noticed them on an empty street.

But their heritage, separated by centuries though it was, had origins in Terlian. They would've felt it when Lady Basilia died.

"I am," she said quietly. "I'm Violet Lyng. And I'm a Terlion."

Five pairs of brown eyes met five pairs of black brows.

"Great Welder be blessed," one of them whispered.

Dag removed his hat. "I didn't know, Dame," he said, wringing the purple fez, "when I gave you passage before. Else I would have honored you, I would have."

"Oh. It's all right. No honoring is necessary." Violet, hands behind her back, nervously scraped at the iron grate. "I'm pleased to meet you. Thank you for taking me on your boat, and for hosting me in your home."

"A Terlion, in my home!" Dag laughed out. "Blessed be!"

The others nodded and murmured their assent, burly frames and rugged features suddenly bashful as they clapped Dag's shoulders and congratulated him on his good fortune.

"Can you tell us of Terlian?" spoke one of the blonds.

"Is she as beautiful as Bar'Talian?" asked another.

"Must be," said Nareg, "having the Lykill all the years gone. Do they know of us, Dame Violet? Do they know of our Lady?"

"May she who sleeps rise again," the others murmured together.

Beneath the expectation of these five hopeful loyalists, Violet's courage failed. She could think of nothing to say but the truth: Terlian was ugly, dying, and nobody knew anything about the Hasteins. She looked toward Alikar, hoping he'd read the scene for once and provide a necessary distraction.

"Yes," he said slowly. "Many things of Terlian can be said—"

"When we are not at the mercy of time," Nikos finished. "What a wondrous reunion! Alas, the hourglass ever exhausts itself. Good sirs, shall we plan?"

Only Nikos would presume to take charge in someone else's house. His presumption wasn't lost on Dag, who appraised Nikos with none of the warmth he'd shown Violet. From his friends, four additional scowls emerged.

"What do you think, Dago?" Nareg spoke. "We plan?"

Dag readjusted his fez. "We plan."

Nikos took the divan, leaving space only for Dag, who waved Violet over. Alikar shoved Nikos off, even after Violet insisted that she was fine standing. But no one would hear of that, so she sat beside Dag, who brushed off the cushion for her, beaming.

Is this what it feels like to be royalty?

"What fine specimen of Arat!" said Nikos. "It is expedient that we hurry. Shall I tell you of my plan?"

Nareg turned to Dag. "What's the plan, Dago?"

"I don't think they like you, Linus," Violet heard Alikar murmur.

"Well." Dag rubbed his whiskered cheeks. "Give us the stock, Kristapor."

The other blond nodded. And Violet, relieved that the planning was finally underway, forgot her discomfort and focused. Here was how they'd make their plan to capture Yakiv. This could all be over in a few hours.

"Twenty barrels," Kristapor said. "Twenty-six if we lose my haul."

"Put yours with mine," Nareg said.

"So you can say you made good catch today?" joked Arek or Hazar. The others laughed while Nareg rolled his eyes.

Kristapor, however, seemed the serious and single-minded type, for which Violet was grateful. "Twenty-six barrels, then," he told Dag.

"So we roll the barrels downhill, knock him over," Nareg said.

"Then throw a ten-webber over him," another suggested.

"That's a shark net, true and true."

The men laughed.

Violet sat amid the joking of fishermen, hoping there was more to it. It seemed the plan was to knock Yakiv off his feet with some barrels, then capture him with a net.

"Be most merciful to this interruption," Nikos spoke. "Your plan is robust and hearty, and would be most beautifully complemented by a Goldentongue. You are wary of my liryn, for which I cannot fault you. But it would serve us well against Stefanos, who will not be expecting a Goldentongue. He has one in his service, has he not, Dame Violeta?"

She nodded.

"You don't catch fish by telling them to jump in your net," Nareg said gruffly.

The others nodded, fiercely.

"Dame Violeta," Nikos said, "perhaps you would like to offer your opinion on Goldentongues?" His focused gaze told her he wanted her to back him up.

She would, only because she agreed with his point. "I do think having a Goldentongue will give us more equal footing. Linus can distract Yakiv's Goldentongue to make sure she doesn't interfere."

"Pardon, Dame Violet, but . . ." Dag fidgeted with his hat again. "This fight against Yakiv, it's a fight for loyalists. And the Janlions . . . they're no friend of our Lady. Not when they're no friend of her son."

"And niece," Nareg added.

The others gave vehement assent.

Violet observed the men's scowls with a new light. This wasn't so much about liryn as it was about loyalty.

She said nothing more, and neither did Nikos. The planning continued, namely discussions of barrel weights and whether Nareg or Hazar could throw farther. Jarek chimed in on occasion, and his opinions were considered. If only the men knew he was an ex-cord thief.

Throughout the discussion, Violet couldn't ignore her own restlessness. These attack plans were no good. She wasn't a military strategist, and even she could spot the issues. But Dag and his friends—and their new ally, Jarek—weren't open to suggestions outside of "Attack Yakiv with heavy artillery, then charge." Fresh air and silence called, where she could think up some tactic for getting Dag to see reason. She was a Terlion; he was a loyalist. He might listen, if she could say the right thing.

Violet stood. "Excuse me. I would like a breath of fresh air. I'll cover my face," she added quickly, "and I won't go far."

"All right." Alikar started buttoning his coat.

"I meant alone," she said.

He paused, eyes on her. And in them, she read sorrow for Kelispar and worry for Meliora.

"Okay." Violet nodded and began wrapping Alikar's scarf around her face.

Escaping Dag's house involved acknowledging five separate head bows and "Dame Violets." She thanked each of Dag's friends, unsure why, and finally made it outside.

She drew in cold air, feeling a bit dramatic as she did, like June gasping in the AC after an afternoon jog. They walked the sloped path toward the lake, traveling subdued streets. Violet saw curtains moving in peoples' windows; she checked her covered face.

"You're quite the celebrity, Lady Terlian," Alikar said.

"They're being stubborn. A Goldentongue would be useful."

"Is it such a vice, loyalty?"

"When it keeps you from being logical, yes. For instance . . ." She wouldn't have dared touch on such a sensitive topic with anyone else, but Alikar's open manner, while it should have put her off, somehow made him easier to approach. "Don't hate Jarek for the wrong reasons," she said.

Predictably, his face became one giant scowl. "He's a cord thief."

"*Was* a cord thief. Are people not allowed to change?"

"She chose him." Alikar kicked a pebble. It soared and thunked against someone's yard fence.

"I think the situation was more complex than that," Violet said. "Either way, Jarek isn't to blame for her decision."

"So I should blame Melly."

"No, you should let it go. There's already been enough pain. Meliora is your friend. You care about her."

Alikar slowed, frowning at the road.

"She needs you. She has no one else."

He massaged his brows. Then, he straightened with a nod and continued walking. Their pace was slow, and it worked like a bellow on Alikar's frustration. Every step was another gust of surrender. At last, he sighed, though the sound resembled resignation more than anger.

"What a wise counselor you are." He bumped his shoulder against her, smiling.

She smiled too. "What do you think of the plan?" she asked, and not so much to distract from the heavy conversation, but because she truly wanted to discuss the idea with someone other than herself.

"The prophecy states that you will restore the Lykill. Therefore, it must work."

"The prophecy doesn't say whether or not I'll restore it before I'm eighty."

"That would be the sight." He hunched over, descending to Violet's height, and poked an imaginary cane at the air. "Yakiv," he croaked, "you hand me that pendant this instant, or I'll whack you!"

She smiled again. There was a freedom in being teased. Though they shouldn't have made so light of things, not when they were in the midst of battle plans.

Alikar straightened, rubbing his lower back. "Do you ever laugh?"

"Sometimes."

"Over what, maps with too wide of margins, or books with too few words?"

"I laugh when something is appropriately funny."

"I'm nearly out of ideas." He booted a hunk of ice that had dislodged itself from someone's yard. "I could sing. Or tell you about the time Nikos accidentally tried wooing his own aunt."

"Please don't sing. And let's not talk about Nikos."

They drifted farther from the residential area. Buildings shaded them, and the air grew quieter, safe from the wind. Their camaraderie was starting to feel comfortable. It made Violet miss June, and wish she could miss Oliver—that her brother had been a friend. The fault wasn't entirely his, though. If he'd stopped trying, it was because she'd never given him a fair chance.

"Are you troubled?" Alikar said.

Violet couldn't talk about Oliver. "You didn't want to be an Advocate," she said. "You were never trained. But you're still Advocating."

"As King Asbed said, the liryn supplies the aid."

"But you can refuse to Advocate, and your liryn will stop working."

"Yes."

"I didn't even know I was welded, but somehow, sílfar was still affecting me."

"That's the difference between *nehfey* and *da'atan*. Liryn of *da'atan* is akin to fire, which can be summoned or doused. But *nehfey* is . . ." Alikar peered upward, downward, and then said, "Water. Ever-moving, even when it appears still. You're better off asking Ezio."

"He tried talking to me, while everyone was out."

"That's quite the miracle. What did he say?"

She pictured the lamb, a representation of herself, running away from the Lykill. "Yakiv is a shoe."

Alikar snorted.

They walked until the quiet Borku began to awaken with noise. An alley led into a street out of the Wild West. Commotion swelled: jeers, singing, and the chipper tunes of an accordion. Smoke poured from a dingy building. It was the only lively building on the street. The Separatist logo was painted on its grimy window. Alikar scowled at it.

As they passed the tavern, its presence felt akin to a giant peering over Violet's shoulder. The feeling lingered, a dog in her steps, a shadow she couldn't shake. Violet tried, rounding a corner and checking behind to make sure the tavern was out of view. It still felt as if the building was caught in her hem.

They took a few more turns. The sensation of being followed shifted, and she was relieved—until the feeling settled in her belly, and she rounded a bend and saw the tavern in front of them.

"Are we going in circles?" Alikar said.

Dare she tell him, or should she ignore it?

"Fiiii-leet." Alikar nudged her. "Is this sílfar? Was this walk all part of your elaborate plan to indulge your liryn?"

Violet closed her eyes, afraid of that very thing. Wind teased her clothes—a stranger's clothes. She was out of her element, stripped down to a girl chasing a feeling.

"There's something in that tavern," she said.

"Are you certain? Sílfar can want nothing from a Separatist nest, if I may give it a name so civilized."

"I'm certain."

He sighed. "I'll go, then."

"No, I'll go."

"That's not the sort of place for a lady."

"But you won't know what to look for." Violet adjusted her face scarf. They'd have to be discreet and hope that sílfar made its purpose known quickly. "Tuck your hair under your hat," she said.

Alikar obeyed.

They started for the door. The laughter grew obscene. Alikar grimaced.

"Don't make a scene," Violet said. "If we haven't found anything in five minutes, we leave."

He offered an elbow. "We don't know what types of men are in there. Rather, we *do* know—and, well, you shouldn't appear unattached." His cheeks were coloring.

Violet was grateful hers were obscured. "Very gentlemanly of you," she said, taking his arm.

"Yes. Well." He cleared his throat and opened the door.

At first, Violet wondered if the kitchen was on fire. Smoke burned her eyes. Laughter crescendoed, clogging her ears. Whatever people smoked on Bar'Talian made her sneeze.

"*Ench?*" a man in an apron shouted at Alikar.

He gaped at the barkeep, squeezing his cord. Summoning the flame. "Two beers."

"Louder, man."

"Beers! Two of them!"

The man waved them off.

Violet dragged Alikar to a table in the farthest, darkest corner of the tavern. The sticky tile pulled at her soles like glue, and she had a definite headache by the time she sat on a chair with uneven legs. Their table housed another occupant: a man using his scarf for the same purpose as Violet. Sitting in shadow and smoke, he cut an intimidating figure, which might've been the reason no one else had wanted to sit here. Alikar got one look at him and vehemently shook his head, but Violet was already sitting. The stranger might keep others away.

Nothing of significance was in sight, yet sílfar brimmed with the nearness of her goal. Invisible but reachable.

"Why didn't you order water?" she called over the din. "We can't pay for beer."

"No, we can't afford water. Beer is free. King's law."

"Oh."

A peal of triumphant shouting came from the busiest table, in the center of the pub. Men crowded an image projecting from someone's shell. Violet didn't have to strain to recognize Yakiv. He stood like one giving a speech, but Alikar's liryn couldn't translate, and there was too much noise.

"A toast to Yakiv!" A man hopped onto his chair, tankard raised. "May he hate the monarchs forever!"

The tavern whooped and drank. Everyone except the man at their table.

"May he find the rest of that blasted Lykill," toasted another, "if only to says I told you so!"

The room laughed.

"May he gut the monarchs next!"

That garnered the loudest cheer yet.

Alikar's fists were clenched and his mouth on the verge of opening. Violet kicked his foot. He seethed but kept quiet.

"That's four cottons." The barkeep had found them. He carried two tankards.

A distracted Alikar was slow to register. "What?"

"Two for you, two for your girl."

"I asked for beer."

"So they are. King's law don't stand here. Which you'd know, if you weren't a Unionist. Smelled it soon as you walked in." The barkeep flung the contents of both cups at Alikar's face and hollered, "Four cottons!"

Violet leaned back, in case there was more. A spluttering Alikar yanked off his hat to wring it out. Wet hair dripped onto his lap.

"Say, I know you . . ." The barkeep leaned over, hands on his knees. He peered between Alikar's stringy locks. Then he bolted upright with shock. "The Terlion emissary! He's alive!"

It shouldn't have, but somehow his shout made a dent in the noise. The stranger at their table started forward, losing some shadows. The projection of Yakiv quieted, and the occupants around it swiveled toward Alikar. Violet slunk back into her chair.

Another Separatist came closer. "That's not him."

"Sure it is." The barkeep dragged Alikar to his feet.

Violet was stiff. Her entire body felt like a poster labeled with the words *Violet of Terlian.*

A few other Separatists closed in. Violet looked at her feet, trying to appear smaller.

"That's the brother," someone said. "Saw him at the Vaspu-rakan rally, I did."

"But he's a Muratsan?"

"Not a pretty one."

The jeers were chaotic.

Alikar was shaking. They shouldn't have come here. Violet didn't know what to do. Maybe she should stand, push him toward the door.

"What dragged you in here?" a Separatist said.

"Rat's got nowhere else to hide, not with the Pretenders out of commission."

"Did you hear Yakiv, Muratsan? Says your brother rolled over for him. Didn't put up a fight."

Alikar suddenly flinched. Warm slop splattered Violet's foot. Someone had thrown food at him. He covered his face, but the next blow hit someone else's arm. The man from their table was at Alikar's side, blocking him.

"Go," he said.

Alikar's arm reached back. His hand waited for Violet's. She took it.

They darted, heads down. Noise churned, an angry mob. Dishes clattered and food splattered underfoot, but none of it hit Violet. The stranger shielded them, ushering them along.

Alikar got the door open and pushed Violet through first. She staggered out, sucking in clean air.

"Keep going!" Alikar said.

They ran, clacking over cobblestone, until they came to a corner and ducked around it. There, they paused to catch their breaths. Violet started when she saw the stranger. He'd come with them, and he hadn't let go of Alikar.

He wrenched his arm out of the man's grasp, stumbled, and had to be righted. "I do not require your assistance, sir," Alikar said, unsuccessfully prying himself free. "And I did not require it inside. Now if you would—"

"Alikar."

He froze. So did Violet.

The stranger gripped Alikar by the shoulders, forcing them to match gazes. Then he ripped off his scarf. Violet watched Alikar's uneasy expression crumble, rebuilding itself into shock. His mouth opened. A single word fell out in a ragged, desperate whisper.

"Eliathor?"

CHAPTER TWENTY-NINE

"The few loyalists still in existence have mostly congregated around Vaspurakan, close to Faargard, their 'holy city.'" – Vessel Yal, recitation at Darbinyun Manor

VIOLET HEARD THE NAME, knew what it meant, and still she stared at the stranger. He'd shorn his hair to jagged, ruddy locks, and the braided beards were trimmed to scruff. Yet that shadowed melancholy was his.

Alikar croaked something in Arati. And then they were embracing, a fierce colliding of arms.

Slowly, Violet's feet unstuck. Eliathor was alive. He was here. Against all odds, they'd found him.

No, sílfar had. Even now it tugged Violet, as if wanting to make sure she didn't doubt it.

The two finished hugging. Alikar asked questions, wiping his eyes, and Eliathor answered. Bits of thrown food clung to

Alikar's cheeks, but his smile was full. Violet imagined this was something like getting a brother back.

When Violet shifted, Eliathor finally let his head turn in her direction. Recognition glinted in the gaze pooling with sorrow, rage, and distrust.

"You remember the Terlion?" Alikar said. "Her name is Fileet. Not to be confused with the purple flower."

"I know her name," Eliathor said.

Violet, holding his gaze, felt solidarity with Atlas, forced to carry the sky. "I, um . . ." A greeting was appropriate. But what, *Welcome back to life?* "It's very good to—"

"Someone is Advocating." Eliathor shielded Alikar, scanning the road. His hand found his sword.

"It's me," Alikar said.

Eliathor glanced from the empty road to the purple belt hanging over Alikar's chest. "They welded you?"

"Not a regulation cord, but we were in a bind."

"I am sorry for your sorrow."

Alikar shrugged. Regret—which Violet keenly felt—betrayed his nonchalance.

Eliathor didn't push it. Instead, he took in Alikar again, brushing his shoulder. Then gripping it, like one needing support. "How did . . . Meliora?"

Alikar awaited more, but Violet understood. "She's alive," she said. "She's just not with us. We got separated."

Eliathor's head whipped Violet's way, and Alikar grunted—probably from the force of Eliathor's grip. "Where?" he demanded.

"The Amber Forest."

Copper brows drew together. "She went looking for the gate pendant."

"We found it," Violet said. "But then Yakiv found us. He took me. That's when she and I got separated. He left her alive. We think she's on her way to Dag's, but on foot." This was the most she'd spoken to Eliathor directly. And to think—he was Lady Basilia's son. Lady Basilia, whom Violet had felt that strange stirring of loyalty toward. With both his parents and his elder brothers deceased, Eliathor was next in line for the throne. Did that mean Violet would start feeling that odd unity with *him?*

That question would remain a mystery, for the suspicious look Eliathor was giving her left no room for any connection. "How did you escape him?" he asked.

"When he uses the pendant, it causes an explosion. He got thrown back."

"And you didn't take the pendant from him before you escaped?"

The not-so-veiled audacity in Eliathor's tone caused Violet's chin to lift. "It was buried in rubble," she said.

"But that's neither here nor there," Alikar said, "because we have a plan. A horrible plan, but it has a beginning and an end."

Eliathor let Violet sit in his accusatory stare another moment before he returned to Alikar. "Tell me while we walk."

So they walked, staying in the shadows that pressed along walls and under awnings. Alikar detailed Dag's plan, expertly refraining from mentioning Nikos or Ezio by name, referring to them simply as "the Janlion representatives." Eliathor quietly listened. He and Alikar walked side by side, Violet behind them, noticing that Eliathor favored his left leg, and that he moved like one who had half a dozen people draped over his shoulders. His sword was unsheathed, something that made Violet wince each time his leg moved and the weapon threatened to impale him. But its point looked dull. Rounded, even. She remembered he'd pulled it from the statue in the Hasteins' throne room. The fact that he hadn't thrown the Terlion heirloom into the nearest sewer indicated his desperation. He had no other weapon—nothing left but legacy.

"Barrels?" he said when Alikar finished. "We should use the Goldentongue."

"Yes, well . . ." Alikar's squirming wasn't lost on Eliathor.

"Say it," Eliathor said.

Alikar visually implored Violet, who was certainly not going to be the one to tell Eliathor that his dead fiancée's brother and cousin were just down the road.

He grimaced. "It's Nikos. He's a Goldentongue now. And . . . Ezio is with him."

Eliathor went still as stone.

"Dag and his friends want nothing to do with them, due to the edict. So, barrels it is."

Violet lowered her gaze, feeling Eliathor deserved to process this without an audience. She couldn't see his expression, but she felt it in the air, taut with affliction.

"I've seen the bounty," Eliathor spoke slowly, a seventh person now wrapped around his shoulders. "It's high. Unexpected. Why does Yakiv seek you?"

A conversation change.

Oh. He was asking Violet.

Now she implored Alikar, knowing she was being a coward.

"For her liryn," Alikar said. "She's welded. Terlian's liryn. Evidently it's a compass. Finds things in need of finding. Yakiv wants her to lead him to the rest of the Lykill."

If Violet's association with Terlian was enough to earn Eliathor's permanent mistrust, being welded was enough to toss her into the Separatist tavern. In a voice like sharpened metal, he said, "You lied to my mother."

"I didn't," she said, loud enough that Alikar uneasily searched the road. "Yakiv took me to that Hand leader, Malokki, who pointed it out."

"A man you had never met knew you were a welded of Terlian."

"He knew multiple versions of the prophecy; he must have reasoned it out. Yakiv told him I was from Terlian. Everything else, Malokki deduced." She matched his steely gaze. Eliathor had no right, assuming the worst. "I'm not a liar," she said.

"Your father used the Lykill to give *her* father the power to weld," Alikar added, with the delicate air of one hoping to be heard and not seen.

"There are no welders but the monarchs," Eliathor said, still eying Violet.

"Malokki claims the Lykill can create new welders, remember?" Alikar said. "He's right."

The staring contest between Eliathor and Violet strengthened her grit with every second. Eliathor could think she was many things, but not that she would lie to Lady Basilia's face. *She's my queen,* niggled a thought threaded with loyalty that hadn't existed a week ago.

Eliathor wrapped his face once more and set off.

Alikar gave Violet a *Dodged a bullet there* look before hurrying after. Violet took her time, exhaling.

"What were you doing in that hog hole?" Alikar asked.

Eliathor booted a stone out of his way. "Listening."

"To what end?"

"To determine Yakiv's whereabouts."

"But you wouldn't have gone after him on your own, surely."

"What else do you expect me to have done?"

"You can't be serious, Thor. He'd have killed you."

"Then I'd have died doing my duty."

"No," Alikar said, "you'd have died for revenge. And then the prophecy wouldn't—"

"I will hear no mention of the prophecy, the Lykill, or Terlian."

Alikar stopped. So did Violet, sensing the emotion that stirred like smoke collecting heat. From Alikar, in the wrinkling of his forehead. From Eliathor, whose voice had deepened.

"The prophecy is real," Alikar said.

Eliathor yanked his scarf away. Anger seeped from him. Violet involuntarily stepped back. "What good has come of faith in the prophecy?" he said. "My father followed it to his death. My mother died defending it. My brothers. *Your* brother. Children who ought to have been shielded from its madness. Examine what the prophecy has wrought. We are forsaken." He raised a fist like he hoped to bash the prophecy into dust. "Curse the prophecy. Let it and the Lykill and Terlian rot together."

Alikar's gaze fell in defeat.

Violet found herself saying, "Terlian *is* rotting. That's why the prophecy matters. It's about more than restoring your family to the throne. It's about saving your realm."

"Bar'Talian is my realm," Eliathor said. "If Terlian is to die, then that is the way of things. Let it run its course."

"You're talking about an entire planet. About billions of lives, people who are supposed to be yours."

"I never asked for their fealty."

"And they never asked for an iron-hearted king." She sucked in her lips, stunned by her audacity.

Eliathor was a wall. Even as she envisioned him grabbing his sword and gutting her, she knew he wouldn't. The lack of reaction was no less unsettling, however. The quiet hung louder than any shout. But Violet wasn't relieved when Eliathor broke it.

"Terlian has no king."

He continued walking, leaving Violet and Alikar beneath an awning. A sea breeze puffed the fabric up, stretching the image on it.

A sheep.

Any excitement that might've come from learning Eliathor was alive had dissipated. As far as Terlian was concerned, he might as well still be dead. And Terlian was just as dead to him.

"Come on," Alikar murmured.

They left the awning just as the wind stilled, making the sheep sag.

Dag's house looked paler, cast in the light of a sun-hidden cloud. On the threshold, Alikar spoke in Faartunga. Violet caught Jarek's name, then *Nikos* and *Linus*. Eliathor shook his head and put his palm on the door, like one ready to push it open.

"Basilia," Alikar said.

Eliathor's shoulders fell as he opened Dag's door.

The chatter ceased as soon as Eliathor made his appearance. Dag and his friends were stunned in equal wonder, while Jarek nervously fidgeted. Nikos, on the other hand, held himself so poised, so indifferent, that Violet could've guessed he was completely unaffected—except for the fact that he was staring determinedly at the floor.

"*Ark'ayazn Eliathor*," Dag whispered. He dropped to his knees, followed by his friends. Together, they repeated the name.

Eliathor turned and closed Dag's door, perhaps to keep the men from seeing the turmoil in his twitching face. But, by the time he turned back around, he'd mastered himself, greeting the men in broken Arati.

" . . . your hospitality," Eliathor said.

"I could not withhold it." Dag, clutching his fez to his heart, stared up at Eliathor. "How did you survive, my prince? The good monarchs of Bar'Talian said most were lost."

"Your deference is not needed, Dag. I am no prince. Rise, please." Eliathor squeezed his hilt.

The men rose. Violet edged around them, planting herself near Jarek and Nikos.

"I have heard your plan," Eliathor continued. "I understand your reluctance to work with the Goldentongue, but he is useful. We shouldn't reject his aid. If he is still willing."

"I am willing," Nikos said simply—to the floor. Did the edict prevent him from even looking at Eliathor?

"Then I propose a new plan. Be at ease and listen." Eliathor waited for Dag and his friends to relax. Futile, though they did try, shuffling in place like they were releasing nerves.

Eliathor squared his stance. "Jarek"—Jarek flinched— "will contact Yakiv through the mirrorgraph and show that Violet is in his possession. He will demand that Yakiv show himself at the Ashtarak. This should pose no difficulty for Yakiv. He has the pendant. And he is near. The mountains tremble."

Violet swallowed. Yakiv was already here, looking for the gate.

"Yakiv will suspect treachery," Eliathor said, "so he will come prepared. How many keep his company?" he asked Violet.

"Four," she said. "Including a Pillar."

"Five total. Four will be strengthened by the Pillar. So we fight the force of twenty men. Weapons will not penetrate." Eliathor politely refrained from mentioning the barrel and net idea. "Unless the Pillar is weakened, we cannot hope to match Yakiv's strength."

"What if Yakiv hides the Pillar out of sight on the other side of a gate?" Alikar interrupted.

"Gates disrupt liryn," Nikos spoke. "Stefanos must have the Pillar nearby."

Eliathor was right. These were horrible odds.

"If someone is being strengthened by a Pillar, can they still use their own liryn?" Violet asked.

"No," Jarek answered.

Finally, a weakness. "Then it's possible not all of them will be strengthened. Yakiv might want his Goldentongue for negotiating about the price of the bounty. And, if that's the case, he'll also need his Advocate for translating. That leaves just two strengthened by the Pillar: Yakiv and the Chair. So, the force of ten men."

"Unless Stefanos has been collecting donations for the cause," Nikos said, "I would not rely on the depth of his pockets. Greed knows only greed. He'll arrive at the rendezvous, verify that Dame Violeta is in Jarek's possession, and then kill him."

Violet snuck a sideways glance at Jarek. No visible trepidation.

"I'll take the risk," Jarek said.

"Do as you wish." Nikos shrugged.

Uncertainty creased Alikar's forehead.

"We must assume all four will be strengthened," Eliathor said. "Incapacitating the Pillar is our priority. Once Yakiv realizes that his Pillar is endangered, he will see to his protection."

"That's supposing another Separatist crow doesn't flap to the Pillar's aid," Alikar said.

"Our Goldentongue will see to preventing that."

"And Yakiv's Goldentongue? She'll be unaffected."

Then a Goldentongue couldn't hook another Goldentongue?

"She will be our next target, after the Pillar," Eliathor said.

"I rely upon an Advocate," Nikos interjected.

Violet had forgotten that limitation. All Nikos' hooking would be for naught if no one could understand him.

For the first time, Eliathor appeared unsure, inspecting Alikar's purple cord. "Is there an Advocate in Borku who would help us?" he asked Dag.

Alikar waved his arm. "You've forgotten. I'm welded."

Eliathor ignored that.

"Not one I trust not to snatch Dame Violet for the promise of cottons," Dag said.

That further perturbed Eliathor's expression. But he said nothing about whatever his reservations were, instead announcing, "Before I continue, there is no objection to using the Goldentongue?"

Dag and his men shared glances. There were some mumbles, some shoulder shrugs and swinging of arms. Finally, Dag said, "Prince Eliathor, we do not trust the Goldentongue. But, at your word, we will consent. So long as the Goldentongue makes a promise in the sight of the Seer."

"What do you ask of me?" Nikos said.

Gentle Dag's features calcified. "No using the cord against us, and no disrespecting his lordship."

The room felt stuffy again; Violet nearly shed her coat.

"I will fetch the Seer," Nikos said at last. He left. After a minute, two figures re-entered Dag's sitting room. Ezio came slowly, his feet shuffling.

Eliathor drew in breath and didn't release it. The ancient shadows were there on his face, but so was something softer. Fondness? An embittered fondness, someone welcoming an old friend who'd once betrayed him.

"Janlian's heart shares in the Hasteins' sorrow," Ezio murmured. Like Nikos, he wouldn't look at Eliathor directly.

Eliathor's eyes roved over Ezio with indecipherable feeling. "All homage to the Eagle King," he said.

Ezio flinched.

"Seer." Nikos snapped all attention back to him. "You have been summoned to witness my vow, after which you will return my cord. And so"—Nikos pressed three fingers to his chest—"in your sight, I pledge that my liryn will not be used against those present. And I pledge that I will give no disrespect to Eliathor Hastein, son of Lady Basilia, rightful heir to Terlian."

"It is witnessed," Ezio mumbled. He began removing Nikos' cord, but it flew off his chest before he could finish and zoomed toward Nikos' outstretched hand.

"The Seer too," Dag said. "Let us hear him pledge his respect."

Violet saw a furtive glance pass between Eliathor and Alikar. Now worried, she wondered if Ezio would protest on the grounds that he couldn't be bossed around because he was a prince—which Dag didn't know.

But Ezio's air was so demure that it seeped out through the face covering. "I would never disrespect the Hastein household," he said quietly.

Dag eyed him keenly, then Eliathor, who nodded. Ezio's pledge was accepted.

Further planning commenced. The "Ashtarak," where Jarek would tell Yakiv to meet him, was an antique, tower-like monument in the lake, easy to spot from the mountains. Violet's reminder that the Ashtarak would be destroyed by the gate was brushed off. What could Yakiv do, Nareg asked, against history?

A lot, she thought.

And then it was finished. Their plan had been tested, ten people (Ezio would not accompany them) practicing their roles in Dag's stamp of a backyard. Bushes were trampled, but Dag didn't complain. Violet's arms began to ache from being constantly pinned behind her back by Jarek. He grunted an apology the first time.

The sun was fleeing fast. Nareg commented on it. Those who manned the mirrorgraph would retire with the daylight. There was nothing left to do but act.

Violet couldn't fight a shiver. *The prophecy says Terlian will be healed,* she reminded herself. That meant they'd get the pendant from Yakiv.

Not necessarily today.

"Who are the Advocates in this town?" Eliathor asked Dag.

Alikar crossed his arms. "Eliathor. I'm up to the task."

"You need to find Meliora."

"She's not in any immediate danger. Fileet can help us find her, when this is over."

Eliathor pressed Dag like Alikar hadn't spoken. "There must be an Advocate who can be paid for discretion."

Timidly, Dag sought support from his friends, none of whom gave a suggestion. "Well—"

"You're overcomplicating the situation," Alikar said. "I am our Advocate. We cannot risk another."

"I cannot risk your life." Eliathor stared at Alikar, whose frustration relented with a sigh.

Dag broke the silence. "There's no other Advocate, my prince. I can ask my sister to search for Dame Meliora. She'll see it done."

Eliathor scraped a palm through his hair.

"What will you do with the pendant, Prince, when you take it?" Nareg asked him.

"Let the Seer decide what is to be done with an object of liryn."

"But you will see it restored to the emperors, Prince?" Dag said. "As the prophecy says?"

"If others wish to chase the prophecy, that is their business. I will have no part in it."

Violet stared at the mountains that hid Terlian's gate.

"No part?" Dag squinted, though the sky had grown dim. "I don't understand. The prophecy is what gives us hope for Terlian's restoration."

"Terlian is your hope. Not mine."

Dag's head tilted, puzzled.

"Why does the shunned one not fight for his throne?" Ezio's soft voice was confused, like a wounded creature uncertain why its pain is there. "My sister would be very sad. She would cry, and I would not know what to do. I did not like to see her cry. The shunned one makes her cry."

Dag's yard was quiet. Eliathor, whose expressions Violet thought she could count on one hand, showed a new layer of anguish that widened his eyes until she could discern the blue. Then they closed.

"Light's going," spoke Jarek, his words like the pick-up of wind. "Are you ready, Violeta?"

She met his gaze, her partner in this plan. What did Meliora see in Jarek? Violet saw a grubby, impetuous boy who'd stolen a cord so he could befriend Meliora without having to learn her language.

Cheater.

A boy who'd given up his stolen cords when Meliora discovered his shame.

Repentant.

A boy who had promoted a plan that might result in his death.

Honorable?

Violet nodded. "Yes. I'm ready."

CHAPTER THIRTY

"The liryn of *basareth* requires the appropriate ritual and *da'atan* intense concentration, but *nehfey* wants only your permission."
– *Liryn on a Mission* by Vessel Augustinia

DAG AND HIS FRIENDS collected their gear, offering a fishing spear to Eliathor. He declined, indicating his sword.

"I've not seen this." Alikar bent over, running a hand along Eliathor's blade. "Stone? You need a better sword. This isn't remotely—anak!" Alikar, having loosened the hilt from Eliathor's belt, immediately dropped it. The weapon slammed to the ground, nearly crushing his toes. "What in Barikad Forest! How much does that weigh?"

Eliathor collected the sword without difficulty. Nareg chuckled, causing Alikar's cheeks to burn red.

"We will meet you at the rendezvous," Jarek called as he edged toward Dag's front door.

Violet was suddenly wishing she had not eaten so much bread.

"Wait, I . . ." Alikar stepped forward. "A word with Fileet, please. Outside."

"Be quick," Jarek said.

Surprisingly, Alikar's nod came before his scowl.

Violet appraised their little army. They were the ones willing to match Yakiv, this random mixture of Bar'Talions, Janlions, and Terlion.

"May you find the road to us again." Dag gave her a little bow.

"Thank you," she said. Her eyes found Eliathor. He watched her. No words of encouragement to give. "Goodbye." Violet slipped out the door.

The moons had swapped shapes since she'd first arrived on Bar'Talian. The leftmost had waned to half its size, and the other had grown almost full. What with everything new on this world, Violet hadn't spent much time getting used to the sight. It was surreal, like she could blink and realize that the second moon had been an illusion all along.

"What is it?" she said as soon as Alikar pulled the door shut.

"I only wanted to tell you to be careful."

"Thanks. You too."

"And to trust your liryn."

Violet's throat plugged.

Alikar was quiet, a shadowed smudge on the dim evening. "Give me your hand," he said.

"Why?"

"So I can bite it."

"What?"

He sighed. "Trust me. Please."

Violet relented. His grip was warmer than hers.

"Was that so impossible?" he said.

She wanted to tell him to hurry his point, but her voice was locked.

"You're still in control of your fingers," he said, wiggling them around. "You haven't lost them. But you've entrusted them to me because you know I won't misuse them. Liryn expects the same."

It probably did, yes. Maybe she could relinquish full control if she were a different person. But she was Violet, too stiff to bend.

"The prophecy calls me iron heart," she said, turning her head.

Soft whooshing, the combination of village noises, floated by.

"Well," he said, "a fact about iron: It's actually quite malleable."

"Is it?"

"And can withstand a good bit of stretching. Very durable, iron. But gentle too. It's also rather bossy, but we forgive it because it's got such a nice sheen."

She tried to smile, but she felt more constrained than ever.

"Let me see your cord," he said.

Relieved at the new task, Violet was slow in retrieving her pocketed pendant.

"Why aren't you wearing it?" he asked.

"The chain broke." Her pendant couldn't even reflect Dag's porch light. So much for having a nice sheen.

Alikar touched the flower. "A violet, I presume?"

She nodded.

"It ought to be around your neck and not stowed away. Liryn does not like to be ignored."

"You make it sound like liryn has feelings."

"Not *feelings.* I don't know the word. I'm sure Kelispar has . . ." His momentum fell away.

Violet's heart seemed ready to knead itself into something flat.

After fidgeting with something under his shirt, Alikar pulled out a chain and freed its ring. "Wear your pendant."

"But that necklace is yours."

"So it is. Take it, Fileet, else I'll throw it away."

"You're so dramatic," she said, but she accepted the chain. "What about your ring?"

"I'll wear it. Mother wanted me to, but it feels so cumbersome on the finger. I could never do anything with it on. You see this? The Muratsan crest." He showed her the ruby stone and the curly letter.

Violet slipped her two pendants onto Alikar's chain. The moons' light pinpointed his serious furrows. He looked closer to Kelispar than he ever had.

"Don't do this alone," he said.

But I've done everything alone.

She opened Dag's door and called for Jarek.

F IRE GLOWED IN THE streetlamps, painting an amber residue on the snow. It clung like fog.

Jarek hadn't handcuffed her yet. He'd do that once they were in the mirrorgraph. She couldn't look captured before then, lest the employees at the mirrorgraph call the police. Or Yakiv.

Their footsteps sloshed. Somewhere, crickets chittered.

Are there crickets on Bar'Talian?

Alikar would probably roll his eyes and say of course there were crickets.

The mirrorgraph building was small, a one-story cone not far from the Separatist tavern. The man sitting behind the table at the entrance had his feet propped up and disinterest all over his absent greeting.

Jarek spoke first, in the language of Piast. The man replied in Arati. So Jarek pointed beyond the table, toward a telephone booth-shaped cubicle built out of copper and crystal. The man pointed to a bronze plaque on the wall. Unrecognizable written characters, somewhat reminiscent of Greek, encircled a golden sun whose rays all converged together, pointing at one character. A sundial.

Jarek argued by dumping a sack of cottons on the table, courtesy of the Janlion treasury.

The man leaned forward and peered inside. Then yelped, "Anak!"

Jarek took that as his cue to proceed. He smirked at Violet. A unifying, celebratory thing.

Violet tried to smile back and probably made him think she was chewing bitter herbs.

The word "mirrorgraph" had called to Violet's mind a device like a phonograph, only with some mirrors attached. The actual thing itself was not a device at all—it was a room of mirrors that made Violet dizzy and reminded her of a carnival fun house.

Lines like rainbow crystals were embedded in every mirror, following a circular track. A stool sat before the center of the spiral, where a snail shell of rainbow-colored crystals came to a tight end. In front of the stool, on a table, were some copper dials.

Jarek ran his fingers over the dials, frowning. But then he nodded, withdrawing the fabric they'd practiced with. Violet pulled the silky fabric over her face.

"*Przebacz,*" Jarek said somewhere by her ear. Then he yanked her arms behind her back.

She put up a struggle—now was the time to pretend. Through the thin fabric, she saw Jarek's hazy arm as he fidgeted with one of the dials. The inlaid crystal in the mirrors lit up, so bright she squinted despite the covering.

"Yakiv Stefanos!" Jarek yelled, and Violet increased her fake squirming. He spoke again, saying her name before he yanked off the covering. Violet blinked as a kaleidoscope of light clashed in her vision. Jarek gripped her by the back of her head now, shoving her closer to a mirror, and proceeded to give his demands.

She knew this was a ruse, had practiced these movements with him a dozen times. Still, she was grateful June wasn't privy to Bar'Talion radio broadcasts, and even more relieved when the lights petered out and Jarek let her go.

He scooped up the discarded cloth, keeping his head down as Violet casually stretched her sore arms. Her body hadn't caught on to the trick; it remained tense, her heart pattering. The mood in the mirrorgraph was awkward and strained as the two of them fidgeted. The mirrors were beginning to fog.

Then, Jarek looked at her, the shame in his face reflected an infinite number of times from above and below. "*Przebacz,*" he said again, and she thought it might mean *I'm sorry.*

"It's okay," she told him. Then she gave him a smile—an actual one, sans bitter herbs. "We should hurry." She tapped her wrist, then realized he would only understand the gesture if he'd seen a wristwatch.

But he got it. Jarek yanked open the door, letting her escape first.

They hurried past the man at the table. He would've heard Jarek's yelling. Maybe he'd seen the broadcast and now knew exactly who Violet was.

Outside, they forwent nonchalance and ran.

They raced past the Separatist tavern, bypassing the residential area, downhill toward the marina. But they didn't clatter onto the dock, instead turning, sprinting alongside the lake in the direction of the trees. Violet remembered that forest, having traveled through it a few days earlier.

Jarek slipped on ice once, and then Violet. Neither helped the other.

At the border of the woods, they slowed. The cold grew colder; dirt masked the smell of salt and fish. They stumbled in the dimmed sunset light, purplish shadows on tree trunks and on snow patches that resembled bruised earth. Jarek kept plowing northward, but Violet knew they needed to turn eastward, toward the lake.

"This way," she called, beckoning him and telling herself that the nudge in her gut had nothing to do with liryn. Likewise, it wasn't liryn coaxing her left, nor did sílfar have anything to do with it when she sensed they'd come to their destination. She tried to feel surprised at finding Eliathor standing in her path, between the trees, like he'd always been there.

He recognized them and let go of his hilt. Alikar, Nikos, and the rest crept into view.

"All went well?" Alikar anxiously asked her.

She nodded.

The ground sloped uphill, toward a path of mountain boulders that gave access to the lake below. Protruding from the water was a slim tower, shorter than a lighthouse, its bulbous golden dome like some sultan's single-turreted palace. Its base lay submerged in sloshing water that had weathered the stone and flung algae up its walls. The Ashtarak wasn't wide enough to serve much purpose except as a monument. Perhaps someone had built it to quietly stand and be admired.

It might've been solid enough, submerged enough. Maybe that's why Dag and his friends thought it could withstand the gate pendant.

She stared at the tower, imagining how it would look bathed in gold light. How long—

The ground shuddered.

They'd been expecting that, but even so, bodies pitched as their footing threatened to rip away. Someone secured Violet's elbow—Dag, she guessed. She gripped his arm too, automatic self-preservation. It wasn't as embarrassing as it had once been, holding on to another for help. A stranger, even. And, as the wind made chaos and the earth continued coughing, she didn't mind the tiny ripple of unity that came from them supporting each other. Maybe it was their Terlion blood that caused the strange, inexorable pull. Two loyalists, braced against nature.

After half a minute, the rumbling slowed. Violet straightened, releasing Dag's arm, and turned to thank him. Her gratitude died, dead as the wind.

Eliathor.

He stared at her without any of his usual certainty. He was still supporting her elbow, his head washed with red as the sinking sun found him.

Then he let go and moved back into the shadows.

Violet pulled her arms close. No time to ponder that. Yakiv had come.

"Come out, boy," floated a voice from somewhere in the Ashtarak's direction.

She and Jarek eyed each other. If only Meliora were here with a reassuring nod. Violet was suddenly aware that she needed one.

Jarek captured her arm. His hand quivered. She tried not to notice it, nor think about Nikos' warning—that Yakiv would sooner kill Jarek than hand over a bounty.

The others were tiptoeing into position. She paid them no mind, focused on the path to the makeshift bridge.

And then Yakiv spoke again, his voice as calm as the lake. "Anything unexpected and this tip goes in deeper."

He must be using his Advocate, Violet thought; Yakiv didn't know Alikar was here. Or had Kora spotted Jarek's stolen cord when she'd first tailed him, and they assumed he was Advocating?

Violet was reasoning out these things, trying to settle her wayward pulse, and didn't immediately realize that Jarek had gone stiffer than the packed snow. She only noticed when he let go and darted toward a break in the trees.

Hurriedly, she joined him. Peeking around Jarek's shoulder, Violet's breath failed her. A shimmering gate stood where the Ashtarak had once been, the tower severed like its top had exploded. The missing half of the monument must have already sunk. Destroyed, in less than a minute.

But then Violet's eyes adjusted to the glow, and she forgot the Ashtarak entirely. Kora, Boh, the slack-jawed Denys, the weakened Slav—they were all there, but so was someone else, the reason Jarek's breath was coming out in jagged bursts. Yakiv stood directly before the gate, and he wasn't alone. He had a shield, one hand around Meliora's neck and the other around the dagger in her side.

CHAPTER THIRTY-ONE

"A crown can kill a man. Keep him weak. Dependent. Tell me, monarchs, how there's any dignity in that." – Yakiv Stefanos, speech at Lake Karap Park

F OR A MOMENT, ALL was silent but for the thudding in Violet's ears.

She had reassured Alikar. Had told him Meliora was still on her way.

But Meliora *was* here. Captured by Yakiv, with a tainted knife in her side.

Her expression was hard to determine, half obscured by dusk, the other half weirdly illuminated by the gate. Her stance said enough. She was slack, arms by her sides, not bothering to resist. Defeated. Just as Violet had left her in the Amber Forest.

"See that your mind's made up fast," Yakiv called. He shifted his dagger hand.

Meliora moaned.

"Stop!" Jarek shouted. "I'm coming." He dragged Violet to the descending path.

Nikos stepped in their way. "Wait," he murmured.

Jarek's pace went from frenzied to nonexistent in one second. Violet lurched, caught off-guard.

Nikos was calculating Jarek like a hunter who's just withdrawn his lasso.

Violet searched for Eliathor and Alikar, wondering why they hadn't knocked each other down on their way to rescue Meliora, and found both of them locked in the same rigid stance as Jarek.

"You swore before the Seer," whispered Dag. He and his friends crowded Nikos, all manner of leeriness.

"I never swore to be honest. Now, none of you will move." Nikos spoke in a voice no different from his usual one. "Danger is nigh."

Dag and his friends let their grips loosen around the fishing spears. Eight people under a Goldentongue's sway now, all accomplished by a few unimpressive words.

"Dame Violeta."

She tensed, eyes locking on the remaining light around his purple cord.

"You must be alarmed. But I mean no harm. These men are rash. We must follow the plan, or Meliora will die. Will you come willingly? I cannot divide my focus endlessly." Indeed, his voice had grown softer, his words slower.

Violet nodded.

"Good," he said, tucking his cord beneath his shirt. "You will lead, and you must appear to be in my clutches. A spectacular show for a critical audience. Can you do this?"

"Yes," she said.

"Then . . . we go. Now." Nikos' vision had drifted, giving him a lazy-eyed appearance.

Violet extended her wrists for him to capture.

He didn't move. Perspiration speckled his skin. She really *would* have to lead.

After situating his hands, Violet walked, dragging him along. The captive, leading her captor.

Exactly what Yakiv expects of me.

Focused on guiding Nikos while pretending it was the other way around, Violet's mind had little room left for fear. That, she relegated to another corner to be dealt with later. They stole over the dirt and then the bridge itself: wide, uneven blocks of brown stone that might've been part of the mountain at one point, now reaching toward the lake like a lonely arm. Down Violet led Nikos, making sure to stumble, painting her expression with discomfort and hoping he wasn't stupidly staring about.

"Where's the boy?" Yakiv called.

Nikos didn't answer.

Violet caught Meliora's stare, or tried to. It was like catching water. She resembled a waif, an enervated shape. Then, Violet met eyes with Yakiv and gaped. He watched her from a face half painted in white, which completely colored his neck and made his black stubble look like pepper on snow.

Nikos finally got something of a grip on Violet's hands and pulled her to a stop. "My companion is emotionally conflicted at the moment," he replied, though the only conflict Violet was aware of sat in Nikos' voice—strained and slow, crystallized syrup struggling to drip. "He sends me in his stead. Linus of Janlian. Friend of the Hasteins; enemy of Separatists, murderers, and those who refuse to rinse their teeth. Now I must ask you and your party to be still and cease all use of liryn. And you, Stefanos, must remove that weapon from Meliora's skin."

Violet could hear his panting.

"A Janlion?" Yakiv said. He leaned on one foot, redistributing weight. In doing so, the white hand around the dagger loosened. "Kin of Basilia?"

"No relation," Nikos said. "Do you know why I prefer to call you Stefanos, rather than by your chosen name? No, you don't know. I admit I am stalling. All the way removed, Stefanos. I want to see the tip. Yes. There it is."

Violet was staring down the dagger, though the shimmery blood made her stomach twist. He'd withdrawn it entirely. Slav the Pillar was standing now, and Denys the Advocate was pondering Violet, which meant only Alikar was facilitating this conversation. Yakiv's team had stopped using liryn.

Perhaps Goldentongues weren't *wholly* obnoxious.

"Got a lot of words, don't you?" Kora said.

"Drop the dagger," Nikos continued. "It's Greek. Your surname. Do you know what it means? No, you don't. Yes, drop it. I insist. Thank you. Do you understand irony, Stefanos? It can be beautiful." His voice had dissolved into a fractured whisper.

Violet squeezed his hand, reminding him to hold on.

"You urine bucket," said Kora. The unaffected Golden-tongue loped her way around Yakiv. "You're a Golden-tongue."

"Am I to understand that you are a Goldentongue yourself, my glittering star?" Nikos eked out.

"He's hooking you," she told Yakiv. "Got his cord hidden."

Nikos gripped Violet tighter. "Let me teach you to better your art. My lessons will cost nothing but a kiss."

His flirtations apparently knew no restraint. Yet Violet, forcing herself to inspect Yakiv's alabaster face for any shift of awareness, didn't have time to roll her eyes. Yakiv looked confused, and he hadn't made any move to capture Violet, but the sharpness of clicked-together puzzle pieces stirred behind his gaze.

"You're a slop pile," Kora told Nikos.

"So I am called. And still I persist, battling fate with a fool's heart, hoping for one crack in the crown." Now his grip was slack, and his words had turned wet and cracked. Was he . . . crying?

Kora laughed. "Pathetic." She moved in.

"Violeta," Nikos whispered. "Take Meliora and run."

She needed no encouragement to escape Kora's incoming fist.

Violet broke apart from Nikos before the punch made contact and made straight for Meliora, despite her proximity to Yakiv. She pushed Meliora away from him, even as she recognized how foolish this was, putting herself directly in arm's reach of the man who had a bounty on her head. So Violet couldn't truly blame him for snatching her. Even as she wrestled against his hold, she knew the logical thing would have been to come nowhere near Yakiv.

Nikos told me . . . did he hook—

She didn't have time to wonder before Yakiv shoved her through the gate. It deposited her into an equally dim outdoor setting. Her feet slipped over gray stone carpeted by moss and snow, and she bumped into another figure. Violet stumbled back, arms defensively raised by some unknown instinct that clearly expected her to punch someone. Fortunately, she recognized the figure before she struck. Yakiv had thrown Meliora through the gate too.

Violet took her arm, swiveling around in search of Yakiv, but they were alone with the wind and boulders. Should they make a run for it, or should they dash through the gate to reunite with the others? To what end, though? Violet and Meliora were safer escaping.

And abandon the others?

It's not abandonment. They would want you to save yourself, and Meliora, rather than hand yourself back over to the lion's jaw.

Logic and emotion and exhaustion and sílfar's inevitable tug whirled together. And Violet did absolutely nothing.

Perhaps either plan would have failed. In another few seconds, Jarek came barreling through, his momentum carrying him several feet past Violet and Meliora before he slowed. Then came Denys the Advocate, toppling like he'd been kicked. Kora's head appeared as she backpedaled into view, lugging Slav the Pillar along with her. And then it was Boh's turn, his entrance a confusing tangle of fighting limbs as he and someone else rolled their way through the gate. Yakiv stepped after the pair and immediately spoke to the golden light.

Violet yanked Meliora back. Neither made it far before the ground revolted. Meliora got blown out of sight, but Violet's legs somehow steadied her, like two trunks with entrenched roots. Though the wind blew off her scarf—Alikar's scarf—and her muscles absorbed every rumble in the earth, she remained upright.

Luck, Violet figured, until the air settled and she spotted Yakiv, Kora, and Boh standing just as she was, while the others were scattered. Kora was still carrying the weakened Slav. He'd strengthened them against the gale. Violet didn't take it as kindness. Yakiv wouldn't want his Compass broken.

His eyes found hers, so dark in contrast to the pure white. The discoloring had crawled further up, almost at his eyes. He didn't bother restraining her, and she didn't bother escaping. The absolute indecision unnerved her, yet she couldn't bring herself to do anything but stand. A prisoner awaiting execution.

He spoke to his team with a jerk of his head. They dispersed, shadowed forms moving on mountain rock. Violet could comprehend it now, the scenery—starlit trees and pale-gray rock and the sound of rushing water far off. These were the mountains across the lake. Yakiv had come here to find the gate to Terlian.

Yakiv's team came back, each dragging along a figure. Violet took in her fellow prisoners with scientific detachment. Meliora, whose emotionless face likely resembled Violet's. Jarek, hard-set in the jaw. And . . .

Alikar. He must've been the one tumbling around with Boh. Of the three, Alikar was the only one resisting, straining against Boh's grip with that wild, horse-like mania.

Here were three weapons Yakiv would use against Violet.

He stooped, tugging at Alikar's purple cord. "*Zakhyshchay.*"

Alikar's response was a glare.

Yakiv stuck his dagger beneath Meliora's jaw and repeated the word.

Alikar's glare remained fastened, but Violet knew he'd relent. Yakiv knew too. He turned to Violet. "You understand?"

"Yes," she said.

"It's simple, Terlion," he said, tucking the blade into his belt. "Take me to the Lykill or your friends suffer."

The ultimatum failed to surprise her. It failed to do anything, not to her iron, iron heart.

"Ignore him," Alikar said.

But she couldn't, not with that eerily white face looming at her. Violet exhaled and managed to say something reasonable. "Even if I wanted to help, I don't fully understand my liryn. I can't guarantee it will work."

"An ant can carry a mountain if he's motivated." Yakiv pointed his painted fingers in Meliora's direction. "She'll be first."

Alikar reared against Boh and almost managed to stand. "You'll start with me, you putrid coward."

Yakiv didn't even acknowledge his existence.

Violet couldn't speak past the cinch in her throat, couldn't think beyond the cloud in her head. He'd kill them. All of them. Even if she helped. Yakiv wouldn't want the extra baggage.

"Start with the thief," Boh said. "Let's squeeze him out."

Jarek didn't bother squirming. "Meliora," he whispered. "I'm sorry."

"The cord thief's not part of this negotiation," Yakiv said. "His life is already forfeit." Out came the dagger again. "A demonstration, to motivate you," he told Violet.

A gust straight from Helheim could not have made her any colder.

"I returned them, Meliora. I—" Jarek grunted as Kora pulled back his head, exposing his neck. But he resigned himself to the discomfort and eyed Yakiv as best he could from his oddly angled position. "Do you know who I am?"

"Vermin that's going to know justice," Yakiv said.

"Jarek Mieszko. I'm sure the name means nothing. I doubt you remember. But I do. You dragged the pieces of my pa's body down Krótka Street. My ma made me collect them. I never found them all."

Yakiv paused.

"Piast?" Kora said. "You're Mieszko's son?"

Yakiv shook his head like he was disappointed. "I can respect vengeance. Honor it, even. I would have let you try to kill me. But you had to become a thief too. And now you'll go the way of your old man."

"No I won't. He didn't regret a thing." Jarek tried turning his head so he could see Yakiv head-on, but Kora wouldn't let him. "I wanted to kill you. My whole life. I was going to try. Then I thought, what's the point? He'll kill me first. So I decided I might as well go out trying to do something worthwhile."

"Find the Lykill?"

"The prophecy, Terlian—that's for the Hasteins to sort out. Whatever that pendant is, it's not yours. You're a thief too. What a joke." Jarek's laugh was humorless and jittery. "And you're wrong," he said, voice cracking. "You think you're the hand of justice, but you're not, because everybody's got two hands, and you only use one."

The familiarity of the words brushed Violet like a bittersweet breeze. One of the taut, unmoving chains around her panic broke. She blinked at Jarek, seeing him differently now, no longer *the cord thief* but *another flawed human, just like me.*

A voice as fragile as fraying thread entered the silence. "I forgive you," Meliora whispered. Her stupor cracked. The smallest fraction.

Jarek smiled. His shoulders relaxed. Then spasmed as Yakiv slashed the blade across his neck.

Violet rammed her eyes shut. The image stayed fast. She stood there, going cold again, so cold that she couldn't shake, frozen as she was.

There was a laugh from Boh and then a *thump.* Someone cheered.

One by one, new chains secured Violet's emotions, their pressure as firm and constant as she'd always known. Yet she found no comfort in them. Too much had already come undone. Since coming to Bar'Talian, she had endured more swings of the heart than she had in the past ten years. Sorrow, shame, regret, and even humor had broken through, and they would not go back to their shackles easily.

She thought of Meliora, unable to bear her own feelings, who didn't realize Eliathor was still alive; who had lost aunt, cousins, Kelispar, and now Jarek. Could she deflate any further?

A voice penetrated Violet's thoughts, familiar, yet not.

"Men like you always fail," Meliora said.

Violet opened her eyes. Immediately, she saw Jarek, mercifully face-down. Beside him, Meliora's chin lifted like a bud unfurling, steady and sure. She gazed at Yakiv with every ounce of energy the gate pendant had sapped from her. "The Lykill cannot be under you. You must be under it. If you are not, you will die."

Yakiv rolled a shoulder, disinterested, and touched his wet dagger to Meliora's cheek. "Give your answer, Terlion."

Meliora let the weapon dribble Jarek's blood down her neck. She didn't blink.

Neither did Violet. Nothing came to her—no flash of inspiration, no train of reason by which to change Yakiv's mind. She was empty of all ideas, an actress thrust onstage and having no memory of her lines. Completely and utterly useless.

Her mouth opened. Panic trapped her words. They wouldn't have been inspiring, most likely *Please don't kill Meliora too.*

"I will give you one—" Yakiv gasped. The dagger dropped, steel tip bouncing onto stone ground. He gripped his arm near the elbow.

"Yakiv?" Kora said.

For a moment, Violet wondered if Nikos had interfered, then remembered he was miles away.

Yakiv was slowly exhaling, the sound like a dying whistle. He'd gone as rigid as Violet.

"You were right," Meliora said. "You can see it, in the eyes. I understand you now."

"Quiet."

"Do they know—"

Yakiv backhanded her.

Alikar shouted obscenities a nobleman shouldn't have known.

"Quiet!" Yakiv kicked Alikar in the chest; he crashed into Boh. "Stop—talking—" Yakiv seized his arm again. Then, he made a gate right there.

No one had time to prepare but Yakiv, who dragged Violet through before the quaking began. She stumbled into sunlight, but Yakiv heaved her along before she could register anything but dirt, twigs, and leaves beneath her feet—that is, until this side erupted too. Thrown in the dirt, Violet let the angry gate batter her. Sounds of destruction threatened violent impaling, but she was spared of all but bruising and wind burns. When the commotion calmed, Yakiv yanked her upright with two white hands. Briefly, she glimpsed a dingy house of yellow stone walls before they were inside it.

She'd never understand Yakiv. He hadn't given any warning, not even to his own team, before he'd tossed a grenade at them.

They entered a dank room with an unmade cot and a nightstand. The curtains were drawn. Dust floated in the shadows. There, Yakiv shoved her to the floor. She caught herself; but, seeing Yakiv, she stumbled back, butting her head against the wall.

His mouth gaped, his eyes swelled, taking in something she couldn't see. Whatever it was raised the veins in his skin and brought terror to his face. Pure fear, the kind that shows before something so awful that no amount of pride will keep the fear at bay. His lips were moving, pushing out broken whispers.

"*Nye, nye, ne moneh . . .*"

The feeling was contagious; Violet's nerves pricked with unease. If something could reduce Yakiv Stefanos to trembling, she was done for. But there was nothing there.

Yakiv fell sideways. His limbs curled, forming the fetal position. "*Ne relno!*" He banged on the floor. Then, he pushed himself up and clawed at his jacket. Off it came. Off came his shirt too. Yakiv searched himself, scratching at the white that stained his chest like he could scrub it away. The pure white color had painted his whole torso, though it hadn't covered the scar stitched around one arm like a jagged bracelet, nor the purple tattoo of a book on his back.

Violet stared at the tattoo, the mark of a Vessel in the same spot Yakiv's scapegoat grandfather had received one. The same grandfather who'd cut off his own arm.

Or maybe there had never been a grandfather.

Yakiv stumbled toward the nightstand and dunked his face in a bowl. Violet took this as her cue to flee. She darted to the door. The wash basin smashed against it. Yakiv blocked the door. His voice was low, a tiger's warning, his face red and sopping.

Violet didn't move. He was unhinged. The sort who'd attack the smallest movement.

He slapped her across the face.

Violet cried out and tripped sideways.

Then the door slammed. Yakiv was gone.

CHAPTER THIRTY-TWO

"Then the reluctant child will come. And this reluctance will be shed, and the Lykill will be found beneath a twin silvered sheen." - Prophecy of Thulian

VIOLET'S EAR RANG AND her jaw throbbed. But her pulse throbbed harder. Seeing Yakiv whimper like a child should have made him appear weaker, but he was all the more terrifying.

Yakiv was welded, a Vessel. A barren Vessel. That story he told—it was his own. *His* mother had offered him up as a scapegoat so she could get money. *He'd* cut off his own arm, hoping to die, anything but fear. Fear of living, dying, breathing, suffocating. His crown was fear, an unpredictable panic, which struck him without warning and turned the calm, cool Yakiv into a shivering man screaming on the floor.

She pinched down the wrinkles in her skirt. No matter how long she pressed the fabric, the wrinkles remained.

Yakiv would return, as soon as his episode passed. If she didn't help him, he'd kill Meliora. And then Alikar. One by one. Now was the time to plan, to plot some method of outsmarting him. Perhaps she could lie, promise to take him to the Lykill but in actuality—

No. Boh was a Chair. He'd see right through her.

Violet sat on Yakiv's dirty floor and waited for inspiration. It never came. She was depleted, flattened out, unable to muster any fervor.

"*Don't do this alone,*" Alikar had said.

Her last hope was sílfar.

She felt for Alikar's chain. What could a Compass do—show her a trap door in Yakiv's floor? A hole in the window? What if there was no ideal path? What if the only route forward was death? Sílfar hadn't stopped Jarek's. Lady Basilia's or Kelispar's. Fa's.

Please. Violet squeezed her flower. Then, because thinking to sílfar felt ridiculous, she muttered to it, which wasn't much better. "There has to be a way to prevent anyone else from dying. If the prophecy is right and I'm supposed to reunite the Lykill, that means there's a way to get the gate pendant from Yakiv." She paused, focused on the feeling inside her gut where sílfar liked to stir. It would nudge left, toward Yakiv's window, or right, toward the door, which Yakiv would have accidentally left cracked.

Sílfar didn't prod. It sat there—she could recognize its presence now like a smudge on glass—and failed to call attention to any other path but the one she'd been on for days: *Find the Lykill.*

"That's what I'm trying to do," Violet told her pendant; desperation left little room for embarrassment. "All I have to do is unite them. But how can I get the gate pendant from Yakiv? How can I trick him?"

A flashing arrow didn't burst into the air. Nothing happened, actually, other than Violet peeking around Yakiv's room, feeling foolish. There was nothing in here but an unmade bed, a nightstand, an unbreakable window, a door with no knob, and a shattered washing bowl. Could she use the shards to cut her way free?

Violet crawled to the broken pieces, having no energy to stand, nor even much excitement over an idea that was nearly improbable.

The bowl had broken neatly; its five pieces didn't look much sharper than a pencil. Violet tested the edge of one, simply to reassure herself that she was doing something other than mope in the corner. Dull. But she could reassemble the bowl, at least, though she had no glue, and Yakiv didn't deserve to have this fixed.

Halfheartedly, she pushed two pieces together. Purple splotches conjoined on the porcelain background. Her fingers stilled. A confusing earnestness threatened to unsnap another chain around her heart, but she quelled it, finding a third piece with purple and connecting it triangularly to the others. She knew what the purple splotch would form, even before she finished connecting the fragments.

A violet.

She stared at the half-formed bowl and its only decoration. Why did a murderous Separatist own a bowl that could've belonged to someone's grandmother? Why had he thrown it? Why had she decided to investigate?

Violet knew that answer, too.

Her pendant floated to eye level before she could reach for it. There it hovered, letting her see it. *Really* see it, the liryn Fa had given to her, whether or not he'd fully understood the consequences. Violet had no weapon against Yakiv but sílfar, a tool she'd never wanted. But it was here, telling her to use it, though she didn't understand how.

Prodding the gap between her brows, she worked to lower her resistance, which felt very much like exposing her neck to a knife. Yakiv wanted the Lykill. Something in that seemed significant, so she repeated it until, probably exasperated with her, sílfar let the link slide into place.

So take him to the Lykill.

But she couldn't bring Yakiv to Helheim, to the research station, where Utkin might be killed.

Don't worry about where the gate will lead. Let sílfar decide.

She could not delay this moment any longer. Violet and sílfar needed to reach an understanding. What other option did she have? That question brought relief and discomfort. She could give in, but that felt like giving up, and Violet couldn't see the difference between the two. Not at first. But if she stopped looking at the whole thing like a math problem, the answer came simply. And, because of the simplicity, she grew warier and surer that the last thing she should ever do was stop trying so hard.

But Violet was tired. People were depending on her, and she couldn't let them down. She *had* to trust sílfar. She had to surrender to it.

Iron was malleable, Alikar had said. Not a shape fixed in stone, but something willing to reform. But into what? Violet was afraid to see who she might become if she allowed her heart to breathe. If she let herself go, she might never find herself again.

Her palms lay flat, fighting the habit of clasping her flower. Fa had given pendants to June and Oliver too, but he'd given sílfar to Violet. An act of gratitude because she'd worked so hard for him? Yet Fa had been a Compass, welded with sílfar, and sílfar was a guide. It had wanted Violet, in spite of her flaws. In spite of her ironness.

But what would sílfar do with her once she gave it the reins? *I won't misuse you.*

It wanted her trust. This liryn demanded it.

She exhaled, a surrender in and of itself. The movement didn't ache. She didn't fall apart or lose her self-awareness. Sílfar didn't want a robot. It wanted Violet.

Okay, sílfar, she thought. *You can lead now.*

It didn't answer—of course not. Liryn didn't talk. But she sensed that triumphant smugness and could have guessed that sílfar was thinking, *Of course I can. That's what I've been doing all along.*

CHAPTER THIRTY-THREE

"'Harð' is often translated as 'stone,' to denote the great sword's composition, but it can also mean 'hard.'" – *Relics of a Bygone World* by Dr. Mariemma Crawley

T HE DOOR OPENED AS soon as she reached her decision. Violet flinched, scooting away.

Yakiv's entrance was slow. Measured. Carefully, he shut the door. Calmly, he strode toward his bed and picked up his shirt. Slipped his arms into it. Buttoned it.

Violet didn't watch, though his presence was impossible to ignore. The Vessel who'd lost his liryn before it had been truly his. No wonder he'd asked Malokki if the Lykill could unweld. Yakiv didn't want power; he wanted peace.

But he wanted vengeance too, revenge on the emperors who'd done this to him. His vengeance had a price: the lives of anyone who got in his way.

And now I'm going to give him what he wants.

No. Violet clutched her necklace and bottled the thought. She was going to trust sílfar.

She sensed his watchful eye and forced herself to meet it. His face was placid again, that familiar nonchalance. A mask, one that couldn't hide the story his eyes told. Meliora must've seen it there too. His crown. His curse. His motivation.

They shared the tense silence. Yakiv showed not one hint of shame over what Violet had witnessed. Instead, she read his silent threat. Unnecessary—she wouldn't tell anyone about his panic attack. She wasn't the type to blackmail. Not like him.

He dragged her out of the house, through the gate in his ravaged backyard, and back to the mountain. The switch from afternoon to night stung Violet's eyes; though, with two gates now shining on the mountain stone, her eyes adjusted quickly.

Alikar and Meliora had been given the allowance to sit side-by-side on the ground, now twice disturbed by gates. Jarek's body was covered with Alikar's coat. Violet surveyed the lump, feeling an identical one in her throat. Alikar hadn't lost the kindled ire of loyalty, but Meliora looked on calmly. Dirt smears failed to obscure the confidence shining in her face.

Confidence in what?

Yakiv got Alikar to Advocate. "Your answer?" he asked Violet. He didn't have to hold her captive; the crossbow aimed at Meliora's forehead did the job.

Violet knew what she had to say, but her surety wavered. How could taking Yakiv to the Lykill be what sílfar wanted?

She found Meliora, who gave a tiny smile and nod.

Violet breathed. Borrowing some of Meliora's certainty, she announced, "I'll take you to the Lykill."

"Fileet, no!" Alikar said.

Yakiv's frown showed he wasn't convinced. "Where is it?"

"Not far from the Terlion gate," she said.

"Guards?"

"Just one."

"And you'll take me there."

"I said I'll take you to the Lykill."

Yakiv sought Boh.

"I see a key and a sheep," he said. "She's truthing."

"Wise choice, Terlion," Yakiv said.

This time, he led her some distance away before he made another gate. Slav strengthened them. Violet withstood the hurricane, her interior equally unflappable. Yet, when the gate twinkled, a star waiting to be touched, her calm cracked.

Sílfar, she thought. *Lead me.*

It had been waiting. At once, a hinge within her loosened. It didn't collapse; it didn't burst. The peeling away came gently, a knot softened by warm water.

She stepped forward, not envisioning Helheim. Not envisioning anything but a compass pointed north. For a moment, Violet hovered in a comfortable hush. Just her and the gate. Reluctantly, she pressed on and waited for the calamity.

But Yakiv pulled her back out of the gate. He was waiting for the other side to settle. Smart.

Sílfar felt differently, however. It wanted her to move.

Violet didn't consider the consequences of darting into an area that was currently in the middle of a catastrophe—she just obeyed.

Yakiv might've shouted after her; she didn't hear, having slipped through the gate and been immediately assaulted by a clashing sound of dozens of rocks colliding and splashing into water. She saw nothing but her windswept hair as a gust knocked her over. Yet she didn't face plant onto the rocks. Someone caught her. Steadied her. Violet gripped the arm securing her own and recognized it.

Eliathor?

He'd planted his sword vertically, and somehow the ground didn't cough it back up. The weapon anchored him as the wind thrashed and the earth threatened to fold. That was good and well, but Yakiv was going to pop out any moment.

"Hide!" Violet shouted, and she pushed against Eliathor's torso. Though she might as well have put her shoulder against an elephant, he was actually thrown off balance, losing his hold on the sword. Once he let go, they were at the wind's mercy. Eliathor tried retrieving his weapon, but Violet shoved him. They staggered over rattling rocks, sloshed over a stream, and came to the base of a mountain slope. *Are these the same mountains?* Violet wondered, a mental note she'd return to later, once she contemplated the fact that she was pushing Eliathor around like a shopping cart.

Without pause, Violet hurried up a makeshift trail, one surprisingly formed and flattened for being in the middle of nowhere. The wind was slowing. Panicked, she motioned for Eliathor to follow; then, in a mental state that was both certain and confused, she squeezed through a gap beneath an overhanging ledge and found herself inside a cave. A small, bathroom-sized cave that was illuminated by a glowing gate.

Violet stared, hardly noticing Eliathor's entrance.

Sheep's wall.

Eliathor inquired, gesturing.

"Terlian," Violet said. For days, she'd wanted to find this spot. Now she was here, footsteps away from familiarity. Eliathor must have been hunting for Yakiv and unwittingly come close to the place he wanted nothing to do with.

But why had sílfar taken her to him?

Eliathor spoke again. He pointed to Violet, then the gate. He was telling her to go home.

It made sense. She could return to Helheim, warn Utkin about Yakiv, have him put the pendants under top security. What more could Violet do on Bar'Talian? The farther she was from Yakiv, the safer the rest of the realms were.

Eliathor gazed upon the gate, whose bright rays showed the discontentment in his expression. Yet his face was not entirely without feeling. Violet thought she spied longing.

His boot edged forward, closer to Terlian.

Then he turned around and left.

Light had a way of playing tricks on faces.

Violet lingered, though she was averse to wasting time. Slowly, one leg moved toward the gate. Sílfar pulled from the opposite direction.

Not again.

What did it want from her? She'd listened, and it had taken her nowhere in the proximity of reason. The logical thing to do was find Utkin, not go back to the trap that awaited her outside.

Violet tucked her hair behind her ears and rubbed her forehead. Then she went after Eliathor.

Peering out of the cave's narrow entrance, Violet took in the uprooted landscape: the boulders, now strewn out of place; the stream, now swollen with plant debris; the shrubs, now crooked from being bent so harshly. Yakiv, carrying Slav, had come, searching with Kora and Denys.

Violet ducked back into the cave and caught her breath. Cautiously, she peeked again. Eliathor was hiding among some shrubs, so plainly visible from her vantage point that she couldn't guess how Yakiv hadn't spotted him yet; the shine from the two moons fell right on him. But the Separatists were distracted by the sword. It stood like a spear, very obviously not a part of the landscape. Denys tried to free it and failed. Then Kora landed a kick on it. The sword didn't even waver. She yelped, hopping. Then it was Yakiv's turn. He grasped the hilt and tugged. No movement.

Were they not strengthened by Slav's Pillar liryn? Alikar had accused the sword of weighing too much, but he was dramatic. Eliathor wouldn't have been able to lug around a weapon that even someone strong with liryn couldn't handle.

A memory came to Violet, so familiar that she felt the comforting relief of remembering a quiz answer at the last moment.

"Harðgjǫrð doesn't like to be carried by anyone but its master," Fa had said, years ago in the basement, buried in all the random assortment of pamphlets and trinkets he'd found. Oliver had walked out shortly after that comment, but Violet had stayed, June on her lap, scooting over Fa's hand so she could better see the drawing of the stone sword.

She peered across the yards at the weapon stuck in the ground. The top of the hilt was rounded, and though Violet couldn't make it out from this far, she knew what was etched there: a key.

She sucked in air. It *was* Harðgjǫrð. The statue Eliathor had gotten this from must have been King Borgfastr, Earth's first monarch. Borgfastr was its original owner, though it hadn't turned to stone until an enemy used it to execute Borgfastr's friend. The blade got stuck in the executioner's pillar and sat there until the 6th century, when another Terlian king reclaimed it. Only the true king of Terlian could wield it.

An outlandish idea branded across her thoughts: *Harðgjǫrð is the Lykill.* Some people in the Order believed that. Perhaps sílfar hadn't been entirely confused when it led her here. But it wasn't the sword itself that was special, according to Fa. The power was in the one who carried it.

Violet thought about the painting above Malokki's unlit fireplace, that king wielding Harðgjǫrð as he opened a gate. She remembered Malokki's recitation that Violet would find the Lykill aided by the blade. She broke down the Old Norse compound word as she'd done with Fa and Dr. Mariemma a dozen times. Harðgjǫrð's meaning tumbled into memory at the same time as a line from Bar'Talian's prophecy, both competing for Violet's attention. They didn't fight for long, blending into the same meaning.

"With the hard cleft, the Lykill will be found."

Or, one could say:

"With Harðgjǫrð, the Lykill will be found."

Yakiv and his Separatists gave up trying to carry off the weapon. They dispersed. Then he made yet another gate. Judging by the nearby avalanche a moment later, his new gate was somewhere at the top of this mountain.

Eliathor didn't jump out immediately. He was probably making sure Yakiv had really gone.

Violet stared at his form, highlighted by the moons, seeing not so much Eliathor, but Lady Basilia. She had known three versions of the Lykill's location: with the hard cleft, where water meets sand, and at the sheep's wall. Two of those currently worked, as Yakiv was here with the Lykill's third pendant, near the hard cleft—Harðgjǫrð—and the sheep's wall. What about "where water meets sand," however?

Yet, hadn't Violet and Meliora determined that the prophecies weren't describing any single part of the Lykill, but its whole?

Her head throbbed, but Violet treated the ache like an irrelevant nuisance. When she'd first learned that the Lykill was the pendants, she'd found that idea confusing, but she'd accepted it. Even though Chief Halfdan had collected all three, he'd failed to deliver them to the emperors, and so Earth continued to deteriorate.

And Fa continued looking elsewhere.

Her father had been a Compass, but he'd never been drawn to the pendants. Either he'd ignored sílfar as much as Violet, or . . . the pendants weren't the Lykill.

But Harðgjǫrð? Violet truly was a horrible Compass if she'd walked right past the Lykill without noticing, yet sílfar had no problem directing her toward things she wasn't looking for. She'd certainly managed to find Eliathor countless times.

Where water meets sand.

She'd found him at the shoreline when she first entered Bar'Talian. She'd found him with the hard cleft too. Aided by the blade. *He* was aided. And he was here, at the sheep's wall.

Carefully, she slipped out of the cave and let the night air sharpen her thoughts. Another theory was growing. This one did not surge like something trying to prove itself. It hovered in that quiet, insistent, determined spot she'd relegated to sílfar.

Violet hadn't found the pendants where water meets sand; she'd found Eliathor there. Again she'd found him in the Separatist tavern. Again in the woods. Again here. Again and again. When searching for the Lykill, she'd found Eliathor.

For the first time, her thoughts and sílfar's tug were seamless. A single source of power. A lineage, a throne, given by King Eirìkr to govern the twelve realms.

The three pendants were not the Lykill.

Eliathor was.

Having made that mental affirmation, she repeated the idea: *Eliathor is the Lykill*. Even as a thought, it sounded so natural that she couldn't understand why it had taken her so long to conclude it.

King Eirìkr had not imbued three objects with his power; he'd imbued Terlian's royal line. *That* was what needed to be restored. She wouldn't lead the pendants back to the emperors—she would lead Eliathor back to his throne.

"Wait," she whispered. He'd freed Harðgjǫrð like a blade of grass, and now he was walking toward the gate to Meliora and Alikar, ignoring Yakiv's newer gate, moving as though every step hurt like a bandage repeatedly ripped off. Eliathor wanted to go after Yakiv, but he had to protect his family. He'd take down Boh, then drag Alikar and Meliora a million miles away. Only then would he come back for Yakiv. At that point, he might not be able to find him again.

It became suddenly clear to Violet—who accepted this with much relief—that she was not the one who had to defeat Yakiv. Eliathor was. But he couldn't do it without her.

She jumped onto the treacherous path she'd tumbled down days earlier and repeated the same mistake, but it was the quickest way of getting to the ground. "Wait!"

Eliathor spun around. His face read confusion, with a touch of exasperation.

"*Farðu!*" he said, pointing again. He was glaring, forcefully reminding her of Oliver. The glare had a way of normalizing him, stripping away his intensity and putting him before her as an overgrown boy running from his responsibilities.

She rooted her legs like stumps. "*Neinn. Þú est—*"

Eliathor shoved her all the way back to the cave. He probably would've tossed her through the gate, but she squirmed out of his grip and yelled, "*Þú est Lykill!*"

The shout surprised Eliathor as much as it did her. It had billowed over, a spark gone too high. Embarrassed, she forced several breaths through her nose.

"*Hvat?*" he said.

"*Þú est Lykill,*" she said calmly.

He shook his head. "*Neinn.*"

"*Já.*"

"*Neinn.*"

"*Já! Þú est!*" Violet felt like a kid trapped in a game of "I know you are but what am I?"

Eliathor tried staring her out of conviction. He emanated doubt like a dead flame releases smoke.

"*Þú est,*" she whispered, then switched to Scandinavian. "I know you don't want it, but . . . you have to. Please. Save Terlian."

He looked toward the gate, letting it highlight the grime and pain and exhaustion. For a long, slow moment, Eliathor watched the door to Terlian.

Violet held her breath. They had to catch Yakiv. They had to rescue Alikar and Meliora. They had to . . .

No. This moment had to happen first.

Finally, Eliathor shut his eyes. Then he dropped Harðgjǫrð, slumped to his knees, covered his face, and wept.

Violet numbly stood, privy to a scene so far outside her comfortable realm that she felt an acute kinship with Prince Ezio. Why was he crying? And what was Violet supposed to do now?

You are the only one who can help him.

Violet's hand twitched. Sílfar was wrong. Eliathor would hurl her away if she tried. She'd sooner comfort a porcupine.

Fifteen more seconds passed in this discomfited noise. Sílfar did not relent. Fighting herself had become like fighting a hurricane. Because she *did* want to help. She was simply positive he'd want it from anyone else.

Violet inched her hand closer and told it to rest on Eliathor's shoulder. It sat there like a bird on a stump, ready to fly at the barest hint of danger.

Eliathor spoke. He might have been talking to her hand. He continued, one endless rumble of Faartunga. She listened, paying attention to the cadence of his voice—where it rose, on words like *Terlian* and *Lykill*. Where it fell, on words like *faðir* and *móðir*.

Father and mother.

Violet's palm was sweaty, but she held on. When he finished, part of her wanted to send him away. The other part longed to tell him she finally understood, and not only because she'd recognized fifty percent of his words. He hated Terlian because he loved his family. It was illogical, but loyalty was blind like that.

She knelt, coming level with his wet gaze. Violet held her breath, then touched his hand. "I understand," she said in Scandinavian. "But . . . *Þat er døkkust áðr dagan*." It came to her, probably on account of sílfar. It was an Old Norse expression; there were dozens of them tacked to corkboards in Fa's basement.

It's darkest before dawn.

His eyes flicked up, wavering and uncertain. Yet he didn't blink.

"You have to fight for Terlian. Now, pick up your sword. Um . . ." Scandinavian hadn't borrowed this from Old Norse; what was the word? "*Sverð*."

Eliathor inspected it, and Violet received confirmation in the key etched into its rounded hilt. "*Konungr nú ok Konungr a-lengðar,*" he read, touching the Ókunnigr runes at the top of the blade. Whatever that meant caused a chain reaction of emotions Violet struggled to follow. First he sighed, then frowned, then shook his head, then chuckled with a lighter sigh.

Finally, he stood, offering a hand. Violet let him help her up. "Terlian?" he said.

She shook her head. "Yakiv."

Every hard, determined line in his expression read *I was hoping you'd say that.* Eliathor scooped up Harðgjǫrð, having no idea he carried a legend.

They left the cave. He let her lead. Automatically, she side-stepped to let him take over, but Eliathor was content to follow. She decided she was content to follow, too.

At the second gate—not the one toward Alikar and Meliora, but the other—she and Eliathor paused. He put out his arm and told her to stay. The command carried a warmth his others had lacked. He wasn't sending her away because she was a burden; he wanted to protect her.

Violet closed her eyes, seeking inward. What did sílfar want? *Stay.* With the Lykill.

She looked at him and, forgetting to be embarrassed by her broken Old Norse, said, "*Ek ferr þú.*" *I'm going with you.*

He exhaled, and then nodded, assuming the lead. Eliathor entered the gate.

Violet hesitated. Maybe Yakiv was expecting them. Maybe this was as good as walking into a snake's wide-open jaw. Her nerves somewhere in her throat, Violet vanished into the gold.

On the other side, Yakiv was waiting.

They were in the same snow-touched mountains, some-where above the gate to Terlian. The elevation put Yakiv closer to the moons, which highlighted the white that now covered all but a sliver where his forehead met his hairline. He said nothing, surveying them without any sense of urgency. He knew he had them pinned. They could run, but he could run faster. They could fight, but he could fight harder.

Denys stood in his zombie state, nothing keeping him up-right except liryn. Slav was there too, gasping for air against a boulder and muttering the words that made Yakiv as strong as five men. A breeze made those words sound gentle. And Kora? Where was she?

Yakiv studied Eliathor. Confusion brushed his face. "Thought I killed you days ago, Pretender," he said.

Eliathor said nothing.

"You want this?" Yakiv held up the pendant. The moons made it shine.

"Do you feel any remorse?" Eliathor asked.

"Would you, if you were killing one of mine?"

"If any of yours were children, I would refrain."

A weary pain pricked when Violet remembered Liam.

"Children die in wars, Pretender. That's what makes us fight like we've got more oxygen than we do—the innocent lives." Yakiv's spectral face grew harder to interpret. His voice quieted. "But why should a child of Terlian be spared when other children aren't? You call that cruelty. I say it's justice."

Eliathor lifted Harðgjǫrð. "I'll fight to that."

Yakiv's head gave its slow shake. Still so calm, so indifferent. He held a weapon like a grenade, and if that failed him, he'd fight with a giant's strength. "You'll die to it. And then I'm taking the Terlion."

"No." Eliathor moved in front of Violet. "You will not have one of mine."

She stared at his shoulder blades. A shield. For her. She wasn't a Muratsan or a family member, but a Terlion. Eliathor finally found that something worth protecting.

His loyalty stirred her own. This plan *had* to succeed. She'd led him here. He'd trusted her. But he couldn't match Yakiv on his own. He needed help. Hers? How did she think she could help? Violet spied around, searching for some stick she could pretend was a weapon.

Yakiv charged before she got the chance.

She stumbled back, but Eliathor held his position, swinging Harðgjǫrð wide. The enhanced Yakiv would bat the weapon aside, then rip it out of Eliathor's hands and throw it off the mountain.

Instead, Harðgjǫrð thwacked Yakiv in the stomach. He stumbled back, but his head shot up immediately. He ran again, to the same obstacle. Harðgjǫrð didn't care that Yakiv fought under a Pillar's strength. Five men or one—Harðgjǫrð hurt them all the same.

Yakiv didn't need another blow to the stomach before he recognized his deficiencies and changed tactics. Harðgjǫrð defied him in strength, but Yakiv was faster. He darted around before Eliathor could react and plunged a fist into Eliathor's side. Had Harðgjǫrð not stabilized him, Eliathor would've gone flying from the force of that blow. Instead, he merely staggered.

His advantage realized, Yakiv swept in again. Eliathor had guessed Yakiv's move and cut Harðgjǫrð over, but Yakiv was already making his next strike. Palm hit rib. Eliathor's return swing was chaotic, misguided by pain. He missed.

And so their dance continued. Eliathor did his best to fend off his opponent, but Yakiv had no problem zipping around the sword and attacking from behind. Eliathor became a rag Yakiv was using to beat down bugs with. Prey to Yakiv's swift, strong beating, Eliathor grew welt after welt, dripping all manner of sweat and blood. Harðgjǫrð was the only reason he was still standing. He couldn't keep this up much longer.

Violet searched for aid, hoping sílfar could make a hole in the ground for Yakiv like it had for her. She only saw Denys, drooling, and Slav, muttering. Her focus zeroed in on

Slav's Pillar cord. Could she take it? Maybe theft wasn't wrong in self-defense. She was unsure. Instead, she'd drag his body through the gate, severing his connection to Yakiv.

The man was shaking like one having a seizure. Any pity she might've felt got pulled like a loose root when she remembered he was the reason Eliathor's family was dead. As she got a grip on his wrists and hoped he was lighter than he looked, someone else got a grip on her.

"Can't do that, Terlion," said Kora in her ear. Violet didn't have time to bemoan not acting sooner before Kora pinned her arms behind her back and shouted, "I got the Terlion!"

Yakiv didn't bat an eye, but Eliathor did. For one moment, his focus faltered, turning Violet's way, grip on Harðgjǫrð slackening. Yakiv only needed that blip of a distraction to duck around Harðgjǫrð and kick. It was like watching a cartoon horse kick a cartoon villain. Eliathor dropped his weapon, went airborne, and crashed against mountain stone several feet over. He struggled to rise. Injuries defeated him. He lay in pitiful inertia.

Steady on his feet, Yakiv wasn't even panting. He walked toward Eliathor. Violet squirmed against Kora and forced the girl to stumble forward with a hissed curse. But Yakiv aimed for Harðgjǫrð. He bent to retrieve it. Violet basked in satisfaction to see him uselessly tug.

"Why can't we pick it up?" Kora called. "Come on, Slav!"

In response, Slav gave a shivering mutter, and then rolled off the support of the boulder, unconscious.

Kora sighed. "Great."

Yakiv turned to check on the Pillar. Violet tried doing the same for Eliathor, straining to escape Kora, to run to the Lykill's aid. He wasn't moving. Was he . . . No. It couldn't be so. Violet had to bring him to Terlian.

But, she reasoned within herself, *the Lykill is Terlian's bloodline. There are still others. The Hastein grandchildren. They would suffice. It doesn't need to be Eliathor.*

Yes, it did. It needed to be him.

Yakiv was kneeling by Slav, attempting to revive him. Violet forgot Kora's sweaty grip, instead staring at Eliathor like intense eye contact might wake him up before Yakiv threw another dagger at him. How could someone destined to heal a dying planet, to restore order to the twelve realms, someone born of a lineage chosen by the High King himself—how could he have no power before a man whose only strength came at the expense of others? Even the Lykill, strong as he was, was powerless without pendants.

There, sílfar seemed to say. *Stop there.*

Pendants? What about them?

Eliathor is the Lykill.

I know that, she returned. The strangeness of talking to herself was overshadowed by the drive to understand.

What powers does the Lykill wield? sílfar prodded.

It doesn't matter. He doesn't have Terlian's monarch cord.

Neither did Chief Halfdan.

He used the pendants, she thought.

Where's the evidence? The cave where his gate formed should be caved in. His corpse should have been stained, like Yakiv and Meliora.

She considered that. Though he'd been found in the river, water wouldn't have washed those stains away. Lady Basilia had never mentioned those disfigurements. Perhaps she'd never seen his corpse.

But Violet had seen Halfdan's gates, both the one in Helheim and the one on Bar'Talian. Both stood in intact caves. Undamaged. Somehow, he'd used the gate pendant to no ill effect.

Was he a descendent? No, he was the Lykill. Power over the gates was his by right. The gate pendant—all three pendants—held power that should have been his. And if someone was the rightful owner of a liryn pendant . . .

Violet tried to move before remembering that Kora kept her restrained. "Eliathor!" she cried. "Wake up!"

Yakiv glanced her way, then toward Eliathor. He rose, began walking—to the unconscious Lykill. Though not unconscious anymore. Eliathor was stirring. He struggled to sit up.

"Eliathor!" Violet pressed forward. Kora tilted, grabbed Violet around the waist, and together they fell. Squirming to free herself from Kora's weight, Violet called out, "It's yours! They're all yours! Summon it!"

Yakiv reached Eliathor. "A crown can kill," he said. He bent, gripping Eliathor's wrists, and dragged him across the jagged ground. Not without difficulty; Slav wasn't strengthening him anymore, and Eliathor was no feather. "You think that's a beautiful thing?"

Eliathor resisted. Yakiv pulled faster, rougher. They passed by Violet. She and Eliathor were both prostrate, pinned. Their eyes met.

"It's yours, Lykill," she whispered.

Then he was dragged away. She twisted, crawling out from under Kora's weight, only to feel the Goldentongue clamp down on her legs.

"Summon it!" Violet cried again. Of course, it wasn't as if Eliathor knew how to use the pendant. However, holding it meant holding one advantage over Yakiv.

But this was the man who'd slaughtered a family. A pragmatic move, by his own admission. Pragmatic men did not care for extra baggage.

Yakiv toted Eliathor to the broken, crumbled ledge that the gate had recently fractured. "But in the end," he said, panting, "a man's two hands can do just the same as liryn." Yakiv crouched and put his weight against Eliathor's shoulder.

Then he shoved him off the mountain.

Horror got trapped in Violet's throat. Horror and pain and sorrow. Her iron heart threatened to reform, this time locked with fierce, unwavering shackles.

Sílfar, you promi—

A golden halo burst into existence above Harðgjǫrð and dumped out Eliathor.

Violet gasped. On top of her, Kora said, "How . . .?"

Eliathor bent and retrieved his sword. Then he rose, gripping a white triangle in his unstained fingers, focus narrowing in on Yakiv like a lion who's just spotted a mouse.

Violet's mouth hung.

Kora's grip lessened. She bolted upright and ran. She didn't make it far. Another gate popped to life in her path. Eliathor stepped out of it. Kora's momentum carried her through. The gate closed, and she was gone.

Relief was still unwinding Violet's nerves when she was jerked to her feet. Yakiv captured her in a headlock and began pulling her backward with him. She fought, scratching his arm.

"You won't get here in time," Yakiv called to Eliathor. "A blade moves swifter than a gate." She saw his dagger rising. Pointing. Aiming. He must've figured he'd lost—but he'd take Violet into death with him.

She wanted to close her eyes, but couldn't.

Yakiv's blade touched her neck. His arm jerked. He hissed. Her knees locked; she teetered back, into his chest, wondering why her throat wasn't on fire, wondering how long it took to bleed out. Dazedly, she saw Eliathor running for her. He knocked Yakiv's hand away and pulled her into safety.

Her emotions were numb. She couldn't feel any wetness of blood. But then again, she couldn't feel much but cold fear.

Eliathor tilted her chin, searching. The sight satisfied him; he let her go. Either Eliathor was heartless in the face of her death, or . . . or she was fine.

Violet brought a trembling hand to her neck. No blood. No stab wound. Then why . . .

"No, no, no, no, no . . ."

She followed the sound of the gasping voice. Yakiv was holding the dagger in a violently shaking hand. A mad terror lit his eyes. Like straw set ablaze, his whole countenance roiled, turning spastic and jittery. He mumbled incoherently with the pleading of a child, his head turning this way and that.

Violet looked at Eliathor, forming words to explain Yakiv's crown. Her attempt never made it past her throat. There was no pity in Eliathor's face. He watched Yakiv and waited for it to end.

Yakiv stumbled back. He gripped his head. His own dagger slashed against his cheek. Blood glistened. "No! No! Not . . .

real!" He stumbled again, closer to the edge. Another stumble. His feet slipped.

Violet turned her head. Yakiv shrieked all the way down. And then silenced.

For a long moment, she calmed herself with quiet, rhythmic breathing. Somewhere uncomfortably near, a wolf howled.

"*Vargr*," Eliathor said quietly; the Advocate must've finally passed out.

"*Vargr?*" Violet repeated. That was Scandinavian for "wolf," a derogatory word. She'd thought Old Norse was "*ulfr.*"

He nodded.

Violet shivered, remembering the wolf that had chased her not far from this very spot. Perhaps it was the same one.

Eliathor picked up Yakiv's dagger. Without hesitation, without perusal, he threw it after its owner. He watched its descent long after there was nothing to see. "*Rotna í Helheim, vargr.*"

She checked her neck again. Still dry. Yakiv's crown had saved her life.

And taken his own.

Her knees gave. She crumbled into an awkward position, sitting on her feet. It was over. Yakiv was defeated. Eliathor had the gate pendant. Terlian was safe. Violet thought some mention of these victories was appropriate—or would be, if she was the boldly speaking type. Alikar could be the one to jubilantly exclaim when they told him. Violet could be quiet, and that was okay. An iron heart was a heart nonetheless.

She looked up at Eliathor before averting her gaze from his tears. Crying was okay too. Maybe she'd remember how to do that again.

He knelt and put a hand on her shoulder. Startled, she tried pretending it wasn't there, then gave his hand a pat of acceptance.

Together, they overlooked the dark landscape across Lake Vaspurakan. She spied the lights of Borku glinting from the northeast. None were as bright as Bar'Talian's two moons and the haze of foreign stars.

A familiar sensation made itself known. She assumed it was sílfar, but it was only solidarity. Violet and her king. The connection didn't embarrass her like it once had.

Eliathor looked at her. He felt it too. He surveyed her, long and intent. Somehow, she kept from blinking. Then he stood, hands folded behind his back, and exhaled. "*Þǫkk, Violet,*" he thanked her.

"*Gerðu svá vel, Lykill.*"

He chuckled but didn't refute it.

And Violet, feeling oddly content, smiled.

CHAPTER THIRTY-FOUR

"Harðgjǫrð has touched the hand of every Terlion king since Björnson ('*Konungr nú ok Konungr a-lengðar,*' or 'king past and king to come'), who reclaimed the stone sword after its 500-year absence." – *The Reign of Terlian* by Dr. Mariemma Crawley

T HE FEELING OF VICTORY is short-lived when one is attempting to balance someone with a Viking's girth. Eliathor almost fell off the mountain, forcing Violet to jump to his aid. She couldn't relax until Alikar and Meliora were safe anyway. After that, she had to bring Eliathor to his throne. But which one: the one in his family's burned estate, or the empty spot on Terlian where it had stood a thousand years ago?

Can Earth really heal?

With Yakiv defeated and the Lykill leaning on her shoulder, Violet's heart began straining with hope. But first things first.

Her plan was to drag Eliathor to Yakiv's gate and try not to stumble. His plan was more straightforward. Eliathor created a new gate right next to them.

Violet would have to get used to that.

Now that she was close, she heard him muttering the ritual. He glanced at the pendant for verification. Was he *reading* Ókunnigr? Hadn't Malokki said no one could?

Oh. Except the Lykill.

"Come on," she said.

He resisted, doubled over.

"Eliathor?"

He was trying to reach Harðgjǫrð. Then, he gave up and grunted something. She recognized *sverð*.

"*Þú*, Violet."

She sighed. He was asking her to retrieve it. He must not have realized how Harðgjǫrð worked—or didn't work. Shifting away from his weight, she reached for the hilt. The stone was hot and moist. Violet gave a half-hearted attempt, not willing to strain a back muscle. Harðgjǫrð lifted. And Violet, caught off-guard, almost dropped Harðgjǫrð on their toes.

Eliathor rescued the sword with a "*Þǫkk*."

Violet gawked at her palm. Better not tell Alikar about this.

She led them through the gate, thinking of Meliora and Alikar and not Boh—until she and Eliathor drifted into the dark setting and found him gawking at them. Rather than attack, he flung himself aside and dashed away. Violet wasn't dumb enough to assume he was terrified of Eliathor's crippled self and her; no, he was running away from an explosion.

It never came. And Boh, so intent on escaping, didn't have the chance to stop before he plowed through the gate that materialized in his path. Eliathor closed it before he could run back out.

"Eliathor," came a tight whisper that reminded Violet why they'd come.

Meliora and Alikar were standing, and then they were running. Violet didn't have time to tense before she and Eliathor were smothered by limbs. Alikar's chatter, weaving in and out of Arati, assaulted her eardrums. Violet hadn't felt this content in a long time. Unable to say so, she hugged them back.

Finally, she extricated herself, with difficulty; Meliora was holding on to Eliathor like he was a tree during a tornado.

"Come on," Violet said, ushering Alikar away to give them privacy.

He glanced between the two gates Eliathor had just created and inquired in Arati.

"*Já,*" Violet said, having no idea how she'd explain it all but not worrying about that for the moment. She'd never been so happy to see Alikar. What an unexpected relief a friendly face could be.

He continued rattling incredulously on; so Violet, thinking he deserved a taste of his own medicine, said the longest Old Norse sentence she had memorized, some idiom about howling with wolves.

He stared at her. "*Hvat?*" he said, Faartunga now. He might've understood the expression, and now he thought she was crazy.

Violet gave another idiom. *A fair wind at our back is best.* Why she was teasing him like this, she couldn't say, but her mouth hurt from smiling, and she was very much enjoying his confusion.

Eliathor spoke, leaning heavily on Meliora. Then, he noticed something on the ground and frowned.

Violet's uncharacteristic enthusiasm ebbed. She knew what Eliathor was looking at.

He knelt, with Meliora's aid, and peeled back the coat that hid Jarek's body. This time, Violet found herself able to watch as Eliathor touched Jarek's head. He spoke unintelligibly to Meliora.

Violet nudged Alikar, indicating his liryn cord. He obliged.

" . . . his mother," Meliora was saying. "But . . . not like this." She turned her face toward the cloudless night. "I don't know," she whispered. "Our home is gone."

Violet nudged Alikar again. He read her gaze and knew what she meant.

"Bring him to Muratsan Manor," he said. "We'll see to his cleaning. To everything."

Meliora's flat expression tumbled into something between confusion and desperation. "I was going to tell Kelispar yes."

Alikar gathered her close. "I'm sorry, Melly."

She squeezed him tighter.

Eliathor remained kneeling. He couldn't stand on his own. Violet offered her hands.

"We need to find you a Balm," she told him as he pulled himself upright in a fashion that nearly dislocated her arms.

"Muratsan Manor first."

"Fine. *Then* the Balm."

"At your wish, Lady Terlian." Two gates formed. Then, Eliathor sunk downward and passed out.

WARILY, BECAUSE HE STILL didn't understand how Eliathor could create gates with ease, Alikar walked through the first gate. They followed him into a richly furnished sitting room, carpets everywhere. There, he laid Jarek on some floor cushions. He and Violet left, giving Meliora a moment. Violet entered the next gate in search of a Balm, asking sílfar to lead. She didn't linger, returning quickly to help with Eliathor. She and Meliora gripped him by the ankles, Alikar by the wrists; and, in that undignified way, they swung the Lykill into a bedroom of purple carpet, floral wallpaper, and two gawking Janlions.

Prince Ezio had removed his turban, revealing the full force of shock on his round, tan face. He was *much* younger than Violet had thought; he couldn't be any older than June.

Nikos was holding a hand towel that he forgot to wipe across his damp face. He and Ezio wore matching white pajamas, loose pants and a tunic—though Nikos was only wearing pants.

"What in Barikad were you thinking about when you walked through that gate, Fileet?" Alikar eyed her accusingly.

"I am flattered beyond expression, Dame Violeta." Nikos winked, finally drying his cheeks.

She almost dropped Eliathor. "I wasn't—"

"You seek a Balm for he-who-is-shunned? Yes, I'll retrieve one." Nikos flung the towel aside, summoned his liryn cord, shimmied into his tunic, and pointed at Alikar. "Explain nothing until I return. See that this gate disappears." With that, he exited.

"Bed," Violet mumbled. They hoisted Eliathor onto one of the two beds hanging from the ceiling. She guessed this was a hotel room.

Meliora stepped toward Ezio, but he skittered back. "Do you remember me?" she said.

He nodded.

She got on her knees. "May I pay homage to the Eagle King?"

"The Eagle King would refuse homage from she-who-is-shunned," Ezio said.

Meliora's shoulders sank.

Ezio's face, now that it wasn't covered, proved to be one of open and varying expressions. The strongest was confusion, until something between guilt and sorrow won out. "But the Eagle Prince does not refuse it." He removed his liryn cord and let her kiss the eagle pendant.

Meanwhile, Violet shook Eliathor awake. He opened his eyes long enough to mumble the closing ritual before he fell back asleep.

Nikos returned with a Balm who may or may not have been hooked into helping them. The Balm shooed them away. Meliora protested. The Balm insisted. Nikos said a few mild words, and the Balm relented.

"Your luster is becoming dark, Nikos," Ezio said as they exited the room, Violet leading them in search of somewhere private.

"Stop staring at it," Nikos said.

"My father will be angry when he sees you. You must not hook unless—"

"Dame Violeta, where are we going?"

Somewhere private, according to sílfar, was a storage clos-et. They crowded among giant dusters that might've been brooms, shelves of silver cloth ("Layinthai," Alikar told Violet), unknown objects made of crystal, and some copper buckets. Violet made room for the prince to sit, but he chose to stand. She felt obligated to remain upright. Nikos, however, had no qualms about lounging on an overturned bucket.

"What happened here?" Alikar's finger brushed Violet's cheek, the spot where Yakiv had hit her.

"I, um . . ."

Alikar's face was so close. Somehow, Violet both didn't mind and tremendously minded.

"You, um, what?" He smiled. When had his smile started looking like Kelispar's?

Never mind that Ezio was standing. Violet could sit. She escaped and settled on a bucket beside Nikos.

"Plenty of room beside me." He winked.

"Why are you so skittish?" Alikar asked Violet.

"I believe she—" Nikos started.

Violet whacked his arm.

What in Barikad? She'd just hit a practical stranger.

Nikos laughed.

Fortunately, Meliora and Eliathor soon arrived, and every-one shifted to make room. Eliathor's welts were either ban-daged or gone, one of his wrists was wrapped, and he wore a florid shirt.

His eyes found Violet. In that quiet, confused gaze, Violet saw that he understood.

"The Lykill has to be restored," she told him—just him. Her awareness of the others faded. They were like shadows cast from another room. "So Terlian can heal."

He nodded. "Where?"

"I don't know. Sílfar will show me."

"Then we must go."

"Now?"

"Yes. Now."

Good. Terlian had waited a thousand years already.

"Hold one minute," blared Alikar's voice.

Violet winced, turning her head.

"We know where the Lykill's got to be restored," Alikar said, "to the emperors. So let's retrieve the remaining pendants and finish this."

"The pendants are not the Lykill," Eliathor said quietly.

"Say that twice?"

Violet gathered her thoughts. She had no idea how to explain it, especially with Prince Ezio in the room. As Lykill, Eliathor could rule over Ezio's father, the king who'd publicly shunned him.

"So," she said. An excellent start.

"He-who-is-shunned is the Lykill," Ezio said simply.

Her mouth shut.

There was a beat of silence, and then, "I beg your pardon?" Alikar said.

"The Lykill?" Meliora said.

"Come now, Ez, we've talked about saying ridiculous things," Nikos said.

"It is not ridiculous," Ezio said. "He has used the gate pendant, but he isn't tainted."

"Let me explain," Violet said.

They turned to her with an assortment of crossed arms and dubious eyebrows.

"My father was a Compass. All his life, he searched for the Lykill. But he didn't give the pendants a second thought. When you told me they were the Lykill, I accepted that he was wrong. He wasn't."

"Yes, but—" Alikar started. Violet kicked his foot. "Anak. What's gotten into you, Fileet?"

"The Lykill belongs to Terlian's throne," Violet continued. "It *is* the Terlion throne. Eliathor's bloodline. He's the Lykill. Chief Halfdan was too. And Lady Basilia, by marriage."

"What in Barikad Forest?" Alikar drew back his foot, as if Violet might kick again. "Eliathor—the one with the patchy beard—he is blessed with the powers of the High King?"

"Then maybe," Meliora said, eagerness overriding her doubt, "the pendants are Terlian's monarch cords."

"No." Ezio shuddered. "They are tainted. He-who-is-shunned should not use them." He peeked at Eliathor's trouser pocket, then covered his face. "I do not like it. My parents did not like the liryn pendant either. They saw it, when the father of she-who-is-shunned found it. My mother wished to destroy it."

"I don't understand," Meliora said. She was wearing gloves, Violet noticed—Alikar's gloves, the ones given to him by the Unionist couple in the woods.

Nikos cradled his arms behind his head. "Look at the gate pendant, Ez, and tell us what you see."

"I do not want to."

"Don't make me hook you."

"A true servant to the king, you are." Alikar rolled his eyes at Nikos. "I'm certain hooking the prince is illegal even on Janlian."

"But we aren't on Janlian," Nikos said. "I'll give you three seconds, Ezio. One, two—"

"I see a shadow," Ezio blurted, not uncovering his eyes.

"Good," Nikos said. "The pendant is dark?"

"It is a shadow. A . . . a . . ." He rose to tiptoe. "It's black and broken and bleeding. Decaying. Like our gates."

Alikar eyed Meliora, his expression suggesting *Not this again.* "Prince Ezio," he began, "might it be that your sight is, well . . ." After some seconds, he gave up.

"Don't be shy, Muratsan," Nikos said. "I'm sure the son of the High Seer could learn much from a fledgling Advocate."

Alikar snatched a broom handle, like he might weaponize it, then changed his mind.

"I could not learn anything from an Advocate," Ezio said. "His liryn is of *da'atan.* And his luster is very feeble. He still fights his liryn."

Nikos grinned at Alikar's flushing face.

"The spirit of she-who-is-shunned shows the same stain," Ezio continued; it took Violet a moment to realize he was still analyzing the pendant. "She used it."

Meliora stiffened.

"You needn't voice *every* observation, Ez," Nikos said.

Ezio's hands dropped. Doubt flooded his expression in abandon. "I said something wrong."

"It's all right," Meliora said softly, hiding her gloved hand under her skirt.

"You say I am not tainted," Eliathor said to Ezio.

The prince was too absorbed by his mistake. Nikos had to repeat the question before Ezio shook himself and said, "No. You are not."

"Then I think I understand," Meliora said. "The pendants resemble a shadow because they're an imitation of the High King's powers. But those powers are only meant for the Lykill. Not the emperors. The pendants shouldn't even exist." She pursed her lips to the side, uncertain. "We've been lied to."

The statement hovered above the shelves like a crow.

"But the pendants were made for the emperors," Alikar said. "History can't lie. We have Vessels for this sort of thing."

"Unless Vessels of the past intentionally obfuscated the truth," Eliathor said.

It made sense. Vessels had infallible powers of retention. They shouldn't have been able to misremember facts. Unless they'd done so intentionally. Why else did none of the realms realize that the Lykill was Terlian's throne?

Violet thought of Malokki, who had some grasp of a language only meant for the Lykill, and then the philologist who'd parsed out sílfar's welding ritual for Fa. They were proof that information about the Lykill was not as accurately stored as the realms believed.

"You can read First Tongue," she told Eliathor.

"No he can't," Alikar said.

"I can now." Eliathor withdrew the gate pendant. Ezio hissed and turned around. "It says, 'I loose thee, oh gate, from which all life flows.'"

How many books sat in Fa's basement, books Eliathor could translate? Violet wasn't the envious type, but she couldn't help feeling that this aspect of Eliathor's powers would go highly unappreciated.

"We have manuscripts," she said, "on Terlian. The oldest ones are in First Tongue. They might shed light on this. I'll make copies, though I don't know how I'll get them to you." A previously unexplored realization occurred to Violet: How would she stay in contact with them?

She glanced at Alikar, who was yawning, and Meliora, who rubbed her bracelet-free wrist.

Nikos sighed, kicking out his legs so that everyone had to shift. "She needs a gate crate," he told Ezio.

"A gate crate?" Judging by Alikar's awe, a gate crate was the equivalent of a private jet.

"Yes."

"King Giannis would never allow that," Meliora said.

"The emperors are the ones who have to authorize a gate crate," Alikar said, "and they wouldn't. Not between Janlian and Terlian."

Nikos didn't reply. After scanning the room like one enjoying the last vestiges of freedom, he climbed to his feet. "Come, Ezio. We have to speak to your father."

"The child of sílfar must restore the Lykill," Ezio said.

"Then we will leave her to it."

The prince's face fell. "But I want to see."

"I have work to do, kings to hook, laws to exploit. Come."

They exited the closet, back to the corridor of floral wallpaper. Garish though it was, it was cozier than any of Fa's hospitals.

Nikos skirted around Eliathor, shared bows with Alikar, and kissed Violet on both cheeks. "We'll need organic material from Terlian," he told her. "Give it to Muratsan. He'll give it to me. Then the gate crate can be made. It'll be delivered to you. Eventually."

"You're not omnipotent," Alikar said, "even if you are a Fork-tongue. You can't commission a gate crate."

"Your doubt wounds me immeasurably," Nikos said.

"I can communicate with this crate?" Violet asked.

"Imagine a shining box. You put things in, the king of Janlian takes things out."

The king of Janlian? Violet wanted to communicate directly with Eliathor. "And the king will pass my information along?" she said.

"To a shunned one? Certainly not." With that, Nikos moved on, leaving Violet distinctly unsure. Looking vaguely toward Meliora, he said, "The loveliest dianthus in all of Patmos was always Lady Basilia's niece."

Meliora smiled sadly.

"What syrup," Alikar muttered.

Eliathor appraised Nikos like he'd just noticed he was wearing a Separatist armband.

"But you said the gardener's daughter was the loveliest dianthus in all of Patmos," Ezio said.

Alikar's chortle was so violent, Violet worried for his throat.

"Muratsan, Dame Violeta," Nikos said with additional bows, "may eagles bear you."

"Send our greetings to the gardener's daughter," Alikar said.

"Willingly. Come along, Prince."

Ezio hesitated. "Lord Alikar," he said, "tell he-who-is-shunned that my sister would be pleased with him."

Alikar swallowed. "I will."

Eliathor's face revealed nothing.

In silence, they watched the Janlion representatives move farther down the hallway. Violet wondered how long gate travel took if one had to pass through the Bar'Talion palace. Perhaps their familiarity with the monarchs would speed up the—

"Wait," she called. "Prince Ezio. May I speak with you privately?"

The way he stiffened made her cringe at her own forwardness, but she didn't want to send the message through anyone else.

"Do you speak Greek?" Nikos asked her.

She looked at Alikar. "You can Advocate while not listening, right?"

He frowned. "Why can't I listen?"

"Because I said so."

He rolled his eyes but conceded to covering his ears.

The others gave them some space, and Violet was forced to approach Ezio, as the idea of speaking privately to her had apparently caused his legs to fail. After making sure Alikar's palms were firmly over his ears, she said, in a whispered rush, "Please tell the Bar'Talion monarchs that Meliora had a conversation with Jarek that night. Yakiv's ally eavesdropped. That's how Yakiv knew about the Hasteins' plan. None of the monarchs' attendants betrayed them."

Ezio shook his head. "I don't like this. I don't want to know it."

"It was an accident. It's not their fault."

"Accidents hurt people."

"But you'll tell the monarchs?"

"Yes."

"Thank you." She stepped back, relieved. Violet expected Ezio to crawl away, but the prince hesitated.

"Your luster is strange," he said. "Lord Alikar's crown has not come, but I see the bud. You do not have a bud."

Meaning Violet would never get a crown. After hearing about how tainted the pendants were, she wasn't so sure she'd gotten a good deal. But there was nothing she could do about it.

She and Alikar returned to the others, who fortunately refrained from any questions. They probably thought she'd asked a question about her liryn, which suited her. This was one secret she'd jealously guard.

Eliathor was staring at the gate pendant. The smudges under his eyes had come forth.

Meliora touched his arm. "Just a bit more, and then you can rest."

He stood taller, resolutely clenching the pendant, and eyed Violet. "Take me where I need to go."

CHAPTER
THIRTY-FIVE

"When the great peace spreads over the land, the sun and moon will mingle for ill. A great rift will disrupt the provinces. Terlian will turn barren. But what is fallow can regrow. First, the man in white must resign that which evil has wrought. Second, the parched man must water his own soil. Third, the hole must be dug out. Then the shackled flower will bud. And the flower will find the Lykil blooming where the ground has been upturned. Only then can all lands flourish. And the shepherd will reclaim his pasture." – Prophecy of Filian

V IOLET WORRIED SHE'D IGNORED sílfar when she entered a black landscape that even the gate failed to brighten. It smelled of old eggs. Immediately, a frigid gust knocked her back through the gate. She tried again, but grounding her core didn't stop the wind from trying to throw her back to Bar'Talian.

The others came through; she could feel their shifting forms. Hands clasped hers. She held on in the icy black void, trying not to go flying. Sílfar was tugging her onward, into the unnerving emptiness. She obeyed, treading the rough, downward-sloped ground, until she bumped into something hard. There, the tug relented.

One of the figures around her moved—and nature responded.

The wind flattened her against the ground, where she scrabbled for anything to hold and failed miserably, her body spinning like she was on some carnival wheel.

A sliver of light pierced the darkness. Violet thought of lightning and covered her head. Another sliver came, then another. The blackness cracked apart, like she was in a tomb and someone was hammering at the coffin. Light trickled, then poured as a mighty swell dispersed the darkness.

All at once, the wind died.

Several strained blinks finally allowed Violet to see. Sun rays were falling from a periwinkle sky. The color was familiar, a proper Terlion shade. It was stretching, pushing against the black clouds. Darkness receded as the overcast sky cleared in fast motion.

Violet barely noticed Alikar help her up. They stood in a massive crater of black-crusted rock, but even as they shored their footing, the ground rumbled. Alikar steadied her as the crust fractured, splitting, shrinking. Something pulverized the rock into dust, which caked the earth before a breeze returned to clear it away. The crust had concealed white stone, gleaming as if recently waxed. The whole crater was constructed of it.

As Violet shifted and her shoe glided easily, she realized it was marble.

A crater. That familiar wind, the ominous black, the sulfurous stink . . .

She scanned the lip of the crater and the steep incline that led up to it. She needed to see from the top, to know if she was where she thought she was. Unfortunately, her soles refused to grip. "Come on," she told Alikar. "I need your help."

"You . . . need . . . my . . . *what?*"

Violet ignored his smirk and took his arm for balance.

They inched up the slope. Violet was too focused to mind that they were holding hands. Anticipation wrenched with so much hope that it ached, but she wouldn't allow herself to consider what for. Not until she was certain.

The hike was arduous. Violet was flushed after a minute, despite the cold.

"It's remarkable that I was shivering a moment ago, and now I'm wet with sweat," Alikar said.

"I don't need to know how sweaty you are," Violet panted.

"Yes you do, so you can appreciate my manful labor. Now, let's run the rest." And he dragged her to the top. The sight stole what remained of Violet's breath and held her hope in a fragile cocoon.

They were elevated hundreds of feet on a mountain, which allowed her to take in the strange phenomenon in every direction. Shadows on the ground were chased away as clouds dissipated, giving the landscape a rippling effect. The sun shone over black stone and ash, dark puddles and smoking sulfur pits. There was no grass, no trees, no crystal-blue springs. Violet recognized this view. Everyone had seen the aerial photos.

They were on Mt. Rof. Terlian's throne was in Helheim, where the sun had not shone since Ragnarök. Where blue skies could not exist. Yet both were there to defy the statistics.

Violet's throat was too tight for speech, her gaze too transfixed to notice anything outside the view.

Whenever she'd imagined the reversal of Earth's deterioration, she'd pictured it in a laboratory, some chemist crafting the right fertilizer. Never had she entertained the Order's expectations of a magical melody sweeping through countries, causing plants and animals to spring up out of the soil. They'd both been wrong. The initial moment had happened as a violent wind, but now all was calm. Trees weren't bursting to tall heights; flowers weren't dancing out of the ground. All that had really changed was the sky and sun. But it was enough for Violet to know, for her to hold Fa's dream one second more before releasing it into the land he'd loved.

The last chains over her heart, the ones lingering out of habit, fell away. Everything became bright and hazy, until Violet couldn't see. Her cheeks were wet.

There were voices, Alikar's hand on her shoulder. Eliathor was a few feet away, quiet wind stirring his hair. His shoulders were straight as he overlooked Helheim. He stood like a king.

Violet stepped toward him. "Thank you," she whispered. Then she curtsied, not even feeling ridiculous.

"Don't," he said vehemently. "Not to me. You brought me home. And so I bow to you."

And so he did.

Violet kept blinking, but that just made her vision blurrier. The build was too much; she had to succumb, lest her throat close up entirely. So Violet covered her face and cried in private. At least, as much as she could manage. It was strange to let go after all these years. But it was wonderfully satisfying too. She cried for Kelispar, Lady Basilia, little Liam, Eliathor's brothers. For June, who'd grown up too fast, and for all that had broken with Oliver. And, at last, she cried for Fa.

A strong hold bound her together. Eliathor held her. Violet wetted his chest, feeling awkward and mortified while oddly peaceful. Hugging him was not like hugging Jeremy Stiggs. This was nothing romantic, nothing butterfly-inducing. This was a hug of pure safety.

Additional arms wrapped around her, gentle and lithe. Meliora said nothing.

Alikar, on the other hand, was indignant. "You stop this instant, Eliathor. You're making her cry. I won't allow it. We haven't any handkerchiefs."

Violet wanted to laugh, so she did. Nothing outrageous, like an Alikar cackle. The small chuckle suited her. "I'm all right," she said, leaning back and feeling sheepish. There was nowhere she could safely look—not at the emotion straining Eliathor's composure, nor Meliora's warmth, nor at Alikar, whose ire couldn't hide compassion.

"Well." Violet cleared her throat. "I'm going to investigate the crater."

"There is no 'I,' Fileet." Alikar took her elbow. "Shall we?"

Finding the thing Violet had bumped into was easy; there were only two objects in the crater: marble chairs finished with gold.

"They're thrones," Meliora said. "This is a throne room." She pointed to the ground.

Perfect, man-made circles were carved around the crater where numbers on a clock would have sat, each circle etched with a different design. Violet walked to one. Her heels brushed the talons of an eagle.

"That's Bar'Talian," Alikar said, striding toward a knife. "And there's Matlian."

Violet walked around the crater. Sure enough, each circle held a realm insignia.

"These indicate where each realm representative would have sat," Meliora said.

"It's a marble foundation, seamlessly laid," Alikar said.

"We always thought this was a volcano," Violet said. "No one's ever climbed to the top. Too dangerous."

They rejoined Eliathor, who hadn't moved from the thrones. They were so wide that one chair could have fit him and Meliora both. A king was painted on one chair so that, if Violet squinted, it appeared that a giant man was peering at her. A queen sat in the other throne. Both had an arm raised, and both wore necklaces, but it wasn't sheep pendants hanging from their chains. Their pendants were Viking keys, identical to the key which formed the Order's logo.

Key necklaces. Fa had known. These were the cords of Terlian's monarchs, the necklaces Fa had hunted for. But they'd been confiscated after the Rift. Somewhere in the emperors' vaults were two necklaces that held power beyond their size.

"Why don't you sit?" Alikar asked Eliathor.

But Eliathor wasn't staring at the king's seat. He was staring at the queen's.

"I have failed everyone I know," he murmured. "And even those I don't. I am not worthy of this throne. I am not worthy to be the Lykill."

Violet waited for Meliora to say something profound. To her consternation, Meliora was watching *her*.

She bit her lip. "Well . . ." The words burned her throat, but Violet voiced her shame. "I never believed Fa. I thought he was wrong. But for some reason, the prophecy chose me. And when I realized I was welded, I fought it the whole time. Alikar can vouch for that."

"It was an admirable fight," he said.

"The point is, it's not about feeling worthy. It's about trying to do what's right, and I think you're capable of that."

As Eliathor studied Violet, some of his melancholic cloud dispersed. "You have faith in me?" he said.

"I do."

He smiled. She smiled back. That was enough.

Eliathor couldn't leave Terlian without the other pendants. His new gate led to the small room at the outpost Violet and June had slept in, where two exercise mats still lay and June's clothes were scattered like a thrown deck of cards. Odd—had she left in a rush?

"How fascinating." Alikar reached for the tool shelf. Meliora dragged him back.

Something thudded on the building. Eliathor stepped in front of everyone, drawing Harðgjǫrð, and cracked open the door (Violet had to point out the knob). A glass canister floated inside and hovered by his elbow. The red and purple triangle pendants clinked together as they strained to escape.

"I am immensely confused," Alikar said.

Violet started to explain, then laughed.

"You shouldn't use them," Meliora said as Eliathor freed the pendants.

"I'll use the gate pendant today, but no more," he said.

"What!" Alikar said. "But the liryn pendant! You could be a Chisel! A Pillar! A Sprite!"

Meliora shook her head. "You heard Ezio. They shouldn't be used. What he needs are Terlian's cords."

"I'm sure the emperors will be delighted to return them."

"It won't matter if they do," Eliathor said. "Every monarch must be crowned first. Even the Lykill."

"The emperors must have the coronation ritual," Meliora said.

"Perhaps. But who would crown Terlian?"

Meliora's answer got trapped in her throat before she gave up.

"Who can?" Violet asked.

"Only another monarch," Meliora said.

"You don't think the Bar'Talion monarchs would?"

"Not without their emperors' permission."

Which the emperors wouldn't give.

Then Eliathor was still several steps from being the Lykill. With the pendants, he had power, but a stained power. His true cord was locked away, but it was useless until a monarch officially crowned him.

He was studying the pendants with a focus so concentrated Violet could nearly feel it. Then, without preamble, Eliathor created a gate. He stepped through. Half a second later, another gate appeared against the back wall, and Eliathor emerged. He muttered something. Both gates began to shrink. Just before they vanished, Eliathor threw the pendant through the gate nearest him. It came out of the other gate and clattered onto the floor next to June's haphazard pile of toiletries.

"What was the purpose of that?" Alikar said.

Eliathor scooped up the pendant from amid June's hairdryer and toothpaste. "That is how the gate pendant came to be in the Amber Forest." He turned to Meliora. "Your father never used it. My father did, and he sent it after yours before the gate closed."

Perhaps on another day Meliora might've shown more reaction to this suggestion, but her response was simple. "But why did your father stay behind?"

"To face their attacker."

The word pulled Violet from her mental organization of June's chaos. What attacker?

Eliathor watched his fingers as they slowly turned the gate pendant over and over. "Uncle Niall must have been injured. My father gave him a way to escape, and to hide the pendant. Perhaps they'd gained ground on their pursuer." He turned to Violet. "How close was my father to the gate when he was found?"

"Not far," she said. "Maybe twenty yards."

"And he was already injured?"

"Yes."

"You're suggesting there was a third person on Terlian," Alikar said.

"One who murdered both our fathers. That is why mine gave the Tome and the pendants to Violet's father. For safe-keeping."

The ancient light bulb overhead shone on the pendant, staining it a sickly white.

Violet couldn't deny that Eliathor's theory held, given the odd circumstances in which Fa had found Chief Halfdan. Bleeding alone in the sand, without any obvious explanation for his injury? Yet, despite passing out, he'd roused up the strength to crawl to the gate while Fa had run for help.

Unless someone else had dragged him there.

Meliora spoke up. "This would mean their murderer has known about the gate to Terlian for two decades and kept it a secret. That's highly unlikely."

"Chief Halfdan might have killed him," Alikar said. "At least, he might have if this man actually existed. It's a very wide leap, Thor. You have no proof."

Eliathor closed a fist around the pendant. "There was no mention of Uncle Niall's body carrying a white stain. That tells us he did not wield the gate pendant. And I have never been satisfied with the explanation that he killed himself." His forehead furrowed, like one confused or upset or sad, or perhaps all three. "My father's shameful death was easier to believe," he quietly ended.

Alikar's mouth was open, skepticism ready to unleash. Violet touched his arm. He eyed her, then sealed his lips. Alikar could argue all he wanted—later. The mood was already heavy enough.

Indeed, Meliora looked like she had to struggle to push out, "What do you propose we do with this theory?"

Eliathor stopped staring at his hands and seemed to notice the dense air. He made an effort to clear his expression and came close to smiling. "You will do nothing," he said, tapping Meliora's nose.

She did not even attempt cheer. Exhaustion was potent, hugging her like cling wrap. She leaned on Eliathor's arm. "Let's go home."

His gaze tightened. "I don't know where to take you."

"Muratsan Manor has plenty of room," Alikar said.

"Then it's time to say goodbye," Meliora said.

Oh. Violet wasn't sure why the idea surprised her. She had only meant to stay with them one day. The additional time wasn't the length that lasting friendships were built on. Or was it?

Meliora faced Violet, who saw so much loss that no one could mend. But Violet could try. She dug into her pocket and found Jarek's bracelet. Words failed her, but Meliora didn't need them. She slung her arms around Violet's neck.

"Thank you," she whispered.

Next, Violet acknowledged Eliathor, but that wasn't any easier. Even with unkempt hair and a patchy beard, he emanated poise, though it showed some cracks in his wan eyes. Violet wondered if Oliver had tired eyes too. The more she studied Eliathor, the more she missed her brother. She thought she'd stopped missing him years ago. Somewhere on Bar'Talian, she'd forgiven him. Now, she wanted to see him, to know him. If he'd let her.

"Thank you for saving Terlian," she said.

"Thank you for saving it first."

In this room of mismatched clutter, the internal magnet awoke, the same that had driven Violet toward Lady Basilia.

It must have sensed their imminent separation and was giving one last hurrah.

Violet wasn't sure she'd ever get used to it, this pushing and prodding. Sílfar was the last option she would've picked. But it had picked her.

"I'm pretty certain the book your father gave mine was the Tome of Rites," Violet said, trying to drown her senses with something practical. "That probably has your coronation ritual, plus a lot more. Someone stole it, years ago. I'll start looking."

For that, and for the philologist. She needed to have a word with him.

"Then I'll wait for you to find it," Eliathor said. He had faith in her too.

Violet twisted the tip of her braid. Then she moved toward him. At the last moment, she lost her nerve, turning her attempted hug into an outstretched hand. "Goodbye," she said.

He surveyed her palm. "A Terlion farewell?"

"Oh. Yes. It's called a handshake."

Eliathor waved his arms, imitating her failed hug, then stuck out his hand too.

Violet was mortified. "Only this part's necessary," she said, shaking his hand.

Now it was time to say goodbye to Alikar. They stared at each other, then away.

"We'll give you a moment," Meliora said. She and Eliathor backed toward the gate.

"I'll . . ." Violet noticed the loudness of her voice and tried quelling it. "I'll see you all again."

"You will." Meliora smiled.

They stepped into the gate and were gone before Violet was ready.

Alone with Alikar, she didn't know where to look. He was suddenly too bright, standing in the golden glow.

"Well," he said.

Violet sensed a surge of emotion she was ill-equipped to handle. "Goodbye, then," she said.

"I'd rather not—"

"Violet!"

It took a moment to register that the voice had shouted from behind her, through the ajar door. Violet spun around and peeked outside.

Gawking in the snow were June, Oliver, and Utkin, bundled and mud-splattered as if they'd just hiked Mt. Rof too. June and Oliver were *here?*

"Hold on," she told Alikar, then hurried outside. June met her halfway, smothering her with two arms in a puffy jacket, pouring out an explanation of Violet's supposed death-by-lightning, how the National Guard had flown helicopters over Helheim, and why Helheim was the worst scrap of land that had ever existed.

"But then the sky cleared." June leaned back. Her face was a mess of tears. "And I knew you'd found the Lykill. You did it."

Violet's heart reached the pinnacle of straining. She made several attempts to speak and came up short. Then, she managed to say it. "Junie, I missed you."

"Us too. Especially Oliver. He . . ." June glanced back. Oliver had kept his distance. Shame. Violet had seen Eliathor wear it too. "Talk to him," June whispered.

Violet was already moving.

Uktin was barking into a walkie-talkie, his Russian intelligible now, thanks to Alikar. ". . . Yes, yes, the girl's alive, but did you hear me? Blue sky!"

Oliver's whole presence seemed to retract as Violet neared. When she stopped, they stood at the same height, due to his slouched posture.

"You're supposed to be on duty," she said.

His face fell. "Violet . . ."

"He looked for you every day and night," June called. "He even stole Utkin's truck, which was really awkward. Ollie hasn't spoken one word except to yell about taking too long in the outhouse, I think because he's worried I'll get struck by lightning. Anyway, he'll kill me for saying this, but I caught him crying last night, which I never thought—"

Violet didn't hear the rest; Oliver's jacket crinkled with too much noise as they hugged. Somewhere in all the shifting of fabric, he said he was sorry, and she said she forgave him.

"I never would have left you here, Violet. You're my sister."

She hugged him tighter.

When they finished, both were blinking fiercely. "Here," Oliver said.

Through a glossy film, Violet saw a handkerchief embroidered with a *QL*. "That's one of Fa's," she said.

"June sewed a million of them."

"She did," Violet said, laughing. Then, the handkerchief reminded her of Alikar. "Oh. My friend. He's in the room. Um." How could she explain him?

"Your what?" Oliver said.

"I thought I saw someone else!" June said. She yanked open the door just as a leg disappeared through the gate and the golden glitter vanished.

"What was that?" Oliver shouted.

Meanwhile, Utkin's rapid-fire Russian accompanied the drawing of his gun.

Anak.

Without preamble, Violet said, "Fa wasn't lying, and he wasn't crazy. That was Alikar. Eliathor probably had to close the gate, but he'll make another so Alikar can say goodbye. I found them on Bar'Talian, one of the twelve planets. Eliathor's the Lykill. I brought him here to his throne, which healed Earth. That's probably all you need to know for now."

June and Oliver's gapes were identical.

Over the next few minutes, Violet did her best to answer questions. Utkin cut her off eventually, saying a ferry had been summoned and should arrive within the hour. While Violet's explanation made June giddy and erased some of Oliver's frown, it appeared to have personally offended Utkin, who wanted to hear of nothing else but their itinerary home.

The Lyngs packed their belongings, Violet awaiting Alikar's reemergence at any moment. In hindsight, it was a good thing he'd disappeared before Utkin got his sights on him. Once ready, they stood outside, admiring the sky.

"Do you think it looks like this in all the Blacklands," June asked, hooking her arm around Violet's, "or only here?"

Oliver took out his phone and scrolled. "It'd be on the news if everywhere was healed. Guess it's just Ground Zero."

"Iceland," Violet said. "That's its proper name."

Oliver replied, but she was too busy thinking. The prophecy said the Lykill must be restored. Coming to Iceland had only been the first step. Eliathor needed to be crowned. Only then could the rest of the Blacklands heal.

"I think Ragnarök is done spreading, at least," Violet said.

"How do you know?" June asked.

"Terlian's king has seen his throne."

Oliver ruffled Violet's hair and called her crazy. She didn't mind.

Twenty minutes passed. The Lyngs were ready, and Utkin was readier. He waved them toward his truck so he could drive them to the shore, where the ferry would dock. If he noticed his tea canister had gone missing, he didn't mention it. Likely Utkin didn't care if anything vanished from the outpost, so long as the Lyngs vanished with it.

"I don't think he likes us." June nervously laughed while Oliver loaded their bags. "By the way, why are you dressed like a medieval peasant?"

Violet surveyed the outpost. What was taking Alikar so long?

"All right, let's get off this rock." Oliver hoisted June into Utkin's truck, then held out a hand for Violet.

She took it. But she hesitated, looking back. Eliathor wouldn't know where to create a gate if Violet left. Sílfar could help him, but she doubted he'd use the liryn pendant just for this.

"Hold on," she said, hopping back down.

"Hurry up!" June called.

"It's fine," Oliver said. "It's not like we'll leave without her."

Violet smiled as she ran.

Back at the storage building, she wrenched opened the door. Dark. No Alikar.

Violet stood there as long as reason would allow. Alikar didn't come. Maybe he wouldn't. Maybe some emergency had called him back to Bar'Talian. He had people to visit, pieces to pick back up.

Slowly, Violet exited. Closing a door had never felt so final. If only she hadn't been so awkward, she might have managed a proper goodbye. Now, she had no idea if or when she'd see him again.

Her eyes burned. Crying was silly. It wasn't as if he was her longest, dearest friend.

But he was a friend. Violet's first, outside of her family. And they'd barely had a moment to see how true that friendship could become.

The door flew open, smacking Violet's toes and clipping her forehead. She yelped and hopped on one foot, pain smarting her eyes.

"Fileet!" A figure, blurred by her tears, steadied her shoulders. Gold flooded the area behind him. "Did I hurt you?"

She squinted. A blond mess of hair and a purple belt over his chest. The pain dulled to a gentle throb. "You're here," she said.

"Of course I'm here. Melly was worried that I'd alarm your family, so we . . ." He trailed off. "You thought I'd gone?"

"Well I . . . you're busy. I understand." Violet was beginning to fear she'd hug him, so she knotted her arms behind her back. She blinked, a terrible mistake. Quickly, she wiped the freed tear. Somehow, her hand got tangled with Alikar's. He'd been going for the same tear.

"Oh, I did hurt you. You're going to have a welt." His fingertips brushed her forehead.

"It was an accident."

"I'm prone to those." He sighed. "I forgot to acquire a dirt sample. For the gate crate." He crouched, skimming the ground with a hand. "We can communicate through the crate, you know."

"You and I?"

"Yes, by letters."

"But I can't read Arati, and you can't read English."

"Then we'll have to write in Faartunga, won't we?" He smiled.

"I only knew a little, and I imagine the writing system is entirely different between Terlian and the Hasteins." Violet pondered the Younger Futhark runes and their eventual growth into medieval runes. Who knew how written Faartunga had been reformed among Eliathor's ancestors? "You can write in Faartunga?" she asked, a mite jealous.

"I've never tried, but it's the same alphabet as Arati. Mostly. I think they added a few letters."

"It is?" she said eagerly. "Not a runic alphabet, correct?"

"Er, I don't know."

"But I recognized the runes on the portraits in the estate. Maybe the Hasteins originally wrote in Futhark but eventually adopted Arati's alphabet. That makes sense, after a thousand years in your country . . ." It was incredible. Faartunga's alphabet would look nothing like its roots.

Alikar chuckled. "What did I say that fascinates you?"

"I like languages." Violet worked to reel in her enthusiasm.

"I didn't know that. I look forward to learning more about you."

Hope for continued friendship soared up, then dove back into hiding once Violet remembered that her mail would go directly to the king of Janlian. "What about the king?" she said.

"King Giannis is never going to see that crate. Nikos is a weasel. But, as his weaseling ways will facilitate our communication, I can't complain." He gathered a fistful of dirt and shoved it in his pocket. "It's settled, then," he said, rising. "I'll pester you monthly in Faartunga."

"Monthly?"

"You're right. Weekly would be best."

Violet bit her lip. He could never learn how relieved she felt. But relief was hardly the word. Happy?

No. She couldn't admit that.

Yes. She could try.

"I would like that," she said.

He grinned. She could say a bit more.

"Thank you for being my friend, even when I was difficult."

"You proved the better one," he said.

"That's not true. I'll . . ."

"Miss me?"

"You don't have to look so pleased." She fiddled with her necklace.

"But I'm immensely pleased," he said, swinging his arms. "I'll miss you too."

"Oh. All right."

Alikar's smile made her heart work harder. "May I, er . . ." With a groan, he covered his face. Terlion mud smudged his cheeks. "Kelispar would have disowned me," he muttered.

"I'm sure he wouldn't." Violet had no idea what Kelispar would have done, or why. Her fingers were nervously twitching. Maybe she should leave now, before the thing currently embarrassing Alikar embarrassed her too.

Her legs refused to obey. She blamed sílfar.

He drew in a forceful breath and let it collapse out of him. Then, staring her down with alarming confidence, he said, "Your hand, Fileet."

"Violet," she said. "Vi-oh-let. Not Fileet or Manishag or Violeta."

"Vi-oh-let?"

"Yes." She let him have her hand. If Alikar could collect himself, so could she.

"Well then, Violet." He secured the tips of her fingers.

She'd held his hand already. Why was this different? Why had she not noticed before how focused his touch was, like a craftsman intent on his tool?

Alikar met her eyes and didn't squirm. "May you find the road to me again." He bent his long torso over her hand. Stray hairs tickled, and he kissed her knuckles. Not as softly as Nikos, and not so firmly that it felt obtrusive. "Oh, I've dirtied your hand. My shame." He brushed off the speckles, taking his time.

"Gentleman," she said.

"I'm glad you think so." After her fingers were more than clean, he edged back. "*Hrazhesht*, Violet." Then, Alikar stepped into the gate and was on Terlian no more. Her first friend, transported to another planet.

She cupped her hand, careful not to wipe away the spot. *Silly.* But that little patch of skin stayed unperturbed.

For seconds, she waited, wishing she'd said something more conclusive than *Gentleman*. Maybe he'd come back and she could redeem herself.

The gate blinked out of existence. He was gone, and that was how it should be. He had a life to start cultivating. So did she. This time, she wouldn't attempt the journey on her own.

Violet felt her necklace. She'd forgotten to return the chain to Alikar. The two pendants were still there: Oliver's and hers. Sílfar hadn't left her. And it wouldn't.

She smiled. Maybe she had a friend on Terlian after all.

EPILOGUE

I T HAD TAKEN fiFTEEN years, but his father had found the Tome of Rites, one of his last useful acts before death took him. The Terlions called what Rafe had done theft, but one could not steal one's own possessions.

Malokki found the page that had set these events in motion. The man on Terlian had copied the welding rite for sílfar and splayed the sacred words on a table where lesser, mundane rituals took place. Eating and drinking. The Terlions were true sheep, bleating what they did not comprehend.

Malokki had read the ritual for the man. He had not expected the man to repeat it to his daughter. He had not realized those words would have any effect. Rafe had never discovered that Halfdan had created a lira of Terlian. Malokki's father had not learned many things. An empty Vessel after all.

For a thousand years, the prophecy had lived on, retained in Vessels who did not appreciate it any more than the lira had treasured his grasp at history. None could safeguard truth but the line of the Lykill. None could seize it. Yakiv Stefanos had tried, and it had spat him out like bitter worms.

Gently, Malokki closed the Tome of Rites. The Lykill's birthing had come. The daughter of the lira had found him, had entered his very threshold and looked upon him again, though she had recognized him not. Soon, the realms would have their redemption. The prophecy could not lie. The Lykill would rise. He would save them.

Malokki would save them all.

GLOSSARY

BARREN – someone whose liryn cord has been stolen. Barrens cannot use their liryn, but they still suffer a headache and crown.

CROWN – the particular and unique suffering that comes to someone who is welded.

GATE PENDANT (WHITE) – a triangular pendant that enables the wielder to open and close gates. If anyone but a member of the Nehfey royal bloodline uses the gate pendant, there will be an earthquake and the user's skin will be stained white.

HANDS OF THE LYKILL – currently led by Malokki, the Hands of the Lykill believe that the prophecy's fulfillment is nigh, which means the time of the Lykill will soon be ushered in. The Hands of the Lykill believe that the Lykill will take away the suffering that comes with having liryn.

LIRA – someone with the power to weld the particular liryn they were given to weld. Liras can only weld one liryn.

LIRYN – what some might call a "magical power." There are twelve distinct liryn gifts.

LIRYN PENDANT (RED) – a triangular pendant that gives the wielder all twelve forms of liryn. This pendant can only be rightfully used by those of the Basareth royal bloodline.

Loyalist – someone who supports Terlian's claim to the throne.

Separatist – those who resist the idea that the monarchs are the only people who should have the power to distribute liryn.

Scapegoat – someone who is welded specifically to bear the pain of a headache and crown while someone else uses their liryn cord.

Unionist – those who support the power of the monarchs to distribute liryn.

Valknut – a Norse symbol consisting of three interlocking triangles.

Vegvísir – the "wayfinder" symbol many people call the Viking compass.

Welding – the ceremonial process by which someone is given liryn.

Welding pendant (purple) – a triangular pendant that turns the wielder into a lira, someone who can weld. This pendant can only be rightfully used by those of the Da'atan royal bloodline.

AFTERWORD

Let me just say that this book was supposed to be about a girl who takes on a babysitting job for an eccentric wizard's niece. It was also supposed to be a standalone. Alikar was the wizard, Kelispar was dead, Meliora was the villain who'd killed Kelispar, and Eliathor was Alikar's goofy sidekick. Violet also had a love triangle with the boy-next-door.

I do try outlining, people. I really do. But the story will have its way, and I'm so glad it did, because it allowed me to play with cultures and languages in a way that the original idea wouldn't have. On that note, I'd like to add some clarity to the worldbuilding found within *Iron Heart of Terlian.*

While modern-day Scandinavia typically refers to Sweden, Norway, and Denmark, the Scandinavian Blacklands of Violet's family comprise just Norway and Sweden, with the Lyng family having settled somewhere northwest of our Oslo. Their Scandinavian language descended from Old Norse; although, as Violet's ancestors migrated due to Ragnarök, crossing the Baltic Sea and heading southeast toward Azerbaijan, their Scandinavian picked up Slavic influences. Having studied Russian, Ukrainian, and Polish, I relied mostly on the Slavic influence for the few Scandinavian words we see in the book and enjoyed bringing the Germanic *-th* sound into the Slavic mix!

For Arat, I drew from Turkish, Armenian, and Persian culture. Vaspurakan was inspired by the city of Van (now in eastern Turkey), Van being a prominent city in the ancient Armenian kingdom of Vaspurakan.

Jarek and Yakiv (may the former rest in peace and the latter not) were from neighboring countries on Bar'Talian with cousin languages inspired by Polish and Ukrainian, respectively. *Dziękuję bardzo* to my friend Magdalena, who gave me the idea to use the outdated *Przebacz* when Jarek apologizes to Violet, and who was tickled by the fact that I gave her son's name to the infamous cord thief, Bartosz Mieszko.

Lastly, I am not an Old Norse scholar and must beg forgiveness for any probable mistakes. Given that Eliathor's family has been living in an Arati-speaking country for 1,000 years, his Faartunga would realistically be a strange hodgepodge of Old Norse and Arati, not to mention its own unique Hastein dialect. However, for the sake of convenience, I decided that Faartunga is more or less the same Old Norse that modern-day scholars study today. That way, Violet can use her Old Norse (and Scandinavian) knowledge to communicate with characters both in this book and the sequel. In the same vein, Meliora's Greek is nearly identical to ours. If I were to let both Faartunga and Greek organically develop, it would've been extremely difficult for Violet to learn them, and she wouldn't be able to communicate with her friends in Book 2 unless an Advocate was around. And she wouldn't like that, would she?

About the Author

As a child, Adelaide Thorne was so picky that her family would sing songs to encourage her to eat. It didn't work. All she ever wanted to eat was pickles and canned Chicken & Stars soup. Then she grew up and became a food journalist and restaurant reviewer for the local newspaper. So, you just never know how people are going to turn out.

She once dragged her friends all the way to Iceland to find Fa's troll. Not being a Compass, she never did uncover the gate to Bar'Talian, but at least she got to climb an inactive volcano. Currently she lives with her family in the muggy wetlands of Florida, where she is known to be allergic to palmetto bugs, humidity, and flip flops. Soup is still her favorite food. Find her online at AdelaideThorne.com.

ALSO BY

The *Whitewashed* Trilogy
Book 1: *The Trace*
Book 2: *The Integer*
Book 3: *The Anamnesis*
Memento (companion short story collection)

www.ingramcontent.com/pod-product-compliance
Lightning Source LLC
Chambersburg PA
CBHW022250310726
48973CB00001B/25